Three Women

George, May you always feel the creative energy that is your soul - may you continue to share yourself with us in song & music

Three Women

a novel by

Denese Shervington, M.D.

silver lion press
Atlanta, GA

Copyright Denese Shervington, M.D. ©2002

All rights reserved under International and Pan-American copyright conventions. No part of this book may be reproduced or utilized in any form or by any means, electronic or mechanical, including photocopying, recording, or by any information storage or retrieval system, without permission in writing from the publisher.

Published and distributed in the United States
by Silver Lion Press
931 Monroe Drive
Suite 102-319
Atlanta, GA 30308

www.silverlionpress.com

Manufactured in the United States
First Silver Lion Press Edition: March 2002

Publisher's Cataloging-in-Publication
(Provided by Quality Books, Inc.)

Shervington, Denese.
 Three women / Denese Shervington. -- 1st ed.
 p. cm.

 1. Title.

PS3569.H4375T47 2001   813'.6
                         QBI98-500012

Cover and Interior Design by Ken Maudsley

Dedication

Walter, as I watched your physical body struggle to take its last remaining breaths, I experienced the joy of seeing your true spirit emerge; and in that moment I saw you, God. In that instant I realized that if, with each breath, you are fully present in every moment of your life, when you come to the end of the last one, there will be no regrets.

Thanks for allowing us to experience the complete spectrum of love and exploration of ourselves. We have a perfect love; we completed the circle—from emotional and physical romance, to mental intimacy (that was hard for us two ego-filled individuals most of the time, of course you, more than me), to spiritual union. Our last six weeks together were pure bliss. I will love you forever for eternity.

This book is for you in celebration of the many lessons about love, both painful and joyful, that we shared.

Three Women is also for our daughters, the two wonderful women that you left behind, Shanga and Iman, the products of our love. I know that you join me in hoping that their paths toward healing, body, mind and spirit, are filled with many loving, wise and generous teachers.

Walter, we love you fiercely forever.

P.S. I give thanks and praise to spirit Marlon for welcoming you into the divine realm!

Acknowledgment

As I move forward in the present, Fire, thanks for putting it to me. Thanks for blazing a trail within my soul that burnt away the cobwebs of self-doubt; ones that previously left me hollow in the aftermath, open and empty; hungry and begging. Now my soul space is open and forever being filled with self-love and acceptance. Thanks for igniting my soul's creativity circa 12/4/99. You say that Fire exhibits the kind of behaviors and attitudes that are necessary for black men to successfully negotiate the new millennium. Well, here's Spice, his understudy!

My wonderful sisters and brother in blood and through marriage to Walter, thanks for listening, comforting and drying my tears whenever needed—Aunt Gem, Del, Nicks, Dewnett, Anne, Carol and your many children too. And Marie, my dear friend, thanks for being there always like family. For, that's why we are here—to stand by each other and help soothe the pain of our forever loss. Donna, thanks for doing much of the housework and attending to the needs of my children the many mornings and nights that I labored at the computer.

Thanks to my three women friends, Lisa, Michaela and Mia for taking that trip with me and validating the lessons of spiritual love, growth and healing; and forcing me into the last rewrite. Special thanks Lisa for giving so freely of your editorial wisdom; thanks for the countless hours of breathing life into my words and making the three women come alive. The many truths that we had to learn are indelibly printed in my fifth chakra. Thanks to Rachel for being there from the beginning full of encouragement, humor and support, and giving me a mirror to peep into places that others keep hidden. And thanks to Jackie for oozing much of the sensuality that informed one of my three women; oops, I won't tell which!

Michelle, my first reader, thanks for telling me that you saw a little bit of yourself in *Three Women*, confirming for me that not only was *Three Women* readable, (for you are such an avid reader of black literature), but that the book was going to be helpful in the lives of black women. Your support gave me the green light and confidence to move forward.

My three models, Lisa, Dianne and Jackie, thanks for representing so divinely my three women. Jamie, thanks for being such a passionate photographer. Billie, artist par excellence! Thanks for always being willing to bring visuals to my sounds. SuperClubs Jamaica, thanks for the hospitality during my final writing phase.

Marcy, my loyal, dear friend, thanks for giving me hope that one day, white and black women will unite in womanhood and friendship. Thanks for pushing me into more thoughtfulness with your query upon reading the manuscript: "Do you think all white women are hopeless, or just the ones who fuck black men?" The history of black and white women in the Americas is fraught with the distasteful vestiges of how we were pitted against each other during slavery. And this issue still lingers quite prominently in the psyche of many black women, which is why I chose to open it up in Three Women. No, I don't think that any white woman is hopeless, you being a prime example of the potential for positivity when white women operate in awareness, love, humility and a willingness to respect the divinity in all women; in other words, when white women exist within their own true, divine self. So too are black women not hopeless when we act from our divine selves.

Shange, my dear publisher and first editor, thanks for supporting my vision of love and healing; the truth is, it is a shared one, it is both ours. Thanks for believing in me that glorious morning in Providence when us two colored women opened up our hearts to love and shared our dreams and aspirations. Without your support, there would have been no "Three Women." May the lioness always keep roaring! Kiini, my second editor, thanks for believing from the very first go around and pushing the story to its very best. Thanks for completing the soul triumvirate—the three women creators of *Three Women*.

And for all those others that I have, now, or will ever love, thanks for the lessons and the stories. *Three Women* is the voice of so many sister friends all across the diaspora whose stories and voices I am trying to bring out of silence.

Namaste,

Denese Shervington (Dspiral)

Prologue

Once upon a time, three beautiful, colored women traveled together on a beautiful island in the sun, in search of themselves, each other and whomever else. They had totally forgotten that once before, long ago, in far away lands, they had committed to always reunite after their travels took them far apart.

"Around the year 200 AD, in a small village in Ethiopia, the women would gather along the banks of the Nile every full moon at midnight to celebrate and give thanks. They were led in song and dance by the high priestess Sarantha, in praise of Isis, their creator, who blessed them with children and food. Men were never allowed to attend, except for the few who served as musicians.

One night, in the midst of one such celebration, strange-looking men with pale faces and stringy hair invaded their gathering. These men stopped the dancing and forced everyone back into the center of the village. There, they killed all the males, including children; the two musicians were spared however, because they were dressed like women for the ceremony. Next, the strange men raped as many of the young girls as they could. When they were finished with all their pillage, they bound Sarantha into captivity and took her with them. Se, the drummer and her lover, tried to rescue her as she was dragged away on the horse. He was stabbed mercilessly in his chest.

Janius, the general and leader of the invasion fell in love with Sarantha on the journey back to his homeland up North; he loved her dark skin and wide hips. When they arrived, he declared her his concubine and took her to live in his primary home. He lavished her with fine jewels and clothes, but kindness could not cure her blues. She missed her daughter, lover, people and their customs. In the beginning, she oftentimes tried to run away, but she always found herself lost in the strange terrain. She did not know where she was nor was she sure which direction she had come from. Her feet failed to lead her in the right direction. Whenever she was found, the strange men would bind her wrists and carry her back to Janius.

In an attempt to make her love him, Janius built her a temple like the one he found her in the night they raided her land. He thought this small, profound reflection of home might make her happy. He was right. Soothed by her temple, Sarantha's blues began to lift. After a while, she even came to love him—almost as much as she loved Se, her old lover. Yet no matter how much Sarantha had grown to love Janius, she refused to bear his children. Whenever she found herself with child, she aborted Janius' seed with extracts of myrrh.

One day, the king's wife became very sick. Word spread that Sarantha had special powers from the gods, so the king summoned her to the palace. He begged her to heal his dying wife. In her temple, Sarantha called upon Isis to infuse her with the wisdom of healing. She guided Sarantha to a willow tree. Sarantha made a *brew of the willow's bark and placed a few drops upon the queen's lips. As the willow-bark brew saturated the queen's royal mouth, she opened her eyes and arose from her deathly sleep.*

The next day, the queen was completely healed. The townspeople celebrated for 35 days. The queen made Sarantha an attendant in her royal court and appointed her the task of training royal healers. Sarantha chose seven women to be her disciples. As the women learned the wisdom of the sun and moon, Sarantha grew in power and influence. Within years, everyone had forgotten Sarantha's arrival as a captive and revered her as a powerful holy woman.

Many years later, a new religion that had only men at the center swept through the land. A few generals, who had grown tired of the king's deference to the power of women, embraced the new religion and started a bloody battle to force all the townspeople to adopt the new ways. The king and Sarantha's husband refused to become converts, so they were killed.

The new generals put out an edict that anyone who did not convert risked having their heads cut off. Sarantha and her disciples went underground. One night, during the secret moon gathering, their makeshift temple was raided. The commanding general threatened to have all the women killed if they did not rebuke their worship at once. One of the priestesses screamed in defiance. The general grabbed her and attempted to rape her. As he fumbled with her disciple's skirts, Sarantha summoned her Isis warrior power within. She seized the general's sword from his waist and stabbed him through his groin. She then cut his penis off and threw it into the pot of burning frankincense. He bled to death.

PROLOGUE

The following morning, Sarantha set her house and temple on fire. She bribed a few of the remaining loyal men to take them back to her homeland. After all those years of refusing to show her the way home, the men nobly escorted her and her disciples South in honor of the dead king. As they neared familiar terrain, a new joy overtook Sarantha. The length of her absence did not diminish the love she felt for her homeland. She was very happy to be returning at last. She hoped her daughter might still be alive and prayed that they might make a home for themselves in the land of Sarantha's birth.

Sarantha and her disciples eventually reached her village after several weeks of travel. Famine, illness and death had decimated the village. The only face she recognized was that of Sau, the other musician, and sole person remaining from the old circle. His face twisted into a painful smile when he recognized Sarantha. When Sarantha asked for her daughter, Sau's eyes went blank. In trembling tones, he informed her that he had married her daughter when she came of age. Together, they hoped to repopulate their land after the invasion. Sarantha demanded to see her daughter right away. Sau opened his arms helplessly. His voice faltered as he told Sarantha that her daughter died giving birth to their first child. The news filled Sarantha with overwhelming grief. She did not want to lay eyes on her grandchild, for she did not want to ease her hurt. Without even a glance at her disciples, she ran to the river and threw herself back to Yemoja."

Diaspora women
nuh fret;
nuh cry;
come soar up high
with Sarantha,
your Sun-Moon goddess,
your true I and I.
Sistren, I know
what you seek most
is love,
to give and to get.
So come listen to the tale
of three women,
who from their spirit source fell,
and how love's magic
raised them back with its spell.

1
Saturday

ANN

His scent disarmed her.

"Madam lady in red," he whispered in a husky baritone voice. Little did he know that his essence had preceded his voice—he did not need to speak to grab her attention. Sandalwood was the underbelly of the cologne worn by her late husband, James. "Allow me to buy a drink for the most beautiful woman in the house."

"Thanks, but no thanks," Ann replied, turning around to be greeted by a very seductive grin. "I do not accept gifts from men whom I don't know." Ann persisted in spite of his playful wink, "not even when they lavish me with such sweet compliments."

"And I do not give gifts to women with whom I am not familiar," he responded.

Speechless, Ann threw him a quizzical look.

"We definitely are not strangers. Not after the way I felt you looking through me when you walked into the room. It was such a knowing stare, I had to come over and find out where we had met before."

"I did do that, didn't I? My bad." Countless times before,

others had told her about the way she seemed to stare right into their souls. She softened her defensive posture.

He nodded his head, welcoming her admission. "I like black women who know what they want and go after it," he said teasingly, grinning even more mischievously than before.

"Please believe that I was not trying to pick you up," she said, her annoyance returning. "For a brief moment I honestly thought that you were someone else."

She felt him ignoring her pleas of innocence so she quickly continued, "I am sure this has happened to you before—mistaken identity?"

"I sure am glad that it happened to us," he replied, reaching over to shake her hand. "We can ease your discomfort right here and now."

"My name is Spice," he told her. His glistening teeth emitted sparkles that signaled her tongue to come and explore their abode.

"Your name sure does explain why you are trying to impress me with sugar and all things nice," she said, fumbling to camouflage her quivering with words.

"I am going to take your words at face value and not entertain the possibility that bitterness lies beneath those sweet remarks," he replied. He squeezed her hands tightly, keeping her firmly locked in his grip, and he continued, "I am not going to let you go until I know your name."

"I don't have a poetic retort," she said. "I come plain and simple; my name is Ann."

"I am sure that a redheaded, black woman with freckles and dreads is filled with complexities and contradictions," he replied, still not letting go. "How about I give you the poetry and call you my sweetness?"

His assumption of familiarity coupled with his comfort with physical intimacy was beginning to irritate her. A sweat was building in her palms and an electrical storm was feverishly moving up her wrists and spreading through her entire body. She was also annoyed that she had only struggled a little against the captivity of his large hands. "It's time for you to let go," she ordered forcefully.

"If you insist," he smiled and gave her hand a soft caress before letting go. "Remember, this is all your doing. If you had not beamed me over here with those knowing looks, I would not have succumbed to this infatuation. You must know how intoxicating your beauty is."

"And you must be equally aware of how intoxicating your charm is," Ann said, trying to regain control. "After all, performance is your game."

"What I want to know is, why are you trying so hard to avoid this spice between us?" he asked.

"You want the truth? I am probably old enough to be your mother, that's why." She stepped back, afraid that he would hear her heart thumping. His persistence slowly chipping away at her veil.

He reached for her hands and again pulled her close, "I am not put off by your age, my dear lady, even if you are. Virgin grape is not my thing. I find it much more intriguing to sip finely aged, full-bodied red wine." His eyes bore into her even more, "I love how it flows mellow down my throat, then goes straight to my head."

Ann was finding it difficult to keep her head clear. It felt as if a magnetic field had developed between them and she was being sucked into the charge. As she was about to extract herself from his hold, a whiff of his intoxicating body musk pulled her back in. Subdued, she held her breath for a second; it seemed to stretch into eternity.

"This is happening too quickly for me," she said, feeling weakened and frightened.

"It is fast but true. From the instant I saw you seeing me, you became my guitar."

Ann found herself falling for his words—they seemed too rich a poem to have been contrived from a book of well-worn plays. She attempted to diffuse his seriousness. "Is that what you are trying to do? Play me, hit me with your music and strum my senses out of me?"

"So that I can show you that the only player in me is for my guitar, can we get together after this last set? Spend some time with me. See how for real I am." She could not stand her eagerness to believe him.

"That sounds like player move number one to me," she replied, laughing out loud. He was not amused.

"Ann, I do understand your caution," he said. "Even though it seems like I am coming at you with abandon, I too am a bit wary."

She looked at him a bit confused. He was saying all the right things. And though she kept telling him she thought he was a player, his words were so similar to the thoughts in her very own head. She feared he could feel the burning attraction she was trying so hard to ignore.

"I would be a fool to not take a chance and find out why you draw me so," he continued. "Maybe this is one of those chemical attractions that don't go further than the skin, one of those that would make no sense if we were not in a club with a few drinks in both of us. Since it seems you are not going to give me the pleasure of seeing you later tonight, give me a chance and let me ring you tomorrow when the sun is shining. Who knows, we may talk until sunset."

Even if the bartender had not saved her by returning with her refill, she would have had no reply. She couldn't find an honest word to deny how she felt. Over his objections and happy to change the subject, she insisted that the bartender charge the drink to her room. She took several large gulps while he ordered himself sparkling water. The momentary reprieve that the liquid spirits brought was welcome relief. The fire that had sprung up between them was threatening to burn out of control, and she was not ready for another charring. So why then was she allowing him to hold her hands and guide her back to her table? She concluded that it must be the spirits—vapor and liquid—that had turned against her.

"Since you did not give me the honor and pleasure of buying you a drink," he said as he seated her, "I will sing you a song when I am back on stage. It's free of charge."

"Just remember that I am not," she replied, winking a bit suggestively.

"You are not sure what to do with me, are you? I can feel your push and pull."

She looked away trying to find the words to lie, but returned to his gaze with truth. "It's going to take me a little while to figure this one out."

"Remember that much of life cannot be explained," he said. "The beauty lies in the mystery of it all." His words reminded her of the advice that her friend Cassandra had given her only two days earlier—that she should flow with life and love it for those things that she could decipher and let go of those things that she simply had to allow to be.

"I wish that I could sit here with you and explore the mystery of this meeting tonight. I do hope that you will give me the chance to spend some time with you." Ann could feel herself being drawn into Spice's web; there was nothing she loved more than men who knew how to reason and play with words. He reminded her of her stepdad, a brilliant writer and philosopher who was ahead of his times and stung by the racism in New York. She had to get out before she got any more tangled in his magic.

"I won't have much time tomorrow or the rest of the week for that matter," she replied. "In the morning, two of my girlfriends from the States will be coming for a week's visit. I came a night earlier so that I could be well-rested."

"If the truth be known," Spice said, the wicked wink appearing one more time, "you came early so that you could meet me."

"Trust me, my name is not Stella and I am not trying to get my groove on," she replied, becoming irritated once more by his undaunting confidence. Thalia and Sara would think she was absolutely crazy if she let this go any further.

"Why don't you at least stay until I finish this last set so that I can sing a song for you and only you."

"Speaking of singing, all of the band is back on stage except you."

He reached for her hands and kissed them both. "You running and you running, and you running away, but you can never run away from love."

She glanced over at the table next to hers. She met with the envious stares of three, sexy young women with 'come fuck me' halters and bikini shorts. She suddenly became very self-conscious about being in the club by herself. She had come to the club tonight with no intentions other than to sit and watch the ocean and listen to some sweet Jamaican fusion. Instead, she realized that it was time to make an exit.

As she stood up to leave, the band began to play "Cherry-O Baby," one of her all time reggae favorites. Even though she tried not to make eye contact, she could feel his words piercing through her skin. He even had the nerve to change the final stanza to: "Pretty lady in red, you gone straight to mi head. I want to love you real nice; mi a the grand master Spice." She gathered up what little was left of her drink and left.

She walked briskly down to the beach, afraid to look back. The song 'Every move you make, I'll be watching you', kept resounding in her ears; but she was unsure if it was his voice or the imaginary ones inside her head. She found an empty chaise lounge, laid down and listened to the waves. As they crashed against the shore, she implored them to smash inside her head even more forcibly and erase all memory of what had just occurred.

"How could you allow yourself to become attracted to another man?" she chastised herself. "How could you be so disloyal?"

Vowing to cut it off right then and there, she walked slowly back to her room. She welcomed sleep; her newest best friend, safe haven and comforting reprieve.

She jumped up from slumber, heart pounding and body drenched in sweat. She sensed someone's presence, but scanning the moonlit room, she saw no one. Her anxiety rising, she jumped out of bed, walked to the window and looked outside.

The low-hanging moon greeted her as it slowly made its way across the star-studded sky. Convinced that the smiling face silhouetted inside its cocoon was James', she begged the moon to come closer and bring him to her. There was so much that she wanted to say to him.

Instead she heard a voice saying "Goodbye my love, it is time for us both to go." As a blinding light immediately encircled and wiped out his image.

"Come back, please, please, please …"

But there was no answer.

Panic rolled through her chest as her heart and her thoughts began to race. She had to kneel by the window in order to steady herself. Was she hallucinating or was James really there?

Anguish bubbled up from her tormented psyche and enveloped her. The piercing pain that had gripped and crippled her a year ago when she had labored along with James as he struggled for his last breath once more resumed full residence in her heart.

Overcome by the darkness, she could feel the limp, heavy night air descending upon her grieving heart. A coarse fluttering moan escaped her lips, followed by a dam of tears that had welled up behind the floodgates in her eyes. Pinned beneath the weight of the sorrow herding down her face, she surrendered to the floor and to her pain.

She wept for James, her nude body writhing uncontrollably against the hard, cold tile. Her head filled up with multiple images of his journey through suffering—from the moment that he got the bad news of his incurable cancer to the moment of his death; and lying still in the coffin, refusing to get out and tell her that it was all a dream.

The pain became so intense it consumed her entire psyche, crushing and blurring James' image into all the other loved ones that had been taken from her before she was ready to say goodbye—her father, her nephew and her mother. And, with the image of her mother, came images of her becoming a mother. The pain that up until then had represented the hurt of the sting of death, spiraled downward to her umbilicus and transformed into that of the joyful labor of bringing forth life. Almost immediately, Ann's tears of woe changed to showers of joy as she remembered how happy she had been at the sight of the final leg of Ahsima's birth.

With the birthing process still floating in her subconscious, Ann felt herself breathing through her vagina as the center of her consciousness sank into her lower pelvic area. With each inhalation, she imagined herself taking in the joy of life. Likewise, with each exhalation, she visualized herself releasing the fear of death. Finally, she was able to drift off into a peaceful sleep.

A fierce clap of thunder jolted Ann back awake. She took a deep breath and noticed that the room was filled with the scent of James' cologne. More tears started gushing from her as Ann worried about her sanity. Tonight, not only was she seeing spirits, hearing their voices, and talking back; now, even worse, she was smelling them. She wondered if she was on the brink of psychosis, but she knew however that she could not afford the self-indulgence. Ahsima needed a fully functioning parent and, without the security of her partner and companion, she had to be all there for herself. From her many years of being a psychiatrist, she recognized that she had to let her pain work its way through and out of her; or else, she was going to unravel and slip into major depression.

Ann sat on the cold floor in her hotel room and allowed all the remaining tears to flow out and through her. When she was all dried up inside, she took off her dampened nightshirt and went out to the cottage's back patio in search of a sea breeze.

Finding no breeze, she jumped into the private pool that came with her cottage. It welcomed her naked body with its cool waters. As she swam, her mind began to race again, vacillating between guilt and sadness. She wondered why James had appeared to her tonight. This was the first time since his death a year ago. Was his visit prompted by his anger at her for being attracted to another man, as short-lived as that was? She began to feel resentment take her. Why hadn't he come to her those nights of darkness; countless hours when she was so filled with anger and despair at God for taking him before she could find the cure for his illness. "Where were you then?" she yelled out in the night to James. As she expected, there was no reply.

She quickly became fatigued after only a few laps of swimming. She could feel the weight of her sorrow pushing her beneath the buoyancy of the water. She flipped over and tried floating on her back, unwilling to give up the water's cool embrace. She could feel the guilt returning as images of Spice started to dance in her subconscious. Suddenly her legs began to cramp making her body so taut that it began to sink. She rolled over on her stomach and slowly started doing another lap of the pool.

She was able to reduce her desire for Spice to a dull throbbing, but she could not figure out why she allowed herself to be swept up in his rapture. She had promised James, as he laid gasping for his final breath, that she would never again give her heart to anyone else. How could she be so weak? Was it his lazy, brown eyes, the wildly locking Afro, or the close to wicked, dangerous smile of his? Searching for a way to overcome the almost irresistible seduction, she did something that she had not done since James' death; she prayed. She prayed to never see Spice and all the added anxiety he brought ever again.

"Don't worry, my forever darling, our love will never die." She was not sure where the voices were coming from, but this time she was not worried. Instead, calm descended upon her as she felt herself surrounded by James's eternal love. She became one with the dark mysterious night. "Maybe, I am a moon child," she thought to herself as her energy began to soar.

Lost in time, swimming beneath the moonlit, star-dusted sky, a thunderous roar jolted her from her short-lived reverie. Mindful of the dangers of swimming during lightning, she knew that she had to get out of the pool. As she reached the steps and lifted her head out of the water, she heard footsteps approaching. In a split second, all the warnings about crime in Jamaica blasted in her head. Trying to disguise her fear, she asked in as calm but forceful a voice as she could muster, "Are you lost?" Remembering that she had no clothes on, she remained underwater, covering her bare breasts with her folded arms.

He continued walking toward the steps of the pool. "How could I be lost, when it's you I'm looking for?" He brazenly picked up her towel and handed it to her.

There was no mistaking the velvety crackling husk in Spice's voice. Embarrassed about her nudity, she quickly grabbed the towel from him and wrapped it around her as she pulled herself out of the water. She sat on the ledge of the pool, towel halfway in the water. "What are you doing here and how did you know where I was staying?"

"No mountain is insurmountable when we become mesmerized by beautiful women like yourself," he replied as he sat next to her without being invited.

"Is this supposed to make me feel good?" she asked moving away. "Your trespassing and showing up at my pool unannounced and uninvited makes me very nervous."

"Well, I didn't exactly break in. I am staying in the cottage next to yours."

"And you're going to convince me that was a coincidence? Fate or something?"

"A little bit of luck, my dear, together with a lot of connections," he replied. "The hotel manager is a high school buddy of mine."

"Still …"

"I inquired about the striking redhead. You see, you don't exactly blend in. You so increase the island's beauty with your presence."

"That is a breech of my confidentiality and privacy," she interjected. Damn if she was going to let his poetic words cover-up what was such a violation and intrusion.

"Look, why don't we both admit that there is a natural mystic happening here tonight. Lay down your arms and give up the fight."

"Has it occurred to you that I'm fighting because I'm not interested in you?" she asked.

"It has, and that makes me very sad," he said softly. "The thought of never seeing you again feels like a black hole; the death of something that burns fiercely inside."

She wondered how he knew just what to say to reach her. "It is weird that you mention the word death," she replied, recognizing that he was beginning to pierce her armor. "I have been haunted with death and spirits all night."

"Let me chase them away for you."

"I don't know if you can."

"I know I can. What is happening between us is on a higher order."

This time, his confidence reassured her. She surrendered her battle gear and signaled him to continue with her now engaged eyes.

"Ann, believe me, this is very unusual behavior for me. This is not about a catch for the night. If it were, I could easily have found bite for my bait."

"I did see them, breasts and behinds anxious to be caught; to use your vernacular, virgin grapes waiting to be plucked," she remarked as she remembered the three women sitting next to her at the club. She noticed that her returning annoyance was tinged with a bit of jealousy. "Maybe you just like the challenge of pursuing women who resist."

"Whether or not you want to admit it, our chemistry has already bound us together."

"Maybe we are both just a bit mad," she chuckled, bursting out laughing. "All evening, I have been struggling to maintain my sanity. Maybe I have fallen over the deep end."

"Mi turn fool too," he laughed, slipping into his Jamaican tongue. "Like the old folks say here in Jamaica, it feels like 'duppy swell mi head and tun mi round!' You have obeahed the hell out of me, cast a wicked spell on me."

"It makes for a great story doesn't it, psychiatrist turned witch doctor," she said, thinking of Cassandra, the obeah woman whom she had met several weeks ago at a woman's health seminar at the university. Ann sensed that her work, indeed, her life, was headed in a new direction.

"So you could just wave the magic wand and release me from the prison of my infatuation with you."

"My obeah woman friend would say that all you need to do is change your feelings to true love and it will set you free," Ann said.

"So you have finally admitted to the possibility that just maybe there is some love stuff happening here," he remarked.

She paused for a moment, surprised at how quickly and how much she had opened up with him. "I will admit that I am charmed by a smooth talking island man, and …"

"Go on."

"Maybe that's not so bad; tonight at least. Maybe it wouldn't be so bad to have someone's arms around me in case the spirits return."

He delivered his knowing smile but said nothing.

"Would you believe I was deep in thought about you at the moment that you turned up?" Ann said.

"Then mek wi celebrate our good fortune den nuh," he said, shifting again into his Jamaican accent. "For mi feel the fire bunning, fire bunning, fire bunning..." Heat waves went surging through her body.

She splashed water on her face to neutralize her hot flash. "This menopausal woman is trying not to lose her cool. It must be the intensity with which you sing." She turned toward him in earnest and said, "Spice, your earlier rendition of Marley's 'Woman Nuh Cry' is the best that I have ever heard. I loved the violins; they always cry so much better than I ever can."

"Violins cry so much better than the human voice," Spice agreed. "I always allow it to lead my singing. And I sing this song with passion for all women because to me it is so symbolic of your healing from all the pain that you have to bear."

Without any warning, his words triggered an outpouring of sadness from her. Tears began streaming down her face. He wiped them and gently laid her head against his shoulder.

"I feel you, Ann. I feel your pain," he said, holding her firmly against him.

When her tears began to slow their descent, she whispered, "You are very intuitive. Underneath this shell pounds an ocean of pain. At times it has been so turbulent, I felt as though I was going to be catapulted into nothingness." She told him enough about James to serve as warning.

"Let me help you reverse that flow," he said wiping her eyes as she finished.

She sighed deeply and relaxed more into his embrace. Timidly but with certainty, he reached for her face and slowly caressed it. Time stood still in its long moments as their chests moved again in unison; each breath mirroring the other.

"Sweetness," he said after an eternity of silence, "I am running my hands all over your face so that I can study it. I want to always have your memory imprinted right here in my hands." Tenderly, he caressed her face over and over, occasionally moving up to rub her head. He brushed his lips against hers, "And yes, let me remember the feel of your velvet lips."

As she surrendered her lips, he crushed his mouth onto hers. With much urgency, he pried her lips apart and ran his tongue deep inside her mouth. She allowed all her muscles to relax as she welcomed him in and savored the faint taste of mango that lingered in his mouth.

They kissed hard and hurriedly, hungry for each other. She could feel herself surrendering to her tantric zone.

"Spice, you taste like sweet nectar sent to me from the gods."

"As only a goddess could know, my dear. Let me feed you some more."

The skies could no longer bear the burden of heat. Several flashes of lightning brightened up the dark blue skies, followed by mighty roars of thunder.

"The Great Spirits are mirroring the fire burning between us," he told her.

Suddenly, the skies opened up and a light drizzle began to fall. "I want to make love right here in the rain," he said, holding her back as she tried to run inside.

"Isn't it dangerous to be so close to water with the lightning?" she asked.

"Correct," he says hesitantly. "Okay, so Mr. Sagittarius here tends to get a bit carried away with his passion."

He pulled her toward him as soon as they made it inside. Her towel fell to the floor. He eyed her well-toned body longingly. She however was embarrassed by her stark nudity. It had been quite a while, decades, since she had come so close to sex with anyone other than James.

She ran to the bathroom and put her robe on. Instead of returning to the living room where she heard him getting comfortable, she went to the kitchen. She needed a drink, or food; anything other than him in her mouth. She decided upon the fruit punch that she had concocted earlier from oranges, tangerines, mangoes and pineapple.

"Have you run away again?" he joined her in the kitchen. "You seem so tense. I won't try to pressure you into going anyplace that you do not want to go."

"The intensity and quick pace has slightly wrecked my nerves," she admitted, as she poured the fruit punch, much of it spilling. "I think I need to add some rum to this punch."

He kissed her gently on the forehead then stepped back to give her some space, "Sweetness, I am all the spice that you need right now. Trust me, I too am smitten; it happened this fast."

"But isn't this how it always happens for guys like you?" she asked. The uncertainty was beginning to seep back in.

"I understand the doubt that I hear in your voice; so I am not going to be offended," he said. "Believe me though, as I said earlier, if all I wanted was some pussy, I would not be here. I could get that very easyily without all this work."

"Don't rub it in," she said.

"All that I want to rub into you is my loving," he remarked. "Trust me when I say that this feels different and special. I am not exactly sure where this is coming from, or going for that matter. I have this strange feeling that this is a second chance that I am getting to do right by us so that we can be together again. It must have been I who messed things up the time before."

Ann moved into his outstretched arms and relaxed once more in his embrace. She whispered in his ears, "It's hard for me to admit it, given all that I have gone through in the past year, but I feel as though I want you right this minute, Spice."

She took a sip of the punch and squirted some in his mouth. He begged for more. When she finished feeding him, they walked back into the living room toward the sofa. She sat down; he knelt by her side.

"You like naseberry?" he asked, noticing several of the ripe fruit in a bowl on the side table. "I'll feed it to you."

"They are my favorite," she replied. She looked at him with begging eyes and ran her tongue slowly along her lips."

He took a bite and chewed it lightly. With the crushed berry on his tongue, he rubbed it all over her lips. He rubbed some along her neck; then her ears, and her arms. He parted her robe while looking deep into her eyes. She shrugged out of it, offering her breasts up to him. He lingered at her nipples. When he moved down to her tummy, he squeezed the juice from the remainder of the berry into her navel and licked it until it was all gone.

He continued his journey south, then paused, "May I enter?"

"Yes!"

He slowly ran his tongue along her legs up to her thighs. When she felt his breath close to her vaginal lips, she was unable to wait much longer. She pressed against him urgently. He kissed her bud slowly and deliberately; then he stroked it with the tip of his fingers. "Stroking you this way reminds me of strumming my guitar," he told her.

"You have just struck the right chord," she moaned as she moved beyond her senses.

"Sweetness, come for me! I want to taste your flowing juices." He lapped it all up.

She could feel her fingers tingling as sparks of electricity ran through them. Her toes curled and her shoulders braced forward. She entered nirvana feeling alive and dead all in the same moment. She felt sure that she the goddess had met her god in flesh.

After she returned to consciousness and regained her equilibrium, she moved on top of him and said, "Spice, I want to love you back."

"Yes," he replied, "Love me so that from this moment forward I am a changed man. Love me so that when I walk out of this room, I will know we are joined in a special way forever."

She ran her tongue lightly over his nipples.

"Yes, suck them," he moaned. "How did you know that I wanted you there?"

"And here," she added. Slowly and deliberately, she ran her tongue down his chest to his pelvis. His manhood, now at full attention, greeted her. He directed her to a condom in his shirt pocket. She fetched it, put it on her tongue, and with one swooping movement pushed it firmly up his penis with her lips. As she licked the tip of his penis through the condom, she could feel the juices eagerly awaiting their release. She licked and sucked until he was ready to explode and implode.

But not wanting to just yet, he asked her to sit on him. "I want to remind you that it is a pum-pum you have, not a pussy," he whispered in her ears, regaining a bit of his composure.

"Spice, you are the man I waited for to guide me back to joy," she told him.

After several minutes of her riding him almost to orgasm, he lifted her off him, turned her on her belly and entered her from behind. "This is how I want us to come, your man guiding you from behind."

After what seemed like timeless eternity for them both, he rode them straight to glory's door, as together they came. Worn out, he slipped out of her. They lay side by side in each other's arms. He whispered in her ears, "From this moment on, no matter how hard you try to run, you are my woman, and I your man.

"I don't want to run anymore," she said. "I want what is blossoming between us to free us into becoming who we truly are," she told him.

"You have no resistance from me, my sweetness," he replied. "I am not interested in love that binds us unto becoming who we want each other to be."

They remained silent as the sound of rain falling upon the roof crept between them. "Maybe it is the sound of the heavens crying that is bringing tears to my eyes now; but they are happy tears, tears of rejoicing. Water to feed and enrich the soil for our love," he commented.

"If this is a dream, don't pinch me, I want to sleep forever," she whispered as she snuggled up against his neck.

"Except, as soon as the morning light hits, I will awaken to love you again and again. Let me sing you one last little lullaby." He hummed Marley's, "Woman Nuh Cry" once more as they both drifted off to sleep.

THALIA

The snowflakes swirled in the mild breeze until they grew tired and fell, covering the earth with their milky sheath. The barren trees welcomed the powdery cover, trying to escape their naked freeze. Thalia jumped up from her sleep unsure of where she was for a brief moment.

Scanning the room, she saw Lee sitting in front of the fireplace, stoking the fire. Yellow flames were crackling and leaping ferociously from the red-orange burning logs. She could not help but notice the polarity between the snow falling so smoothly outside, and the fire burning so briskly inside. The room was warm, the mood mellow. "This night could not be any more picturesque," she remarked to Lee.

Lee silently admitted that watching Thalia reclined on her sofa like a true sleeping beauty was as picturesque as it got. Thalia probably would have been more comfortable sleeping in the guest room, but Lee did not want to disturb the ambience that was so picture perfect. "I feel blessed," is all that Lee could muster.

Thalia blamed her being bad company and falling asleep on the two glasses of wine that she boxed down very quickly, especially since she drank so rarely. Lee acknowledged having drifted off too, only to be awakened by Sade's 'No Ordinary Love' playing on the CD. "So, I have been just sitting here mellow, playing with and watching the fire, watching my thoughts, watching you, and watching me watching you."

"I was watching my unconscious thoughts, and it was not pleasant," Thalia replied. "I was having such a terrible dream, I forced myself to get up."

Lee asked to hear more. "Even though I am not a doctor like you, I can be pretty insightful myself."

"Hey, I am only a neurologist, not a psychiatrist," Thalia replied. "I deal with the physical aspects of the brain, not the mental."

Lee teased that she would still be considered a head doctor.

"In that case, you are a soul doctor," Thalia teased back. "Seriously though Lee, one of the reasons why you are such a great performer is that you are a scholar of the emotions. Your ability to interpret and give back mood is remarkably incredible."

Lee thanked her, adding that taking care of the soul, being a soul doctor, was the core of any good black musical experience.

Thalia agreed. "Your recordings and performances make a lot of people feel better. That's why they clamor to see you. I used to listen to your music all the time during my divorce. The lyrics on your latest album really helped me to let go of the past and move on."

Pulling up a chair next to the sofa where Thalia was reclining, Lee jokingly asked if Thalia would prefer a song or a listening ear. "After all my years of therapy, I am an expert."

"So that's why you seem so in control," Thalia remarked. "You've been analyzed."

"It is one of the greatest gifts that I have ever given myself," Lee said in a very contemplative tone. "I got a great deal of benefit from having another human being focus their attention on me three times a week for two years, trying to help me understand myself better."

"One could label that as self-indulgence," Thalia remarked.

"And what's wrong with self-indulgence if it results in

your being in control of you, and not just being run ragged by your emotions all the time?" Lee asked.

"Viewed in that light, not a damn thing," Thalia said soberly.

"Well, let's get started with you, Ms. Davis, what brings you here this evening?" Lee asked Thalia, remembering the opening stanza of therapy with Dr. McFarland.

"In case you have forgotten, doctor," Thalia replied playfully, "you are the one who invited me to spend the night so that you ..."

Lee interrupted before she could finish, "So that I could take you to the airport in the morning. I can see already that avoidance is a great ally of yours, Ms. Davis; and we have not even gotten to the hard stuff."

"Okay, so I try to avoid dealing with my painful issues; one up for you, doc, great insight," Thalia replied. "That's perhaps why I always have such vivid dreams. But let me be a good patient, unlike you when I was your doctor, and follow your orders. I will stop my avoidance techniques and get back to my issues."

"Compliance has never been one of my virtues, but I can see that it is one of yours," Lee laughed. "Yes, go on."

"As I was saying before I was so rudely interrupted," Thalia continued, "the dream that I was having earlier has been recurring since high school. In these dreams I am always desperately looking for a toilet so that I can pee, and when I find it, there is so much mess I cannot use it." Thalia stopped and noted to herself that this is when she would always wake up for fear of wetting her bed. A couple times however when she was younger, she did not always get up on time and would have an accident. In tonight's version though, she did manage to find a clean toilet.

"Is that all?" Lee asked, noting that Thalia had drifted off to some unknown place.

"I am sorry," Thalia apologized. "I became flooded with memories of some of the other dreams. Tonight, I did find a clean toilet. But, as soon as I began to pee, a serpent reared up from the toilet bowl. It shot its tongue out onto my vagina, licked me and then squirted me with its venom. That's when I woke myself up. It scared me shit-less. Actually, pee-less, might be the better term." Thalia laughed at herself.

It did not seem like a laughing matter to Lee. "Thalia," Lee said gravely, "in spite of your attempt at levity, you look like a frightened little girl."

"I guess I was trying to disguise my pain."

"Try letting it out," Lee said reaching over and holding her hand. "I am right here with you. Let it go, whatever it is."

"That is much easier said than done," Thalia said, collecting herself. She hated that she had allowed her weakness to show. "I really don't know how. I don't even know if I want to."

"I'll tell you what I do," Lee said, trying to be helpful. "Whenever I am sad and blue, I dance. Something about the movement, letting my body go to whatever rhythm it wants to create, helps me to not be afraid."

"Now I see why you are such a good dancer," Thalia remarked, once again trying to bring some mirth into the moment.

"Please leave the interpretations to your doctor, who just so happens to have one for you right now," Lee ragged.

"I am anxious to hear."

"I think that your recurrent dreams have something to do with your sexuality," Lee said. "Peeing is symbolic of flow and release."

Thalia was silent for quite a while. "That's quite a stretch," she replied in disbelief. "I feel pretty solid about my sexuality." Lee remained silent.

Images of Thalia's ex-husband crept into her mind. She recalled how, as she blossomed into her full identity as a black woman, it was hard to be with a white man. She kept feeling like a 'mammy.'

After a long space of silence, during which there must have been an exchange of brain waves between them, Lee asked Thalia the reason for her divorce.

"The main reason why I left Reggie was because I did not want to be married to a white man any longer. I feel bad about my actions now, because my leaving hurt him deeply. Plus, I know that he loved me. But then again, his white privilege does give him the freedom to love freely, a liberty that many brothers do not have."

"You did not fully grasp what you were getting into when you married a white man?" Lee asked, a bit stunned at her reply.

"In the beginning I was only thinking about myself, the individual. But, as I have matured over the years into my blackness, the group collective issues have become more important."

"Going back to the dreams," Lee persisted, "I still think that they represent some deep personal conflicts around sexuality. Snakes are very phallic objects."

"I can see that your therapy did you well," Thalia replied sarcastically, somewhat miffed by Lee's persistent probing. "To think that all this time I did not realize that I was in the company of an amateur psychiatrist." Thalia thought about her real psychiatrist friend, Ann, who she would be seeing in less than twenty-four hours. A smile sneaked upon her face.

Lee was happy to see that Thalia's anger had dissipated almost as quickly as it had surfaced. Lee reached over and began massaging her arms; Thalia began to relax. She thought about what had transpired between them and realized that Lee was simply trying to help. Why then did she get angry so quickly? It was so out of character for her. When Lee was finished, Thalia took another gulp of wine. Her mood was much lighter and the queasiness in her stomach had dissipated. She had to admit that she preferred to let sleeping dogs lie; that had been her modus operandi all these years.

Lee returned to the seat in front of the fireplace. Feeling guilty about having pushed Thalia away, Lee suggested that they share a little brandy and soft music before they went to sleep. Thalia however was all stirred up and wide awake. She wanted some answers. And she wanted them quickly because she had a plane to catch early in the morning.

Lee went downstairs to put on an Enigma CD. Thalia decided to rekindle the fire during Lee's absence. As she watched the fire come back to life, she hoped that in a similar fashion, Lee would warm back up to her. She really had not meant to snap at Lee, but the pretend therapist pseudo-psychiatrist stuff had gotten to her, for she knew that issues were not always as simple and available for one cheap interpretation as they seemed. And how dare Lee accuse her of being confused about her sexuality. Thalia forcefully stoked the logs, bringing the flames to a fierce crackle and roar once more.

Lee returned shortly and poured the brandy. As the dry, liquid warmth spread throughout her body, Thalia could not believe how uptight she had become. A few minutes later, she could not believe how loose she was becoming. Lee gently reminded her that the invitation to dance was still on the floor. Thalia explained that she was not trying to be difficult and withholding, but that she found it somewhat intimidating to dance in front of one of the highest acclaimed jazz singers and performers in the world.

"With you, I am none of that, " Lee said, maintaining a gentle tone. "Just an ordinary, caring friend."

"I seem on the edge, don't I?" Thalia asked.

"That's why I suggested dancing in the first place," Lee replied. "There is a dancer lurking inside all of us waiting to loosen up our minds, bodies and spirits."

"Unfortunately, this one will do her dancer poorly," Thalia said. "I used to get teased a lot during high school that I danced like a white girl. That's probably why I am so shy now." Thalia took a bigger than usual gulp of brandy.

"Try and remember that I am a loving and caring friend and not a jealous classmate."

"Why are you being so supportive when I am seeming so ungrateful?" Thalia asked.

"Like you, I had a lot of fear," Lee explained. "I used to have terrible stage fright and had to always have a swig of brandy to get my nerves together before I performed."

"No one would ever know," Thalia remarked.

"That's because I learnt a trick about how to control it," Lee explained.

"Care to share?" Thalia asked.

"One of my old piano players noticed my jitters and decided to share one of his tricks of the trade with me. He told me that he would always shut his eyes and would create a loving and appreciative audience in his mind's eye at the beginning of each performance. He would envision the faces of the kids in his neighborhood. They used to love to come to his house to hear him and his Dad, a world famous trumpeter, perform. With that image locked in his head, no audience could scare him. There he was, still performing for his friends."

"Well, did it work for you?" Thalia inquired.

"I looked in Daddy's face that was all filled with pride watching his first born perform, and it has worked ever since," Lee told her. "He was the one who recognized my talent and always encouraged and supported me." Lee drifted once again into an earlier world, filled with loving memories of Dad, in spite of his bouts with depression and alcoholism.

In the ensuing silence, Thalia noticed the pain in her stomach had returned. She got up from the sofa and went to the window. The snow was still falling, creating a white, glistening blanket on top of the earth. As she watched it, the idea popped into her head that she should imagine the snow as Mylanta inside her burning stomach. To her surprise, the aching gradually subsided.

Thalia went and sat next to Lee, who was once again stoking the fire.

"When I closed my eyes like you suggested, it took me back to a very bleak period in my life, so I did not want to stay there," Thalia explained.

Lee apologized for making Thalia uncomfortable, who in turn apologized for seeming to fail at Lee's suggestions.

"Darling, you fail only if you fail to try," Lee replied. These were the exact words that mother used to say when she would give up on her piano lessons. Thalia shook her head knowingly.

"I am sure that in order for you to be where you are now, a brilliant doctor, you must have won most of your battles," Lee continued.

"Part of my winning those battles was to put a very tight lid on all the emotional turmoil that was constantly brewing around me," she said. "After my mother died, I discovered that if I immersed myself completely in my studies, there was no time left to mope and be sad."

"I understand where you are coming from, because I used to do the same thing," Lee said. "Only, you turned to books, I to music. Like you, I excelled at my work and was doing great. But that all came to a stop five years ago when my father died. You see, he and I were extremely close, almost inseparable. When he died, so did the music inside me. I became so depressed I lost all my will to live. I couldn't eat, sleep or get out of bed. As much as I wanted to die, lucky for me, I was too weak to kill myself. My manager, bless her, saved my life." Lee paused for a while, remembering this turning point. "She came by one day and literally had to drag me out of the darkness in my room. She drove me straight to a psychiatric hospital. At first, I didn't want to be there, but I did not have the energy to try to get out. Thank god I stayed. After a few days, I began to appreciate the opportunity it gave me to take time out. For the first time in my life, I slowed down enough to begin listening to me."

"Like you're trying to get me to do now," Thalia remarked.

"It wasn't until the therapy that followed after I left there that all the things that I had avoided for so long, mostly out of fear and shame, began to unfold," Lee continued. "Then I realized that they did not have the bite I thought they did, which is why I was trying to forget in the first place. I discovered also that these negative feelings had been directing me all my life; I just was not aware of it. As I gradually began to understand who I had been and why, I became freer to chose and create who I wanted to be, and who I am at any given moment in my life."

Thalia became overcome with painful memories. Unable to hold back the tears any longer, she shared an incident that she had long forgotten. "It happened during my freshman year. I can still hear the boos and the jeering."

Lee reassured her that she did not have to go there until she felt ready. Thalia knew that at this point there was no stopping it now. "I had entered a beauty pageant at the insistence of my hall sisters, most of whom were from the South. My very 'Nordic' features, 'bright skin' and 'good hair' and green-hazel eyes had always guaranteed my top billing in all black beauty circles. I am sure it had bought me a ticket to the final round that night. The other finalist was a drop-dead gorgeous, beautiful, dark-skinned Afro-styled sister. I am sure that a few years earlier she would not have been allowed to enter a beauty contest, and might not even have thought that she was beautiful. But this was the beginning of the newly emerging 'Black is Beautiful' consciousness.

That night, as we did our final walk down the runway, a group of women in the audience, all wearing dashikis and sporting Afros themselves, started booing and yelling out to me that I should get off the stage with my honky-ass, no-tail, white self. One of them yelled out that I was not a real sister, just a product of the white man's rape. I was so humiliated; I did exactly what they said. I turned, walked, no, I ran through the curtains, and off the stage. I kept running all the way to my room, packed a bag and took the train back home to New York. I never returned. I was so humiliated."

Even now, she could still feel the hurt. She took a minute to regain her composure. "A week later, my aunt and my best friend went back and got the rest of my belongings. I returned to the job I had during high school as a laboratory assistant at one of the ivy-league universities for the rest of the semester. I had applied and been accepted there with full scholarship, but because I was dead set on going to a black college, I declined. Lucky for me, they accepted me back the next semester. I did summer school for two years and was able to catch up with my class. That's also the college that Ann, my best friend, was attending so I was very glad to reunite with her. We had been going to the same schools since middle school."

Thalia took another breather. "So, you see what being on stage evokes in me—lots of shame and pain."

Lee reached over and hugged her. "Thalia, that story is a true example of how we black folks act out our self hatred, nothing other than internalized racism turned against ourselves and each other. The good news is that things are different now. We are much more accepting of all the ranges of our color, from ivory white to jet black. Blackness is defined more by the soulfullness of our being, than the physical appearance of our skin color. But that's just recently. You got caught in the pent-up rage of those of us with negroid features. Believe me, we caught much more hell for looking black than you did for looking white."

"On an intellectual level, I agree with you," Thalia replied. "I have, and still do get a lot of privileges because of looking so fair, so 'Nordic'. I do believe that it's not only white people who must come to terms with their privilege, but many of us light-skinned blacks. On an emotional level though, it gets very complicated for me. You see, that night, I saw my mother in the audience screaming at me too. She was a part of those other dark-skinned sisters who were attempting to reclaim the power of their darkness. Up to the day that she died, my beautiful black-velvet mother had always hated herself for being so dark. I am sure that she married a white man because she did not want to have a child look as black as she did. Plus, of course, many dark, black men are not attracted to dark women because they do not want to have dark-skinned children; they want to have 'bright' children."

"It's incredible that you turned out looking so white," Lee remarked.

"I took all the white recessive genes that I could from my father, including, unfortunately, my flat behind," she said. Thalia sighed, wishing that her Mom could have seen her real beauty, even if it meant she had to reject the norms by which she, her daughter, would be labeled pretty. Thalia realized that this would have been the first step in her mother to reclaim her blackness, which was probably why she put her Mom into the crowd of jeering women. She was convinced that her Mom's inability to accept her true beauty contributed greatly to her death.

Her tears began to flow. Lee held her firmly and rocked her until there were no more tears. She thanked Lee, "I do believe that we need to have safe spaces to talk about our pain. I seem to have opened up a kettle of worms!"

"Snakes, darling" Lee replied. "Just a little humor to lighten up the mood and stop all this heavy-duty stuff. Your hour is up anyway."

"How much do I owe you then, doc?" Thalia said, smiling for the first time in a long while.

"Nothing," Lee replied.

"Then it won't work," Thalia joked back. "They say that if you don't pay, you don't value the lessons. Plus, I charged you for all your visits when I treated you for your headaches."

"All I want is your commitment to our ongoing friendship," Lee said. "Even though we have been kidding, I am very glad that this is not a professional relationship, because then we could not be friends. My therapist made the boundaries very clear to me when she realized I was developing a crush on her."

Thalia quickly became embarrassed as she noticed how intimate the space between her and Lee had become. She inched away as unobtrusively as she could from Lee's embrace, all the while trying to reassure herself that her friendship with Lee was okay, because the power dynamic in the practice of physical medicine was so different from that which existed between a therapist and patient. "Unlike our psychiatric colleagues, we are allowed to have friendships with our patients. No one thinks that it is unethical; in fact, it is not so unusual for an internist or a surgeon to marry a former patient."

"You don't have to feel too guilty because we were already friends before I came to see you," Lee remarked. "Plus, I am the one who has been pushing this friendship along, always inviting you to come to my performances."

"Notice that you have never had any resistance from me," Thalia replied. "I have always been in awe of you. The first time that we met at that dinner party and you shook my hand, I felt like a school girl with a crush on a movie star."

"I must confess that I was drawn to you because I have a thing for green-eyed beauties," Lee said.

"There goes that Nordic privilege again."

"Not totally this time," Lee said, in a notably somber tone. "It's a bit more personal with me. You see, my mother had the saddest and most beautiful green eyes."

"My time now to play therapist," Thalia said, glad that she had opened up the space between them and they were no longer sitting up against each other. "You obviously are searching for your mother in your relationships. It sounds a bit incestuous to me."

"Aren't we all!" Lee said. "And by the way, how did the lady who denies ever having any sexual conflicts move so quickly into the physical realm with this?"

Thalia's annoyance resurfaced immediately. "I was strictly making reference to emotional intimacy."

"And so have I," Lee replied. "I hope that you are not feeling uncomfortable by some of the things I have said about us."

Thalia turned and grimaced at Lee, "So you mean to tell me that you don't find me physically irresistible. My feelings are hurt."

"Thalia, no, do not play with me in this half-serious way," Lee said, showing her anger for the first time. "One foot in, but one foot out in case you have to make a quick exit. Don't put me in a bind and leave me with no way out. If I had tried to force myself upon you, you would have probably felt that I was taking advantage of your emotional vulnerability. Make up your mind Thalia, which is it?"

"Lee, I was being playful, as I thought we both were," she apologized. "But, maybe you are right, maybe I am being a bit dishonest. Maybe there is some wish beneath all of this. Maybe the snake is rearing its ugly head."

"You have to decide if you want this to go any further or not," Lee told her. "I am clear that I do. And by the way, you have just the right amount of curves to balance our silhouette; I have a lot for both of us, and more. I have always felt that I have too much ass, which is why I admire your not having as much. Between us, we have enough."

Thalia stood up and gestured to Lee who was still sitting by the fireplace, "Come dance with me and help me find that space where I can let go."

"I will. I will do and be anything you need me to be right now."

Lee kissed her lightly on her cheeks. She closed her eyes.

"Make me into whoever you need me to be right now," Lee told her. "Why don't I remove your beautiful, silk scarf from around your neck and use it to blindfold you. It should make your fantasies easier. No need to be afraid. I would never hurt you."

"Right now I am in a trust zone," she told Lee. Lee tied the scarf around her eyes.

Without asking, Lee reached behind and began unzipping Thalia's gray, woolen dress. Thalia was amazed that even though her mind was telling her to give Lee the brick wall, her body signaled Lee to continue. Blame it on the damn blindfold, Thalia thought to herself. Lee grasped her elbows and helped her to step out of her clothes that had fallen into a puddle at their feet. As Thalia allowed Lee to slip off her panties and her bra, she was surprised that the shame she often felt about her naked body had melted away.

"You are so very beautiful," Lee whispered, joining Thalia in her nakedness

"Now, let your body go limp on mine and just flow with me to the music." Lee said, kissing her lightly on her cheeks. Once again, Thalia noticed that her mind and body were going in opposite directions, as she opened her mouth and invited Lee in.

"With each breath, blow out all your fears and place them right here in my mouth. I will exhale the pain for you," obviously welcoming the invitation.

Thalia breathed a sigh of relief as their mouths moved closer to each other's. "I like this Lee. I could stay here dancing with you like this forever."

"All we have is right now. So let's live as fully as we can in it," Lee said, breathing harder and heavier.

When the music stopped, blindfold still in place, Lee laid her on the sofa. "I want to love you, to adore you, like never before in your life. I want my loving to erase all the painful memories; I want to lick them all away."

Lee kissed her breasts and sucked each one until they were fully erect, suggestive of the sweet juices that were flowing down under. Each nerve cell in Thalia's body was firing, making her more open and alive than she had ever felt. Their charge quieted all the queer voices that had been conversant in her head all night. The background noise gone, Thalia found the courage to come out of hiding and be fully present with her pleasure. She gave herself freely to the ecstasy of the moment; there was no turning back now. Thalia pulled off the blindfold. Lee's loving wink greeted her.

Lee plucked a feather from one of the pillows on the sofa and ran it down Thalia's thighs. There definitely was no turning back now. Thalia let her body go limp as she relaxed into its tingling. Lee tongued her entire body from head to toe, returning to her navel to lap it for a while. Thalia screamed in ecstasy, her remaining breath becoming shallower with each touch. Just when she thought that she could not breathe any longer without exploding, Lee told her, "Hold on, there is more!" Lee then went and fetched some whipped cream and squeezed it all over her body; then licked it clean. Lee pulled her big toes together and bit them, sending her into a nosedive. Thalia's clitoris began to pound out of control, heralding a tail spin. "Lee, I cannot wait any longer," she panted. "There is electricity running all through my body. Now please, now!"

Lee calmly told her, "I have breathed away the pain and licked away all your sorrows. Come enter rhapsody with me now." Lee began licking her clitoris in a circular motion. Thalia sank deeper and deeper inside her pelvis, allowing her breath to flow from her vagina with each swirl of Lee's tongue. When her breath, mixed with the motions of Lee's tongue crescendoed to the boiling point, she erupted like a volcano, pouring her hot lava all over Lee's face. The sensation catapulted Lee into nirvana with

Thalia, and together they came. "I have tasted my milk and honey," Lee told her, "I have found my heaven."

They lay numb and motionless on the couch for several minutes, enjoying their shared bliss before they both fell off to sleep.

Thalia was the first to awaken. Her appetite having been whet, she suggested that they make love one more time. "This is my first orgasm since … I can't even recall," she explained.

"I could die from total bliss," Lee warned. "I don't think that I could tolerate more than one orgasm. You just took all my life away." Lee looked into her begging, green eyes and continued, "But I would be a fool wouldn't I, to turn down such a beautiful lady. How sweet death would be to die in the arms of such a beautiful woman. Let's go upstairs to my bedroom so that we can slip into sweet, uninterrupted sleep."

They locked hands, as Lee led her upstairs to the bedroom. Lee lay on the bed while Thalia went to the bathroom. When she returned, Lee pulled her on top and they lay cuddled in each other's arms for a long while.

Thalia slipped into a dream-like state. The serpent from her earlier dream appeared again, however, this time, she was not frightened. Suddenly it occurred to her that perhaps she had not been finding clean toilets in her dreams because she had been going into the wrong stalls. She wanted to be sure to ask Ann for her interpretation.

She kissed Lee deeply, allowing their mouths to familiarize themselves with everything there was to taste and feel in them. Thalia wanted to make love again, "Forgive me if I seem persistent," she said, pouting a bit, "but shouldn't I make love to you too? I do not want to be the only one that was pleasured."

"The only one that was pleasured!" Lee exclaimed in amazement, "Some women just don't get it, do they. Every now and then Thalia, it is okay for only you to receive. I got my total pleasure and orgasm from giving love to you. Making love to you was also making love to me. I don't need any more loving right now, honey. It's sweet of you to be concerned about me, but let someone else take care of you for a change." Lee kissed her tenderly once more and then suggested that they go to sleep so that they could make love again in the morning before Thalia left for her trip. "I love making love in the morning, just before day breaks."

"I won't use whipped cream then," Thalia joked, "I should tell you that I am a pure chocolate lover."

"I am sweeter than chocolate," Lee replied. "When the time is right, you will discover that I am much better and twice as addictive."

"I can't wait," Thalia said. She attempted to revive herself for one more round, but as Lee predicted, sleep overtook them both.

SARA

The sky was filled with dull, gray clouds. A fierce wind blew from across the mountains, bringing with it cold, wet rain to the California coast.

When the raindrops began blowing onto the balcony, Sara got out of the hammock and went inside. She was forced to relinquish any remaining hope for one of those Southern California sunsets in technicolor and panavision. It would have been such a wonderful backdrop for the romantic evening that she was planning to spend with Don. This evening, the horizon refused to be sandwiched between the red-orange skies above and the deep, blue ocean below. Instead, every place was sullen, and sulking in a brownish gray hue.

She answered the phone. Don was on the other line.

"Honey, I may not be able to get home in time to take you to the airport," he said. "Jessie just called and asked me to make rounds on one of our patients over in the Valley. He is still in the operating room and ..."

"Why can't Rob cover for him?" she asked. No answer. "I bet that you are trying to get out of our plans for the evening!"

"Woman, why do you always ask me a question and then answer it yourself?" he said getting very angry. "I shouldn't even bother to reply, but since I have nothing to hide, I'll tell you why. Rob is not answering his pager or his phone. When he left the office this morning he said that he was going to be rehearsing all afternoon for his upcoming concert. He is probably blowing that trumpet so loud he cannot hear the phone ringing."

"Whatever, Don," she said in disgust. "I was really hoping that we could spend a quiet and romantic evening together since I am going to be gone for over a week."

"And you'll be back won't you?" he said. "We'll have plenty of time then."

"Dr. Kelly did tell us that we should let our relationship take priority over our work, at least once a week," she scolded him. "At least I am trying to keep my end of the bargain."

"Dr. Kelly can't tell me shit about how to live my life," he replied bitterly. "That quack probably got his Ph.D. from some correspondence school. And what gave you the right to imply that I was not keeping my end of the bargain?"

"I'm sorry Don, I didn't mean to," she said apologetically. She realized that she had ticked him off and needed to appease him if she were ever going to get her way with him. "It's just that I am leaving tonight and …"

It did not work. He became even more enraged, "Sara, I am goddamn sick and tired of always having to jump to your demands. Sara always has to have her way, no matter how much I am inconvenienced." Unable to hide his exasperation any longer he yelled at her, "Can't you see that this is the root of our problems. It is always your way, or the highway. Kaboom with anyone else's needs."

"Don, I don't want to get into another fight with you," she said.

"Then stop being so fucking controlling," he screamed in her ears.

"If I seem controlling, which, by the way, I do not think that I am," she said, still trying to cajole him, "it is only because I miss you. We don't spend time together anymore. I love you very much Don and I am just fighting to save our marriage."

"Well, this is certainly not the way to do it," he said,

calming down somewhat. "Sara, you're going to have to trust me and give me space if this marriage is going to work. Stop trying to change me."

"Don, I don't want to change you," she said. It occurred to her that what she probably needed to change was her plans to go to Jamaica in the morning. "How about I cancel my trip? I would much prefer to use this time off around the house being a real wife to you; pampering you and loving you like I have always wanted to."

"I would love that too," he said. "I don't think that your girlfriends would like that though. If they found out that you canceled this trip on my account, they would probably have me killed. Ann in particular."

"No, they wouldn't," she said, "I am sure that both Ann and Thalia would understand; they've both been married."

"Honey, we'll have lot's of time when you get back. I could use some down time alone right now. Even though I make fun of your idol, Dr. Kelly, this counseling stuff gets to me sometimes."

"Guess what," Don said, "I'm going to try my best to track down Rob. Let me get off the phone now and go drop by his home to see if he is there; it's on the way to the hospital, so it should not delay me much in case I have to go make some lightning rounds."

"Don, come home as soon as you can, baby, I'll be waiting," she told him, hanging up the phone and trying to mask her rising anxiety.

She made herself a vodka martini. She needed to calm down before he got there. She was sure that he had made this all up so that he could go to Rob's house. Her private detective told her last week that Don was spending a lot of time at Rob's house. He was pretty certain that Don was having an affair with Rob's sister Melanie, the jet-set fashion model. Sara had seen the way that Don kept looking at Melanie the night at the opera when Rob introduced them to her. She had heard Melanie's loud announcement that she would be staying at Rob's house for a while until she decided whether or not she was going to return to Europe or move to New York.

She gulped her martini for solace. Even though his affairs hurt, no matter what the race, the thought of Don being with a white woman rubbed the salt a little deeper into her wound.

She turned on the television. A very attractive blonde, blue-eyed anchor was reading the news. She turned it off angrily. "Why the fuck do you give me a white woman at this very moment that I am wishing that they would all disappear from the face of the earth!" she shouted at the TV.

With her anger and agitation escalating again, and her drink finished, she went over to the bar to make herself another. The repetitive motion and noise of shaking the martini temporarily quieted her nerves. She realized that another reason why she was feeling so on edge was because she dreaded the upcoming trip. She had doubts about spending such up close and personal time with Ann after all the years of their estrangement. Since they were roommates in medical school, almost twenty years ago, she and Ann had not spoken to or seen each other, until James' funeral. She had felt obliged to attend the funeral. Unbeknownst to Ann, she and James had dated each other while attending a pre-med summer program for minority students in Boston. It didn't go much beyond a few dinner dates because neither one of them particularly liked each other. She didn't like how nerdy he was most of the time, and he didn't like how disorganized and spacey she was at times.

That day however, as she saw James again after twenty years, lying so still in the coffin, images of her father lying in his coffin kept inserting themselves into her memory, reawakening a lot of long forgotten grief and guilt. So, when Thalia suggested at the repast that all three of them should have a reunion and try and patch things up, she agreed. It seemed like a great idea then because she was feeling that life was too delicate to waste time being angry with those that you love. But that was a little over a year ago. Now, as she nervously waited to say goodbye to her husband the night before the reunion, she wasn't sure anymore that she wanted to dredge up the painful past with Ann.

As she sipped her second martini, she felt it hitting the spot. Her neck and shoulders felt much less tense. She went upstairs and put on some Miles Davis because music always helped her unwind and pass the time. Tonight she was going to forget Reverend Morton's constant warning about the evil of booze and devil music—jazz and R&B.

When she went back downstairs, Don was standing in the hallway. "Honey, thank God you're home," she said as

SATURDAY

she went toward him. He was soaking wet. He handed her his coat and umbrella. She took them to the powder room.

"I am going upstairs to dry off and put some comfortable clothes on," he yelled to her. He was shocked to see that she had loosened up and was having a drink. What had gotten into her? All the good times they used to have drinking, smoking weed and doing an occasional hit of cocaine went out the door when Sara got seriously involved in their church. He did not comment however, because he did not want to mess up the flow. Instead, he asked her to make him a martini also.

She wasn't sure if it was all that devil's nectar in her that was distorting her view, but something about his voice and the way he looked at her made her feel that things were going to get better. So, she shook martinis for them both. She did not want to stop the magic.

She would pray for forgiveness tomorrow.

He returned to the living room wearing the warm-up suit that she gave him for Christmas and sat on the sofa next to her.

"Honey, I am glad to see that you finally wore that jogging suit," she said as she handed him the martini. "You look so sexy. Burnt orange is a very good complement to the gold undertones in your skin."

He took the martini and raised his glass, "Sara, let's drink to us. Things are a bit tough right now, but if you take care of me the way you are doing now, it's gonna be all right. Come sit on Daddy's lap," he motioned to her.

They intertwined their hands and sipped from each other's glass.

"To us, Don," she said. She kissed his ears and whispered, "My commitment is stronger now than ever before. I will do whatever it takes to make things work."

"In that case, you're going to have to be more understanding honey," he told her. "You have to believe that I love you as best that I know how to love a woman." He cuddled up close to her and gave her that special wink that he always did when he was in a sexy mood. "In spite of all the many problems we have had over these years, I need you to always be my wife."

His words were like sweet music to her ears. How could she have doubted his love? She tried to explain the reason for her jealously so that he could forgive her. "I know that I have been impatient at times and have gone away. It's just that it is so hard for me to think of you with other women."

"Sara, why do you always go down that road?" he asked as he pulled away.

"Because that's the road that we started on," she replied. "There was someone else then and there has been someone else ever since."

"That's a bunch of bullshit!" Don said angrily, his voice several decibels above normal. He jumped up from the sofa and started lecturing her, "You black women never give black men any slack, do you? Take tonight for example, have you shown any appreciation for the fact that I worked out the coverage and came home to be with you? Not to mention that I have been desperately trying to show you how much I want us to be together?" He answered his own question. "No! You are just waiting to show me up and blame me for all our problems. Of course you, the newly converted righteous bitch, never take a look in the mirror." She got up and tried to hold him, but he pushed her away and continued the lambasting. "Our problems have to do with us, woman, not the other people that you accuse me of seeing."

She had enough. She was tired of always having to take the blame along with all the other black women, for not being accepting enough of her man's need, no right, to screw around. She shouted back at him angrily, "No, you take a look in the mirror too. Why did you have to go down that road? You black men are always so predictable. Always casting black women as castrating Sapphire bitches so that you can have an excuse for fucking white whores!"

Don pushed her back toward the couch. "One look at your past and you will see that you are the number one bitch and whore. So open your legs and give me some pussy."

She tried to pull away from him. She knew exactly which road they were going down now, but there was no turning back now. "I am neither a bitch nor a whore, and I am not a feline, so I don't have a pussy to give," she snapped back. "Your dirty talking is probably a turn on for your new whore, Melanie, but it won't work for me." Covering her ears, she yelled even louder, "Most of those nigger-loving white women are nothing but freaks; all they want is your big fucking dicks. But maybe that's all you niggers have to give."

Don wrestled her firmly down on the sofa, spilling both their drinks on the side table. "There is nothing nasty about pussy, my dear Sister Sara. Like most men and lesbians, I love it," he gloated. He pushed her away then continued, "That's another part of our problem. Sex is always dirty to you. What's wrong with wanting a little pussy and asking for it?"

"I have never said that anything was wrong with the act," she snapped back at him. "It's the words that you use to describe it. I am sure that no woman wants to be disrespected. At least, let me speak for the women that I know."

"And most of the women you know are fucking uptight broads," he snapped back. "There, is that word better?" His anger was close to boiling point now. "The ones that you accuse me of fucking, at least they know how to keep a man wanting more of what they got, enough so he is willing to risk being caught."

"There you go again throwing your goddamn affairs in my face," she retorted. "Well guess what, you can leave now and go fuck that white bitch one more time. I'm sure that she cannot get enough of that big black dick of yours. Trust me, this is the last time that I am going to allow you to disrespect me. I don't have to take this; I am a very successful doctor."

"Yeah, say it," he yelled. "Say that you earn more money than me, even though you give half of it to that goddamn church. Well let me show you who still wears the pants in this house and had the penis the last time that I checked." Don pushed her off the sofa onto the floor. He slapped her across her face a couple of times. When she tried to cover her face with her hands he grabbed them and pinned them by her side. He shouted at her, "You're nothing but a castrating black bitch, not even worthy enough of the title, whore. They know how to make a man feel good when they fuck him."

"Get off of me," she cried. "Just let me go."

He hit her once again, this time in her groin area. He screamed at her, "I guess it's all that abuse shit that you have been talking about in counseling that has you so messed up. And that goddamn counselor, calling himself a spiritual counselor, he needs more help than the both of us; he is nothing but a repressed homosexual."

She yelled at him to shut up, but he kept on going. "I don't care anymore. I am leaving; I have had enough. I should have stayed at Rob's house like I wanted to. Instead I came home to try to patch things up with you, and what did I get in return? Your non-appreciative mouth telling me that I am not good enough because I don't make enough money as you. Well, I hope that you find some Jamaican man whom you can control with all your money. I won't be here when you return."

Her body ached all over, and she no longer had the mental energy to argue with him. She tried to kick him in a last ditch effort to get him to let her go. He grabbed her feet and sat on top of her. She gave up then; she could no longer defend herself from his brute force. Her body went limp. She curled up in the fetal position and started rocking her head.

He began to slap her again, shouting over and over "See what you make me have to do to you to gain a little respect." She laughed in his face. His abuse did not hurt anymore.

Images of her father started to float back into her mind's eye. She numbed her body and let her mind take her far away to the beach in Florida where she and her brother used to play. She moaned in an almost inaudible and rambling voice, "Please, please forgive me for being a bad girl. I should not have said the things that I did. I have a big mouth. I don't know what gets into me. I am sorry to make you have to hit me. I don't want any other man and I don't want you to have any other woman."

He began to calm down, "Then come fuck me woman, and this time, give it to me bare-back."

Still lying on the floor, and not caring anymore, she moaned, "Take me whichever way you please."

"That's what I want to hear," he said, pulling off her robe and mounting her on the floor.

She sucked her thumb. The spreading numbness was complete by then. She did not feel anything. She heard him say as he came, "Now you know who really is in control."

She drifted away to unknown times and unfamiliar faces, until the sound of Don's snoring brought her back to life. She looked at her watch; it was 10 p.m. She jumped up and rushed to get ready so she could catch the red eye flight to Miami. She tried to awaken Don to have him take her to the airport like he promised.

"Please call a cab. I'm too tired," he said, without opening his eyes.

SATURDAY

She called a limousine. She marveled at how numb she had become; how empty she felt inside. Nothing seemed to matter much any more. She thought about canceling the trip, but then felt that she could not stay in the house with him any longer. She prayed that she would be able to hide these bruises from Ann and Thalia, especially Ann.

2
Sunday

The smell haunted Ann.

It mixed with the scent of new luggage and the sweat of those not ready for the heat of paradise. She tried to block it out and the thoughts that it packed with it. Troubling thoughts of the night just past that she was not yet ready to deal with.

But it was under her skin. And every time she moved, it moved with her and wafted from her pores into her wide-open nostrils and reminded her.

Fortunately, none of the bustling travelers, hurrying into waiting vans, leaving flights and welcoming arms, were concerned with this tall, red-headed black woman with furrowed brows and anxious eyes. But she knew Thalia and Sara would be. Distance and troubles aside, they had been best friends for so long, been through so much together, Ann feared that they would see right through her.

Ann took a deep resolute breath and squared her shoulders. Hoping that their flight was delayed, for she was almost an hour late, she rushed over to the arrivals board. She let out a big sigh of relief when she saw the 'just landed' sign. The weather must have been as nasty in Miami as it had been in Jamaica. She went up to the waving gallery to see if she could still catch them as they disembarked. Her eyes wandered from traveler to traveler, as she tried to make out the faces of her girlfriends.

She had seen them both last year at James' funeral, but the service and the grief had given them no real time to talk. Thalia had returned to the States and taken up residence in Washington DC, only a few months before James' death. Even though they had so little communication during the ten years that Thalia had made Africa her home, her connection with Thalia would be easy. But Sara was a whole other story. Despite her California home, closer in physical distance to Ann's New Orleans base, she might as well have been the one on a different continent. They were going to have many miles of friendship to traverse over the upcoming week.

Ann paced along the rails looking for Sara's face. Having no idea how willing Sara would be to heal their friendship, Ann wanted to digest Sara's presence before they greeted each other. After several minutes of searching in vain, Ann figured that they must have been among the first to get off the plane. She decided to go back downstairs and wait by the customs area. Remembering what Sara was like in their med school days, she would have insisted on traveling first class. Then, even though they were all struggling students, Sara always managed to land in the front of the cabin. Now that she was a wealthy gynecologist, first class and the Concorde was probably the only way she flew.

Ann made her way through the ever-growing numbers of tourists with people. She almost laughed out loud at the tourist faces painted with superficial grins to conceal their anxiety at being totally enveloped and outnumbered by blackness. She wondered if the plastic smiles and 'Welcome to Jamaica' songs of the local singers dressed in traditional costumes did anything to assuage their fears. She wondered how Thalia would react to this show of Jamaican plantation mentality. Many of Thalia's letters from Africa had suggested that the racial identity issues that had plagued her from their days in elementary school had blossomed into a passionate analysis of society at large and the racial ills that slavery left behind. The pages had been filled with disgust at the colonial infrastructure that still dominated the economic and social systems. It was only now that Ann noticed how empty the same pages had been on news of Thalia's own life. And she, consumed by her own feelings of victimization, had not asked. But still, she didn't worry about reconnecting with Thalia. Sprung decades ago out of a melee from which Thalia had rescued her, their friendship was tough and resilient. And now that Thalia was living in the same city where Ann's daughter, Ahsima, was attending college, she was sure they would be seeing a lot of each other over the coming years.

Ann's roving eyes rested for a moment on a porter. He was obviously trying to pick up more than the luggage of the visitors to his island paradise, as evidenced by his particular interest in the suitcases of attractive women unaccompanied by males. Watching him return unfazed from his most recent failed attempt with the blond woman he escorted to ground transportation, Ann could not help but

SUNDAY

marvel at the daring and persistence of Jamaican men. Having seen no sign of Thalia and Sara, she decided to risk becoming the new object of his flirtations and ask him to look for her friends when he went back inside the restricted customs area. If she was lucky, his interest was directed primarily at the white women.

Her wishes were short-lived. "What can I do for the woman wid the sexy smile and pretty glow all around her," he beamed as she approached him.

Ann stiffened a bit as she remembered how a similar line last evening had turned her life upside down. Ann asked for his assistance, making every effort not to appear too needy.

"If they look anything like you, the pleasure would be all mine."

Ann could not help but smile at his pseudo-American accent. She would gladly unload hers on him, in exchange for a permanent infusion of her first true cadence, her Jamaican tongue. Soon after arriving in New York at the tender age of eight, she had realized that she needed to let go of her foreign accent if she were going to survive and be accepted in school.

"What a pretty smile you have," he continued to lay it on, "If you should need any more services, you know, that of a real man …"

"Sorry, but I have one already," Ann interrupted, in her delicate, reconstituted Jamaican accent.

As the words rolled off her tongue, Ann realized that it wasn't simply a routine answer that she had given. She had to struggle to hold back last night's memories, they were threatening to take precedence over her conversation with the porter.

As soon as the porter went inside, Ann headed toward her car where she told him she would wait. She tipped the policeman who had been watching it for her, making sure to avoid any eye contact with him. She could not deal with another man coming on to her right this moment, no matter how innocent and playful. As she walked the short distance from the policeman to the car, she became very conscious, maybe a bit paranoid, about her gait. Spice's parting whisper sounded in her ear, 'if anyone ask why you walking so sweet, tell them it is because you and your man just do it.' Damn Jamaican men and their arrogance, she thought, angrily slamming the car door.

She leaned her head against the headrest. But, rather than washing his memory away, the few light sprinkles that began to fall, and the clap of thunder that followed, flooded her with the images, sounds, and smells she was attempting to ignore. Tuning in to the sounds of the rain, she tried to block out visions of Spice. She forced her mind to sink into the rhythm of the raindrops. Her imagination soared upwards and she visualized herself drifting upon a puffy white cloud. Journeying through the never-ending sky, she arrived at a crossroad. The street to the right was named Desire; the other, to the left, Full Street. Desire Street—with its straight roads, flat land, and neatly manicured trees and shrubbery—was crowded with people with smiling faces. In contrast, Full Street was bumpy, curvy and lined with untamed shrubs and trees. There were but a few passers-by on this less traveled road. She was instantly drawn to the neatness of Desire Street, until she noticed that the smiles were frozen on the faces of the numerous inhabitants. As she went from person to person, their effortless, mechanical movements surprised her. She halted when she recognized herself. Looking into her eyes, only death reflected back at her. Shocked, she realized the mask of happiness that she wore on Desire Street was a reflection of her everyday life as she went through the motions of living. Her smiles and hellos toward her fellow human beings were plastic, empty and meaningless. For if she really cared, why had she not done more to help others see that love was the only anecdote for all the evil and violence that had gripped the world?

Glancing over at Full Street, Ann knew it was where she belonged. The unmanned growth of the bushes echoed the free moving spirited stroll of the few that walked along. There was a pleasing sense of comfort and contentment that everyone exuded as they looked each other in the eye, something no one on Desire Street had done. They seemed confident in their love of self and each other.

Ann could not ask for a more revealing metaphor for her life. Everything that had happened over the past year had catapulted her to this crossroad. This potential journey onto 'Full Street' seemed to have begun with her inviting her friends to reconnect with her in Jamaica. She, like Thalia and Sara, had much to acknowledge and confront if she was to begin her walk through life on her true path, one in which she was going to replace her fears with love. In that moment, she promised herself to start each day in full awareness that death sat on her left shoulder. Lost in the quietude of her thoughts, she made a silent promise to the heavens: "I feel ready now for 'Full Street'. I am ready to begin living again."

Ann felt someone tapping her on the shoulder. She jumped up, startled.

"Thalia, Sara," Ann said. "He found you!" She rushed out of the car and hugged them both while the porter looked on beaming. Ann was not oblivious to the lack of energy in Sara's weak-hearted hug, but she refrained from commenting.

"Jamaican princess, you couldn't have seen us," Thalia replied. "You were somewhere far over and beyond the rainbow."

"I must have dozed off while waiting," Ann said apologetically. Right then and there, she made a vow to stay fully present in each moment with her friends.

She quickly opened the trunk and supervised the porter as he placed their luggage in the car. She was so glad she had rented a SUV. Sara had packed for at least three months.

SUNDAY

"You have Miss Thing over here to thank for the wait," Sara said pointing at Thalia, "As usual, she had to look for something to eat as soon as we got in the terminal."

"The food that was handed out to the flight proletariat was not fit for human consumption," Thalia rebutted.

"That's why I only fly first class," Sara shot back, confirming Ann's earlier thought.

"And if I were a surgeon like you instead of being a plain internist with no procedures to bill mega bucks for, I would too," Thalia replied, though her wink told Ann that she knew it was more than food quality that had Sara flying up front. Fortunately, Sara missed it.

"Ladies, I promise that here on this beautiful tropical paradise, we will all feel like princesses, divas, even," Ann decided to move on. Sara would probably not have dismissed the teasing with a roll of her eyes like she did in the past. The philosophical divide between Sara and Thalia had contributed to many passionate late night debates and friendly girlfriend bantering. After some of their most introspective arguments, the women used to rise and head off to breakfast together, cranky only from lack of sleep. But their theoretical differences probably would not manifest the same way after all these years of separation. To pretend that things were the same now as they were back then could only ensure that the chasm would grow wider.

"I was not kidding earlier when I called you a princess, Ann," Thalia remarked. "You have a beautiful aura about you; sorta like you have been fairy-dusted."

"It's a sharp contrast to the last time we were all

together," Sara piped in. "Paradise must really be helping you to put the past behind you."

Ann marveled at being told for a second time today that she glowed. She felt very blessed that she was able to get away from all the concrete reminders of her life with James. Being able to trick herself that the reason she and James were not together was because she was traveling, did indeed give her the space she needed to begin the healing process.

Thalia went over to Ann and gave her another hug. "Keep doing whatever you need to do to buy time," she said. "You know I've had my share of pain. And I know first hand that time is the best healer."

Sara ignored this part of the exchange between the two and walked over to the porter who finished loading the bags. She tipped him handsomely and sat in the backseat.

The porter walked over to Ann and Thalia. "You weren't lying about your friends being gorgeous," he said pointing in the direction of Sara.

"Thanks for your help," Thalia said.

"All you ladies pretty the same way to me," he stalled. "I would pick any one of you, or all of you." Looking at Ann he continued, "If your man wouldn't mind sharing."

Ann shook her head. "Thanks anyway, but I think he would mind."

"Doesn't he understand goodbye," Sara shouted from the car. "I'm ready to get out of this miserable heat."

He hesitated, held his heart in an exaggerated heartbreak, and shrugged his shoulders.

Ann and Thalia laughed and headed to the car as he headed back into the airport, after his next prey.

Thalia and Ann joined Sara in the car. "There you go spoiling our friend's desire for not just a ménage-à-trois, but a ménage-à-quatre," Thalia chuckled.

"He sure went for the gusto, didn't he," Ann agreed. "No foreplay, no nothing. His testosterone must be over the top if he thinks that he can handle so much estrogen."

Thalia and Ann burst out laughing. Sara did not seem amused.

Ann looked at her through the rearview mirror, but the darkened sunglasses hid her eyes. Ann could not tell if she was joking until she angrily continued, "I can't believe that you feminists find it funny that men still treat women as chattel. And by the way, he probably figured out that our combined estrogen level added up to perhaps only one."

"Sara, when did you start getting so testy about your age?" Thalia asked. "Anyway, we were just laughing at his childish arrogance."

"I'm sorry that he upset you," Ann added. "After being here for a while, you learn to let it roll off your back. Jamaican men just want to think that they are knights in shining armor having to rescue damsels in distress."

"Then he should wait for our SOS and not make assumptions," Sara continued.

Realizing that this must be a sore spot with Sara, Ann started up the truck. "I don't have to assume that you are ready to hit the road."

"I am sorry for seeming like a spoilsport," Sara said with only a touch of conviction. "It must be the heat and the jet lag. Anyway," she brightened a little, "this is a women's get-together. Let's not even think about men right now."

"We should be at the resort in about forty-five minutes."

"I hope you guys won't mind if I relax a little," Sara said. "It's been a long night and morning for me."

Ann did mind. There was so much she was eager to share with Sara. But she said nothing as Sara slipped on her discman. Sensing her disappointment, Thalia slapped Ann's thigh playfully. "So girlfriend, where have you been hiding this man that our friendly porter made reference to?" she laughed, thinking Ann had been lying to the porter. "No matter what you said, he just kept trying. Men, I tell you."

"I could tell you a few stories," Ann said vaguely.

"I bet!" Thalia changed the subject without catching on that Ann was holding something back. "What have you been doing with yourself over the last six months? Did you really just need to leave New Orleans to clear your head? Or is there something more?"

Even after six months, driving in Jamaica was still quite an adventure, so Ann asked Thalia to hold the conversation for a while until she got into the flow of the traffic.

Following orders, Thalia drank in the magnificent scenery that opened up almost as soon as they got on their way—the cobalt blue sky with an occasional white puff of a cloud; the many shades of green trees and shrubs; the rainbow of wild flowers that lined the streets; and, of course, the sparkling turquoise blue sea encircling them alongside their left.

After Ann felt comfortable on the road, she slipped into catching up on Thalia's life and talking about her own. Unavoidably, they soon arrived at the painful past year.

"I'm not going to lie, Thalia. Up till about six months ago, I was traveling down a path narrowed by the pain of losing James. Believe me, his death stripped all the trust and faith that I had. Sometimes I have even felt as though I was heading toward self-destruction, totally out of control and with no ability to stop it."

"You should have called more. You knew you could, didn't you?" Thalia was sad that she even had to ask.

"I did know, I did," Ann said somberly. She patted Thalia's knee, and even though she would have liked for her hand to linger there and remember the comfort they used to give to each other, she had to return it quickly to the steering wheel. "But you know that making yourself call is all a part of it. And that's the hard part."

Thalia nodded in full appreciation.

Ann thought about how constricted she had become from her pain; until that hot, humid night in New Orleans when she listened to a little voice inside that kept telling her it was time to follow her heart's longing. Having hit rock bottom, things could not get much worse. So a few weeks later when the opportunity to take a sabbatical year abroad presented itself, she knew that it was her golden moment. She had become more and more interested in the interface between spirituality and mental health, so she designed her research to examine the contributions of pre-Christian African spirituality to the mental health of peoples of the diaspora. Most important of all, she needed to get away from the constant reminders of her twenty years with James.

"Where are you girlfriend?" Thalia asked. Ann seemed to have moved into another zone.

"I was thinking about how coming to Jamaica has turned out to be one of the best decisions of my life," Ann said. "Except of course, my decision to become a mother during the beginning of my residency program. That was a very difficult period in my life."

Thalia nodded silently, realizing that she had not been there for both of the most intense periods of her best friend's life. She had asked why Ann hadn't called her, but she realized she should have known Ann needed her and called. That had been her role in Ann's life when they were children—to protect her from pain. Before Thalia could mention her guilt, Ann had moved on.

"God, you don't know how thankful I am that Ahsima and Olu ended up at the same university," Ann said. "He has taken such good care of her, especially at times when if she had needed me, I don't know what I would have been able to give."

"Yes he has," Thalia concurred. "Since their reunion at the funeral, they seem to be hanging out a lot in the same circles. Maybe the crush he has had on her ever since you guys visited us in Harare has resurfaced." Thalia smiled as she recalled how Olu, at the awkward age of twelve went to such lengths to hide his crush by always making fun of Ahsima's expectation that Africa would be like a scene from the Discovery channel.

"From the bits and pieces that Ahsima has shared with me about their relationship, I gather that Olu is like a security blanket for her, safe and warm, just like it was with her Dad." Ann became saddened and happy all at the same time as she recalled how close Ahsima and James were.

"Olu's soul is wise and old," Thalia proudly boasted. "His African nanny, Yeala, always used to say that he was already born an elder."

"Ahsima so needs a friend whom she can trust and not some wise-cracking guy who will take advantage of her vulnerability."

"She found the right guy then," Thalia reassured her. "You would not believe how Olu has turned into a solid rock of support for me since I divorced his father." Thalia reflected on how careful she had been in making sure that she did not burden him with more than he could or even should carry. For he was still her son first and friend second and it was difficult for her to deal with the table being reversed. It was hard for her to think of her son caring for and protecting her, rather than the other way around.

Hearing some traces of hurt lingering in Thalia's voice, Ann inquired about how she was handling the divorce.

"I still struggle with a lot of guilt and regret," Thalia

told her. "Now that I am not so angry at Reggie anymore, his whiteness in particular, I can see how very hurt he was by my leaving. Worse yet, by taking his only son away with me back to the States. He and Yeala wanted me to leave Olu in Africa. And although I would have loved for Olu to grow into his manhood there, there was no way that I was going to have my son living on another continent apart from me."

"I couldn't do it either," Ann agreed, recalling how hard she tried to get Ahsima to transfer to the university back home in New Orleans after James died; she had felt so completely alone then.

"Why do I get the feeling that our children are probably dating?"

Ann was uncomfortable at Thalia's inference. "I don't get that feeling at all," she darted back. "Maybe we are projecting our needs onto our children."

Thalia was shocked and confused by Ann's negative response. Not wanting to risk getting her feelings hurt, she did what she always did when she felt rejected, she went running in a different direction. Taking a 180 degree turn, Thalia reminded Ann of the time during college when one of her boyfriends turned up at one of their parties in psychedelic hot pants and a purse. Given that it was not Halloween or a costume party, they concluded that he must be a transvestite. Ann was so humiliated in front of all of her friends, she broke it off with him right then. Thalia and Ann burst into belly-up laughter as they wondered if he was now Michaela instead of Michael.

SUNDAY

The sudden outburst after what had previously been a quiet conversation disturbed Sara's nap; she had fallen asleep long before the last tune on her CD faded. Waking to a splitting headache and soreness throughout most of her body, Sara felt waves of nausea rolling in her stomach. She prayed that her discomfort was in response to the disconcerting feeling of dread as she watched Ann driving on the wrong side of the road, coupled with the speed with which other vehicles attacked the very narrow and winding road. Hopefully, it had nothing to do with the previous night.

"I hope you guys won't think I'm as lousy a traveling companion as I seem to be, but I hope we are almost there," Sara warned. "I'm afraid if I don't get out of the car pretty soon I am going to get pretty sick."

"Is it the jetlag?" Thalia turned in her seat and looked at Sara with concern.

"Probably; plus the sticking heat."

"It does take a while to adjust," Ann concurred, glancing in the rearview. "Hold on, we're just about there." A few minutes later, Ann pulled off the main road into a narrow gravel-lined street. They arrived at the gate not a minute too soon for Sara, who was about to ask Ann to stop the car so that she could get a breath of fresh air to ease her nausea.

The security guard waved them through the magnificent entranceway, lined with huge white-washed coconut trees and all colors of towering bougainvilleas. Sara could feel herself becoming revived the closer they got to the sight, sound and smell of the ocean. It immediately took her back to her parents' beach home, a place of refuge during her early years growing up in Florida.

A pretty, young woman greeted them the moment they pulled up in front of the lobby. She introduced herself as Marcia and informed them that she would be their personal attendant during their stay. She helped them out of the car, took the keys from Ann and hailed a bellman. She then placed garlands of sweet smelling orange blossoms and dahlias around each of their necks. Sara, Thalia and Ann hugged each other tenderly. In less than five minutes at the resort they had already understood the concept of being pampered.

Their embrace wiped the slate clean for Ann. She had been tense and worried since they all came face to face at the airport. Now she felt that their reunion had a chance after all. Stretching her tension-stiff shoulders, she toughened her resolve to let each moment flow just like Marcia's gait—slow and deliberate. And for the rest of the week she would become one with the Jamaican mythos—'no problem, man' and let what is to be, be.

Marcia led them into the reception area. Sara immediately went to the restroom. Upon Sara's return, Marcia offered them champagne. Sara declined and asked instead for ginger ale; her stomach needed a bit more soothing. A three-piece banjo band, with members who appeared as old as the almost forgotten Jamaican folk songs they were playing serenaded them while they sipped their drinks.

Marcia swiped away their next paychecks, as the three women sat around in the lobby resting and taking it all in.

When Sara indicated that she was ready, Ann beckoned Marcia over. When she saw the waiting trolley, Sara was relieved that they did not have to walk to their living quarters. The ride took them through a gumbo of breathtaking tropical sceneries: floating lily ponds; a brook filled with lazily, meandering red and orange fishes; several gardens boasting blazingly, colorful tropical plants: zinnias, crotons, allamanders, orchids and birds of paradise. She was pleased the resort lived up to its claim of being a haven for the rapidly disappearing fauna and flora of the Jamaican countryside.

Ann particularly loved the sight of the peacocks, brilliantly and perfectly plumed, strutting and strolling out on the lawn like landowners surveying their property. To her, they were so reminiscent of Jamaican men; one in particular.

From the look on Thalia's face, Ann could tell she was pleased. It was hard to read Sara though; her eyes remained hidden behind her immense sunshades.

After what seemed like a timeless ride through the Garden of Eden, Marcia delivered them to their accommodations—a beautiful rendition of a Jamaican country cottage circa 1900. It boasted a wooden frame and thatched roof, surrounded by a sprawling verandah filled with potted plants and creeping vines. Inside was equally as charming. The furnishings were all mahogany and rattan, accompanied by white lace, tulle and voile fabric trimmings.

Marcia disappeared as unobtrusively as she had appeared with the trolley, but not before ensuring that the three women knew where everything was located. After she left, Ann suggested they sit on the verandah and enjoy what was left of the afternoon breeze. The bellman still had to arrive with the luggage.

Sara hopped into the hammock. She shared her concerns about the single telephone. "Don't get me wrong, I find this rustic, two-bedroom cottage very charming indeed, but CNN and an internet connection would make it even better."

Ann sat next to her in a rocking chair. "Do you remember when we decided on an island versus a city setting for this trip?" Ann asked. Sara shook her head, feigning ignorance with her puzzled look. Ann noted that in spite of twenty years, Sara's 'dumb, pretty woman' avoidance tactics remained the same. "In case you have forgotten my dear Sara, let me remind you that you were the first to suggest that we needed an environment conducive to de-stressing."

"Not being able to contact the outside world could do the opposite and become quite dis-stressing," Sara quipped back.

"That is music to my ears," Thalia rebutted, flopping next to Ann on a lounging sofa. "I need to slow down and catch my breath. I am totally ready to stop thinking and just be totally spontaneous."

"I am not being unappreciative ladies, this place is picture perfect. Don't you all remember how much of an organizer and stickler for details I am; I even need to plan how to do nothing." Sara lightened up momentarily. "Shoo, what worries me is that the world could get blown up and come to an end and we wouldn't even know it," she joked.

SUNDAY

"Shit, this is the perfect place to be if the world were to end. Whohoo." Thalia laughed and gestured to the lush fauna rushing up to their patio.

Ann was about to get annoyed with Sara's resistance when she remembered that when she first arrived, it had been hard for her too. Initially, she also resisted emptying her head and allowing the natural beauty and relaxed Jamaican attitude to soothe her aching soul. Lucky for her, life in New Orleans all those years helped; both cultures seemed to share a similar ethic regarding leisure—you work to support living, and not the other way around. She remarked to Sara, "being away from the constant pressure to always plan for some project, workshop, or something has really helped me." There was no reply, for Thalia indeed wanted to just be, and Sara did not understand exactly what Ann meant; and did not care to find out either.

Thalia took in the scenery. She recognized how important living in environments with lots of color had become for her. As far as she could see, there was less than six degrees of separation between the motherland and the people scattered throughout the diaspora. Little wonder that when she returned to the States from Africa she had to live in chocolate city, DC. "I tell you, although we are scattered throughout the Americas and the Caribbean, the blood runs thick," Thalia mused. "Even with the slave traders dropping us off in different places, we still have one mind, one heart."

"Speaking of slavery, I did make some plans for us for tomorrow," Ann said.

"Let's hear them, oh dear Ann, who just a minute ago brushed aside my need to have plans and structure."

"I did no such thing," Ann replied smiling. She was not going to let Sara spoil her joy, not just yet, and hopefully, never. "A dear friend of mine is going to be visiting a cave close by where slaves used to gather and plan rebellions, so I told her we would try to meet her there."

"But you told us earlier that there was no agenda," Sara complained.

"It all happened serendipitously," Ann said contritely. "If you all don't want to go ..."

"Lighten up Ann, I am sure that Sara is just messing with you," Thalia interrupted.

"Thalia is right Ann, I was just being playful," Sara lied, not wanting to admit that she was having second thoughts about coming on the trip and leaving Don still angry with her. Maybe she should have stayed at home in Los Angeles and worked on making things right with Don.

Ann was glad to hear that Sara was okay. She realized she still had a lot of work to do on being less sensitive to what she perceived as rejection. "Believe me, I am fully committed to us flowing with how we feel each day and being totally spontaneous. I promise, that other than tomorrow, I have no other plans. Of course, there are some incredibly beautiful places and experiences I would love to share with you, but the bottom line is that we don't have to do any of it."

Sara adjusted her tone. In spite of all that had happened between them, Ann still seemed so eager to please and take care of those that she loved. "Of course I am game for all that you have on tap for us," Sara said with fifty degrees of earnestness. "You should know from way back that when I travel I am the tour and excursion type. I just need clarity about what to expect so I can plan things out in my head."

"At the risk of being accused of being corny, I am going to suggest that we open ourselves up, metaphysically speaking that is," Ann grinned and winked at Sara. Sara winked back. Ann seized the pleasantry as permission to continue. "Why don't we consider this journey as a kind of vision quest that is going to lead us to deeper layers of self-discovery."

"Come on now Ann, I did not sign up for a new age getting in touch with your inner self trip. I have already done so through my lord and savior Jesus Christ."

Ann was taken aback by Sara's religiosity. Even though she knew that Sara's father was a minister and that Sara had always kept close ties to the church, she did not know that she had gotten in so deeply in the past twenty years. Given how unpredictable Sara could be at times, Ann knew to leave well enough alone.

"Seeing that I don't yet have a savior, my biggest worry is that once I open myself up, I might not be able to close the lid," Thalia sighed.

"Maybe I can help you open up your hearts to the lord while I am here," Sara told them. "We could do some bible studies in the morning."

"No thanks, Sara," Thalia quickly jumped in and out of her usual role of agreeing with and protecting Sara. "Why don't you practice something that I know is hard for you Christians to do—drop your presumptions and judgments about what's right and what is not. Respect my choice to believe or not believe; stop trying to convert everyone."

"I can see that we are all going to have to agree right here and now to let religion and politics go," Ann warned. "Otherwise, Sara's prediction of distress is going to become a reality."

"Sounds reasonable to me," Thalia said, pulling back.

Sara did not commit, but she let the conversation slide. "I know I have been bitching a lot, but all the traveling from coast to coast and now to the Atlantic has left me feeling a bit under the weather. Believe me, I am grateful to be here, plan or no plan." Sara took a breather and became aware of the ocean in the background. She thought that perhaps more than everything else, it was the ocean that was going to de-stress her. "Being close to the ocean always helps me to put distance between myself and all the shit that always seems to surround me."

"It cools me out too," Thalia agreed with her, finding common ground again. "Tranquility is definitely the space I need to be in now, especially after all that I have been through in the past couple of days."

Ann wanted to ask about her experience, but resisted pressing too early. She had to work hard at not coming on too strong as a therapist, at the risk of ignoring her need for love and support from her friends. So she offered her vulnerabilities out alongside with her friends, "I need a whole lot of serenity to keep healing."

"How do you start?" Sara inquired earnestly.

"From a place of love and forgiveness, of ourselves and each other," Ann replied.

"We used to love each other deeply, once upon a time," Thalia remembered, tears beginning to well up in her eyes. "I want to reclaim that energy that existed between us. I mean, I think we still do, but there is so much that has happened in each other's lives over the past few years. We have a forever of catching up and a forever of forgiving for not being there more for each other."

"Once again, that is easier said than done," Sara cautioned them. "It is not going to be that easy to wipe the slate clean and just pick up from where we left off in our friendship."

"A year ago I might have agreed with you Sara, but not anymore," Ann countered. "I now believe that the detours and wrong turns that we make in our lives are there to help point us in the right direction. Mistakes and failures become lessons that show us where not to turn."

"That's all well and good," Sara said skeptically. "But the truth is, some of those lessons I would much rather do without."

"I know what you mean," Ann agreed. "I used to feel that way about James' passing. But it now occurs to me that in some ways his death has helped to prepare me for my own. I now understand all the way through to my bones that this mortal existence has a beginning and an end. Once you've signed up for life, you've also signed up for death. That's why I have made a commitment to try to live each day fully, knowing full well that death is sitting on my left shoulder and could tap me at anytime. Life is very delicate; it could be snapped away at any moment."

"Okay, Ms. Castaneda," Thalia said. "This is way too deep for the rest of us tired travelers to ingest, especially on empty stomachs."

"Tomorrow when you meet my friend Cassandra at the caves, you will see how much of a novice I am," Ann replied.

"I am dying to meet her. Maybe she can lay some wisdom down on me and help me figure out the twists and turns my life is taking right now."

"What's up, Thalia?" Sara inquired.

"Later," Thalia shrugged it off. "It's a long story. Way too long for our tired bones. I need to take a nap and get some food; especially if I am going to be able to hang later."

"You won't get any opposition from me," Sara said, her jet lag beating out her curiosity. "I am ready to lay me down to sleep."

The bellman finally arrived with their luggage. Ann volunteered to give up the master suite to either of them who might want it. Sara was tempted, but before she had a chance to take up Ann's offer, Thalia announced that she needed to watch over Sara. Not wanting to be accused of being ungrateful any more, Sara offered no resistance. Instead, she changed into loungewear and laid claim to the double bed with the best view of the ocean.

Ann's mind was in too much turmoil to shut down and invite sleep in. She ordered lunch for Thalia and Sara, then headed toward the beach. She was not yet ready to break her fast; she wanted to stay with the meal Spice gave her in the early morning.

Like Thalia, she wasn't ready to discuss the occurrences in her near past. For now, she needed to meditate to help clear her mind and provide her balance to deal with Sara's swinging moods. She could see Sara struggle to contain her anger by escaping into bitchy remarks and a sour attitude. But even as a psychotherapist, she was not looking forward to coaxing Sara's real feelings out. Not when she battled so many pent up emotions of her own.

Ann followed the lead of the few wise sun worshippers who sought refuge under the cabanas. By now, the early midday sun had burnt through all the clouds and was mercilessly scorching everything and everyone in its path.

A local woman passing by with a basket of mangoes on her head brought back even more memories of Spice. Ann pulled out her journal—her self-prescribed therapy from childhood.

Dear Spice,

After the remarkable night we spent together, the glow of love is trying to appear once again in my persona. I should eagerly welcome it back into my life, knowing as I do that love is what truly connects us to the life force. In those moments of your loving me so completely, you helped me touch the divine. But I am scared to listen to my heart. My intellect cautions me and wants to steer me away from reading too much into the wonderful time that we shared.

I hope that soon I will find the courage to give this love the space to grow. But I am scared that once love is unleashed, like a river, it will flow into all spaces it encounters in its path. I am not sure if I am yet ready to surrender.

If I were a musician like you, I would create a symphony to express in sound the infinite, vibratory waves that alighted from my soul in your presence. But I only know how to create words.

So here is a poem that I hope to send to you whenever my heart breaks free:

> *Spice, my gallant prince*
> *Stroll through my blooming garden*
> *Smell the tender fragrance*
> *Of love, young in bloom*
> *Spice, my fearless warrior*
> *Climb up my steeply rising mountain*
> *Witness raw passion aglow*
> *Of love, burning free*
> *Spice, my naked knight*
> *Wash in my flowing river*
> *Taste the sweet nectar*
> *Of love, pure and true.*
> *Spice, my majestic emperor*
> *Swim in my unending ocean*
> *Feel the exhilaration*
> *Of love's mysteries revealed.*
> *Spice, my regal king*
> *Rest on my satin pillar*
> *Hear the melodious serenade*
> *Of love's eternal flame.*

SUNDAY

Ann's writing was interrupted by the presence of someone standing over her. Cynthia, the local woman who she met the day before, was back again offering her services. As tempted as she was right then and there, she wanted Thalia and Sara to experience Cynthia's energy-packed magic fingers. She arranged for Cynthia to come by their room later that night.

After Cynthia left, Ann picked up her pen to continue writing, but drew a complete blank; her rhythm was gone. Rather than fight it, she went swimming in the sea. The water was calm and crystal clear, a striking contrast to the day before when it rolled around turbulent and murky. Ann hoped that, like the sea, she too would find her calm after the storm last night.

She swam long and hard, making her way quite a distance from the shoreline. She floated for a while among the fish, until fatigue and hunger steered her back to shore. No longer able to fight sleep, she laid down on the bare sand. The feel of the gritty, raw force of nature beneath her reminded her once again of Spice; how he held her so firmly yet gently against the coarse hairs on his chest. She wiggled her pelvis against the grains until she fell asleep. She probably would have slept until eternity if it were not for the sound of thunder announcing the daily afternoon showers.

Ann made her way back to the cottage to the serenade of crickets doing their dry run for the evening symphony.

The phone was ringing as she entered. She ran to get it so it would not disturb her sleeping guests. Thalia was totally knocked out on the sofa, connected to the outside world only through her sonorous snores. Ann had to step out onto the back verandah so she could hear the person on the other line.

"Hello sweetness."

"Spice, I am so relieved to hear from you and know that you made it back into Kingston safely."

"I know that you were worried about me driving back after so little sleep last night. But believe me, all I had to do was think about making love to you as I took those sharp turns around the corner and up the mountains, and I would get this incredible surge of energy ...."

His deep, baritone voice bringing back the events of the night immediately sent shivers up her spine.

"Please don't go there now," she had to put out the fire.

"It sounds like you are not missing me half as much as I do you."

"How could I not!" Ann said. 'Let's just say I haven't had a chance to because every time there is a quiet space in my consciousness, you creep right in,"

"Good. Be forewarned that I plan to take up permanent residence." The confusion began all over again for Ann. His play on words always sent her spinning. She had to steady herself so as not to topple over into the pool. Totally oblivious on the other end, he continued, "I hope you and your friends will decide to come to Kingston soon. I can't wait to see those beautiful, brown eyes again and kiss those sweet lips."

"I am going to be patient because the longer I wait, the more your spices seep in and tantalize my taste buds."

"Mmmm, speaking of taste, yours is an addictive one. I am definitely craving you right now."

"Spice, don't make this harder for me," Ann begged, as she felt herself losing control. "I need to focus on reconnecting with my girlfriends and not be off in fantasy land somewhere with the most sensuous man to make his way onto my radar screen in the past year. So if we make it to Kingston, it probably won't be until Friday.

"Sweetness, don't fight us. We are hundreds of miles apart, yet I can feel your spirit all over and in me. I am crazier about you now than I was last night. You better believe that you are the woman of my dreams; you are my shanty woman ..."

"Whoa, you are way ahead of me," Ann stopped him. "I feel the intensity too, but I have to go a bit slower. I have just come through some difficult times."

"From the little you told me about your husband's death, I know that it must be rough. Maybe I was sent into your life to help you weather the storm."

"How kind of you to be so understanding," Ann told him. "My guardian angel must have sent you to me. She probably saw that I was flipping out."

"He sure did," Spice said.

Before Ann could ask what was up with the pronoun, their conversation was interrupted by a call waiting beep. Knowing how eager Sara was about access to the outside world, Ann clicked over. But it was for Thalia. Since she was still deep in sleep, Ann asked Lee to call back in an hour. When Ann clicked back over to Spice, he was not on the line. She tried to call him back but kept getting a busy signal.

Ann's anger at not being able to reconnect with him disturbed her. She wondered what the hell was happening to her. A part of her kept warning her that Spice was too good to be true. Unquestionably, something about him reverberated deep in her body. She felt him in places that answered to more than just lust, but she didn't know how to silence her doubts. How could he have fallen in love with her, after just one night? Especially someone like him who could have just about any woman he wanted. It was hard to believe that he would want the same things that an ordinary looking, middle aged woman who had grown beyond the stage of puppy love and awestruck adoration would want after the initial infatuation wore off.

Ann went and sat by the pool. Just as she was about to reconstruct the events of the night before for the umpteenth time, Sara joined her.

"I didn't sleep as long or as hard as I had hoped."

"I am sorry if the phone woke you up."

"It didn't," Sara replied. "I was already stirring when it rang."

Rather than awakening refreshed, Sara seemed to be very agitated. She kept breathing hard and sighing. Ann got the feeling that something other than jet lag was bothering her. "Sara, are you as nervous as I am about seeing each other again?"

"Yes I am. I'm afraid to stir up the ugly past. I'm not so sure I want to go back there."

"Neither do I, Sara," Ann consoled her. "But I have learned through all my suffering this year, that once you realize that you have more control over how you feel now, as compared to how you were feeling when the pain happened then, it is not nearly as painful."

"The truth is Ann, when we decided to do this, it was at a time when we were all very emotional. Funerals have a way of doing that to you. Faced with the reality a year later, I am not so sure if it was the right decision."

"Look, the bottom line is, whether we rehash things or not, whether we work through the issues here on this trip or not, I will always love you." Ann paused for a moment as Sara looked away from her, seeming to block her outpouring of love. Ann persisted, "When I walked into that chapel at the funeral home and saw you viewing James' body, I knew that in spite of all that had happened, we would always be family. I made a promise to myself then to work on forgiving us both. We were just victims of our passions."

"Be patient with me Ann," Sara said. "I may not show it all the time, but I love you too. You and Thalia both. But it's going to take me a while to get to where you both seem to be. I am feeling very confused right now and have a lot of sorting out to do. I am barely on first base with knowing how I feel about most things in my relationships, so I can't make it to home plate just yet; which I guess is where forgiveness lies. That's why I turn things over and put them in the hands of Christ."

"Jesus is a great example of being able to forgive the ones who hurt you the most." Even though Ann had just declared that they were going to stay clear of religion, she could not help using the moment to show Sara that the potential to be just like Christ existed in her.

Sara was shocked that Ann, who had years ago declared herself as an agnostic from their medical school days, made such a positive statement about Jesus. Maybe her daily prayers asking the Lord to bring both Thalia and Ann back into his light were beginning to pay off. Sara couldn't help asking Ann where she was drawing down all that strength to keep living. If Don were to die, she was sure that she would die too.

Ann explained that dealing with James' death was the turning point in her life. She felt she finally made it to adulthood when she was able to accept death as inevitable for everyone, herself included. That realization began to force her into living life more truthfully and lovingly; tomorrow is not promised. "One day, as I sat by James' side, I realized that I had wasted a lot of time. I spent so much of the time we could have spent loving each other being angry with him over insignificant things—'ego bruises' I call them. There he was, dying, and I would have given anything to have those moments back, to replay them in harmony. It was no longer important then who was right or who was wrong. I made a decision then and there to begin to forgive myself and all the people that I loved, so I could spend more of my time loving them. That simple little attitude adjustment on my part allowed us to spend the last two months of his life recapturing the rapturous love we once had when we first met."

"I just have so much to uncover, Ann. So much I haven't dealt with," Sara said wistfully.

"Like Thalia advised me, you too should make an effort to lighten up by unloading some of the burdens you have been walking around with," Ann told her. At this point in her life, she was firm in her belief that friends should help one another search for ways in which to create and be who they are, and not who others want them to be. "I meant what I said earlier about us finding ways of being emotionally supportive to each other," Ann continued. "I know we can't fix everything in one week, but we can certainly help each other find a bit more joy in our lives."

But Sara backed away once more. "But isn't that stressful, all this emotional upheaval? I'm not sure that I want all this stress during my vacation. Remember, it was you who said this trip was about pampering ourselves."

"Sometimes holding on to pain is much more work than letting it go," Ann said. Encouraged by the honesty with which she and Sara were relating for the first time, in spite of Sara's reservations, Ann seized the moment to push the envelope. "Sara, there seems to be much more going on in your head other than just your anxiety about seeing me and reviving our falling out."

"I thought I just heard you say you wanted to be supportive. What I need more than ever right now is a friend and not a psychiatrist." Sara raised her hand in a 'brick wall' gesture, "Your little psychiatrist self needs to go far away so that we can make this a real stress-free vacation."

"As your friend, I cannot help being analytic some of

the time," Ann said. "It is very hard for me not to seize an opportunity to help a friend better understand why they feel, think and act the way they do. Especially when I have seen time and time again how insight helps to give us better control over the choices that we make. Unfortunately though, as you just confirmed, most people don't want to know their truths; they would rather live in the lies."

Knowing that she was guilty as charged, Sara looked away from Ann again and stared at the ocean. In her escape, she recalled how happy she used to be when her mother would pack them up and take off for the beach. But it all changed when she tried to tell her mother about the footsteps she heard at night. Her mother told her that it was because she was not saying her prayers. That was the last time they ever went to the beach.

Sara took a big breath and returned to her present conversation. As stressful as it was avoiding being analyzed by Ann, it was much less stressful than those memories of her early life that seemed bent on finding their way back into her consciousness. As she exhaled into the silence between them, she promised herself that at some point she would try to tell Ann the truth about her marriage. But right now, she was not so sure Ann would believe her, much less be able to support her. She herself found it hard to believe that Don had been such a terror these past few months.

Accepting that they had come to a neutral crossroads in their conversation, Ann left Sara and went inside to awaken Thalia.

SUNDAY

Upon opening her eyes, Thalia immediately declared her state of hunger. Since they were all still somewhat fatigued, they agreed to order in. Steamed fish, callalloo, boiled yam and rice and peas were the choice, accompanied of course by a bottle of white wine; and port for afterwards. Ann called in the order, while Thalia hurried to the bathroom to freshen up.

The phone rang as soon as Ann hung up from her conversation with room service. The loud reggae music blasting from the cottage next door made it impossible for Sara to overhear Ann's conversation, but from the look of annoyance on Ann's face, Sara worried that it was Don on the other line. She knew that he and Ann had not spoken to each other in years. Sara let out a sigh of relief when Ann called Thalia to the phone. Placing the phone on the table for Thalia, Ann headed to her room to get dressed for dinner, and Sara did the same, saying a silent prayer that Don would not call her until she felt strong enough and had the courage to ask him for a divorce.

When Ann returned to the living room, Thalia and Sara were playing scrabble. Marcia arrived very soon thereafter with the dinner trolley. After she set up their dinner, Marcia poured the wine. She offered to stay and serve them throughout dinner, but Ann told her it wasn't necessary.

The wine and food were exactly what the women needed. Famished, they concentrated on the delectable meal left for them. While the wine diluted their soul-searching conversations, they filled their mouths with lighthearted reminiscences of their first two years in medical school.

After they feasted on everything there was in sight and all the wine was gone, Thalia suggested that they go for a walk along the beach. With the several glasses of Sauvignon Blanc fully saturated throughout her system, Sara quickly assumed her old role as group comedienne. Within minutes, Ann and Thalia were in stitches, as she colorfully recounted some of their many adventures, adding color and exaggerating wherever she chose. Neither of them checked Sara on the truth. That was for tomorrow. Tonight they were trying to remember why they had all been such close friends so long ago.

They returned to the cottage a few hours later. There was a note pinned to the door for Ann. "Shit," she exclaimed, "I got so frigging drunk, I totally forgot that I made plans for us all to have late night massages."

"Not to worry, Ann," Sara said lightheartedly, "It's all about the moment, isn't it?"

"So right," Thalia joined in. "And right now, we have made Bacchus proud." Ann, Sara and Thalia wandered off to bed without Ann remembering to check to see if Thalia had gotten to the phone, like she had intended to do earlier.

3
Monday

Ann woke to a shrill cock-a-doodle-doo. Reluctantly she admitted that the tingling all over her body was due to Spice's sleepy whisper the morning before telling her that this would always be their wakeup call for love.

She was determined not to call him. She couldn't allow herself to get swept away by his magic, once again. Moaning and groaning in her somewhat hung-over stupor, she realized that the perfect cure for withdrawal from Spice was right there at her fingertips. She closed her eyes and imagined they were his tongue. She slowly moved them from her breasts, past her navel, to her pum-pum, lingering for a while in the plateau of her pleasure.

Waking more fully, she reoriented herself to the wakening morn, withdrew her fingers and decided to spend no more time flirting with the sweet memories Spice left on her body. Quickly slipping on her swimsuit, she went out to the pool to wash away his claim on her body

Ann was surprised to see Sara lying by the pool. Ann tapped her gently.

Sara jumped up startled. She had just drifted off into a light sleep. "I couldn't sleep so I came outside to listen to the ocean. Believe me, it's much more soothing than

Thalia's snores. My age must be showing. It never used to take me this long to get over jet lag."

"What is showing, Sara, are your bruises," Ann declared, trying to conceal how frightening Sara's face looked.

Sara sat up and began to feel around for the shades she had worn all of yesterday until late into the night. She had been surprised that neither Ann nor Thalia had questioned her about it, especially when she still had them on at dinner.

She tried to speak, but words were not forthcoming; just tears. Ann sat down beside her and stilled her with a hug. "Sara, no matter what has happened between us, I meant it yesterday when I said that we are family; I am here for you."

Unable to hide any longer, Sara released the stiffness in her body and relaxed into Ann's embrace. The tears flowed more freely now. Ann didn't ask any questions. She already knew the answer. Her insides wrenched itself into a knot as the faces of so many of her clients flashed through her mind; only now, one of her dearest friends was added to the overwhelming statistic. Ann knew only too well that as different as each plot was, the story was always the same.

"I know this is very ironic coming from me, but you are lucky to be rid of Don," Sara eventually ventured. Ann did not reply. Sara continued, "Gee, some prize I landed! God must be punishing me for what I did."

"Sara, don't even go there; no one ever deserves to be hit." Ann consoled her. "As I understand God, I do not think she would ever ask that one human raise their hand against another. I cannot believe that she is judgmental or punitive."

"Until judgment day," Sara shrugged.

"Sara," Ann grasped her shoulders and turned her squarely to meet her eye. "My mother-father god is merciful and forgiving. I no longer buy into that 'eye for an eye' patriarchal he-god construct."

"Ann, that is pure blasphemy," Sara recoiled from her grasp, energized by her fear of what Ann was saying. "Aren't you afraid of burning in hell?"

"Not if you pray for me," Ann replied flippantly. "But seriously, Sara, you look like you've been through your own personal hell. How long has this been going on?"

"This is the worst—well physically, that is. Usually it's just a shove or a slap or so. But even when he's not hitting me, it's like you said, just hell. For a while when we were in counseling things seemed like they were getting better. But then he stopped going and now he is acting out all this rage against me. And it's just getting worse and worse. "This," she pointed to her bruised face as new tears began to fall, "was my going away, 'see you in a week honey' payback. Everything I try just … I don't know what to do anymore, Ann."

"Let's begin by washing off all that makeup and cleaning these cuts."

"I don't know if I can face the world with my battle scars, I have to keep them covered," Sara said.

"I can see that you do, but at least you need to put some healing medicines underneath."

"It's stupid and vain, isn't it? Trying to hide the bruises."

"It's not stupid, Sara. It's human. No one likes the world peering into their backyard and passing judgments. But you're around friends here, and we've promised to come and heal together. So let's start by taking off the rest of your mask."

Ann guided Sara into the bathroom. She wiped off her face with a warm washcloth, revealing more distinctly the large bruises around both her eye sockets. Ann thought that the bruises needed topical antibiotic to prevent them from becoming infected, but neither she nor Sara had traveled with medical supplies. There was none in Thalia's traveling case either. Sara could not believe that she was so unprepared, but then she had to admit that the night she packed, she was more focused on covering up her injury than treating it. Ann suggested using aloe instead. She had seen a huge patch growing in one of the nearby gardens. Ann made a mental note that she was going to buy some nutmeg next time they were close to a local market. Several of the older country folks had informed her that ground, young nutmeg was a miracle cure for cuts and bruises.

While Ann went outside to cut the aloe, Sara succumbed to the idea of the healing plant, even though she had very little faith that it would do much. Upon her return, Ann cut the thorns off the side and rubbed a piece of the leaf that was laden with aloe gel gently into Sara's bruises.

Neither of them saw Thalia sleepwalk into the room. Nor did she notice them. After several yawns, stretches and cold water to her face, she eventually noticed Sara perched on the toilet with Ann stooping beside her. She slipped her contacts in her eyes to get a closer look. She gasped audibly upon coming eye to eye with Sara.

"What the fuck happened?"

Sara's bewildered look was all she needed.

"Holy shit. I can't believe you hid this from me all this time! Damn, I kept wanting to take those god-dammed ugly sunglasses off."

"Thalia, you seem more upset about my not telling you than about what happened."

"What the hell is that supposed to mean," Thalia retorted angrily. "I have always been there for you, Sara; you don't think it should upset me that you don't trust me enough to tell me about this, especially when we've all come here to bare all with each other?"

"Thalia, you don't need to go there," Ann said, knowing that with her secret about Spice she could not cast any stones on those grounds. "Sara is just trying to make you angry so that she can deflect your attention away from the truth about what happened."

Sara didn't deny Ann's analysis. She sighed, "I was just telling Ann, Don and I got into a fight last night right before I left; he hit me a couple of times."

"Hit you a couple of times!" Thalia exclaimed in disbelief. "Sara, he must have been trying to kill you, the goddamn bastard." Thalia took a few deep breaths and tried to regain her composure. She gently examined Sara's face, and became enraged when she discovered how close one of the lacerations was to Sara's cornea. "That dick-head coward almost succeeded in blinding you!"

"Don't be too mad at him, Thalia," Sara replied. "A lot of it was my fault."

"Sara, don't even say that shit," Ann jumped in quickly.

Thalia walked away as she felt herself losing control. She went outside and took some more deep breaths, hoping that the pure morning air would contain her rage. Returning to the bathroom minutes later, she said in a much more subdued tone, "You are doing exactly what my mother did. If she would have stood up for herself, she would probably be alive right now." Thalia looked away but not before Ann noticed a tear escape one eye, and her fingernails an inch from digging right into her palm.

Ann attempted to hug her.

"No, this is about Sara." Thalia tried to push her away.

"No, Thalia," Ann responded. "There is enough room for all of us."

"But ..." she gestured towards Sara.

"I know, you appointed yourself Sara's caretaker eons ago." She smiled sadly and slid her hand under her friends chin, forcing her to look her in the eye. "You can't pull this one over on another black woman. You know that I know all about how we put people's pain ahead of ours. We are the caretakers of the world." Ann hugged her and emphatically added. "We've paid dearly. All of us."

Ann looked over at Sara who was nodding her agreement. Ann released Thalia and continued, "Our healing is going to have to be about becoming more self-centered and caring for our needs."

"I don't know how," Sara said in angry desperation. "I keep asking but don't seem to be getting any straight answers. Where the hell do I begin?" The anger quickly turned to more tears. "I am so confused, I don't even know why I am crying any more."

"You're crying because you are scared," Ann said.

"I am not scared, I am terrified. Terrified about what I might discover. That must be why I keep moving and am always on the go."

"From one fender-bender to the next," Thalia cut in, having regained her center. "But this time we're here with you Sara, to help steer you away from the big crash; that is what always comes next."

"We used to do that for each other." Ann recalled how they used to stay up all night planning and strategizing their lives.

"Why don't you finish it and say that it used to be that way until I fucked it up," Sara threw angrily to Ann, surprising them both at the hostility that had crept between them unannounced. "Let's just get it all out now; now that we are being honest and open."

"Sara, if you bring that stuff up now, it's on you," Ann said. "I have accepted your warning that we should be careful about how we dredge up the past."

"Well, I am ready now," Sara stood up and braced her hands on her hip. "I can't stand dancing around this shit anymore."

"Sara …

"Don't stop me," she shouted at Thalia. "You want to know all my hidden shit? You got it girlfriend. The reason Ann hasn't spoken to me all these years is cause I fucked Don when she was still with him. Okay? That's why they broke up. Happy now?"

Silence tied up everyone's tongue. Ann turned her back and leaned on the washbasin, wishing she could vanish down the drain with the drops from the faucet. In one way or the other by her constant probing of Sara, she knew that she had asked for this; but, did it have to be this hard when it finally arrived? She looked herself in the mirror and silently reminded herself, yes—the truth, especially after it has been tightly restrained and buried, creates shockwaves and volcanic eruptions when forced out in the open.

Turning to face the others, Ann looked at Thalia, who had sunken to the floor and sat with her head back against the door frame, tears betraying her frozen pose as they ran unchecked down her face. Ann's heart went out to her. The newness, the shock of it all. She remembered how raw it had felt to her when she first caught them in bed. Before she could go over to Thalia, Sara continued.

"The irony about it all is that in the beginning I was not trying to take Don away." Ann turned to look at Sara as she continued, "Believe it or not, that night when you came in and found us in bed together, I was doing it for you."

Ann was dumbfounded by Sara's revelation. After she regained her voice, she said, "Run that by me one more time. Are you saying you slept with my boyfriend as a favor to me?"

"Yes," Sara replied. "In my messed-up head at the time, I thought that you would see how insincere and 'no good' he was for you if you saw with your own eyes what he was secretly bugging me to do. I thought that our friendship was strong enough to withstand it."

"I want to believe you, Sara, I want to believe," Ann said, trying to cling to all the training she had been through over the past six months. At times like this she wished that Cassandra could be there to bring some spiritual sanity to life's messes. "But it doesn't make a hell of a lot of sense. If you knew that he was so bad for me, then, why did you think he would be any better for you? If it was just to show me a lesson, why not just fuck him that once and walk away from him?"

"When have you ever known life to make much sense," Sara said. "I don't know, Ann, I was really messed up. Maybe I just thought you were worth more. Then, with each passing moment, I just kept making bad choices and became more and more stuck in the drama. You know how that goes don't you, if not in your own life, in that of your patients?"

"But you're not one of my patients. You were one of the people I trusted most in life. You made everything a lie. I had no idea how long it had been going on or what had started it or anything."

"I know. When I saw your reaction it triggered something in me. I wanted to explain, to talk to you. But I don't know if I would have made anymore sense then than I am now. It would have been the same story. Then you called me every kind of bitch that you could think of, and I was speechless. I just watched you storm out. I never thought it would take twenty years and James' death for us to talk again. I always thought I would be able to make you understand. But I never had the words, and much like now, I never wanted to face the truth. I never called. And neither did you."

"I am sure you understood why," Ann replied and Sara nodded. "You knew how madly in love I was with Don back then; I was consumed by him. I didn't think that I could breathe without him."

Ann stopped for a while as she remembered their first meeting at a medical convention. He had somehow managed to catch her eye and offer her a knowing invitation without words. His gaze led them to his hotel room. A few weeks later he was professing his undying love for her and asking her to become pregnant with his child. At the time, she was not particularly interested in having children, but if bearing his child was the ticket to his love, she was game.

Ann shook her head in amazement that she had not seen through him earlier. She should have paid closer attention to all the signs of his arrogant ego that kept popping up. She instead chose to ignore them, chalking up his narcissism to being a victim of the white man's system. But hindsight is so much better informed.

Ann sat next to Thalia. She needed the reassurance of Thalia's familiar China Musk scent. She needed an anchor before admitting to Sara what she had come to discover during her analysis years ago, but quietly kept to herself.

The brutality of the conversation left her at the point of no return; no more cover-ups, no more lies.

"The truth is, it was very easy to fall out of love with him," she confessed to Sara. "The real hurt that lingered and which kept me away from you both came from my feelings of betrayal, by you Sara. You see, up to that point in my life, you and Thalia were the only women with whom I had ever shared such an emotionally, intimate friendship; with whom I had ever allowed myself to become so vulnerable." Ann could not hold back her tears any longer.

"It was special for me too, but I didn't how to handle it," Sara said. "My boundaries became so blurred that sleeping with Don felt like part of our little group." Sara's admission reminded Ann of the stories many twins had shared about sleeping with each other's partners. For reasons not yet obvious to Ann, her anger dissipated and changed from sibling rivalry into sisterly love.

"So much so you screwed him right there in her bed?" Thalia spat at her.

"It made me feel close to her," Sara responded.

"I don't buy that Sara." Thalia had not been privy to Ann's twin tales.

"I hear a tinge of jealousy," Sara replied with an air of self-importance.

Ann turned away and clutched her head, attempting to block out Thalia's doubts. She found herself beginning to flip-flop between her desire for forgiveness and Thalia's unrelenting anger.

"You lied ..."

"Thalia please," Ann pleaded

"Be quiet Ann. You both lied to me," Thalia would not be hushed. She shifted back to Sara, "All this time I never knew what you'd done to Ann. I got so caught up in my anger at her cutting me off like that when I hadn't done anything, I really thought the lame excuse you gave me was the truth."

"I was mad at you too, Thalia," Ann revealed. "It wasn't until last year when Ahsima and I came to visit you that I realized you didn't know the truth. I thought for sure that Sara had told you what happened. By then, you had stuck by your friendship with her for so long, even though I had gotten over my anger with you, maybe because of it, I didn't want to tell you the truth."

Thalia nodded.

Sara got up from the toilet and went over to Thalia. "I'm so sorry. I shouldn't have lied. It only made what I did worse, but I needed you so badly ... I ... There is no excuse. Please forgive me."

"Don't look at me like that, Sara, with those big innocent eyes of yours. You know I can't stay mad at you. But it hurts."

"We all hurt," Ann sighed. She threw her arms around both her dear friends. "Even Sara, Thalia. We have to remember that. It's hard, but we are here to forgive and find each other again. I've missed you both so much." Her tears began to flow again, "I want to do everything in my power to work this all out. Even if that means finding depths of forgiveness I have yet to tap."

The rapping at the door abruptly brought the meeting in the ladies room to an end.

"Who is it?" Ann cleared her throat and stood up.

"Marcia," the faint voice returned.

"It's Marcia," she repeated for the others.

Thalia nodded and stood up, "Breakfast," she filled in. Sara rose as well as they all began straightening up.

"We'll get through this together," Ann quickly squeezed her friends' hands. They shared sad smiles. "Coming, Marcia," she said, raising her voice.

Settled into their own thoughts, they could barely do justice to the delicious cornmeal porridge and harddough bread. Marcia told them she had it specially prepared for them, knowing that Ann was a yard girl.

Their conversation was sparse, each woman secretly glad they had planned an outing that would occupy their attention.

Marcia met them at the S.U.V. with the picnic basket Ann had ordered for the trip. Before they left, Marcia admonished them to be very respectful of the duppy spirits that they would encounter at the cave. She advised that they should not look back when they passed by the cotton tree that was close to the entrance.

Thalia sat up front with Ann again. Sara preferred the back and no one cared to argue. As they wound their way along the coast to the sounds of irie vibrations on the radio, Thalia observed how much more serene and pastoral this scenery was, compared to the trip yesterday from the airport to the resort. Herds of cattle and goats lazily grazing in the pastures along the hillsides set the backdrop for several of the photographs that she snapped with her newly acquired digital camera.

Sara—who was seeing the countryside for the first time, as she had slept during the drive the day before—was mesmerized by the sparkling turquoise sea on one side of the road, and the unending expanse of verdant, green meadows flanked by even greener, rolling hills on the other. The energy she felt here seemed so much more feminine than the California coast. She found herself wishing that she could carve out more time to devote to painting, a passion she had since childhood but had abandoned once she started medical school. Once more, early memories of the beach house started trickling into her awareness.

Ann noticed that her road rage was high. She blamed it on the cattle crossing at their own leisure, but lurking in the back of her mind was the memory of the first time that she and Don met. The chemistry was almost as intense as her meeting with Spice. Thankful her relationship with Don had been halted, she wondered who would save her from Spice. A voice questioned whether she needed saving, but Ann knew she was much too scared to take a chance now.

Ann was pleased to finally see the sprawling, great white house upon the hills that Marcia told her was the landmark for Duncan. The trip so far had taken only thirty minutes, but it seemed as though she had been driving forever. She turned off the main road and headed toward the caves, hoping that Cassandra had been there and left already; they were over an hour late.

About a mile down the side road, Ann saw the open field with the boulders where Cassandra said she would be waiting. But she was nowhere in sight. Ann drove down to the beach to see if perchance she was waiting there instead. No luck. The only people on the beach were a few young boys kicking a soccer ball into a makeshift goal of coconut brush.

Ann turned back toward the caves. She parked under the only shaded area she could find, under the cotton tree that Marcia had mentioned. She hoped that Sara and Thalia had forgotten Marcia's tales of ghosts and goblins.

A jet-black mongrel dog ran to the car when they opened the door. Sara did not want to get out, but Ann reassured her that he was harmless. She also told her that it was a good omen, because in many indigenous cultures, dogs were believed to be direct messengers from God. As if he understood their conversation, the dog calmly began walking by their side.

"We will need a lot of God here today," Sara remarked. "His presence will balance out the evil spirits that Marcia said were lurking around here."

"I did not hear her use the word evil," Thalia said.

"Well, they certainly are not angels," Sara said.

"I can see that we all have a lot of remembering to do about our African past," Thalia said. "Ancestral worship was the cornerstone of our culture back then," she pointed to Sara and testily continued; "and you, a bonafide quarter-blood Native American woman, you should be ashamed of not honoring your ancestors more."

"And you a three times degreed educated woman should know that everything that happened in uncivilized days should not be honored in modern-day practices. That same African past that you have idealized was rampant with them selling people into slavery. Both of you very well know," Sara defended herself, "that the Bible teaches that those kinds of practices are wrong."

"You're going to talk about the Bible and slavery in one breath and take the high road? Don't you know that it was the Catholic Church that sanctioned slavery."

"Thalia, please," Ann said. "Remember, no religious or political discussions. We have enough personal shit to settle between us, so let's not get too sidetracked by issues that are bound to divide us."

At first Thalia just shrugged and turned away, but she knew Ann was right. "Okay, let's do this," she said, turning back with an attempt at a positive expression.

Sara accepted the olive branch and did the same. "Where is this friend of yours, Ann?"

Ann had to admit she didn't know. They piddled around with light conversation about Jamaican culture while they waited; no one wanted it to get personal and heavy again. After about thirty minutes, Cassandra still had not turned up. Ann wondered if perhaps Cassandra had gone inside to wait. She suggested they go into the cave to look for her. Sara was a bit hesitant, so Ann said that she would go by herself. That proposition seemed even scarier to the two ladies. Sara worried about being in unfamiliar territory; and Thalia was worried about Ann's safety. So for very different reasons, they decided to go in with her.

"Then, let's take each other's hand and lead ourselves into the promise of freedom," Ann said quietly, paying her respects to the many slaves who went before her. She thought about how scary freedom is, back then and still today, and how so few people are willing to take the risk.

When Ann pointed out the mouth of the cave, Sara, in her fright, assumed her role as group comedienne and tried to keep things light between the three of them. It also helped stifle the summersaults that were kicking in her stomach with each step closer to the perceived darkness.

"When I was young, about I don't know—nine or ten—my brother Elijah played a mean trick on me. Wait, I must have been six or seven, cause I was real dumb. He convinced me to let him eat my food for me, so I would not have to do the work of chewing "What? Girl I hope you were barely six cause this one is pretty bad," Ann laughed.

Sara didn't disagree. "The worse thing was that as a child, I was close to anorexic—I've told you all that before."

Thalia smiled and listened intently as Sara continued, "Elijah told me that all I had to do was put my toes on his and hold his hands, just like we're doing now, and the food would pass from his body into mine. Oh yes, I remember now. I was seven. And I believed everything my older brother said. I'm telling you, this went on for several months until my mom discovered what was happening. He got such a beating." Sara's voice trailed off, but with the opening of the cave getting closer, her companions didn't notice the smile fade away. She kept the memory of what happened later that night to herself. Her mom had told her dad when he got home, and he stripped Elijah naked, tied him to the bed and beat him until his back began to bleed. Sara could still hear Elijah's screams.

Sara was glad that she had stopped their progression into the cave. They however were holding on to each other, so she tightened her hold onto both of them. Thalia noticed her painful countenance. Aware that Sara was getting increasingly more frightened about entering the cave, Thalia said to her, "You just hold on to me tight girl."

"I will," Sara said, her awareness now shifted back to the inherent danger of the present, "Are there bats in here, Ann?"

"Bats only come out at night, like the freaks," Thalia volunteered.

"How much daylight do you think there is in a cave, girl?"

Ann ignored the sparring between the two. "Lets think of any bats we see as our guides." She informed them that folk legend had it that it was a bat that appeared to a slave one night in his dreams and told him that he was going to show him the path to freedom. The following morning, he followed the path that was revealed in his dreams and found this cave. Being that it was close to the well that serviced the plantation where he slaved, he and others could gather there without raising much suspicion.

Sara lightened up, "I'm telling you all right now, I don't care where they promise to lead me, I'm not following any bats anywhere."

"They'll show you the path to freedom and you'll run in the other direction, right?" Thalia teased.

They all begin laughing. "Damn straight."

When they reached the cave's mouth, a nondescript opening in the ground, they formed a single file—Ann in front, Sara in the middle and Thalia in the rear. Ann slowly led them down the steps into the cave. Darkness descended upon them as they burrowed deeper and deeper into the cave's belly. When they were all the way inside, Ann stood still for a while to give their eyes time to adjust.

"Ann, maybe we should just go back and wait for her outside."

Ann tightened her grip on Sara. "We're close to the light. Hang in there."

Sara was not clear about what Ann referred to until they took a few more steps and, just as suddenly as the dark had surrounded them, within moments they came upon a stream of light coming through an opening in the cave roof.

As they moved toward the light, they saw several trees whose roots had grown down into the soil in the floor of

MONDAY

the cave. Thalia let go, ran up to one of the trees, and wrapped her arms around its trunk. "My lesson for today is that out of darkness will come light if you have the patience to hang with the darkness for a while," she announced.

Ann, worried about Sara who was about to squeeze the life out of her hands with her grip, said, "Mine is that the more firmly rooted you are in your true source, mother earth, the more you can open up and create paths of light."

"I am sorry, but I don't have any pearls of wisdom to add," Sara admitted. "I am not feeling the least bit inspired by any of this. The only thing that I am feeling right now is pounding in my head and nausea; almost like being seasick."

Ann, though somewhat worried about Sara, convinced them that since they had come so far, they should continue down to the lower level. She reassured Sara that it was much cooler there, and much, much more spacious.

"Are you sure?" Sara pleaded for her to say no. But Ann squeezed her hand determinedly and quickly moved toward the path again. Thalia took Sara's other hand once more.

An unknown, flying object darted by right as they began their descent through the narrow tunnel. Sara immediately panicked and began yelling, "Please get me out of here."

"Focus on your breathing," Ann glanced nervously over her shoulder but kept moving.

"Ann," Sara said in a very low and puny voice, "I'm scared."

Ann stopped and turned to her friend. She searched the darkness until she found the dark pools of Sara's eyes. "Sara, trust me," she said softly. "I wouldn't lead you wrong."

Sara's nervousness quieted for a minute. As she held Ann's gaze, they both knew there was more at issue than a cave of bats. Thalia held her breath until Sara whispered back, "I know you wouldn't, Ann. I know you wouldn't."

Ann smiled sadly. Tears welled up in her eyes. "I know you wouldn't either," she said to Sara and meant it, though she knew not from where her trust came. She felt the madness from the bathroom earlier and the anger and frustration that she'd held pent up inside slip away. She wanted to let go of Sara's hands and hold on to her rage, but the darkness was like a weight around her shoulders keeping her hands where they were. She knew she didn't need the anger, but surrendering to forgiveness often was so much more painful than holding on to it.

Thalia reached out with her other hand and tenderly squeezed Sara's shoulder. Without turning around, Sara accepted the gesture by brushing her cheek gently against Thalia's hand. "We should keep going." She was the first to speak again, though her breath was still ragged and shaky. "I don't want to stay in here much longer."

By the time they reached the bottom of the climb, Sara was hyperventilating, though her steps were steady, anchored by some other force. Only when her feet hit flat ground did her knees buckle. "Oh," she moaned.

Thalia quickly put her hands around Sara's waist, but not before she passed out. Ann swiftly fell to the ground to try and break her fall. Thalia instructed Ann to sit on the ground so that she could lay Sara's head in her lap. They were both very thankful that Sara was so light and petite.

"Panic attack?"

Thalia nodded her agreement as she quickly checked Sara's vital signs. Her heart rate was quite fast, as was her breathing—fast and shallow. "She's been so anxious and high-strung, and with all that she's been through, we should get her checked out by a doctor as soon as we get back," Thalia suggested.

Ann massaged Sara's temples while saying a prayer; she knew that her friend would want her to. A moment later Sara regained consciousness. "Where am I?" she asked.

"With your two best friends, Thalia and Ann in a cave," Ann said to her.

"Get me out of here, please," Sara said in a distant, far away voice.

"We will in a few minutes," Ann said. She was sorry that she had insisted that they continue. Especially after just declaring to Sara that she would not lead her wrong. "But right now, you need to be still for a while. Sara, you just fainted."

Sara closed her eyes and lay still for a while. Ann continued to massage her temples while Thalia fanned her. A few minutes later, Sara's breathing was regular again. She announced that she was feeling better even though she still felt a bit weirded out by it all.

"I'm sorry I brought you down here against your wishes," Ann apologized. "I didn't mean for any harm to come to you." In that instant, Ann understood Sara's insistence that she too did not mean to harm her on that infamous night twenty years ago. The true forgiveness she had prayed for all these years, yet had become ambivalent about since Sara's plane landed, rooted deeply inside her heart. She squeezed Sara's hands and bowed her head, letting the feeling fill her.

"I know that you didn't," Sara reached up and stroked one of Ann's stray locks. "I'm actually glad. Okay, so I passed out, but I did it."

"Even if we carried you half the way ..." Thalia teased.

"You didn't?" but it was more of a question than a statement.

"I'm just teasing you, Sara," she admitted. "You were right here when you passed out."

"You all better listen to the drumbeat and lively up yourself, " a voice called out in the distance. "When the slaves used to come down here, it was a joyful time. They were plotting their freedom. That's what we should be doing now."

Ann recognized Cassandra's voice.

"I apologize for getting here so late," Cassandra said.

"I was worried that you had come and gone. We did not get here exactly on time either."

Cassandra made her way over to them and sat down. Ann introduced her to Sara and Thalia. Her close to six-foot frame and regal locks flowing all the way to her buttocks made quite an impression on them both. Amazon lady, Sara thought to herself. Cassandra knelt down and gave them a warm hug, "Ann has told me such wonderful things about you both. Welcome to Jamaica, previous home to some very fierce African warriors."

"I'm sorry, I'm not feeling much like a warrior right now," Sara said, still resting her head in Ann's lap. She wondered if Cassandra had read her mental impression of her. "They tell me I just fainted."

"No worry. I will fix you up with some of my herbal remedies," Cassandra said, squeezing her hands. "Coming from that cool, dry California climate, you are probably having a hard time adjusting to this muggy heat."

Cassandra offered Sara some of the spiced ginger beer that she always carried with her. "The nutmeg in it works like magic for almost every ailment, in particular, upset stomachs." Ann was amazed once again by Cassandra's ESP. Nutmeg was what she had planned to get from the market for Sara's bruises.

Cassandra gently raised Sara up. Thalia moved over and made room for Cassandra in between her and Sara. They all quietly and expectantly sat around while Sara sipped the ginger beer. Sara apologized for drinking so slowly, but explained that the liquid was very hot and spicy. After her last sip, she announced to Cassandra, "Even though I don't believe in magic, your potion has worked miracles. Except for this strange, lingering sensation that feels almost like motion sickness, I feel much better."

Thalia and Ann noticed that Sara indeed began to perk up again.

"What happened to you is not weird or unusual," Cassandra reassured Sara. "I don't know if Ann has told you, but I come here every full moon and conduct a meditation and visioning ceremony. There is always someone in the group who has an experience very similar to what you are describing."

"Well at least I feel better knowing I am not crazy. Tell me how you learned about using these remedies?"

"I am a practitioner of ancient African healing arts that go all the way back to the Ethiopian dynasties. In addition to being a nurse midwife."

Ann recounted to them the story of how she and Cassandra met at seminar on the integration of Jamaican herbal practices into medicine. "We were paired together as partners during one of the small group seminars and hit if off immediately. She invited me down to one of these ceremonies the following week and I have become a student of hers ever since."

"You remind me of my grandmother. She was a Choctaw medicine woman," Sara said, fond memories of her grandmother surging up into her consciousness for the first in many years.

"Maybe you have the gift too," Cassandra said to Sara.

"I hardly think so," Sara laughed. "My dad was a Baptist minister." Sara reflected on how opposed her Dad was to his grandmother's beliefs and practices, and how he always tried to make sure that she and her brother did not spend any un-chaperoned time around her. "He likened it to voodoo and all that other evil pagan stuff."

"Maybe after you experience the healing powers of the herbs, you will change your mind," Ann coaxed her gently. She was sure one of the ingredients in Cassandra's brew was marijuana, but said nothing to Sara because she did not want to alarm her. Ann had been astonished to discover how much marijuana was used medicinally in Jamaica, especially in the rural areas.

"I would love to participate in one of those ceremonies you mentioned," Thalia said to Cassandra.

"Well, you're in luck," Cassandra replied. "The reason why I am here today is because I am having a gathering tonight. You all are welcome to come."

"I would be scared as hell to come back," Sara begged off. "I wouldn't want to go through this again."

"One day when you are willing to return," Cassandra told her, "I will tell you a tale that will help you understand where all this is coming from."

"Well, since I am already here, why not tell me now?" Sara asked. As much as a part of her was telling her to get away from Cassandra, another part was extremely curious to get to know her. Similar to how she always liked to go with her mother on secret visits to her grandmother's, even though she would be terrified that her dad would find out; or worse that her grandmother would cast a spell on her.

Ann was pleased to see that Sara liked Cassandra; she was very worried that she was going to write her off as an evil witch. She was also very concerned about Sara's health. "Are you sure you're up to it? Maybe we should get you back to the resort now that you're feeling better and able to withstand the drive back."

"I really want to hear the story that Cassandra is baiting me with." Sara did not tell them that she still felt quite nauseous and dizzy.

Cassandra uttered a rich laugh and winked at Sara. "You already know part of the story then," she said.

"No I don't," Sara was obviously confused.

"The story that I am going to tell is an old African tale of star-crossed lovers," Cassandra said.

"That old tale is the same as all of our new stories," Thalia interrupted.

"Then you too already know part of the story," Cassandra continued.

"The way things are turning, I am going to be quiet, in case I am the story, " Ann said. They all chuckled, sat and waited expectantly while Cassandra prepared to tell her story.

Cassandra sprinkled some water on the ground and gave libations to the ancestors as she asked the spirits to join them. She instructed each one of them to call out the names of their dearly departed. Ann called out for James, Thalia called out for her mother, Sara called out for her father, and Cassandra called out for her mother. Cassandra instructed them to sit in a circle around her. She began:

"Legend has it that once upon a time, in a tiny village in West Africa, a very beautiful young African princess named Sarantha was promised in marriage to the first born son of the chief of the neighboring village. When puberty came and it was time for marriage, the princess did not want to marry him because she had fallen deeply in love with her playmate, a promising young warrior named Matinde.

Her grandmother Namo, her mother's mother and the elder in charge of performing the rituals for the grand occasion, had always spoiled the princess and granted her wishes. This was her only grandchild; the child for whom she had performed special moon ceremonies, the child in whom the spirit of her mother had reincarnated.

The night before the wedding was to occur, the princess asked her grandmother Namo to give her a spell that would make her sleep forever. The princess would rather die than marry a boy she did not love. Her grandmother told her that she would instead give her a drink that would make her sleep for only a week. She promised the princess that when she woke up, she would be in the arms of the man she really loved.

The following day, the day of the princess' wedding, became a day of double funerals instead. The chief's son, so broken-hearted from the death of his bride, put an arrow through his heart.

True to her promise, a week later, the princess' grandmother with help from Matinde, Sarantha's true warrior lover, dug the princess out from her burial ground. Grandmother Namo shook her gently while Matinde lifted her from her sleeping abode. The princess opened her eyes, as Matinde placed a kiss upon her slightly parted lips.

Grandmother Namo welcomed the princess back to the land of the living, fed her, gave her food and gold for her journey, then sent her and her lover off to the lands by the big ocean. She knew that they had to go far away very quickly to avoid the sure death that would befall them if the chief found out what had happened. She instructed them to look for the vessels with the strange, pale people on them when they got to the land by the sea. These were traders from up North who were always traveling up and down the coast, and they were to give them pieces of gold in exchange for the journey to lands down south.

The princess did not want to leave, for she knew that she would never see her grandmother again. But grandmother Namo told her to go. She was planning to return to her ancestors soon since there was no more reason for her to live. Teary eyed but happy, the princess and Matinde thanked her. Then they set off, glad to have a chance to start their new life together and live blissfully ever after.

For forty days, they journeyed through the forest, traveling with the friendly animal packs during the day and sleeping and making love at night. They ate fruits and nuts that they picked from the trees and drank water from streams. At times, they were so enamored with life in the woods they could have stayed put; but they knew that if they did, they risked being found and taken back to the chief. So, reluctantly, they made their journey.

When they eventually arrived at their destination, they found a ship with people similar to the ones that the princess' grandmother had described. They saw the men with no color and very strange long hair on their heads and faces, unlike the men from their villages who always shaved the hair off their bodies. The princess approached them, showed them the gold and asked if they could take her to lands in the south. She did not have much difficulty conversing with them because one of their men spoke her language. The men eagerly took the gold and told them that they would be happy to take them wherever they wanted to go. The princess and her warrior were filled with joy; freedom at last to love and live together without fear of being conquered.

Soon after they got on board, the princess and her warrior lover noticed there was mayhem everywhere. Hundreds of people who looked just like them were screaming and fighting with pale men who were chaining them to the walls. They both instantly realized that the gods had played a nasty trick on them. They understood that the men had no intentions of keeping their promise.

The princess was immediately separated from her lover and taken down into a dungeon, where she was stripped naked and shackles were placed on her feet. She immediately lost her sense of time and place as she drifted into a cocoon of emptiness. She created her own world in which not even the pain of the daily whippings or the loss of her warrior lover could find any space to occupy. In the few conscious minutes that fought their way into her psyche, the princess prayed to the gods to send her grandmother's spirit. She wished to gain her grandmother's wisdom so she could figure out how to escape into the freedom of death.

One day, as the captain was walking by, he noticed that the princess had a special aura about her; she was different from all the others he had ever seen and desired. The captain imagined she must possess magic to endure the pain and suffering. He concluded that she would be the perfect vessel for the many slave children he intended to breed. He ordered that the princess be removed and sent to his quarters.

The princess was never sent back to the slave dungeons, nor was she treated like the other slaves. The daily floggings stopped, she received regular meals, and was made to sleep with him every night. As much as he wanted her, the captain kept her shackled to his quarters, fearing she would try to escape back to her people. Although he would never admit it, the captain had fallen in love with his slave princess.

A few months later, feeling movement inside her protruding abdomen, the princess realized that her recent dreams were real. In these dreams, her grandmother kept telling her to eat more of her meals because she was with child. But, the only food the princess desired was the wild yams that her grandmother used to feed the young women who asked the gods to take back their bellies. The princess prayed fervently to the gods to bless her with the wisdom to find another way. In the meantime, her captor lover, thanked his father God for answering his prayers.

On the day that the princess's water broke, the captain ordered the elder midwife to the cabin. There had been so many pregnancies on board, the captain had to free this midwife so she could attend to the births. The elder, sensing that the captain was in love with the princess, asked that her shackles be removed. The captain, overcome by the laboring of his slave lover, agreed. He had to leave the room himself.

Upon his departure, the princess screamed for her grandmother and her warrior lover. Moments later, her son was born. When the elder placed her son in her arms, the princess wept as she saw how much he resembled his father—his skin was pale, his eyes were blue. As much as she loved her son, the princess knew she could not raise a child fathered by her captor. When the captain heard his child's cries, he returned to the cabin. He was very pleased to see how much his son favored him. He even entertained the possibility that he would free his son and his mother and let them live in the great house when they arrived in the Americas.

Sensing how happy her captor was with the son she had born him, the princess begged the captain to let her and the elder take their newborn out to the deck so she could bring the blessings of the ocean gods to her child. The princess told the elder that she wanted to place a little seawater on her newborn son's forehead. Filled with love for his slave princess and their son, the captain agreed.

The princess swaddled her baby in her arms, kissed her captor lover, and thanked him for her child. Beaming with love, the captain led the princess, their child and the elder out to the deck. Upon their arrival on deck, the princess, with her son suckling on her breasts, ran quickly toward the rails and jumped overboard. The elder followed soon after too; knowing the captain would punish her brutally.

Right before the princess hit the water, she heard the screams of her captor.

The princess took a deep breath of water and relaxed into the ocean floor. She saw Yemoja sitting with her arms outstretched to greet her. Seated next to Yemoja was her warrior lover; little did she know, he had taken the same fate onto himself. The princess was overjoyed; she had found nirvana again. The princess handed her son over to Yemoja. Yemoja told her not to worry any longer; they had finally found freedom.

Yemoja took the boy and freed the princess to be with her warrior lover. Matinde kissed her tenderly and welcomed her home. When the princess inquired how and when he got there, he told her soon after they boarded, while still shackled, he wrestled his pale captor to the ground and forced him to unshackle him. He then ran to the deck and jumped overboard to his freedom. The princess smiled as she remembered how fierce a warrior her lover had been while they journeyed those forty nights in the woods. She smiled again as she remembered also how tender a lover he had been.

"And that is the end of the story," Cassandra said. From the mesmerized look on their faces, she knew that the three women had lost their sense of time and space and entered into the world of her tale.

"Cass, no wonder I had to stay," Sara said, the first to break the long silence. "I know that this sounds weird coming from me, but I kept feeling as though I had been there."

"I had some kind of déjà-vu experience myself!" Thalia exclaimed.

Ann thought about how much Cassandra reminded her of the stories about the wise spider, Brer Anansi, which originated from West Africa with the slaves. She asked Cassandra if there was a moral to her story.

Cassandra remained quiet for a moment before she spoke. "I am going to let you all figure it out for yourselves. Right now, I think we should get to dancing and eating before you all have to go."

"Cassandra, you're such a tease," Thalia moaned in mock agony.

Ann was thrilled at how intrigued her friends were. Cassandra did not bend, "No daughta, I'm not teasing. You have to remember, all things in time. When you are ready, you will know."

Sara rolled her eyes in jest. "Now I see why you and Ann get along so well."

Cassandra exchanged a smile of agreement with Ann. She walked over to where she had left a pile of bags. From one large, patchwork cloth backpack, she began to extract a jimbe.

Thalia went over to help, and whispered to her while she was out of earshot of the others. "Cassandra, I know this may sound like a stretch, but I was in such a trance while you were telling the story, I started feeling as though I was inside a womb. At one point, when you told about the birth of the princess' son, I imagined going through my own birth canal."

"Maybe you should trust your third eye and not always think that you are imagining things."

"It was just so weird though, cause it was so real."

Cassandra nodded in understanding. "Why did you whisper it to me? Why didn't you share with us all?"

Thalia was about to deny the obvious, but then explained, "It was so intense it shocked me. I don't know, I think Ann would understand, but Sara wouldn't, you know? It's different when we're arguing about things I've studied or read, but this was ..." she trailed off.

"When you conquer this issue you have been having with opening up and trusting yourself to experience new things, you will become more than a spokesperson for a race of disenfranchised people. You will become Thalia."

Thalia's mouth dropped wide open. She felt completely naked under Cassandra's intent stare. She knew Cassandra spoke of much more than the experience she had just had.

Cassandra began walking over to the others. She stopped and beckoned Thalia. "Come, take the first step. Share."

Thalia obeyed. Chasing away the thoughts of Lee that Cassandra had elicited, she cleared her suddenly dry throat and repeated the feeling to the others.

"This is fascinating," Ann said. "Sara just told me that she felt as though she was on a vessel."

"Yes, while Cassandra was talking, I realized the weird feeling I've been having all along was because I felt like I was in the belly of a ship."

Cassandra acknowledged both women with a nod. "This could all be real memories of things long past."

"I want to believe that, because it seemed real," Thalia said. "But I had this strong feeling of being afraid to be born."

"Why?" Cassandra asked.

"I hate to think about why," Thalia said.

"Release the fear," Cassandra reminded her gently.

Thalia thought for a while. "I hope this won't sound weird to you ladies, but I remembered being in her womb and hearing my mother praying that I would take my father's color." Thalia felt it necessary to give Cassandra the side bar that her mother was black and her father white. "The irony is, all my life, all I have ever wanted is to be just like her, in looks and everything else."

They were all quiet until Ann muttered, "Racism sure is lethal. It leaves its ugly teeth marks in us even before we are born."

"Maybe this can help to explain how certain pan-African traitors get born!" Thalia said, trying to change the subject from herself.

They all burst out laughing.

"We're never satisfied though, are we?" Sara mused. "Most of my insecurities stem from being so dark skinned."

"Sara, I think that you are one of the most beautiful women I know." Ann was very surprised at Sara's admission.

"Absolutely," Thalia said. "Remember how we would all go out and everywhere we went, who would get all the attention?"

"Sara!" Thalia and Ann chorused and laughed.

Sara smiled. "Not all the attention. You two sure could pick up your own riff-raff when you wanted to. I'm okay now, though," she got serious again. "But it's a constant battle to reverse the self-hatred that was dumped on a seven-year old."

"Yeah, kids can be cruel," Ann agreed.

"Adults too," Sara said. "I remember plenty of grown ups who would say crap like, 'she is so pretty, but …' or even actually 'if only she wasn't so dark'. It was pretty bad at times."

"If it's not skin color, then its hair," Ann touched her locks self-consciously, "if not hair then, ass, if not that? It's always something. If we don't find peace inside, anyone can tear us down."

"Well said sister Ann. Let's meditate on that statement of truth. Close your eyes and feel the presence of Jah and our ancestors," Cassandra said. "With their guidance, let us help each other free ourselves of our mental slavery." She picked up her drum and beat out a roll, "Let the dancing begin!"

Thalia felt inspired. "I want to dance for all those dark-skinned women like my mother who could not embrace their beauty, and as a result, their lives became marred with self hatred. And for all those light-skinned children like myself, living lives shadowed by shame and guilt, confused by the ambivalence brought on by the envy and praise of their privilege."

"That was beautiful Thalia," Ann remarked to her friend.

Cassandra beckoned for Ann and Sara to get up and join Sara and her. "Let us claim and keep the conscious energy that has been created here today," Cassandra declared with a gavel-like bang on her drum.

They all stood in a circle around Cassandra, shared a smile, relaxed their bodies, surrendered to the rhythm of the music, and let it sway and take them.

It seemed like only seconds before Thalia heard Cassandra calling out to her, "Welcome back my dear, where have you been?"

"Lost in my dance."

"A very erotic one I must say," Ann remarked.

"You sure did take Cass literal when she said that we should imagine ourselves making love to the rhythm of the drums," Sara added.

"Don't be teasing Thalia," Cassandra said. "She has clearly opened up her heart to love; I could feel it flowing to and from her soul."

"That's right, Cassandra, you felt me correctly," Thalia responded. "I was letting love in and releasing a lot of shame and fear."

"I am glad that you have found this experience helpful," Cassandra said.

Ann nodded and put an arm around Thalia.

"I have to admit," Sara said. "I'm glad I did this. I'm really surprised at how relaxed I feel now. I don't usually get into this kind of stuff, Cass. You can ask Ann. This was special."

"Then you will have to return soon," Cassandra said. "And make sure that it is around the full moon. Whatever benefits that you have gained today will pale in comparison to what would happen if you were to participate in the full ritual."

"Okay, now that starts to sound a little too close to devil worship," Sara said.

Ann and Thalia laughed and shook their heads.

"We were so close, Thalia."

"Almost had her, didn't we?"

Sara rolled her eyes at both of them and, putting her hands on her hips, turned her back and pretended to ignore them.

"If celebrating the great spirits that keep us connected to the larger life force is devil worship, then so be it," Cassandra remained serious. "There is no turning back for me; this is how I get the wisdom to integrate all my knowledge of the healing arts."

"I think Sara is just afraid of delving too deep into unknown waters," Ann said and pulled Sara back so she could hug her too.

"Damn right," Sara said. "And ever since I got off the plane, Ann here has been trying to pull me in, but it doesn't work for me like it does for her and Thalia."

"In what way?" Cassandra asked.

"I enjoyed the peace of dancing in the silent depths of the cave. That was really neat. I felt freer than I normally do. And, with the fairy tale legend that you told, I did have that sea-sickness thing that you said other people feel. But unlike Thalia, it did not give me any clarity about what is going on in my life now. So all I walk away with is thinking that this is all strange."

"That's exactly why you need to come back," Cassandra said. "Our journeys all happen at different paces."

"I will think about it," Sara said. "Right now though, I am starving."

"That's usually my line," Thalia said.

Cassandra agreed it was time to leave. She showed them a shorter, less precarious way out of the cave. The journey out was as uneventful as the journey in was eventful. No flying bats, no screams. As they said their goodbyes to Cassandra, Sara thanked her for the remedy. "I love how you call me Cass," Cassandra said to her in parting. "That's what my mother used to call me."

Cassandra headed back into town while Ann, Thalia and Sara picnicked on the beach. Feeling relaxed and at ease with each other, the incident in the morning was quickly pushed away. The three women swam and sunbathed for a while until the afternoon sun cooled down.

When they returned to the resort, Sara and Ann decided to run into town to pick up some nutmeg in case Sara felt sick again later. Thalia opted out and told them she wanted to take a nap. As soon as they left, she fulfilled the burning desire that Cassandra's intuitive statements had aroused—she called Lee.

"Is it still snowing there?"

"Is that what you called to find out?" Lee was angry from "hello."

"No. I was thinking about you, so I called."

"Yes, it shows."

"Lee, you know I'm here to spend time and reconnect with my girlfriends. I never said I would call every hour on the hour."

"Well forgive me for thinking it is common courtesy to return someone's call when they leave you a, actually, make that three messages."

"You're right, I'm sorry," Thalia was the first to let go, forcing herself to heed Cassandra's warning.

There was silence for a while then Lee admitted, "I was beginning to think that you were avoiding me and all the things you whispered in my ears while we were making love."

Thalia wasn't sure how to respond. Truth was, she couldn't remember all the things she had said. That night, things had occurred so rapidly, she was still trying to wrap her brain around what it all meant. "You should be more trusting, Lee," Thalia said. "Either Ann or Sara obviously forgot to tell me that you had called."

"I have not heard a word from you since you left my bed, Thalia," Lee responded. "Yes, I am not very trusting right now; I am upset. And, why didn't you wake me up so that I could drive you to the airport like we planned?"

"You were so sound asleep I didn't want to awaken you," Thalia said.

"I know I am a heavy sleeper, but I would have been happy to get up and take you," Lee replied. Lee began to soften as the memory of their incredible night took over her rationale. "It would have given me a chance to kiss you one more time."

"Don't be mad at me, Lee, I was doing you a favor," Thalia didn't want to remember it all. "It was still snowing pretty hard when I woke up, so I decided that the surest and safest way to get to the airport was to take the underground metro; it was only a block away."

"Thalia, why are you always so practical about everything?" Lee said. "I would not have minded skidding and sliding in the snow so long as you were by my side. Or, were you were trying to run away from what happened between us?"

Thalia was quiet. Lee's voice was dripping with disappointment. "Nailed it, huh?"

"Yes and no," Thalia said. "I do not want to run away from how good I felt being with you. I may not have told you, but Saturday night was my first true orgasm with someone else. That alone makes me want to stay with you forever. But, Lee, this is all very new to me. Saturday night I, a completely heterosexual woman, go to my friend's house because the weather was bad and she lives much closer to the airport. The only thing on my mind was getting the hell out of the snow and being with my friends in the warm Caribbean sun. Sunday morning I'm heading off to Jamaica having just slept with a woman, a good friend of mine,"

"So making love with another woman for the first time has you frightened," Lee concluded.

"What do you expect?" Thalia exclaimed.

"Haven't we been falling in love with each other over the past two months?"

Thalia was unable to answer. As good as the experience felt physically, she was frightened at the possibility that deep inside she was a lesbian. Maybe her dreams had been trying to tell her that the masculine stalls into which she was going was not correct for her. Maybe she needed to check out the female stalls; she might find peace there. However, she was not yet fully ready to accept this totally.

Lee continued, "Expressing it physically, making love that is, was just the next step, Thalia. There is nothing ever wrong with love and loving. Love is the divine state of being human."

Lee made it sound so easy, so natural. But Thalia knew she was way too confused inside. "When you put it like that, it makes sense," Thalia replied. "But, maybe I just need this week that I'm here to digest it all and get used to it."

"So you are saying that we are okay so long as we stay in the closet?" Lee asked.

"I guess so. I don't know, Lee. Maybe in time I'll feel more comfortable and we can talk then about handling things differently."

"Then we don't have to say anything until you are comfortable," Lee reassured her, suddenly afraid that she was going to scare Thalia away completely. "I haven't come out publicly as yet, but I would with you, Thalia. As a singer, anyway, nobody would really care—it's chic to be lesbian these days."

"Well it's still not lesbian chic for doctors, and lest we forget, for mothers," Thalia responded.

"I don't care one way or the other how we handle things right now," Lee responded. "Please just don't leave me hanging like you did."

"I will try not to," Thalia agreed, her heart warming again for Lee.

"Know that we have to be good to each other," Lee told her. "Thalia, I want to be your lover for as long as you will let me. I know that I have a hectic schedule, being on the road all the time, but I would give that all up for you."

"Lee, let's not get the U-haul truck jut yet," Thalia hit the brakes again. "We should not be talking like this now, we have been intimate for just one night."

Lee apologized. "I just don't want to lose you. I guess a part of me is worried that now that you have discovered your homosexual side, you may become very excited and want to go off exploring other relationships. Especially there on an island with tons of women running around in bikinis."

"Lee, don't worry too much about us. I was advised by someone earlier today to release my fears. So I am going to try to not turn away from my truths any longer, as difficult as that may be at times." Thalia heard Sara and Ann returning so she hurried to end the conversation.

"I will only let you go if you send me kisses and promise to call soon," Lee said.

"I'll do my best, but don't worry if I don't. I'll be home soon." Thalia promised.

"You know how to test my love don't you," Lee said lightheartedly. "I guess I will have to be a good, patient girl.

Maybe I'll have to take my toys to bed with me and stay there until you return. I'll pretend that you are my favorite doll that I am always taking care of and feeding."

"Okay, I gotta go."

"Bye, Thalia. I love you."

"Talk to you soon," Thalia quickly hung up the phone as the two women entered the living area.

"I hope that was Lee," Ann remarked flopping into a chair.

"Yes, she ah, called just as I was about to go to sleep."

"You haven't napped yet?"

"No, I've been on the phone."

Sara yawned. "Good, I think we'll both join you."

"What happened to your trip to the market?"

Sara and Ann looked at each other and shook their heads. "I don't know what we were thinking. We're exhausted. We decided to come back and get some rest before dinner."

"Great," Thalia breathed a sigh of relief about the smooth subject shift and the fact she'd still get her nap. "Nap time it is," she announced in a voice a little too loud, attempting to quiet the competing voices of Cassandra and Lee that swam in her head.

Exhausted, the usually astute Ann didn't notice, and Thalia was left only to argue with sleep as she begged it to take her frustrating thoughts away. But it ignored her and soon her conflicted thoughts fooled her into thinking that the warm, sticky Caribbean air was actually the forced heat from the man-made units that night in Lee's apartment. Or maybe it was another heat she remembered. Her mind blanked as she struggled to remember how things had changed between them so quickly. When Lee first came to her as a client seeking a cure from persistent headaches, Thalia felt awkward and distant. As the months passed, the well-known singer had reached out to Thalia until they became good friends. Now, she found herself in something she both liked and was scared of at the same time. Lee's touch was imbedded in all the sensuous spots on her body. Lee had told her that making love with a woman felt very good because another woman knew what it should feel like when it really feels good. Thalia remembered how she felt in Lee's arms as the tiny seeds grew with every sleepy breath Lee took. It had been good, that was a lie. It had been exhilarating. But even the next morning as she silently dressed, the temptation of having another round with Lee was not strong enough to face the questions Lee had in her eyes. The ones she'd voiced on the telephone this afternoon. Lee wanted more and it made her confused.

The problem was, Thalia sighed as she rolled over and looked at Sara's sleeping outline in the dusky room created by the drapes they had drawn, she didn't know how to bring it up with Sara and Ann, though she was dying to bare her confusion on them. Especially now that Sara seemed so steeped in her newfound religion. She smiled at the irony; once upon a time, they used to thrive on their differences. Rolling over on her back, Thalia accepted the beckoning of sleep. Her last thought rested on her doubt that Ann's seven days would be enough to bring everything to the table and have them walk away closer in friendship.

4
Tuesday

The knock on the door startled Thalia, who, unable to sleep, had wandered into the kitchen in search of a snack. She jumped up quickly and, without thinking, rushed to get the door before the others were awakened by the noise.

"Cassandra! Oh my gosh, I was just thinking about you."

Cassandra smiled, but did not respond directly. "Expecting someone?" she said, reminding Thalia that she had only a t-shirt on.

"No, I just didn't want to wake the others and I ran for the …" she stopped, realizing how self-conscious she was being. "I really was thinking about you. I mean that's not why I'm dressed this …" she stopped again, realizing Cassandra did not care about her t-shirt.

Both women walked into the living room. Thalia sat on the sofa and curled her legs under her. Cassandra handed her a bottle before taking the armchair next to her. "I brought Sara some extra ginger beer. In case she needs it."

"That was so thoughtful, thank you. Do you want me to go get her?"

"No let's you and I talk a little. She might rise before I leave."

TUESDAY

"So you live around here, Cassandra? You didn't come a long way to bring this, did you?"

"My work takes me all over the island. My office is the rock faces, trees and coastline. There is no part of Jamaica where I don't want to be, you know? When I bring this here I get to visit the ocean and speak with the ancestors who cast themselves in it so their spirits could return home. But why are you up so early? Didn't you all have a late dinner?"

Thalia nodded, then paused. How did Cassandra know that?

But before she could ask her, Cassandra continued, "What's going on, Thalia? You seem so conflicted."

Thalia released a big sigh, but no relief came from it. "I can't think of a better word to explain how I feel right now." She paused, but Cassandra said nothing. She felt safe talking to this woman she'd only known one day, but still she began cautiously. "Ever since my divorce, I've been healing a broken heart and taking care of my relationship with my son. I've gone out with a few people, but generally men I know I wouldn't fall for, you know?"

Cassandra's nod assured her she did.

"But then, right before I came here, the night before actually, someone, a close friend, well … we crossed that line you know. And this is someone I've grown close to. Someone with whom I've been sharing a lot of my grief from my divorce. I know I can trust them, but now this person wants to start something, and I just don't know. I care deeply for them but, I'm not sure if I'm ready."

Although Cassandra was silent, Thalia didn't think it

was because she was waiting on her to continue. She too was quiet, and soon Cassandra spoke.

"If you and I are neighbors and we sit on our verandas and talk every day and you tell me that you have to get your back window fixed because it's broken. Then one day I notice you have a beautiful new dress. I haven't had a new dress in a while and though you are my neighbor and I care for you, I really want your dress. If I decide to take the dress, to try it on and see if maybe you'll think I look better in it and tell me to keep it, how do you think I'm going to get the dress?"

"That's simple. The back window."

"It doesn't have to be a complex, involved story like the one I told you all in the cave, Thalia. If you leave your back window open, someone will climb in. And they may not necessarily be out to hurt you, but that doesn't mean they aren't looking out for their own best interests."

Thalia was stunned. She hadn't thought about it that way. She realized now how much of herself she'd shared with Lee lately. Now that she thought about it, she was somewhat annoyed that Lee's interpretation of her recurrent childhood dream was completely sexual; she believed there were other possibilities. But despite her discomfort with Lee's probing, she had continued the discussion that night. She now saw clearly how the conversation had led to Lee's bed.

Thalia was brought back to the present by Cassandra's movement toward the door. Before she let herself out, she imparted to Thalia, "I'm not saying this woman doesn't

TUESDAY

really care for you and that you don't feel the same. I'm just saying, don't rush it. There's no need—what is to be will be. But you have every right to be confused. You have every right to want space. If she can't understand that, listen to your discomfort. Don't just ignore it. It's too dangerous to decide she's pushing you 'cause she cares so much. We rationalize when we want to believe, not when we truly do."

Influenced by Cassandra's soothing tone, Thalia felt the tears well up behind her eyes. Thalia had walked Cassandra all the way to the door before she realized Cassandra had called her lover a she. "How did you know it was a woman?" Thalia whispered, incredulous at Cassandra's knowledge. She thought she had played the pronoun game right.

Cassandra turned and took Thalia's face in the palms of her hands. "Don't you know yet, daughta?" she smiled.

Thalia felt warmth radiate through her and fill her with strength.

"Talk to Ann. I think she has something she could share with you about this."

Thalia nodded, but wasn't sure when she would be ready to bring it up with her friends.

"But if you keep coming to the door like that, you're going to have many suitors chasing you." With a slap on the rump and a responding laugh from Thalia, Cassandra was gone.

It was a much more peaceful Thalia who returned to the couch and lay down. She decided she wasn't ready to talk to Ann and Sara. There were enough things happening between them all on this trip. Cassandra's message would help her sort her thoughts before she returned to Washington. Calm now, she was asleep within minutes.

"A very good morning to you Ann," Sara announced her arrival in a very loud tone and equally loud, red swimming attire and a red hibiscus in her hair. Ann was delighted at the sudden turn around in Sara's spirit and health. The swelling and puffiness around her eyes were almost gone, and the bruises on her face were healing nicely.

"To what do I owe such a pleasant greeting?" Ann asked, looking up and smiling with her. "Come sit and spill it all." Ann moved over to make room for Sara on her bed. Just moments ago during her meditation, Ann had resolved to try to be more gentle with Sara and not push or probe as intensely as she had been. She was thankful for the understanding they had reached in the cave. If Sara left today, she knew that was enough. It was a lot to have covered. Trying to get Sara to be more open, Ann recognized, was a subtle and slightly hostile way of doing battle with Sara. Sara was not interested in introspection, and she was obviously terrified about what might come up for her.

"To my phenomenal morning of snorkeling. I could have stayed on the ocean floor and swam with the fish forever."

"I would have loved to join you," Ann said. "Isn't it amazing being isolated with the sound of your breath? It makes me feel very peaceful and one with the sea, the mother of all life. It's almost like being back in the womb."

"Then you should have come with me and forgotten all that yoga stuff," Sara said.

"Today is the first day since the end of the full moon, and I needed to resume my practice," Ann told her.

"I hope that you won't take this the wrong way, but at my church they really feel that things like yoga are devil worship," Sara said.

Ann was in such a mellow mood from her yoga routine, very little could seriously perturb her. "Sara, why don't you try it some day? When I do yoga, I'm simply touching the god inside. As I stretch, I bring in the healing energy of the universe and use my body heat and increased levels of oxygen to release the built up toxins in my body. Does that sound like I am worshiping a destructive force?"

"Put that way, you make it sound the opposite, like it helps to sustain life," Sara admitted. "But then what's up with all that moon business?"

"Come on now, Sara. It's all very harmless when you investigate it for yourself. I mean, what's wrong with marking days by the moon?" Sara had no answer, so Ann explained to her that the moon, stars and sun were used back in the day before calendars and watches. Sara did not put up the usual brick wall, so Ann encouraged her to employ the critical thinking she needed as a doctor to at least begin to look at what she was afraid of discovering, in both her external and internal worlds.

Sara shrugged. "If I did have dark secrets planted deep inside my psyche like you are suggesting, I probably have a darn good reason for burying them."

"Sara, at the risk of having you accuse me of playing therapist with you, it seems to me that you think that digging up the past keeps you stuck there. My experience has been that you can use the process to help you discover why you have been who you are, and then use that insight to guide you into creating who you want to be."

"Yes, but who needs all that pain? Especially when I've found my own way of dealing with it. Even if that's by shutting it out. At least what you don't know won't hurt you."

"That's the myth, Sara," Ann said in calm disagreement. "What we don't know hurts us all the time; our unknown past oftentimes is what controls how we behave in the present."

"But at what point do you move on? When do you stop spending all your time going over and over what may have happened years ago?" Sara asked.

Before Ann could answer, Thalia jumped into the bed with them.

"What am I missing?" Thalia asked trying to work her way out of her sleep fog.

"What you don't know won't hurt your sleepy head," Sara said.

"Ever since we were children, Thalia, you have been sleeping this much and this hard." Ann shook her head in amusement.

"You all just envy me and wish you could have as much beauty sleep as I do," Thalia remarked

"Maybe the rest of us don't need as much," Sara said.

"That's right," laughed Ann. She grasped Thalia's face and moved it from side to side inspecting it. "Hmm, looks like you could use a couple more hours."

"Girl, get off me." Thalia pushed Ann's hand away and rolled onto her tummy. "So what's the topic du jour?"

"Sara was telling me how doing yoga is going to send me to hell."

Rolling her eyes, Sara defended herself. "I did not say that, I just said your involvement in it and a lot of other things you keep talking about is questionable. It's not too late for you to repent or anything though. I'm not trying to preach to you all, but as my friends I wish you wouldn't do these things because …"

Ann interrupted, "Your church said it is wrong."

"Correct!"

Thalia and Ann smiled and while Ann shook her head and decided to leave it alone, Thalia pressed on. "Sara, you are going to have to explain all this born again Christian stuff. It must have happened after I left for Africa, because up to that point you were sinning and loving it."

"How about I turned to Jesus after you abandoned me for Africa," Sara said, smiling coyly.

"I am glad you said that with a smile on your face, Sara,

because there is no way that you could seriously think that I abandoned you," Thalia replied. "In case your memory has failed you, I begged you to come with me. I literally got down on my hands and knees. I told you that what you needed was a total change of scenery, continents for that matter. But no, you felt that you had to go to California, to see if things could work out with you and Donovan. I was so disappointed, pissed is the better word. I have always felt that he is bad news for you. His ego has always been far too large for his short self."

"Thalia," Sara immediately lashed out, "As fucked up as he is, at least I married a black man."

"Touché, Sara," Ann said, "but that was not necessary."

"It's cool," Thalia said. "It's nothing I haven't heard before. At least with Sara I know there's still love between us."

Ann knew that Thalia's feelings were deeply hurt, in spite of her attempts to brush it off. Sara had just struck her Achilles heel. Ann's protection reflexes kicked in. She felt she had to rescue her best friend from what she knew was not totally her doing. "Thalia, I think that your marrying white was scripted more by the circumstances of your family dynamics than your own individual preference for whites."

Sara stared blankly at Thalia, then at Ann, clueless. "Madame Freud, please translate."

Ann checked in with Thalia to see if she understood.

"I think so," Thalia replied. Years ago when Ann visited Thalia in Africa, she had helped Thalia see that many of her issues with Reggie stemmed from unresolved conflicts in her early relationship with her parents. Indeed, it was that insight that gave her the courage to leave Reggie the following year.

"Okay, I admit that I am the one with the thick skull," Sara said. "So will someone please enlighten me."

"Ann is referring to the fact that I have been very angry with my white father for abandoning my mother," Thalia replied. "So, to deal with it, I found myself a white man upon whom I could turn the tables, and also make sure that he never did the same to me."

Ann went on to explain to Sara that Thalia's actions gave her a sense of mastery over a childhood trauma she couldn't control.

Sara didn't buy it. "That sounds all nice and analytical, but no matter how you dress it up, Thalia, I think that being as light-skinned as you are, you didn't value your blackness and were trying to escape it."

"That's always been the verdict handed to me in my many trials in the court of public opinion," Thalia said, reflecting momentarily on how rejected she felt by many African women when she lived on the continent, in spite of their politeness.

"Since you went ahead and married him anyway, why did you leave him if you still loved him?" Sara asked. "I haven't once heard you say that you did not love him."

"I do love him as an individual, but it got harder and harder to separate him from his group and the structures they have put in place to keep us oppressed." Thalia looked sad, so Ann gently squeezed her hand, afraid she was about to cry.

"More important though is that you wanted to do to a white man what one had done to your mother," Ann insisted.

Thalia thought Ann might be on to something, but she was not yet ready to admit that she could have such inner rage. "I know you think I was a crazy radical in college, but a lot of it was learned rhetoric. I believed it sure, but it wasn't until I went to Africa that I blossomed into my full identity as a black woman. During all that deep personal change, it was hard to be with him. I kept feeling like a 'mammy'."

"But you knew all along that he was a white man, even if you weren't so sure that you were a full black woman," Sara remarked.

"Whatever, Sara," Thalia said, somewhat angered by the fact of having to defend her actions again; Lee had backed her up into a similar corner just a few days earlier. "Let's just say that as I got older and blacker, the collective group issues became more important than just my individual needs."

"One of our burdens as black people is always having to carry the burden of our group survival, versus having the joys of individual freedoms," Ann noted.

"You're right," Sara admitted. "Have you ever noticed how when a report of a major crime hits the news, black people are always praying that the perpetrator was not black? You never see white people taking responsibility for the sins of other white people."

"It's that white privilege that I mentioned earlier, which I couldn't get Reggie to see; it was all so normal to him. Thalia thought about the many instances in which she tried to show Reggie how he never had to waste any mental energy trying to discern whether the reason he was not getting his fair shake was because of group stereotypes. He could always rest on the laurels of his expectations that he got what he was worth.

"I can't go there anymore," Thalia continued. "I just don't ever want to live up close and personal to the constant reminders again."

"Thalia, your growth is obvious and inspiring, but remember that it can be a heavy burden to carry the weight of the whole race every moment of your life," Ann remarked. "You have to take care of yourself. It seems to me that you've been focusing most of your energies on Olu and pretending that things are okay."

"Do you have to know me so well?" The women shared a smile. "Actually, our trip to the caves yesterday was very healing for me," Thalia continued. "As we danced, I could feel myself letting go of a lot of anger."

"That's great!" Ann couldn't have been more pleased.

"Speaking of the caves," Sara said, "will we see Cass again before we leave?"

"Oh, I forgot to mention, she came by this morning."

"Oh no, when?"

"Before ya'll got up. I was restless and tinkering around in the living room. She left some ginger beer for you, Sara. I put it in the kitchen."

"I really like her," Sara beamed. "I'm sorry I missed her."

"We can remedy that," Ann said. "I was hoping that you all would want to come and spend the last days at my place in Kingston which is where Cassandra lives too."

"I know that this might sound a bit crazy, especially coming from me," Sara said, "but this morning while I was snorkeling, I had a strange feeling that I have known Cassandra before. I can't tell you how calming her presence was to me yesterday in the cave. Once I heard her voice, I just had this feeling that everything was going to be okay; kinda like a mother soothing a child with bad dreams."

"I felt the same way about her too," Thalia said. "I definitely found a shared rhythm with her drums."

Thalia paused for a while, noting that one of her secret fantasies had always been to be a performer like her mother. It was starting to dawn on her that perhaps her image of her mother as a black female singer had a significant role in her feelings for Lee, also black, also a woman, also a singer. Maybe her interest in Lee wasn't an overreaction to her failed marriage with Reggie, maybe it was an example of her reaching for her mother's love after all these years. "I have spent more energy thinking about my mother on this trip, than I have in the past 10 years. She keeps coming up in my thoughts," she told Ann. "You are going to have to start the clock ticking for my therapy."

Ann thought about how self-reliant Thalia had always been. Even in childhood, it had been difficult for Thalia to let others take care of her. "Girlfriend, we are here to lean on each other, and support each other's healing."

"Thanks for easing my guilt, my Jewish father's gift to me," Thalia said.

"Thalia, why are you still so angry with your father after all these years?" Sara asked. "Other than being white, what else is he guilty of?"

"Sara, my feelings about my father affect every aspect of my life. Because of his whiteness, I will never be able to feel totally Black."

"You of all people should not doubt your sense of blackness," Sara said. "Thalia, you were a card-carrying member of the Black Panther party."

"I never ever told you the full story about why I transferred to Princeton, did I?"

Sara shook her head. Thalia proceeded to tell Sara the story about the beauty pageant. She was sure that her opening up with Lee was what gave her the courage to tell it again. She had never told the story to anyone else, not even Reggie. And if it were not that Ann was involved with packing her things up from Hillman, she probably would not have told her either.

"Thalia!" Sara was surprised at all she'd heard. "I had no idea you'd had so much hell because of your color. I always thought it was just us jiggas that got all the pain."

"Nope, they make sure to dish it out evenly, don't they?"

"Yeah, but still, Thalia, it doesn't seem like your dad really did anything to you. He was just who he was."

"I know." Thalia admitted. "I'm pretty in touch with my feelings about my father. I'm able to understand my anger and why I'm still hanging onto it. Truth be known, it's my mother who is a kicker for me."

"You and millions of other black women," Ann said. "One thing that my many years as a therapist has taught me is that black women have a very difficult time dealing with issues with their mothers. It is a forever and continuous slow paced work in progress."

"But why?" asked Thalia.

Ann paused a second and thought about it. "For most women, it was our mothers who from our early formative years shaped our understanding of life. It was Mom who laid down the framework and the foundation of the people we eventually became. For those of us who were lucky to have had a father in our lives, he helped to add the bricks. And how much is very dependent on the time that he carved out. So, as a result, Dad's role is much less complex and interwoven in our psyche, and therefore easier to understand."

"What about those of us who lost our mothers way too early?" Thalia asked softly. She worked hard to fight back the tears as another lump began to rise again in her throat. "I feel very hurt and guilty about my mother's death." Ann reached over and squeezed Thalia's shoulder gently. A few tears rolled down Thalia's face and she buried her head in her pillow. "I have always blamed myself, thinking that there was something that I could have done to prevent it. But at the time, I felt totally helpless. I can't understand to this day why she gave up so easily. Even though I was just eight at the time, I could have taken care of her."

Ann said to her, "Just imagine how hopeless she must have felt."

"I don't want to," Thalia said, struggling even harder now to keep from falling apart. "To do so, I would have to admit that she could not feel my love and that hurts. It makes me feel like a bad, worthless, useless person."

"Thalia, I can see that you're very sad, but I bet there is a lot of mad too," Ann probed.

"I'm angry all right." After the words came spilling out, Thalia felt the painful need to feel her mother's love rush over her again.

"At the risk of sounding like a broken record, it never ceases to amaze me how difficult it is for black women to look at their anger at their mothers," Ann pushed. "Admitting it makes us think that we are being disloyal. A lot of the black women that I saw in therapy would attack me if I suggested they were angry with their mothers. The ones who could face their anger made amazing leaps of self-discovery."

"Yes, but ..." Thalia shook off the angry thoughts, disguising them in a more palatable form, "there are so many other emotions to deal with. I mean guilt is a big one too."

Ann sat up and made sure Thalia was listening, "True, but remember Thalia, unrecognized rage emotionally immobilizes us. It keeps us in places where guilt and sadness run wild and unchecked. And, when we are in situations of uncertainty, it makes it difficult for us to breathe through and identify our true feelings."

Silence moved in like a black cloud as all three women

checked in with themselves to gauge their rage. Sara broke the heaviness.

"Okay, too much for one beautiful morning. I am not getting into my issues with my mother. That my dear ladies would take forever. I am all for leaving the past alone!" She got up from the bed and stood, waiting for Ann and Thalia to join her.

"I used to think so too," Thalia said. "But now I am seeing that I can't let go of the past till I deal with it." As Thalia rose and stretched her arms over her head she was filled with a warm feeling. "Today feels like a new beginning for me," she said out loud.

Ann suggested that since they had no agenda for the day they could lounge around and talk as much as they wanted.

"Well, that's not completely true," Sara said. She was glad that she had an opening to tell them what she had been dying to say all morning. "Of course we could stay here and hatchet our mothers to pieces, or we could go horseback riding with this very nice guy that I met while I was at the beach this morning. He and his father own the stables a few yards down. He said there were some beautiful trails up over the mountains that lead to a very lush valley below."

"So, I let you alone for a minute and you're out picking up island men," Ann teased.

Ignoring her, Sara pushed on, "Come on, let's all go riding together. We need to get out and feel the wind blowing through our hair."

TUESDAY

"Come to think of it, I would love to go," Ann agreed. "The few times that I have gone horseback riding did wonders for my spirit."

"Count me in too," Thalia said, happy for the break. "I could definitely use some time out. I've only been riding a few times though, so I hope that I will be okay on a mountain trail."

"You'll be fine," Sara's face shone with excitement. "He said he takes all types of tourists all the time. It's safe." Ann noticed Sara's enthusiasm, but said nothing. Sara, nonetheless was battling her own guilt, aware that her curiosity had been steadily peaking about the young man who she had met earlier. "I ahm, I'm going to go to the bathroom, then I'm going to call Don before we go. You guys can go ahead and order breakfast. Just make sure there's something you know I'll eat."

When Sara left the room, Thalia looked at Ann with a question on her face. Knowing her friend so well, Ann responded to the unasked question. "I don't know Thalia. When she asked me yesterday while we were walking on the beach if she should call Don, it took everything I had not to grab her and shake some sense into her." Ann found it disconcerting that her reaction to Sara's victim role was so aggressive. But she was thankful that she maintained her control and instead had counseled Sara to try to follow her head on this issue, and not her heart.

"It's one thing if they'd just had a bad argument or he was just acting like an ass, but why the hell would she want to call him after the beating he gave her. Damn!"

"Many of my abused patients used to exhibit the same behavior. It's really hard for them to separate from their abuser. At times it seemed to me that they needed the pain; it made them feel alive."

"But this is Sara, the doctor, not a patient," Thalia protested. "She is way too smart and beautiful to think she needs that shit."

"Thalia," Ann said calmly, "if there's one thing I've learned it's that this stuff crosses every line you can think of: racial, socio-economic, whatever. You know yourself what an emotional wreck Sara is inside and how she won't deal with it. That, not anything else, is what makes her a perfect victim for Don." Thalia began to interrupt, but Ann cut her off, "Anyway, I promised myself I wouldn't do anything more to add to Sara's anxiety or stress. She's come a long way so far. If the sharing happens naturally, beautiful. But I don't want to keep forcing the issue because that will just force her out of my life, again."

Thalia closed her mouth. She knew Ann was right. She lay back down on the pillow trying to dissipate her frustration.

To her dismay when she returned, Sara saw that Thalia and Ann were making no effort to get going. "Get your asses up. We need to get to the stables early before the good horses get taken," she nudged them on. "Thalia, I can hear your stomach from here. I'm going to make my call on the patio."

Trusting them to get up this time, Sara took the cordless out of earshot and onto the patio. It had been three days since their fight, and she had no idea what mood Don would be in. Her stomach flipped nervously. She had to block the pain. She had to make herself numb again.

The operator came on the line and connected her to her home phone number. Don greeted her as if nothing had happened.

"Honey, I may not be able to get off in time to pick you up from the airport next Sunday. It's my weekend to be on call."

Sara held her breath. That was the prelude to the argument the night of her departure—him trying to use work to cover up his affair.

"Whatever, Don," she said, trying to hide her disgust. "I called to let you know that I did not like how we left things the other night, and I was hoping that we could patch things up when I get back."

"That's on you Sara," Don replied, "I didn't do anything wrong."

"It's always my fault, isn't it? Well guess what Don, I don't need to put up with your male ego bullshit any longer! I don't give a shit whether you pick me up or not!"

"So you get a little Jamaican sun in you, and who knows what other kind of fun with those bitch girlfriends of yours and you start acting like a fucking lesbian, like you don't need no man. I hope that they are going down on you and licking you good …"

Sara could not stand to hear any more of his vulgarities, so she clicked off. She stared at the phone for a minute or two before slamming it down on the lounge chair. She got up and paced along the poolside sorting out her feelings. She was angry, but calmly so. Most of all, she was very proud of herself that for the first time she had the courage to remove herself out of the line of his emotional abuse. Normally when she and Don fought, she'd be distraught for hours trying to get him to talk to her, forgive her, anything to try to smooth it out. Even when she felt she had nothing to apologize for. But not this time! Furthermore, she was not going to take his accusations about her being a lesbian seriously, because he of all people had firsthand knowledge about what a God fearing woman she was.

Sara took a deep breath, put her hands on her hips and stared out at the lush morning sea beckoning to her. A nice swim would have done wonders to calm her emotions even further, but she didn't want to miss her ride with Marlon. She knew she wouldn't sleep with him. She could hear Reverend Morton droning on about the evils of sex. She'd already had way too much alcohol on this trip, another of his major sins; she had to keep it together. She had never seriously thought about getting revenge on Don by having her own affair. But, she realized that Marlon's attention had been good for her. Look how she'd been able to walk away from the fight with Don. She smiled to herself. She'd spent a lot of time pretending that Don and her were the perfect couple. She never would have thought the perfect weapon was to make him think she was fucking around, even if he got the gender incorrect. His ego couldn't handle it and she should have known that.

TUESDAY

All of a sudden, Sara was so glad that she'd made the trip. At least with Ann and Thalia, she didn't have to pretend everything was okay. They accepted her even though they disagreed on so much. And now she'd met someone to take her mind off Don and whatever he got up to while she was gone. She vowed not to call him again. Let him stew on this for a while. She was going to enjoy herself for the rest of the week and deal with Don when she got back. She knew he was probably hunting for the number to call her back; she knew how much he hated not being the one in control. Laughing, she turned off the ringer on the phone. She'd turn it back on before they left for the ride. After all her arguments about needing communication with the outside world, she was glad Don wouldn't even be able to get voicemail.

Giggling, she went inside to get breakfast.

Ann said nothing, but Thalia, in the process of demolishing her breakfast, noted, "Must have been a good call. You all made up?"

"I wouldn't exactly say that." Sara picked up the lids covering the breakfast dishes and screwed up her face at Ann's order of the Jamaican meal of fried dumplings and ackee. "But I've resolved to deal with it when I get back. I'm not going to let Don ruin my getaway."

Sara decided to say no more. Thalia raised her eyebrows but read Sara's body language and let it go. Ann did the same.

"Just try it, Sara," Ann said, offering her the plate of dumplings.

"I'm not that hungry," Sara declined. "All I need is a cup of that great Blue Mountain coffee." Pouring herself a cup, she got ready for the smooth liquid spreading over her palate, light at first, and firm toward the end. Getting a slice of toast and jelly, she pointed out, "Look at Thalia anyway, there won't be any waste here."

When they were finished eating, they put on their makeshift riding gear—long khakis and tennis shoes, and walked to the stables. They had no trouble finding it, located almost caddy corner across the street from the resort. But, the gate to 'Kermit's Horse Farm' was locked.

Disappointment was written all over Sara's face, so Ann picked up a stone and knocked on the gate. Just as they were about to leave, a young gentleman came out from behind a tree to the side of the property and walked toward them. He reminded Ann of the porter that had helped them at the airport, except that this man's dreadlocks were so much longer, almost to his waist, and his shirtless chest was lean and trim; not an ounce of body fat.

He approached Sara. "I am so glad the queen has graced me with her presence," he said. "I never really thought you would take me up on my offer."

"See, women are not as predictable as you may think," she beamed despite herself.

"You would think that I would know that by now," he replied.

"Why?" Sara said.

"The majority of my patrons are women," he replied.

"You must be in the pimping business then," Sara said,

a very defensive tone searing her voice. "Let's get it straight from the beginning—my friends and I have not come here to be hustled."

As provocative as he sounded, Ann took an instant liking to him. As hard as Sara was trying to appear cool, Ann was pretty sure that her acrid tone hid other feelings.

"My, my, I must have touched a sore spot," he replied, not the least bit put off by Sara's venom.

Ann smiled. "I think my friend was reacting to your subtle reference to women as trade."

"My apologies then. I wouldn't want to upset three such beautiful women who have come to rent my horses," he replied, revealing a hint of devilishness.

"You mean you did not think that we wanted to rent you instead?" Sara asked unrelentingly. "We could have mistaken you for the real stud!"

"Don't take me too seriously ladies," he said, repentant. "I happen to be an artist, sometimes clown and most definitely a court jester." He bowed with a flourish. Sara was not sure how to take the charmer and began wondering if what he'd told her about himself earlier were lies.

"And suppose we did come to rent a dread?" Ann asked playfully.

"I am not touching that one after the scolding I just received," he said, showcasing an endearing smile.

"Then tell us about your legitimate job," Sara continued to push. By now she was convinced that not only was he a pimp, he was a drug dealer like the majority of all those other Jamaican rastamen.

"My Dad has always believed that artists are just loafers who prey upon other people's hunger for beauty. So to prove to him that I am a real man, and also to reassure him that I am not gay, I work here at the stables when I am not in a serious painting cycle."

"Sara, would you kindly introduce your friend?" Thalia said, tired of all the hedging games.

"How about letting me be your anonymous guide as we ride off into the mountains?" he asked.

"Sorry to be a spoilsport and shatter the romanticism," Sara remarked. "His name is Marlon."

"Marlon, I would love to listen to your charming lines along the way, but would you mind if we rode in silence. I have always had this fantasy to horseback ride and meditate." Ann suggested.

"Not only would I not mind," he agreed, "but it would be my pleasure. I get inspiration for my art by silently observing how life unfolds in light and shape. Then I interpret what I've seen through my third eye."

"So our hustler is now a redeemed spiritualist," Sara said, not letting up on her combativeness toward Marlon.

"I am both," he replied. "You see, I have learned from you North Americans the science of using sex to get where you need to, even if it is to heaven," Marlon continued unperturbed by Sara's sharpness.

Ann, unsure as to whether Sara could handle Marlon's cool, suggested that they get going. She paid him the necessary money, and he casually thrust it into the back pocket of his jeans without counting it. Then he took them back to

TUESDAY

the stables and helped each of them to pick out a horse suited to their temperament.

After they were all comfortably saddled, Marlon led them on their journey to the valley.

They rode close together along the trail, Marlon in front and all three of them a few paces behind. Sara tried to stay focused on the awesome scenery as it unfolded. She trained her eyes on the greenery and beautiful wildflowers, including her favorite, lilies, so as not to think about the muscles that dominated Marlon's strong back. The fact that his sparring with her had created none of the out-of-control anger that dominated her during her fights with Don surprised her. He also didn't seem easy to anger. Unlike Don, who would lash out at any small thing. Then after she'd gone crazy trying to placate him and given up, he would come crawling back begging for forgiveness after she had not spoken to him for a couple of days.

This time had been different though. She had been the one to call him after the beating he gave her the night of her trip. The memory began coming back. She could remember so much about that night, but could not pinpoint exactly what had angered him so.

Suddenly it came to her. The argument took a fatal dive when they began talking about money, a big no-no for them. It always led to the same place. She could hear Don clearly now. "Yeah, say it," Don had yelled. "Say that you earn so much more money than me, even though you give half of it to that goddamn church. Well let me show you who still wears the pants in this house and who had the penis the last time I checked." Don pushed her off the sofa onto the floor. He slapped her across her face a couple of times. When she tried to cover her face with her hands, he grabbed them and pinned them by her side, and ...

Sara heard someone calling her name. She snapped back to the present. Marlon had come up beside her and was asking her to keep a better pace with the rest of them. She was glad her face didn't betray the nightmare she was remembering. She quickly apologized and promised to pay better attention.

He gave her a soft smile, nodded and resumed his place in front. Lost in their own thoughts, Thalia and Ann were too relaxed to notice Sara's change in demeanor.

Consciously focused on the scenery, and sometimes the movement of Marlon's muscles as they flexed at his instructions to the horse, Sara was able to lock Don away on the remainder of the trip. Aided by her need to concentrate as they descended into the valley, she was already calm by the time they reached a lush, grassy landing flanked on either side by gentle hills and huge trees. Marlon suggested that they stop there and camp out for the day.

He helped each of them to dismount; taking his time with Sara, who again relaxed and smiled flirtatiously at the special attention. They tied their horses to nearby trees. Marlon settled them under a cool shade tree with a brook close by before attending further to the horses.

Ann was the first to speak, "Isn't it remarkable how much silence can teach us about life. It's as if it forces you to hear your own inner truths."

"I am not meaning to make light of the moment," Thalia said, "but I was deadly afraid of those bulls that we kept passing. It took all my energy to keep from screaming."

"I didn't really notice them," Sara admitted, realizing how zoned out she had been.

"That's great, Sara, you must have really gotten to a special place with your thoughts," Ann said.

Sara didn't know if that's what she would call her thoughts, but she didn't want to spoil Ann's joy. She remained silent.

Thalia saved her from having to lie. "I made it okay though because Marlon seems like the kind of guy who would help a damsel in distress fight off the bulls."

"You better watch it, Thalia," Ann joined Thalia's teasing. "Even though Sara won't admit it, it seems to me that he has lined himself up to slay her dragons."

"Your prize bullfighter and dragon slayer is just not my type," Sara dismissed the banter, but admitted to herself that Marlon did look like he could take care of anything.

"Is it because he seems like a nice guy, or because he is not a professional man?" Thalia wasn't completely teasing this time, and Sara knew it. She took it as payback for having chewed Thalia out earlier for marrying a white man.

"Both," Sara said in an arrogant tone, hoping to put an end to the conversation. "I am ready to eat lunch since I did not have much breakfast. Plus, this tired conversation is wearing me out, and Cass is not here to heal me."

"I wasn't trying to be critical," Thalia said to Sara, "but sometimes I hate to see how you allow men to hurt you."

"Then give me credit for not trying to add another one to the list," Sara said haughtily. "I can feel him trying to hit on me, and I am not interested. In the first place, I am a married woman, secondly, as handsome as he is, I don't find him attractive."

"Sara, I am not suggesting that you sleep with him," Thalia said to her, "But you seem to be playing a game with him. One moment you're flirting, and the next minute you're bordering on hostility. I think it's because he's just a stable hand to you."

"Go ahead ladies and accuse me of being fucked up again," Sara said, her frustration taking control. "I always get accused of sexualizing everything anyway. Truthfully, I am sick of all this exploring. I want to declare now that I am not here for therapy; I am none of you all's damn patient." With that, Sara walked over to the open field and lay down in the grass.

Thalia shook her head in frustration, but Ann only shrugged her shoulder resignedly, remembering that Sara had always acted like that. She would always leave whenever she couldn't get her way. The irony was that she didn't seem capable of doing the same with Don.

"Thalia, remember what we talked about this morning," Ann reminded her. "Give her space, man. This is not getting us anywhere."

"I know, I know. I'm trying, but it's so hard."

"It is for her too."

Thalia agreed. She decided not to run after Sara like she had done so many times in the past. Instead, she shared the blanket with Ann and talked about the mountainside they had just passed through. Something about the journey was beginning to make her feel that emotional healing lay close ahead.

Sara returned an hour or so later. Without making eye contact with anyone in particular, she said, "I apologize for being so disagreeable earlier. Sometimes my emotions get the better of me. From now on, I promise to go with the flow and stop projecting my anger at someone else onto everything and everyone." She fought hard to come clean with them. "I had another fight with Don this morning and I didn't think it had gotten to me, but I just realized I'm really upset."

Ann was surprised, "I hadn't even noticed."

"Yeah, I'm learning to hide it well."

"Sara, all I want is to see you happy again," Thalia said.

"The same for me too," Ann said. "And you don't have to hide anything from us. I know my tendency to analyze everything annoys you. I'm working hard at putting that in check. I am trying hard not to."

"In a weird way, I want you to," Sara confessed. "But of course I only want to hear what I want to hear." Sara finally admitted to herself that she was afraid; afraid of her pain. "This morning I tried to pretend everything was okay, and I really thought I was, but it just came rushing out. I took it out on you guys and that's the last thing I want to do."

"What do you say to keeping it very light on the way back?" Ann asked.

"Sounds like music to my ears," Sara said.

"Better still, I am going to be tuning back into silence on the way back too; I liked it coming." Thalia said, "That is unless I see the bulls again."

Marlon returned from giving the horses water carrying a bag full of oranges and tangerines. Together with the sandwiches and drinks that Ann had taken along and Marlon's bun and cheese, they ate a scrumptious feast under the shade tree by the brook.

At the end of the meal, they sat around and made light conversation with Marlon, waiting for the sun to cool before heading back. Thalia quizzed him about the local sights, scenery and happenings that were off the beaten path for tourists. Sara remained relatively quiet, while Ann listened intently, adding more must see spots to her repertoire.

"It's funny, Marlon, I didn't even notice your stables before Sara told us about it and brought us there. I've been in and out of the town a bit over the last six months."

He nodded. "We actually only have the sign on the gate so that people who are looking for us will know where we are. It's not for advertising, that's why it's so small. My father enjoys horses and loves working with some visitors, but he doesn't really want it to be a huge tourist business, you know? He likes not having a huge staff or having to open everyday if he doesn't want to. He used to have some huge stables in Ocho Rios and worked with the hotels. This is retirement to him. He kept his favorite horses and only takes referrals from a few resorts around here.

"So we were lucky to run into you," Sara piped in after a long bout of silence.

TUESDAY

"I feel just as lucky," he said, his charm returning. Sara ignored him and he smiled and continued, "Anyway, if you want to see some other local sights not on the tourist maps, I'd be happy to take you on a day tour to Negril tomorrow morning. I know one place in particular you three might love."

"Why are you being so kind?" Sara asked, still not trusting his motives.

"I must confess that at first I invited you for the ride because of your pleasing anatomy. But since being around you all and seeing that in addition to being fine, you are all so intelligent and down to earth, my intentions are much more honorable. So that's why I would love to give you a taste of the real Jamaica, not the glossy tourist traps."

Sara felt very confused about her response to his confession. She thought that she would have been pleased at his intent to clean up his infatuation with her, only to find that a part of her wanted it to continue. So she did what she always did to cover up her ambivalence; she snapped at him, "And where might some of those places be, or are we just going to exchange the tourist traps for Marlon's?"

"I am sorry that you don't trust me," he responded. Ann noted the hurt in his eyes, so she quickly jumped in to make him feel better. Her intuition told her that he was genuine, a rare find among the "Winston wanna-be's."

"You have to understand that Sara is just being careful," Ann piped in. "She has heard a lot of stories about Jamaican men preying on vulnerable tourists, like how 'Stella got her groove back'."

He shook his head knowingly. "I overstand."

Even though Sara felt that an apology was warranted, she could not go there just yet. She felt Marlon was being honest, but too much confusion still lingered in her head. She thought Don was an honest man too, when she first met him. Instead, she asked Marlon to tell them about what he had in mind. His response disarmed her because it held not a trace of anger.

"I am speaking of those hidden from the beaten path because they are too precious to share. Kinda like the favorite dessert that you hide away and pull out only when your true friends come to dinner. Let me warn you however, that once she gets under your skin, you will never be able to end the affair. Jamaica instantly converts you into becoming her mistress."

"I'm game," Ann said.

"Me too," Thalia piped in.

Sara remained silent. As frightened as she was, she had no choice but to go along with them. She could not let on how touched she was by the sincerity that was evident even as he passed it off as charm. She had a marriage that she needed to save!

Needless to say, Thalia got her wish on the journey home. There was no need for words; they would only serve to distract the truths that were seeking expression in their souls.

TUESDAY

It was late afternoon when they got back to the resort. Marcia met them on the way to their cottage and informed Ann that Cynthia had been looking for her all day. Knowing that she would sink in guilt if she hung her dry another evening, Ann went looking for her on the beach. She found her after only a brief search and arranged Swedish massages for the evening, giving her word that they would be there. Cynthia smiled and uttered, "No problem, my sistah." How Ann wished that she could make those words her reality.

When she got back to their cottage, Ann found Thalia and Sara discussing the beautiful arrangement of red roses that had arrived earlier. The unsigned card had them teasing each other.

"You can take me out of the mystery," Sara said. "My husband would never be so romantic. I am sure that it is from one of you all's secret lovers."

"Maybe it's from Marlon," Thalia said to move the hot seat from her. She was sure that they were from Lee. Who else but a woman, and a wealthy one at that, would be romantic enough to send a secret lover four dozen red roses. Thalia was thankful that she was tactful and respectful enough to not sign it.

"Hah, he's good, but he can't be that good," Sara laughed.

Ann's heart skipped a beat. She didn't really think it was from Spice. The gesture seemed compatible with his style, but he would have signed it. He enjoyed taking ownership of his irresistible seductions. Still, though she had been forcing herself not to, the roses gave her an excuse to count the days before seeing him again.

Locked in their thoughts, the three women remained silent, wondering who could have sent this mysterious gift.

5
Wednesday

The effects of Cynthia's massage the night before were still with Ann as she opened her eyes and lay in bed watching the sun creep in. She listened to the cottage breathing quietly, interrupted only by the sounds of a few idle birds and a faraway voice every now and then. Ann automatically thought of Spice and wondered what he was doing at that very moment. She had slept past the rooster's crow, but it was still early daybreak, still their magical moment. The moment when she realized she had fallen deeply in love with Spice.

In the quietness of the early morn, she heard a rhythmic whistling, which was eventually accompanied by the sound of approaching footsteps. Pulling the sheets around her as she went over to the window, Ann recognized Marlon coming to fulfill his promise as tour guide. She pulled on the slacks she had discarded on her bedroom floor, slipped on a t-shirt and quickly went to the front door to prevent his knocking.

"Good morning," his full smile greeted her without any of the flirtation he had lavished on Sara.

"It could be better," she admitted.

"Too much party last night?" he teased.

"Nothing quite that exciting. Maybe we're showing our age, but we ended our night early after the best massages ever."

"Nothing wrong with that. Sounds much more like a holiday than spending the night jumping round and waking up with a hangover."

"We're gonna need a lot more time to get ready." Ann was sure that neither Sara nor Thalia was awake; she had heard no one stirring.

"No worry. I'll come back in an hour. Make sure you eat before we head out," he said without a trace of annoyance in his voice.

Neither was the fully rested Thalia or Sara annoyed. They rose upon Ann's summoning and ate on the patio while awaiting his return. During the breakfast of roasted breadfruit, ackee and salt fish and eggs, the conversation was light. They enjoyed periods of comfortable silence as they drank in the sea air and watched birds romp in the blue sky.

Ann stretched her hands above her head, yawned mightily and sank back in her chair. "I feel so open right now. I want to tell you both about something I've been thinking about on and off," she admitted.

"Spill it," both eyes were shining with interest.

"Well," she paused, but there were no defenses left after Cynthia's kneading and rubbing. "I met this guy. He's a singer."

"When? Where was I?" Sara was immediately intrigued and leaned forward.

"No, no, not since you've been here," she rolled her eyes and laughed at Sara's enthusiasm. "I met him the very night before you came."

"So where have you been hiding him all this time?"

"I'm not hiding him," Ann wasn't completely sure if that was the whole truth. "He has a busy schedule. Anyway, we didn't plan to see each other again before Friday if we go to Kingston. That's where he lives, like half of the rest of the island."

"Kingston sounds like the place to be!" Thalia said. "I vote that we head there as soon as possible so that I can meet this mystery man."

"I vote yes too, but not for that reason," Sara teased. "I am dying to see Cassandra again."

"Great, then we leave for Kingston on Friday." Ann hoped that the other women did not see the shiver of excitement run through her body. "I know I have been keeping him on the DL. I just have been feeling weird about the whole thing."

"What's wrong? Were you worried about me?"

Ann hoped that there would soon come a time when she and Sara would no longer need to reference the night that caused them such a rift. "No, Sara, trust me, it's all about my feelings for him and my loyalty to James."

"That sounds normal, Ann." Thalia offered. "I'm sure you will feel strange for a while when you start dating."

"It's not just that," she searched for the words. "I really like him a lot. A lot, lot … But a part of me feels that it is disloyal to love another man. My heart still belongs to James."

"And it always will," Thalia said. "But that shouldn't stop you though from moving on and finding another partner."

"Yes, that's true," Ann wasn't completely convinced, "but honestly, this thing with this guy happened so fast that … it's almost crazy."

"Maybe you're just reacting to the pain of being without James."

Ann shook off Sara's suggestion, "No, if it were just that, I could deal. This, this has me scared and trying to run in the opposite direction."

"Wow," Sara was thrilled for her, "look at the way your eyes shine when you think about him."

Ann covered her face and laughed. "I'm so embarrassed." Then as if the other side of her tapped her on her shoulder, her smile faded, "and I'm ashamed too."

"No, Ann, no. You know you have to move on and find another partner. Your love for James was, is something special. But you are alive, girl. You have to keep living and loving. That's what James would want," Thalia insisted.

"I am not sure about that," Ann said, remembering her vision a few nights before. "One thing is for sure, only death could have separated me from James. No matter how angry I got with him over the years, and believe me there were a few times when I was ready to leave, I could never pull apart from him."

"Maybe one day you will thank me for taking the asshole Don away so that you and James could have found each other," Sara said.

"Sara, that day is today," Ann said. "Except when I see

the traces of the bruises that covered your face a few days ago I'm not sure if the price of getting him out of my life was one you should have paid?"

Sara looked away and said nothing. Ann wanted to find out where Sara was with Don since she called him. But, she remembered her promise not to push anymore. She kept it light. "Anyway, truly, James was the right husband for me and an amazing father for my child."

"Things happened so quickly between you two though, and then we sorta lost touch," Thalia didn't go into accurate details, "how do you know he was the right one?"

Ann leaned her head on the back of the chair and stared into the sky. She could almost see herself and James during their early years. "He very much was like my mother."

"I thought we chose husbands who were like our fathers?" Sara said in a voice as soft as Ann's, not wanting to interrupt the obviously delightful memory that registered in Ann's faraway eyes.

Always on the job, Ann snapped back to reality, sat up and began sharing, "I think that we relate to them like we did with our fathers," Ann said. "But on closer exploration, I think most of our partners, our successful ones, have the qualities of our mothers."

"Well, I certainly related to Reggie like I do to my father. I tried to hurt him in every way I could. But even though he loved me, I can't say that he was like my mom."

"How much did you really know your mom anyway, Thalia? You were only eight when she died," Sara pointed out.

"I know."

"And I gotta ask this, 'cause I've never been able to bring it up completely. I tried the other day but ... anyway, Thalia, your mom committed suicide, right?" Thalia nodded her head reluctantly. Sara continued, "Then why are you not angry at her for leaving too. After all, your father was not the only one to leave. I mean, you know what I'm saying. Is this part of what you were talking about yesterday Ann about how hard it is for black women to be angry at our mothers?" Sara looked to Ann for assistance.

Ann nodded, but said nothing, waiting for Thalia's answer.

"I know I have some unresolved stuff about my mom. Ann kinda hit home yesterday, I think," she took a deep breath and reached for the words, but she could only revert back to her dad. "I am angry at him for the way he abandoned my mother. And me. And to a large extent, I blame him for her death, her suicide to be more specific."

"But ..." Ann placed her hand on Sara's to stop her. She could see that Thalia was about to let something else out of the box she'd kept her memories locked up in. Sara's mouth closed, and she looked from Ann to Thalia, and recognizing the same, sat back and gave Thalia some space.

Before she could find words, tears begin to trickle down Thalia's face. Ann scooted her chair over to Thalia's and wrapped her arms around her. Thalia looked over Ann's shoulder at the early morning sun as it peeked out over the horizon. Sun rays spilled across the sky as her mother's blood had spilled onto the bathroom floor. It was only in the comfort of Ann's arms that she would allow the memory to emerge. Tears came gushing like a river whose rusted floodgates had just been opened. As she relived the memory, her tears washed away the decades-old pain festering in her soul.

After a long while, Thalia wiped her eyes and said, "This is the first time I have ever let myself remember all the details of what happened that morning."

Silence reverberated until it was heard. Thalia continued, "I was the one who found Mom."

Thalia was right back in that brownstone in Harlem. "She was very upset when she returned from the courtroom on the day of the divorce. So she took to her bed the rest of the day. When I got home from school that afternoon, I fixed her some leftovers since it was obvious that she had not eaten, but she put it aside. She kept saying she was very tired. Her twin sister, my Aunt Gem, came over, but Mom locked herself in the room and refused to see her. That night, she asked me to sleep in her bed with her. I can still remember her sweet smell—the scent of her gardenia perfume—as I snuggled up beside her. I wiped her eyes and told her not to cry because I was going to take care of her. I fell asleep in her arms. In the early morning I was awakened by a loud noise. I called out to her, but she wasn't in the bed. Something told me to go into the bathroom, which is where the noise seemed to have come from. So I went in there, and there she was lying on the floor. Her head was smashed open and her brains were spilling out; the gun was still in her hand."

"Thalia, you don't have to tell us anymore," Sara said. As accustomed as she was of seeing flesh and blood in a medical setting, she could not stomach the thought of any young person finding a parent dead. It came too close for comfort.

"Yes, I have to. Please, let me finish," Thalia said.

"Okay, okay," Sara said. "I just didn't want you to get too upset." She knew that somewhere in the background, she was also trying to protect herself from breaking down in tears like Thalia.

"I remember falling to the ground, in the pool of blood and trying to revive her, like I had been taught in Girl Scouts," Thalia continued. "They must have taught us some form of CPR, even back then. I think I passed out, because my next memory is of waking up in a hospital and seeing my Aunt Gem standing over me. There she was holding me in her arms and telling me I was going to come and live with her. She said she was so glad to have me, because she had always wanted a little girl just like me. She said she was going to be my new mother and soon I would forget all the bad things that had happened. And I did. You see, she and my Mom were identical twins, so I easily tricked myself into the pretense."

"Remember how old you were when it happened, Thalia," Ann suggested. Her psychiatrist self could not be contained any longer. "Then go ahead and allow eight-year-old Thalia to let her true feelings come out. She needs validation. She doesn't need the pretense anymore that everything is okay, Thalia. It is not fair to continue to ignore how frightened she still is. Allow her to find her voice."

Thalia began to cry again. She pulled away from Ann's embrace, sank down into her chair and, pulling her legs up under her, curled up into the fetal position and began to sob, "All I want is my mommy to wake up, I just want for my mommy to wake up. Why won't you wake up, mommy, why won't you?"

With each wail, an intense veil of sadness and darkness descended upon the women. The new morning sunlight streaming in through the coconut leaves could not find its way through the curtain.

Sara began to weep silent tears.

Ann allowed Thalia a few moments to be alone then reached over to her. She wrapped her arms around her and rocked with her until she was quiet. When Thalia stopped crying, Ann told her, "We are all crying for our mothers too Thalia. We are all scrambling in the dark, searching for her like lost children. We all want her to come and ease our pain."

"Ann," Thalia began to regain her voice as she stared into her friend's eyes, "Something just occurred to me."

Ann nodded her encouragement.

Thalia straightened up a bit and Ann loosened her hold of her, but didn't release her. She turned to Sara and admitted, "The reason I'm angry at my dad is because he should have been the one to find her. He shouldn't have abandoned us. He shouldn't have left me with that as my last image of my mother. He should have fought against my eight-year-old anger at him and stayed in my life. He, he used my words, my angry words at my mother's funeral when I yelled at him that it was his fault. He used that as an excuse to abandon me again. He's my father. He should have known I needed him. With that one bullet, that one judge's decree, I lost both of them. But one of them was alive. Is alive. Yet he chose to be dead to me when I needed him most." She paused, as if surprised at what had spewed from her mouth. "It's not his color, though it really has rocked my world being half-white. But it's easier to call him a white bastard than to call him a deserter. 'Cause when I think of him that way, then I don't feel he felt my love either. Then I have to look inside and try to understand why neither of them loved me enough to stick around, or why they didn't understand how much I loved and needed them."

"Wow," was all Sara could respond.

"Wow is right," Thalia gave a strange laugh. Leaning forward into her hands and letting them cup her face, she flexed her lightened shoulders. Ann rubbed her shoulder encouragingly. Thalia turned to look at her.

"Damn, you're good." She laughed.

"I didn't do anything, Thalia. You just confronted your pain and got to the root of it. It's something we all need to do before we can heal." Ann stole a silent glance at Sara.

"Maybe the hurt will finally begin to lessen," Thalia nodded already feeling comforted despite the vulnerability she felt having bared such truths.

"That much I can guarantee."

Thalia got up and smiled down at Ann. "I'm going to go wash up. I think a good, warm shower is exactly what I need right now."

"We all should start getting ready," Ann began piling the plates. "Marlon will be back soon."

His name was all Sara needed to get motivated. "Don't take forever, Thalia."

Thalia and Ann smiled at Sara who rolled her eyes. "Give me ten minutes, Sara."

She started into the living room, then turned to Sara and Ann as they cleared the table together and stacked the dishes on the rolling cart Marcia had brought over. "Thank you both for being here with me."

The three women slept almost all the way to Negril. Ann, who had sat up front with Marlon was the first to awaken. Just as she opened her eyes, he zoomed around an almost-hairpin turn. Though her heart was beating a little fast, she felt Marlon was very much in control of the vehicle.

"Marlon, does anyone in Jamaica drive at a regular speed?"

"Well, seeing that race car driving is one of my greatest passions, hobbies, and addictions, this is regular speed to me," he laughed.

Ann could only smile and shake her head. "You Jamaican men equate driving a car on the road with driving your you-know-what up a woman's lane."

She didn't miss the fact that Marlon peeked in his rearview mirror to check in on Sara before answering slyly, "Could be true. Except when I man in bed, I'm not always in a rush to get there."

They both laughed hard and long.

Ann's stomach was queasy by the time Marlon pulled up outside a big thatched-roof hut. Ann roused Thalia and Sara while he blew the horn. Before the passengers could fully awaken, an extremely curvaceous woman, with a wrap that ensured that its contents were revealed and only barely concealed, approached them. Marlon got out and opened the car doors for his passengers before moving into her extended arms. Ann and Thalia got out and leaned against the car; Sara remained seated.

"Marlon, mi happy to see you no matter when, but I thought you weren't coming back til Friday," she said to him. Ann and Thalia exchanged raised eyebrows as Pinky and Marlon greeted each other with lips that seemed very familiar and eager to be with each other. Sara looked away, seemingly disinterested.

"Pinky, meet the three women who made me break my word," Marlon said, moving out of Pinky's arms and back toward the women.

Seeing that Sara was still in the car, he offered to help her get out. She ignored his outstretched arms. "I don't need any help," she muttered beneath her breath with an air of annoyance.

Once again, Marlon ignored Sara's acrid tone and introduced them to Pinky with his usual unabashed attitude and smile. Following Marlon's cue, Pinky extended a warm welcome. "Any friend of Marlon's is also a friend of mine," she said.

Thalia and Ann returned her warmth. Sara stayed chilly.

Pinky showed them inside the inn. When she invited them to have a late breakfast, in spite of having just eaten breakfast a couple of hours earlier, they were all thirsty and road-weary. Ann and Thalia ordered ackee and breadfruit again. Sara chose pancakes and scrambled eggs; her stomach was beginning to rebel against all the hot and spicy Jamaican vittles. When the food finally arrived, after a good and long Jamaican 'soon come', everyone ate heartily except Sara who just picked at her meal. Ann made sure that Pinky understood that Sara was a light eater. Ann did not want their host to be offended by Sara's seeming rejection of her food.

Marlon excused himself to organize transportation for a trip over to a little island off the coast. While he went off to locate his friend who owned a powerboat, Pinky took them to the suite that they were to use for the day. Ann invited her to sit on the veranda and chat for a while. The only reason why Sara agreed to the intrusion was because she was dying to find out more about Pinky's relationship with Marlon.

"So how do you know Marlon?" Sara went straight for the gold.

"Marlon and I are very tight," Pinky said, "he is my business partner and co-owner of this joint."

"No kidding," Sara replied, surprised.

For Sara's sake, Ann wondered what tight meant but decided not to ask.

Pinky too was curious to find out about them. Ann gave her the lightest version of how they met in medical school and became roommates and friends. Pinky seemed very intrigued and was obviously probing to see exactly how close the women were. The hint of sexual energy Pinky was emanating disarmed Sara's hostility. It didn't take long for Sara to suspect that Pinky was a homosexual, or at least bi. She noticed much of Pinky's interest was directed at Thalia. Although she was repulsed by the thought of anyone thinking that any of them was lesbian, she was secretly thrilled to learn that the coast was clear with Marlon, if she decided to play.

"I can see why Marlon wants to take you all to the island. You and your friends are what we here in Jamaica call 'roots'; you are real cool and down to earth," Pinky said to Ann. "I like that. You wouldn't believe how some of the black guests who come here act. They want to make sure we don't think that just because they are black, they are down with us."

"We're down all the way," Thalia replied. Sara rolled her eyes. Did she detect Thalia returning Pinky's flirtations?

"You're going to love Emerald Key. We don't share her with everyone."

Sara was convinced her conclusion about Pinky was correct. Why else would she refer to an island as 'she'? Ann was worried about the aggressively sexual energies tingeing the conversation. She forged ahead on the topic of blackness to steer them in a safer direction. "Unfortunately, for some of us black folks, as soon as we start climbing up the success ladder, we forget those we left behind or stepped over on the lower rungs. As soon as we get a chance, we escape and deny from whence we came."

"That's because that place was so painful," Sara said taking the bait and moving the talk further from sex and deeper into politics. "Who the hell wants to go around remembering when they lived in captivity?"

"The Jews have made that the base of their religion," Thalia said. "That's one of the reasons why they are so successful, they never allow themselves or anyone else to forget their oppression."

"That's true," Sara admitted. She knew she wasn't likely to win a disagreement on religion with this bunch, so she switched the subject back to the personal realm. "Does Marlon share the same view about Black American tourists, women in particular?"

Ann was dead-set on getting them back to neutral territory. She butted in before Pinky could answer. "Marlon told me that you are one of a handful of black locals to own a resort in Negril. How did you manage to pull that off?"

Pinky told her good luck story about how she rose from local girl to nightclub singer to innkeeper. She described how her ex-husband Hans, a German art dealer who used to visit Jamaica frequently, introduced her to Marlon, one of his suppliers. Immediately, they all three became good friends. Hans bought Pinky the inn as a wedding present. After their divorce, a couple years ago, she received the inn as part of her settlement. Recognizing the need for a partner to help ease the burden of running such a large, successful establishment, she sold Marlon a percentage of the business.

Thalia wouldn't have minded sitting the entire day talking to Pinky. As the islander shared herself with them, Thalia saw many similarities between her and Pinky and so many parallels in their lives. Unfortunately, the more Pinky's company appealed to her friends, the more it seemed to irk Sara.

At some point when the conversation lulled, Sara announced that she wanted to get into the water. "Let's go diving off the cliffs before Marlon gets back to take us to the island," Sara suggested.

Pinky was no fool. She smiled warmly at Sara, informed them how to get to the cliffs, and returned to her office. The women changed into bathing suits and wraps and set off for the sea. Along the way, they picked up snorkeling gear from a small shack Pinky referred them to.

The sea was stunningly beautiful, boasting several cobalt-blue swimming alcoves within the rock formations. As they approached the cliffs, Ann noticed a beautiful red tail perched on one of the trees. Bob Marley's song 'Three Little Birds' danced on her lips:

Woke up this morning, smiled with the rising sun

Three little birds, beside my doorstep
Singing sweet songs
Of melodies pure and true
Singing, this is my message to you, you, you
Singing, don't worry, about a thing
Cause every little thing is going to be allright.

When they got to the edge of the cliffs, Sara was the first to dive in, followed by Ann. Thalia, being afraid of heights, walked down the steps that were chiseled in the rocks and joined them in the water.

After they were all outfitted in their gear, they headed out toward the coral reef that the young men who worked at the water sports counter had recommended. It was one of the few remaining reefs in the area that had not been totally wiped out by the pollution.

They arrived at the reef some fifteen minutes later. Oblivious to what had existed before, they were extremely impressed by the dazzling array of multi-colored fish that surrounded them. At first, Thalia was somewhat jumpy when some of the fish swam up to her feet. She had never snorkeled before. But once she took heed of Sara's coaching and became comfortable with her breathing, she quickly became hooked. She loved the relaxation and discovery.

Sara, in one of her favorite places, felt very blessed to be one with the heavenly grandeur of the flora and fauna lining the seabed. After about an hour, she could feel fatigue beginning to set in, so she joined Thalia and Ann who had already swam back to the cliffs.

They sunbathed for a while on one of the rocks. Sara rolled over and laid her head on Ann's lap. Ann welcomed her intimacy; but sensed that Sara had spun into a somber mood. "Sara, is something bothering you?"

"Thalia's wails this morning were very disturbing. As much as I have been trying to shake the feeling, it stirred up a lot of issues having to do with my family," Sara replied.

"When you get good and ready, you'll be able to face those things and let go," Ann reassured her.

"I hope so."

Ann pointed out to Sara how much lighter Thalia appeared after facing the parental issues that had plagued her for so many years.

"You are so right," Thalia confirmed. "I guess I just stopped worrying about 'what if' and started facing 'what is', the reality that I find myself in. By unloading all the heavy stuff, I feel so much better, so much lighter. While we were out at the reefs, several schools of yellow-striped indigo fish darted around me, to and fro, in and out. They created quite a surge of electricity in the water around me. A few times it seemed as though they were trying to impart some of their wisdom upon me. I swear at one point I felt a charge seep inside of me, and I suddenly had the realization that freedom does come from letting go and becoming bare to the bones. I can now appreciate Janis Joplin's lines, 'freedom is just another word for nothing left to lose'. The truth really does set you free."

She stopped for a breather then continued. "I know it

was painful to hear, but as I was crying out to mother, I felt her presence. She held me and told me that it was going to be okay. She told me she was sorry that she had to leave me. She said she couldn't continue the journey on this path anymore, because she had run out of energy. Her physical self had become too worn down. I asked her why she did not take me with her, and she said that it wasn't yet time for me to leave. I was still full of life's energy. She said that by leaving her earthly body and entering the spirit world, she was much better able to protect and guide me."

"Thalia, you held on to the pain for so long, it must be a relief to finally let it go," Ann said. She and Thalia had become friends a few months after her mother's death, but this was the first time Thalia had told her about finding her mother dead.

Thalia nodded. "At that time, I had to forget. I could not go around constantly bombarded with all those memories of death." Thalia became silent again. "What I did was channel all the pain into taking care of anyone, person or animal, who needed to be rescued."

"That was perhaps to give you some sense of mastery over the failure you felt about not being able to save your mother."

"Correct again," Thalia remarked to Ann, remembering how she desperately tried to blow breaths into her mom's mouth when she took her last gasp. Images of her banging her head against her mother's chest, begging her to let her try one more time darted forward into her memory. Thalia had to take several deep breaths.

"I can even understand now why I chose to be a doctor. I am still trying to save my mom."

"So much of our lives makes sense when we deal with our issues," Ann agreed. "We tend to act like our life is one thing and tragedies are separate entities. But they are a part of our lives and they influence everything about us. We have to claim our pain, our tragedies, everything, if we are to truly know and love ourselves."

"Alright then," Sara said. " I will close my eyes, take a deep breath and just go wherever my mind takes me. I won't hold back."

"Remember, I am right here holding you Sara," Ann reminded her. "Lean on me as much as you need."

"All I see is a black hole," Sara said. "There is nothing, just darkness."

"Try harder," Thalia said.

"A part of me is still very afraid of my truths, and I can't understand why," Sara said.

"You are probably afraid that the pain will overwhelm you," Ann responded.

Thalia inched closer to Sara and took her hands. "Pain is relative, Sara. All this time, in my big world in my little head, I thought that I was the one with the heaviest cross to bear. I felt that God singled me out for punishment. But my cross is no bigger than yours, and yours no bigger than mine. "

"Yeah," Sara agreed. "It is very relative, and subjective."

"Believe it or not, I also have been plagued by my feelings of abandonment—maternal abandonment. Except unlike Thalia, I have named it for a while."

"What kind of abandonment?" Thalia inquired. "I thought you grew up with your mother."

"Before that. When I was two years old my mother left me with my aunt and migrated to New York," Ann explained. "I have no memory of seeing my mother again until I went to live with her when I was about seven years old. She tells me, however, that she used to visit me in Jamaica at least twice a year." Ann recalled how upset she was when she got the news that her mother had sent for her to go to the States. She hated leaving her cousins Delroy and Daphne. But then, she was happy to leave her aunt. For, even though she was just a child, Ann could tell that her aunt did not like her. She had later learned from her cousin Delroy that even though his mom, her aunt, hated to miss out on all the money that Ann's mom sent every month to Jamaica, it was she who had told Ann's Mom to send for her. Delroy felt certain that his mom was jealous of all the attention that his dad used to give Ann. "No matter what the reason," Sara piped in, "at least she got you out of there."

Ann shrugged her shoulders. That was a whole other story. She continued with the one at hand, "New York was total culture shock for me in the beginning. Imagine, I went from a tiny Jamaican country village, where there was no running water and electricity, but was full of laughter and joy, to the most cosmopolitan and anonymous city in the world. My first year in school there was awful." A slight band of tightness encircled Ann's forehead as she remembered how the kids used to taunt her; how they made fun of her accent and peculiar way of dressing in bright clothes, even during the winter.

"Remember, that's how we became best friends, Thalia, you came to my rescue; my knight in shining armor." Thinking of Thalia rescuing her reminded Ann of the similar role that Olu seemed to be playing in Ahsima's life. But as warm and genuine as Ann felt about her friendship with Thalia, she had to fight hard to brush aside her annoyance with her for suggesting that their children were romantically involved. Explaining the complexity of Ahsima's birth was the last thing that Ann wanted to deal with right now. Fortunately, Thalia was totally oblivious to the friction.

"Lucky for me that I did," Thalia responded. "You and your family became the kind of stability and security that I was in desperate need of. My aunt, bless her heart, could not keep a husband longer than the honeymoon. When the fun was over, so was her commitment. Then she would start searching again for romance, and of course it was always in the wrong places." The many faces of her Aunt Gem's husbands, several of whom she downright hated, paraded through Thalia's mind. Ann's home was such a welcome escape. She snapped back to reality, "Continue Ann, forgive my interruption."

"My first year at school, that was before you and I met Thalia, I studied real hard. I was always number one in all my classes. Turning to books was how I compensated for my loneliness. But, my book smarts only made the kids resent me even more. It wasn't until after you and I became friends my second year that the other kids accepted me. You helped me get over my anger and sadness."

"I had no idea I had such a positive effect on your life," Thalia said. She thought it ironic that Ann was so grateful to her—she thought she was the one that benefited most from their childhood friendship all these years.

"It was rough going for me and my mom for many years though," Ann continued. "Looking back now, I can see that not only was I angry at her for leaving and then expecting me to just pick up the pieces and become the perfect daughter, I was also angry at her for not understanding how overwhelming it all was for me, adjusting to the American culture. I was also angry with her many times for always ignoring racism and thinking that being West Indian made her better than American blacks. From back then Thalia, you helped me to see through that divide and conquer strategy."

"Ah ha, so it was Thalia who turned you into an activist," Sara playfully accused.

"It is no joke that I was born a Black Panther."

"Well, she wasn't completely to blame," Ann smiled back at Sara. "So was my step dad, Trevor," Ann continued. "I really grew to love him. He was a displaced intellectual and scholar who could not deal with the vagaries of American racism. He also did not act like some of the West Indian men who were afraid to fully immerse themselves into the black American culture. He was the one who paid attention to the struggles that I was having fitting in. He tried his best to help me navigate through it. Mom, she did not want to hear any of it. She deafened herself to the problems and kept busy working as many jobs as she could. She really did think that acquiring wealth and being an accommodating black person would make her more acceptable to the white folks."

"It was not until Trevor got sent to prison for a crime that he did not commit, that she finally learnt her lesson. She died a year later from a massive heart attack, which I am sure was a result of so many of her dreams unrealized. Her death hit me hard; especially since I was just beginning to know her as a real person, and not the mother who disappointed me in so many ways."

"It's hard being black in this world, isn't it? The odds always seem stacked up against us," Thalia said.

Ann sighed as she thought about the many times when she wished that her mother was still alive; how she wished that she could take back all those years that she wasted being angry at her. Especially after living in Jamaica and gaining a much better understanding of the culture that bred her and the circumstances of her life. "It's so much easier to forgive her now that I have let go of all those hurt feelings that I harbored for so long against her."

Sara understood what Ann was saying about her situation, but was not yet ready to apply it to her own. She remained quiet.

"I miss her too Ann," Thalia said. "Sometimes I think that she tried to make up for her failures with you by being a good surrogate mother to me; and I needed one very badly. I went to her on many occasions for advice."

"I on the other hand was always afraid to go to her," Ann said. "I did not want her to see me as weak. So I always went to Trevor."

"Your mom once told me that she wished one day you would understand how much she really loved you," Thalia revealed.

"Now I do, but back then growing up, I did not. In retrospect, I wanted an American styled mother who was outwardly warm and affectionate. She always seemed so cold and aloof. But since being here, I am coming to recognize that being reserved, polite and reticent is part of the culture."

"That did not come from our African heritage," Thalia said.

"Definitely not," Ann replied. "It reflects our British occupation and colonization. What I have always observed on my trips to the continent is how physically close and nurturing African mothers are to their children, especially the young ones."

"Yes," Thalia piped in, "that was one of the pearls of raising my son in Africa. He was always either on the back of his nanny Yeala or mine."

"I wish Don and I had children. It would probably have been good for our marriage."

"In what way?" Ann inquired.

"I am convinced that some of our problems stem from him blaming me for his not being a father," Sara said. "He has always wanted children."

"Sara, do you know why you have not been able to have children?" Ann asked.

"It's a total medical mystery," Sara replied. "All my fertility tests have been normal. Don refuses to do his infertility work up, and of course, I can't force him to do so. He claims that he has all the proof that he needs to let him know that there is nothing wrong with his sperm. When I asked him if it means that he has other children, he just shrugs me off. He is convinced that it is psychological on my part, and he is probably right. Deep down inside, I think that I am scared of being a mother. My mother was not the greatest role model."

"If it is psychological like you both think it is, the good news is that there is hope, Sara," Ann told her. "Releasing some of your issues with your mother would go a long way to getting you started on your motherhood journey."

"First, let me start with a good brisk swim in mother ocean," Sara said. She was not ready to go there, not today at least!

"Yeah," Ann agreed with her dodge tactic, sensing a need for time out. "It will wash the rest of the tears away."

Each time that she submerged her head underwater while doing the breaststroke, Ann could feel the water running over and into every opening in her body. Each time that she surrendered to the cleansing, she felt years of stress being released from her body. She hoped that Sara too was finding more than a swim in this experience in the water.

When they returned to the hotel, Sara announced that she wanted to have her hair braided. Pinky informed them that there were zillions of hair braiding salons down further along the beach. Sara accepted her offer of a ride. She was a bit ashamed about her earlier behavior toward Pinky. She hoped if she was friendlier to Pinky, word would not get back to Marlon about her bad attitude.

When they went back to the room to get ready, Thalia backed out of going with them, deciding to spend the balance of what was left of the morning resting before Marlon came back to take them to the island. She needed to try and ward off the migraine headache that was trying to surface.

Pinky dropped Ann and Sara at the beach, but could not stay because she had to oversee the afternoon meal preparations at her inn. Despite her intentions to be kinder, Sara was relieved that she did not stay.

As quickly as Sara's earlier foul mood had been brought on by Pinky, was as quickly as her spirits soared when she saw the miles and miles of white sand and pale turquoise water. The ravishing beauty left her breathless, spinning her to her usual thoughts of death whenever things seemed too good to be true. "When I die, I would love for my ashes to be sprinkled in these waters. If today were the day, I cannot imagine that heaven could be any more beautiful."

"Well, I am not going to let you leave us today, or any day soon, my dear," Ann said, embracing her. She could feel the tightness in Sara's body. "Soak it all up," Ann whispered to her. "You deserve to have beauty and goodness while you're alive; all of us God's children do."

Sara's spirits were energized by the thought of returning back to Jamaica and just spending her days lazily painting. She could already see that much of what her canvas would capture were the many shades and contrasts of blue. "I love all this blue," she told Ann.

Maybe it was the splendor and rapture of the surroundings, but for the first time since Sara's arrival to Jamaica, Ann felt the joyous love that they once used to share. Before the incident with Don, they had accepted each other for who they were. When they lost their trust with each other, judgment and blame crept into their relationship. Elated, Ann shared her belief with Sara that the blue around them, from the sky and the sea, was leading to inner peace within them and harmonious communications between them.

As they strolled along the beach comforted by their recaptured love, Ann observed that many of the women of European descent were enthusiastically engaging in the rent-a-dread trade. They oozed 'come fuck me' signals to the native men who were ever so eager to make their fantasies real. Ann couldn't help but notice the paradox between this sexually charged hustle and the serenity of the motionless sky and the gently flowing sea.

Sara eventually chose a braider from the several women who approached her. When the braider introduced herself as Marlene, Sara and Ann looked at each other, both marveling about the coincidence. Marlene's name brought Marlon to Ann's mind and his name to Sara's lips. "You are going to have to help me put this in perspective," she said to Ann, "I feel like I am being drawn into Marlon's space against my will. I don't want this, I am a married woman, desperately trying to save my marriage."

"The best advice I can give you Sara, and I am trying not to be too biased against Don, is that when past promises and covenants keep you stuck in a place of non-growth and pain, it behooves you to reassess their value in your present reality. Being in a love relationship should be about choosing in each moment to be there, and not about obligation."

"I hear you, Ann," Sara promised. "I am really trying to figure out what my next move with Don should be."

Marlene led them to the little shack where she had her operations set up, along with another woman who gave massages. If she hadn't already had a customer, Ann would definitely have gotten one while she waited for Sara. Instead, she lay in a hammock under an almond tree and fell into a refreshing nap.

Ann jumped out of her sleep at the feel of someone tapping her. She almost did not recognize Sara standing in front of her. She looked absolutely stunning. Her hair was braided up into a bun, revealing her very striking forehead and flawlessly chiseled high cheekbones. Even the traces of bruises around her eyes could not mar her angelic deportment. "Sara, I have never seen you look as beautiful as you do this moment!"

"I don't feel like the woman who arrived here three days ago, body beaten and spirit broken," Sara said. "Thank you Ann for being so patient with me."

"You don't look like her either. That's all the thanks I need."

As much as they would have loved to keep strolling down the beach checking out some of the other wares and offerings, they decided to return to the inn to meet Marlon. Walking along the beach, they past a couple jerk chicken stands that had Ann wishing that she was not vegan; at least for a day. The sun was now in the middle of the sky pouring down close-to-unbearable rays, so Ann stopped at a stall selling freshly squeezed cane juice, and bought a bottle for her and Sara. It took quite a bit of coaxing, but Sara eventually tried it; and loved it! Ann was pleased to see that Sara was finally beginning to acclimate to the local culture.

They stopped at one of the hotels along the beach to get a taxi to take them back up to the inn. Pinky chewed them out mercilessly for not calling her to get them. She gave them the news that Sara had been waiting for—Marlon was back and ready to take them to the island.

Seeing how profusely they both were sweating, Pinky suggested some coconut water before they left. As Sara watched the grounds man climb the tree and pick the coconuts, she was fascinated by his agility, comparable to that of highwire circus acts. She recalled how when they were kids, her Dad would always take her and her brother to see Ringling Brothers whenever they came to town. Sara chuckled to herself as she remembered how scared her brother was of the clowns. She and her Dad used to make fun of him whenever he would start crying and ask to be taken back home. After they were finished with the coconut water, which Sara far preferred to the sugar cane juice, Ann and Sara returned to the room to check on Thalia and bring her some of the coconut water. She was just getting off the phone.

"Sara, I love your hair. You look so beautiful, you're bound to break some young man's heart," Thalia said. Sara brick walled her, leaving no question that she was not interested in any further discussion of her and Marlon.

The phone rang and Thalia jumped to get it. It was Marlon telling them that he was ready and waiting in the lobby. Great timing, Sara thought to herself. They hurriedly washed up and changed into their make-do sailing gear—shorts over swimsuits.

Marlon was waiting for them in front of the lobby, the car door open, "At your service mesdames," he quipped. "I have come to fetch the princesses and escort them to the Emerald Key."

"Should we consider you our gentleman in waiting?" Sara asked lightheartedly.

"Proud to be your servant, ma'am," he replied.

Ann and Thalia jumped into the backseat, forcing Sara to sit up front with Marlon. As they were about to pull out, Pinky came running out with a picnic basket. "In case the men aren't good hunters, you are going to need this." She handed the basket to Sara who passed it on to the two ladies in the back.

They drove down the cliffs in anxious silence. Marlon's driving had Sara and Thalia's hearts beating in their mouths. Their relief was boundless when he pulled off the road onto a clearing along the beach. Sara took a deep breath and said, "Thanks for bringing the concept of cliffhanger up close and personal for me."

They stepped out of the jeep into the smell of ganja. A

twenty-foot-long boat 'Free-I', brightly painted in red, green and gold was docked and waiting. Marlon hailed the man who was sitting at its helm. Out climbed a slender but muscular middle-aged Rasta man sporting blonde-tipped dread locks. As he approached them, the scent of ganja became more intense.

Marlon introduced Weston, their boatman and guide for the afternoon. He smiled warmly and offered them a puff of his smoke. All three women declined. When Marlon told them that it was very good for preventing seasickness, Sara immediately changed her mind. With the ordeal in the caves still fresh in her mind, Sara asked God's forgiveness as she reached for a toke of Marlon's fired up spliff.

"Even though all of oono don't want to join I in giving thanks and praises to the most high, Jah, rastafari, I still happy to see three beautiful black queens from America. It is not often that I get the pleasure of being at the service of my sisters."

Weston gave them each a life vest to put on. When they were all suited up, Marlon helped them step up onto the boat while Weston helped to seat them. Both men sat at the controls in the back. There was just enough room in front for all three women to huddle in the two front seats.

"Let us ask Jah to steer us safely across the waters, away from this Babylon," Weston said as he started up the boat's engine and they set sail.

The blue sky was interrupted only by a puff of cumulus cloud that blanketed the sun and cut down on some of its fierce and piercing rays. The wind was blowing steadily and casting moderate sized waves up against the shore, causing them to have some significant chops in the first few minutes. Sara prayed that the ganja would soon take effect; she had left her scopolamine patches in her bag back at the resort. Lucky for her, there was hardly a ripple when they got out about a quarter mile from shore. The waters were now a dark hue, creating an eerie calm around them.

After they settled into a steady rhythm, about half a mile out to sea, Ann turned around to Weston and broke the silence. "It almost seems irreverent to spoil the beauty with talk, but I must respond to your earlier comment, Weston. You said that you appreciated our beauty as black women. But from my observations here over the past several months, many of your brothers seem to find the women of the other hue more attractive. Especially here in Negril."

"Sister, it's all about economics," Weston bellowed, ensuring that his voice carried above the wind.

"That's just a part of it." This was personal for Sara. "I think that sleeping with white women seem to make black men feel worthwhile. Their self esteem shoots sky high."

"Seen," Marlon said in agreement. "It's like taking a bite from the forbidden fruit. Since the fruit is now available and we not getting lynched any more, brothers say to hell with it; we going to bite!"

"I have bad news for you, but the brothers are still being lynched," Thalia said. "It's just a subtler kind, nowadays. They do it with the hostile social and economic policies that assure that you cannot succeed."

"For many black men, having a black woman does not seem to make him feel as good about his accomplishments as does having a white woman," Sara said, continuing to pursue her line of reasoning. "Since it is white women who the culture projects as the most beautiful and desirable, and being that a man's self-esteem is so tied to the partner that he has, our men, like all other men, are desperate to win the golden prize." Sara took a breather for a minute. She realized that the conversation was upsetting her a great deal. "I guess the weed hasn't kicked in yet because I am beginning to feel a bit sick."

"I hate to tell you Sara, but that little puff you took cannot do a thing. Trust a seventies weed head," Thalia told her. Thalia asked Weston for another spliff; he gladly obliged them. Marlon lit it and handed it to Sara. "This time do not be shy. Take as much as you want."

Sara ignored the innuendo. She convinced Ann and Thalia to join her because she did not want to be the only one high. Marlon and Weston lit their own spliff and engaged in a lively conversation, seemingly in another tongue.

"Do you realize that all the men we have met are Rastafarians?" Sara said, laughing. The weed had obviously kicked in. "Where are all the lawyers and doctors?"

"In Kingston working," Ann said. They burst out laughing again.

Soon everyone came down with the munchies.

"Thank god for Pinky," Thalia said.

"I don't like her," Sara said, uninhibited.

"Is that because she and Marlon have something going on?" Thalia teased.

"And why would that upset me?" Sara asked, turning around toward Marlon. Too high to leave well enough alone, she said to Marlon, "My girlfriends here think that I have the hots for you which is why I don't like your girlfriend."

She was the only one who laughed. Everyone was taken off guard by Sara's outburst.

"I can see that you are in the zone, so I am not going to take advantage of what you just implied, as much as I would love to," he replied, in a very kind tone.

"You mean you don't want to fuck the rich doctor who has run away from her husband and is here seeking some big black dick to forget?" Sara said. This time even Marlon was stunned into silence. Sara's laughter soon turned to tears. Ann put Sara's head on her shoulder and told her to rest for a while. Within a few minutes, Sara was asleep. Ann and Thalia completed the rest of the journey in silence, afraid they would wake Sara. Ann used the opportunity to meditate on directing the healing energy from the sun above and the sea below into Sara's wounded psyche. She also prayed that the beauty of nature all around them would infuse deep into her soul. The lift Sara had gotten from her new look was obviously only skin deep.

They arrived at Emerald Key thirty minutes after setting sail. Marlon and Weston jumped off and tied down the boat. The tug of the boat as it was being anchored into the sand awakened Sara. Her movements were subdued, revealing her reticence about what had taken place earlier.

The men helped them disembark and wade ashore. The low crinkling sounds of the palm trees as they slowly swayed in the mild breeze served as the welcome anthem to paradise. Several brightly-hued iridescent birds flew overhead.

After the men unloaded the boat, Weston waded across knee-deep water to the other side of the Key. He obviously wanted to respect their privacy. Marlon announced that they were settled, he too would go hang out with Weston, so as to give them space. Marlon guided the women under a shaded area at a bend, where they had full view of the entire south coast of Jamaica to one side and an archipelago to the other.

"I feel like we are princesses here on our own private, tropical island," Thalia said. She reflected on a school of opalescent fish swimming by. "It can't get much better than this."

"Can you see why this island is called Emerald Key?" Marlon said. "I know that it seems bushy and overgrown, but if you get beneath that, you can see the raw beauty of nature when man lets her be. There is every possible shade of green here, from lime to hunter's green.

"I can tell that this is one of your favorite spots," Thalia remarked.

"Yes, indeed," Marlon replied. "I'll have you know that the few people I take here are very special."

"How did you discover it?" Ann asked.

"My favorite uncle, Uncle Desmond, used to take me here all the time when I was a little boy," Marlon told them.

"He wanted to make sure I knew how to survive in the wild with only the elements: the wind, earth, wood, water, and stone. I'll show you all a few things like how to start a fire from sticks and stones if we have time later."

"I would love to learn," Thalia said.

"Not me," Sara said. "My cave woman days are over. Give me the Ritz!"

"Sounds like Sara wants wings and not stone cutters," Marlon remarked.

Sara thought that indeed after her little outburst on the boat ride over, she probably should fly away. How could she have embarrassed herself so badly? "Before you head off, Marlon, I would like to apologize for earlier. I don't know what got into me."

"Maybe the truth did," Ann said.

"Whatever, Ms. Psychiatrist," Sara threw over her shoulders at Ann. "Really, Marlon. Please accept my apology."

"I will accept your apology only if you agree to let me paint your portrait," Marlon said to Sara. He explained that he always kept some supplies with him in his backpack, especially when he traveled to places so beautiful. "You never know when the mood will hit."

"I do want your forgiveness, so I guess you got me captive," Sara said adopting humility for the first in a very long time.

"I won't imprison you for long," he explained. "I only need to capture the outlines and the shades."

Marlon's way with words reminded Ann of Spice. The similarity in the way they used words was striking. Even though it had only been a few days, she regretted not staying closer in contact with him. Quietly, she surrendered to the memories of him that began playing in her head.

Marlon went to the boat to get his paints. When he returned, he guided them through the bushes and shrubs to another side of the island. Impossibly, the view there was much more spectacular than on the side where they had landed. The sand was sparkling white, with red-orange seashells sprinkled throughout. The color of the water was so much more brilliant and glistening.

While Marlon scouted for his backdrop, Ann picked wild daisies and bluebells and strung them into garlands with blades of grass. She placed one around each of their necks.

Marlon eventually settled on a grass patch under an almond tree to set up his paints and easel. As if she had been to that life born, Sara instantly struck a regal pose, her head held high and proud. Ann and Thalia left them and set off to explore the water.

They eventually found Weston fishing over on the other side of the island. He waved to them. When they joined him, he already had several fish in his net. Thalia asked if he were as versatile as Marlon and able to start fire with rocks. Without saying a word, he gathered twigs and stones and started a fire. Next, he pulled out his Swiss army knife and scaled and gutted the fish; then he cut some branches for a skewer, cut the fish into square filets, placed them on the skewer and roasted them kabob style.

Ann was filled with admiration at the ease with which he existed as one with nature. An 'Aha,' moment exploded into her being as she experienced the feeling of being 'One with All'. Sitting there quietly under her Bodhi tree watching Weston in his grace, she was overcome with transcendence and love.

Thalia was curious to learn more about his Rastafarian lifestyle, as was he curious to find out how the three of them became doctors. They engaged in light yet deeply meaningful conversation as he cooked.

After they ate, Weston excused himself and went off for his afternoon smoke and praises. Thalia and Ann waded back over to where they left Marlon and Sara. Marlon was already finished painting for the day. He was superstitious about mortal eyes seeing any of his creations before he was done, so he asked them not to look at it as it sat out to dry.

Thalia suggested that Sara and Marlon go and get some of the fish that Weston roasted, because there was still quite a bit left.

"But we still have some of the food that Pinky's prepared, don't we?" Sara asked. Laziness had set in after her long sitting.

"Yes," Marlon said. "I will go and get it for you." Marlon walked over to the tree under which he had stored their belongings and fetched the picnic basket. Thalia and Ann spread a blanket on the ground and unpacked the sandwiches, fruit and cheese. Sara picked at a bit of fruit. Marlon stuffed himself with a couple of the sandwiches, grabbed a couple of tangerines and left to join Weston.

Thalia worked hard to ignore her urge to eat again. To distract herself, she scooted up next to Ann who was sitting with her eyes closed and back resting against the tree. Thalia laid her head in Ann's lap and closed her eyes too. In an unconscious gesture, Ann ran her hands through Thalia's hair and then across her face. Thalia was reminded of the scene from the movie "Better than Chocolate," in which two lesbian lovers painted each other's body. Lee had taken her to see it a few months after they first met. That must have been when the sexual charge started between them, for Thalia remembered how sensuous it seemed to her and how for a few days after the movie she had thought about what it would feel like to paint Lee's body. She had totally forgotten until now. It occurred to her that what Lee had said to her that night was correct. They had been falling in love and lust long before that night. Thalia jumped up from Ann's lap.

"Did I scare you?" Ann asked.

"Maybe Thalia got excited by your stroking her forehead," Sara joked. She moved over and sat on the other side of Ann.

Without realizing it, Sara was pulling Thalia out of the closet. "I did get excited, but not for the reason running around in that dirty little mind of yours, Ms. Sara," Thalia teased back.

"Come on now Thalia, you are not going to tell us that you have become a lesbian," Sara persisted in jest. "Come to think of it, Pinky was hitting on you earlier."

"Sara I'm warning you not to go poking around in places you're scared of," Thalia said.

"What are you trying to tell us?" Sara demanded.

"And if I am?" Thalia queried.

"I would not be here sitting so close to you," Sara shot back.

"Then you need to move away Sara," Thalia remarked, looking her straight in the eyes as she inched away from them both. "The flowers that arrived yesterday were sent to me by a woman-lover."

"I can't believe this," Sara said standing up and openly disgusted. "Thalia, that is so wrong. I can't believe after all these years of us being so close you're turning into a heathen."

"Who are we to judge?" Ann said, coming to Thalia's defense. "If two people love each other, what does gender matter?"

"Since when did you become God?" Sara said angrily.

"I have always been, and so are you and all of us," Ann replied. "You just don't know that you are; which is why you act so ignorant at times." Ann was upset to be losing her bliss with Sara almost as quickly as she had found it.

"I am not going to get into a fight with you, Sara," Thalia said. "Seeing how narrow minded you have become, all this trip I have been trying very hard to be gender neutral with my pronouns. But, I am not going to lie any further, just to keep from upsetting you. Either you accept me as your friend, or, god-damnit, we part right here and now."

"Isn't it messed up that right when one friend has invited me back, the other is threatening to leave?" Sara said.

"I heard you use the word 'friend'," Ann said to Sara. "Then let that inform your actions with Thalia and not let this bullshit morality you hide under come between you."

"Are you ladies suggesting that the bible is wrong? I am going by the word of God!" Sara exclaimed.

"The white man's religion has you all twisted," Thalia remarked. "Sara, you conveniently select a few beliefs to preach and a few to ignore. Let me ask you this, why didn't your bible stop you from coveting and stealing your best friend's man?"

"My father always preached about the evils of homosexuality, and I believe it," Sara ignored her. Sara remembered how he always used to warn her that there were two things that could get her kicked out of her good Christian home—if she was gay or used drugs.

"So your father must not have preached about fornication?" Thalia pressed on. "Is that what made it okay to take Don right from under Ann's nose?"

"Well I have accepted my mistake and have begged Ann's forgiveness. Shouldn't you do the same?"

"Being a lesbian is not a sin, a mistake, or a choice. It's who I am." Thalia said, pounding one fist into the other palm. Trying to regain her composure, she looked out upon the sea. As she reflected upon what lie beneath the water so still, she wondered if she was prepared to always have to defend herself from all of the reproach that she knew lay ahead; especially from close friends and family. Suddenly it dawned upon her that the decision to embrace being a lesbian involved more than just being swept away by one night of pure passion. And in that moment of feeling so all alone and disconnected from her oldest friends, Thalia found herself questioning the label that had been fully thrown upon her and which she had grabbed wholeheartedly as hers. She turned toward Sara and continued in a much less emphatic tone, "At the very least, being a lesbian is some part of who I am. And that person is the same person that you knew and loved five minutes ago."

"Please let's remember that we are each other's friends; not judges," Ann pleaded, looking toward Sara.

Sara nodded and grabbed her head. She was not sure if she could handle that which went against all that she had been raised to believe. But then again, Thalia was the one friend who had stood by her without judgement when no one else did. She had to admit that she did love her, so maybe it should not matter whom she slept with. Plus she had heard it said so often that God hates the sin but loves the sinner. "Damn, I am trying real hard to be okay with this; but you need to know that it is going to take some getting used to."

"I know it's a lot, but I am still trying to figure it out myself." Thalia was touched by the sincerity of Sara's distress. "I need you to be there for me now more than ever, because being gay in such a homophobic world is not easy. So please don't turn your back on me," Thalia said.

For the first time Thalia was exposing her vulnerability to Sara. She had always been Sara's protector, always on top of her game. Sara could not help but be moved by Thalia's humble plea for love. "I love you, Thalia, and I don't want for you to go away. I guess I will have to find a way to deal with this, but it won't be easy."

"That's all I need to hear, that you will try."

"I will also pray that one day you will get over your anger at men, so that you can stop being a lesbian."

Thalia refused to be angered by Sara's ignorance. So she did what she always did to deflect her hurt. "And just maybe the day that you allow yourself to express your anger at men, you will find out that you are a lesbian," Thalia laughed.

"Sara!" Ann stopped her before she could lash out again. "Thalia, I know how hard ..." Ann was cut short by the men's voices beckoning them.

"Testosterone once again to the rescue of all this estrogen raging out of control here," Ann said. She looked at her watch. She knew they were going to have to start heading back to the inn, and eventually back to the resort in Trelawny.

"We're over here," Ann said, walking out from behind the bushes. The boat was all packed and ready to go. Marlon and Weston were sitting on the side. Ann called out to Sara and Thalia to hurry.

When she reached the boat, Marlon told her he was planning to finish the painting by Saturday and give it to Sara as a gift. Ann revealed their plans to leave the resort on Friday and spend the rest of the weekend at her condo in Kingston. She gave him her Kingston address so he could mail the painting in the event he could not finish in time to deliver it. He made Ann promise to keep it secret from Sara.

Neither of them saw her approaching.

"What secret?" she asked. "I have had enough for one day."

"That I wish that you could be mine," Marlon said.

"If wishes were horses ..." was Sara's only response as she walked away into the direction of the boat.

She pretended not to hear him respond, "I would ride mine all night long."

Thalia joined them and they all got on board. Weston revved the engine and began the journey back to Pinky's.

"Jah must be sending you ladies some extra special blessings today," Weston said. "This is the nicest sunset I have seen in a long while." The blazing red-orange ball of fire was laying its tired head upon the azure sky, ever changing her cover from red to orange pink to purple.

As they sailed and rocked upon the sapphire waters, the electrifying air became pregnant with the promise of love and magic. The three women, still heavy with the weight of so many unfinished conversations, could not help but lose themselves in the magnificence of the moment.

"Now, do you understand why they say Negril is for lovers?" Marlon asked as they reached the shore.

"No, please tell us," Thalia said.

"Legend has it my dear ladies," Marlon said while helping each of them disembark, "that when the purplish orange haze of twilight hits, it casts a spell on all those who are close by and in love and binds them together in each other's heart forever."

Sara was tired of all the talk about relationships. She walked ahead of everyone to the car.

Weston helped Marlon unload and reload their stuff into the jeep. Ann paid him handsomely and thanked him for being such a superb captain. "All thanks and praises be to Jah, Rastafari for bringing us back home safe and in one piece," Weston said. "One love."

They arrived at Pinky's hut just as twilight was about to give way to the night. There was a note from Pinky at the front desk. In it, she apologized for not being there on their return. She had to leave on urgent business. She suggested that they dine at Rachel's, a bar and restaurant a little further up the cliffs. Marlon told them it was one of the happening places in Negril, and since this was Sara and Thalia's first time there, they should check it out. Plus, they needed to have dinner before they headed back to Trelawny, since it was about three hours away.

They settled their bill at the inn, got dressed and packed. Marlon met them in the lobby for the ride up to Rachel's. Sara wore a short, tight fitting, mid-riff exposing sundress; while Ann and Thalia went casual in khaki shorts and t-shirts.

Marlon tried hard to hide his growing crush on Sara. To everyone's surprise, when he complimented her on how beautiful she looked, she gracefully accepted and threw him a light kiss. Ann wrote off Sara's pleasant mood to the charge in the air.

Rachel's was buzzing inside and out, filled with hedonistically driven, sun worshipping women, fully tanned and meagerly clad, hanging out with their equally driven, economically focused, dark and handsome young dreadlocked men.

The high energy in the restaurant was contagious. They all welcomed the loud music and frivolous fun after the slew of intense interactions they had been having with each other. Taking a seat at the bar, they ordered drinks while they waited for a table to open up for dinner. Marlon got ready to leave and told them he would be back to get them in an hour. Boldly, Sara invited him to stay and have a drink with them. The gesture was not lost on him, but he declined with the explanation, "I am so sorry, but I should not drink tonight. I want to make sure that we all arrive back home alive."

When their order of rum punch and veggie-patty appetizers arrived, Thalia unleashed her curiosity about Sara's complete reversal with Marlon. "What's responsible for your change of heart with our driver?" she probed as soon as Marlon was out of hearing distance.

"Why do you want to know?" Sara asked. "You are no longer interested in heterosexual relationships."

"Is that it?" Thalia said. "You are afraid you might have some homosexual tendencies, so you are being hyper-heterosexual?"

"There is not a gay bone in my body," Sara said. "I am 'strictly dickly'. I have always needed a big hard dick inside of me."

"How graphic!" Thalia said. "Now I understand why you have stayed with Donovan all this time, he is nothing but a big dick-head."

"Okay ladies," Ann said once again, "time out."

They sat quietly and nursed their drinks for a while. The few times they spoke they limited their comments to people-watching observations. Two rounds of drinks later, the waitress finally showed them to a table.

Thalia and Sara ordered lobster; Ann had the ital stew.

Thalia eventually broke the ice. "I want you both to know that I was very afraid to come out to the both of you, my dearest and closest friends."

"Thalia, I am so sorry," Ann said. "You need our love and support now more than ever, and all that you have been getting is grief."

"One of my greatest worries is that you are going to reject me out of fear that I might have sexual feelings toward you too."

"It does take two to tango," Sara said. "So even if you liked me that way, nothing could ever happen. I'm not worried about that. I'm worried about your soul."

Sara took a huge swig from her drink, then added, "I must let you know though that I don't like the idea of another woman taking your attention from me. I have always been able to count on you being there for me, even at times when you could have easily walked away."

"Like now, right?" Thalia replied.

"Thalia, I am not trying to be judgmental or any thing," Sara said, "but how can you expect me to go against the teachings of the Bible? I grew up in the church."

"And that's why I can forgive you," Thalia said, "you do not know how to have an original thought about the meaning and purpose of life."

"I am sorry that I am not quite the intellectual and philosopher that you and Ann are," Sara said, a hint of demoralization creeping into her voice.

"After how mean you've been to me today Sara, please don't look at me with those sad eyes," Thalia said. She was certain Ann was going to call her on the 'mother rescuing complex', for she could never stay mad at Sara for long. "I guess I am just a pussy for chocolate women in distress. And by the way, no one ever has or will take your space in my heart."

"So who is this woman," Sara inquired, her curiosity getting the better of her.

Thalia breathed a sigh of relief at the friendlier tone in Sara's voice. "Lee is a jazz and blues singer," Thalia said. "We met over a year ago at a benefit concert she was doing for one of the hospitals where I work. We hit it off instantly and have been friends since; we only became lovers Saturday night before I came."

"Thalia, you are not talking about the Lee Coleman, are you?" Sara asked.

"Yes, I am," Thalia replied.

"She is so feminine looking, I would have never thought that …"

Thalia interrupted Sara, "that she is a lesbian. What do lesbians look like?"

"Thalia," Sara replied, "I am not trying to be ugly. I'm just surprised. I have all her CDs. I love her voice, it's so rich and exotic. Wow, I can't believe that she's a lesbian."

"I hope that you are not going to burn them now that you know that she is gay?" Thalia said. "Or even worse, have your church do a witch hunt and burn us at the stakes."

"For a brief moment there Sara, I thought that you were also going to say erotic," Ann said. She had to block another argument on religion from brewing.

"You ladies definitely are not hearing me, so let me say it one more time," Sara said. "I like dick."

"Be truthful Sara," Thalia said, "have you never had any desires to sleep with a woman?"

"Never," Sara replied. She knew Thalia was headed in the direction of the incident with Don and her asking Ann to join them, so she jumped ahead. "That night with Don was about a ménage-à-trois; and it was about Ann and I making love with Don, not about me and Ann making love with each other."

Ann didn't want to make Sara any more anxious by telling her that, from her ménage-à-trois experience, the women oftentimes stayed up making love long after the man had fallen asleep.

"Okay missy," Thalia replied in a frustrated voice. "If you must continue your denial, so be it."

"Thalia," Sara continued, "Even if we were to take the unlikely position that there is a homosexual in all of us waiting to be released, just because you have just discovered yours does not mean that everyone else needs to be on your timetable. You certainly went a long time without knowing. Not too long ago you were a happily married woman, and I am sure that you still are happy to be a mother."

"Well said, Sara," Thalia replied, "and humbling indeed. But I at least got you to admit that we are all possibly bisexual; maybe the choice is about which pole our preferences will be acted out."

"I did not quite say that," Sara corrected her, "but if that will bring this now played out topic to some closure, I succumb to your wit. Plus our food is getting cold, and Marlon should be back soon to get us."

Sara must have summoned him up, because before they could get to dessert, he returned. He was excited to tell them that one his favorite bands was playing at one of the hotels along the strip. He was certain that they would enjoy the music and asked them if they would be interested in spending the night.

"What's the name of the band?" Ann asked.

"Spice Rum and the Chasers," he replied. "It's a great new band. Funk reggae jazz fusion. Sometime when I paint, I listen to their music. It's very inspirational."

Ann could not believe her ears. Intrigue was permeating every space. All forces seemed bent on creating fusion between her and Spice.

"No, please let's just go," Ann said. Fortunately, she didn't meet with any objections.

With that, they paid their bill, climbed into the SUV and settled into sleep.

6
Thursday

Ann opened her eyes at dawn to a symphony of birds. Their ever-present soprano melodies seemed to have created the heavy base rhythms of reggae. For the first time since she and Spice met, longing for Spice was not her first and only thought. She couldn't imagine how she was going to exist without these tropical sounds when she returned home. They had become such a part of her background noise. And of course, right on queue, memories of Spice's tempting lyrics wrote themselves on the melody of the birds. A sense of belonging wrapped itself firmly around her shoulders.

Sunlight was just beginning to stream in through the sheer, white voile curtains. Even though she wanted to sleep longer, Ann forced herself to get out of bed to do her yoga practice. During the opening sun salutation, she gave thanks for all the light and warmth that had recently blessed her. As she got further along and attempted the lotus pose, a moderately sharp pain ran down her right knee and settled in her kneecap. The rest of her practice became quite a challenge, but she did manage to finish. Lying in the corpse pose at the end, she slipped into a long, deep meditation. It took the crooning of a brilliantly, colored hummingbird to jolt her back to reality an hour later.

Ann rose from her repose happy and enlightened. Humming along the way to the kitchen, she put a pot of coffee on to brew, knowing that Thalia would be overjoyed to open her eyes and nose to the aroma; she loved breakfast in bed. As could be predicted, it wasn't long before the lure worked and Thalia came padding into the kitchen, still quite groggy.

"I must have been having an extraordinary dream."

"Smelled the coffee in it?" Sara, much more awake, was right behind Thalia. While Thalia paused to wake herself up more, Sara moved around her and reached for a couple of mugs from one of the cupboards.

"Seriously. I was very aware of being in the bedroom, as if half awake. A very beautiful woman stood over me rubbing my head as I lay in the bed. She told me that everything was going to be okay."

"Must have been Lee."

Thoughtful, Thalia ignored Sara's sarcasm and added to Ann, "Fact is, I'm not so sure that it was a dream anymore."

"Why," Sara was suddenly serious.

"Who was the woman?" Ann asked.

"It was my mother. I can still feel her spirit in the room."

"Weird," Sara said offering her a cup of coffee.

As they all moved into the living room and curled up in the comfortable chairs, Ann decided that was the proof she needed to convince her that the cottage attracted spirits.

James had only just appeared to her a few nights back. She did not want to scare Sara, so she said nothing.

"I've been having some unusual dreams lately, well, really one recurring one, but this is the first time my mother has appeared to me since her death."

"Well we did get really deep when we were talking about her yesterday," Ann reminded her.

"I know, but I think that's part of it, and the fact that you're here, Sara. I always have strong thoughts about my mom when you're around. You remind me of her so much."

"You always say that, Thalia."

"Well it's true. You're both so beautiful and gifted, yet vulnerable and often misunderstood. I have always had this strong urge to protect you because of it."

"Girl, you try and protect everyone." Sara tried to brush off Thalia's comparison. Hearing Thalia's voice make that comment was probably the only thing that had stopped her the two times she considered killing herself. Something neither friend knew she had even thought about. "Isn't that how you and Ann became friends?"

"Superwoman Thalia, my heroine," Ann joked.

"Ingrate. I should have let them beat your ass!"

The teasing was interrupted by the sound of the phone ringing. To Sara's surprise, it was Don. She never expected to hear from him, not after the way she rudely hung up on him. Thalia and Ann went outside and sat by the pool. Watching the morning coming fully alive was a far more appealing prospect than witnessing the latest exchange between them.

"I worry about what will happen when she gets back home," Thalia was the first to comment. "That man is so damn volatile."

"Yup, she really needs to be careful," Ann replied. "Men like Don don't like being challenged. If there is going to be any separation, they are the ones who want to initiate it and do the leaving. The Dons of the world do not like to be left; they become jealous maniacs."

"How did he handle your leaving?"

Ann paused. There was so much unaired discourse about what had happened between the three of them. "I don't know if Sara knows, okay? Initially, he kept trying to get me to come back. I must admit that in the first few months while I was still intensely angry with Sara, I entertained the idea of seeing him again. But I didn't when I realized I was pregnant. Somewhere deep inside I knew the best thing to do was to get as far away from him as I could. I obviously was right."

"Ann," Thalia leaned forward and blurted out in a harsh whisper. "You're fucking kidding me. Ahsima is Don's child?"

Ann nodded. "That's why I stayed away from him and Sara all these years, even times when I wanted so bad to resolve things with Sara. I was so afraid he would put two and two together."

"I can't believe this. Ann, I thought we were best friends. Why didn't you tell me? I would have kept your secret."

"Thalia, I couldn't take any chances, especially since

you continued to be friends with them. James and I agreed that we would never tell Ahsima who her biological father was, unless for some reason she asked, or if there was a medical necessity."

"I knew you were pissed that I didn't cut my relationship off with Sara," Thalia said. "But back then I didn't know the whole truth."

"I was mad at first," Ann said. "Being that we were best friends and had known each other longer than you and Sara, I expected your unconditional and undying support. Eventually, though, James helped me realize that it was unfair to put you in the middle."

"In the middle? How about in the dark, Ann?" Thalia was still sad as she remembered how disappointed she was when she got back home from her month's training course in Kenya to find Ann and James married. She was even more disappointed to find out that Ann and Sara were not speaking to each other. Whenever she brought the subject up with either one of them, they would just shut down. So at some point, she stopped asking. "You made yourself much more scarce than Sara did. I was shocked to see how wrapped up in James you were. We knew James only casually before I left for Kenya, and when I came back he had replaced me."

"Thalia, I don't know how else to describe him except that James was my knight in shining armor. No joke. I'd known he had liked me, and I thought he was great, but at first, I just wasn't attracted to him. Plus I had Don and all. Anyway, that night when I caught Sara and Don, I was on call. Things were quiet at the hospital, so I went home to take calls. When I saw them, I freaked out. Then I ran back to the hospital and James was there in the lobby. He immediately saw that something was wrong, so he took me to the little restaurant next door.

I was so upset I told him everything, and Thalia, he stepped up like you wouldn't believe. He consoled me and let me stay with him so I wouldn't have to go home. Since we only had two months to go till graduation, he let me stay at his place for the rest of the school year. I promise you, it didn't take long for me to notice the difference between him and Don. He was everything Don could never be. Don is struggling to prove he's a man with all this battery and cheating. James knew he was a man from the beginning."

Her soft words made Thalia smile. "I wanted so bad to dislike him, Ann," she admitted. "But when we started spending a little time together, I could see you two were really happy together. It helped make it a little more understandable, you know, how you had gotten with him so quickly."

"Yeah, I remember the first time you came to dinner. I could see him winning you over. Your little wall of ice just melted."

"I really loved him. He was good for you. And Ahsima. I realize that even more when I think of how much like father and daughter they acted."

"He was like that from the start. A few weeks after I started staying with him I began having morning sickness.

I was distraught. After all he had done for me, I couldn't hide my pregnancy from him. I told him I was pregnant and the next day he brought me a diamond ring and asked me to marry him. He didn't care that Ahsima wasn't his. He promised to take care of the baby and me. I fell in love with him right then and there; he was so sincere. A couple of days later we were married, and he never once broke his promise." Ann tried to remember her and James embracing each other on their wedding day; but the only memory that surfaced was her holding him on his dying bed. She tried hard to fight back her tears, unsure if they were tears of joy or tears of sadness.

"It really upset me that you closed me out of such a major event in your life; and also that you were being so secretive. I guess that's probably a big part of the reason why I turned to Sara. Ann, I am sure that if you had told me all that had gone down with Sara and Don, I would have kept a lot more distance from them. All that she told me was that you and Don had broken up, after which they decided to start seeing each other. She said their relationship pissed you off, so you stopped talking to them."

"Just like Sara to twist the truth to her advantage. But I guess there was no way for her to tell you the truth and not lose you too," Ann said. "As messed up as she can be, at her core, she really is a good person. Most of the time, she means well. She doesn't deserve an ass like Don."

Thalia smiled sadly at Ann's picture of their friend.

"I am so glad to have my best friend back strong in my life, I don't know what I would do without your friendship," Ann said. "Even with Sara, as difficult and challenging as she can be, I did miss her high drama and fun."

"I chock up a lot of Sara's acting out to the pretty-girl syndrome," Thalia said. "You know how pretty girls get so much praise for how they look. Then they become dependent on people's adoration, and when they are not the center of attention, they become miserable."

"Quite a few of those so-called pretty women that I have seen in therapy have had pretty awful experiences when they were young girls; many were sexually molested," Ann informed Thalia. Ann paused to wonder if sexual abuse was part of Sara's issues.

"Some men can be such dogs," Thalia responded. "They will stick their dicks in anything that moves."

"We must not forget that many men were victims themselves," Ann said.

Images of her mother and Sara flashed in Thalia's mind. She said nothing. She was in no mood to empathize with those whose method of dealing with their pain was to inflict it on others.

Ann continued. "I must say that the one good thing that resulted from all the mess was my marriage to James."

The tears began to well up in Ann's eyes again. "Can you believe it's been a year and I still can't talk about him without getting all teary eyed? God, when will I ever get over him?"

"You don't have to get over him, Ann. That's what's tying you up with so much guilt. You just have to get on with your life."

"Spice?"

Thalia nodded her confirmation that they were talking about the same thing.

"Thalia, you won't believe this but I slept with him. The very night I met him."

"Ann, please," Thalia brushed away Ann's concern, "We both know that's not your normal style. If I were you, I wouldn't fight it."

"He told me not to fight it too. And I don't think that he was being pushy; he seemed very understanding about my love for James."

"Then for heaven's sake stop beating yourself up Ann. Do you know how many of us would kill to have a chance at two good men? Or women," Thalia added, throwing them both into a fit of laughter.

Ann hugged Thalia.

"Forgive me for not always being honest with you," Ann offered.

"I am just as guilty," Thalia replied. "I was not immediately honest with you about Lee."

"I understand, " Ann said reassuringly. "Homosexuality can be a very difficult issue to deal with, so don't be too hard on yourself."

"Yes, but you're always so accepting and nonjudgmental," Thalia said. "How could I have forgotten?"

"Easy," Ann replied. "I have been so wrapped up in grief over the past year, I have not been very available to you, or anyone else really."

"You needed the time to focus on your healing, and your healing only," Thalia said. "Those of us who are your true friends understand and respect that."

"But you know what? When I was doing yoga this morning, I learned something about myself. During my routine, I felt some pain in one of my muscles and I spent most of the time focusing on it. I realized that it was the blueprint for how I handled all the pain in my life—I allow it to consume all my energy, to the exclusion of everything else, including the pleasure. Just like my friendship with you, Thalia. I'm dismayed at how little I stopped to think about your feelings through the whole ordeal. I never considered all the other things going on in your life that had nothing to do with Sara and I. That's pretty weak on my part."

"Yes, but I think it's a testament to our friendship that we can be apart for so long and be able to come together like this. I think that's stronger than having been present every day. You know what I mean?"

"Yes, I agree. I just wish I had been the shoulder you leaned on."

"You were, just the other day when we talked about my mom. You're always there at the right time, Ann. That's the important thing."

"So how are you feeling about her?"

"Surprisingly, really at peace. Even with the dream I had this morning. Everything feels right."

"Good."

"In fact, I was thinking last night on the ride back, how

important a role my Aunt Gem played in my life, in spite of her not knowing how to be one of those sixties TV mothers. It's easy to look back now and say that all the denial was not good. On some level, we both lived the pretense that she was my mother; but that's what got me through." Thalia reflected on how she was feeling about it all right then, and realized that it no longer hurt as much as it used to. Even though she still felt sad, she did not feel overwhelmed. She hoped that she could live openly with her pain, without closing out her joy.

"I'm really feeling your energy strong and positive, Thalia." Ann remarked.

"You should," Thalia smiled, placing credit where it was deserved. "You know you have a gift, right?"

Ann shrugged, but was pleased.

"Seriously, this whole "oh let's just relax and hang out" bull. You've been working us girl. And every time I try to close down, the places and people that you have surrounded us with get me all wide open again. This has been so rewarding, and I'm not just talking about us getting back together. I think you could do the same wonders if we were a bunch of strangers."

Ann was beaming by this point. "Thalia, I'm really happy you think so. I've been trying to figure out what I'm going to do. I'm really not prepared to go back to my old job anymore. I'm feeling this new work pull me in another direction. I still want to work with the mind, but I'm so much clearer now on how the spirit affects it and how our environment influences our ability to deal with it ..." she trailed off, realizing how she was ranting. "Let's just say I don't want my work to be limited to people laying passively on my couch anymore. I want to take part in a more active, wholesome, healing."

"Holistic."

"Exactly. Now I can embrace it. One important lesson that I have learned from Cassandra is that I don't have to denounce my scientific education. I just need to broaden my approach."

"I find her amazing after just a few, brief interactions with her. That morning she brought Sara the ginger beer, we had an interesting talk."

"About what?"

"I'll get into it later. She actually suggested I mention it to you."

"Okay," Ann was hesitant. She was not sure if Thalia was dodging, or if she just wanted to finish giving Ann space in the conversation.

"So, have you considered staying in Jamaica?"

"Oh gosh yes. There is so little to take me back to New Orleans."

"I bet Spice doesn't help."

Ann blushed. "True, he's becoming yet another reason to stick around for a while. The only real reason to go back is to be reasonably close and stateside to Ahsima."

"She'll be all right though, Ann. Hey, you might even see her more if she was coming to visit you in Jamaica. Who would resist?"

"If she could leave Olu for a minute."

"You know what they're doing now? Thalia said, hoping not to upset Ann again. "They are training to run a marathon together next month."

"She told me about it," Ann said. "She says that she is doing it in honor of her Dad."

"I remember the day they both stopped by and were talking about it," Thalia said. "As we all sat around in the kitchen eating, it reminded me of that time you and Ahsima visited us in Harare. They were fussing at each other like two old lovers, just like they did back then."

Ann smiled as she remembered that Ahsima did not want to go on that trip. She could still hear Ahsima's protests, "Mom, what is a teenager going to do in Africa? It's going to be boring!"

"I think that a little romance is up between them even though they and you deny it," Thalia said. "Your daughter informed me that young men and women nowadays are capable of having very intimate, platonic relationships without necessarily being a romantic couple. Sounds very much like her mother."

"Thalia, when I got upset with you on the ride back from the airport, it was because I hadn't told you about Ahsima's paternity. My mind went straight to worrying about what could happen if she needed an organ transplant. There would be no way I could keep her true genes secret from her husband and you, her mother-in-law." Ann breathed deeply and let out a sigh of relief. Clearing the air with Thalia had even allowed her to get excited at the prospect that their children could end up together.

THURSDAY

The best kind of arranged marriage, she thought to herself.

"I can see how it was hard to tell me," Thalia said in a very forgiving tone. "But what about Sara? Are you going to tell her at any point?"

"Speak of the devil," Ann said, looking up to see Sara approaching them.

"No, make that angel," Sara says, overhearing what Ann said.

"You're in a good mood," Thalia remarked. Sara was smiling from ear to ear.

"I had a great conversation with Don."

"Oh really," Thalia said sarcastically.

"I know that you both think that he is bad news for me," Sara said, looking down and not making eye contact with either one of them. "But we have agreed to give it one last try."

"What number is this?" Thalia asked. "If you can't remember, why don't you just count the scars all over your body."

"Thalia why can't you be happy for me?" Sara asked.

"Maybe because I have been on this crazy yo-yo with you and Donovan one too many times," Thalia said angrily. "But now that he's beating your ass, you can't expect me to applaud."

"Hear me out one last time," Sara pleaded. "I know he can be a bastard. In fact, he even admitted that he took someone to Palm Springs this past weekend."

"Nice." Ann couldn't resist her own sarcasm.

"Jesus Christ!" Thalia swore.

"The only reason he told me about it was because that was what made him realize how much he loved me. He thought about me the whole time he was with this other person."

"Lemme guess. Was he seeing your face while he was fucking her?" Thalia continued.

"Thalia, why are you being so brutal?" Sara asked.

"Maybe I am trying to shock you into reality," Thalia replied. "You had better take that wool cap from over your eyes, especially in this era of HIV."

"Thanks for your support, Thalia," Sara said as she got up. "But scare tactics do not work for me."

"Obviously not," Thalia says. "Look how much he has done to you already and you're still going back."

Ann remained seated and silent. But Thalia could not tolerate Sara's anger and ran after her before she disappeared through the door. "I don't want to see you get hurt again, Sara, you're my sister, I love you," she told her.

Sara let Thalia embrace her, but only relaxed a little. "I know it is because you love me and want to take care of me why you get so angry," Sara said. "Can't you see that I got upset about you and Lee for that very same reason? I don't want to see you end up in hell just because you are angry about marrying the wrong man, a white man."

"It's not about that," Thalia said, shaking her head. She turned Sara's assessment around and wondered if one of the reasons she ended up marrying across racial lines was because she had not been dealing with her sexuality. How many times before had she heard people say that a lot of black men who were with white women were closet gays?

As Ann observed them, she too shook her head. She was flabbergasted at how manipulative Sara was being. She could not maintain her silence any longer.

"That comparison is not fair. Lee doesn't give Thalia black eyes."

"He apologized, Ann," Sara said. "He feels pretty awful about what happened; I believe he is really sorry."

"As well he should," Ann continued.

"He felt so awful, that even though he was going to keep it as a surprise, he let the cat out of the bag and told me that when I returned, we would be moving into that house in Bel Air that I have had my eyes on for the past year."

Ann realized she was about to get sucked down the same dead-end road as Thalia, so she made a quick U-turn.

"Maybe a new house will bring about new beginnings," she said, trying to make peace. "Why don't we leave it right here and hope that you guys prove us wrong?"

It was obvious what Ann was trying to do. Thalia shrugged off the conversation and said she would hit the showers first. Sara smiled tightly, and walked to the pool. She sat on the edge, dangling her legs in the water. Ann almost said something more on the subject, but stopped herself. "I'll go turn off the coffee pot."

"Sounds good to me."

For breakfast, Ann suggested the main dining room. There was no resistance from Sara and Thalia. They both felt the need to be around other people. At that early hour, there were only a few other guests in the dining room. Sara announced that she was quite hungry after all the days of eating very little. So she ordered a big stack of pancakes and scrambled eggs. Ann and Thalia stuck to the usual Jamaican fare. In a rare switching of roles, Sara devoured her food, while Thalia and Ann barely touched theirs.

When they got back to the cottage, they lazed around for a while in the hammocks on the verandah, attempting to pump themselves up for a day in town, shopping for souvenirs and mingling with the local people. Ann recommended they go shopping in Ocho Rios; that way, they could also visit the Dunns River waterfalls.

Thalia inquired if this was the waterfall Ann had been promising to take her to since college.

"Oh Thalia, I'm sorry to disappoint you, but the property that holds the waterfall is now privately owned. We could try to get someone to take us there by boat, but I can't make any promises."

"Don't the wealthy know they are not the only ones who need nature's soothing?" Thalia declared. "Why do they always hog all the treasures and splendors of the earth?"

THURSDAY

Ann told them how for a moment during the seventies, when Jamaica was experimenting with socialism, there was a glimmer of hope that things could be more just and equitable. And for a short while, in spite of the economic hardships, there was an air of romanticism and adventure. It was one of those summers that she spent hanging out at the waterfalls with some incredible artists, poets and thinkers.

"So what happened?" Thalia asked.

"The government got bullied into returning to capitalism and privatization," Ann explained. "The ruling class, with help from their external allies, bunkered down and squeezed the people. As has happened so many times in so many different places, those who were striving for immediate middle-class gratification lost sight of the future ideals of a more humane society. They let their growling bellies catapult them back to the primal lower-level thinking of survival of the fittest."

"Too bad we don't always seize the opportunities for growth and change when we have them," Thalia remarked.

"We miss them because pain has an awful way of shutting down our broader peripheral vision," Ann said.

"Then, letting go of pain and chains should be our theme for today," Sara remarked, joining in the conversation for the first time.

The phone rang. Thalia jumped quickly and answered it. She handed the phone to Ann.

"Mi can see that one sexy psychiatrist lady is trying to drive her man crazy," Spice said in his sexy, rude bwai Jamaican accent.

A shiver ran through Ann's pelvis.

"Why would she want to do that?"

"So that she can have him on her couch forever," Spice replied.

"But a good psychiatrist would not romance her client."

"Ah, so I got you to admit that you are romancing me," Spice said, laughing.

"Yeah," Ann said playfully. "In fact, I want to invite you out on a date with me and my girlfriends when we get to Kingston."

"You mean I go from one to three?" Spice asked.

"Don't go there, Spice," Ann said. "There's some history there that you don't want to stir up."

"Then I won't," he said. "My only interest is in creating a future with you."

"Spice, you are such a charmer," Ann downplayed his statement, though her heart flip-flopped.

"You're pretending my words are just charm because you're scared of the truth."

"The truth is that you are in love with the words of romance."

"Then have a heart and at least allow me to sing them to you," Spice said.

"Spice," Ann pleaded to him, "I will admit that I'm glad you called, even though we agreed I would contact you when I got to Kingston. I've been thinking about you. Just don't lead me down the wrong path."

"Ann, trust your instinct," he told her. "Let it guide

you into as much intimacy with me as you dare. I am sure that I want you, and maybe I even need you a bit. This is all happening very fast, but so has all the great loves of all times. I know you think that all needs are neurotic, but I don't think so; at least not this time."

"Of course you wouldn't, Dr. Freud" Ann said.

"I would have preferred Dr. Feel-good," Spice joked. "Getting back on a more serious note, remember that I understand your reticence, Ann. Just don't use it as a means to run and hide. Give me a chance. I don't mind proving myself."

"Okay Spice, I hear you," Ann gave in. "From now on, I will move with my feelings. I will live in my heart and not in my head."

"Sweetness," Spice reassured her, "your heart will never steer you wrong. I do believe that its one desire is to keep beating."

Ann's voice was sad and low when she said, "And you remember, Spice, that since James's death, I've cut myself off from pleasure in a lot of ways. It'll take me some time."

"That we have plenty of."

"I'm glad you feel that way. I like to think about us as the sun and the moon. When they spin away from each other they are just as connected as when they are eclipsed in each others' path."

"And when are you planning on eclipsing my path?" Spice asked.

"Tomorrow," she told him. "We're coming to Kingston for the weekend, so I'll call you as soon as we get settled."

Spice made sure she had all his contact digits. They blew each other kisses and said goodbye.

Ann hung up the phone and headed for the verandah, her feet slightly off the air. Her rapturous moment was short lived, interrupted by Sara's raised voice.

"Thalia, stop messing with me. Let me pass."

Ann entered their room to find Sara standing with her hands on her hips, a piece of clothing in one hand. Thalia, who was blocking the way into the bathroom, had a mischievous grin on her face that Sara did not.

"No. Change in here."

"Thalia," Sara was obviously annoyed as she attempted to push past her friend.

"Thalia what are you doing?" Ann wasn't sure whether to intervene or not.

"I've noticed ever since I came out to you all yesterday, Ms. Sara here won't change in front of me anymore. I think she thinks I'm going to jump her."

"That's not true."

"Then go ahead and change. You only want to put on a different top. What are you afraid of?"

"Thalia," Ann said gently shaking her head. "Don't do that. If she wants to change in the bathroom, let her."

"I'm not going to jump you, Sara. I'm your friend."

"That's not the point," Sara began.

"It doesn't matter what the point is," Ann interrupted, a trifle more annoyed at Thalia; she should know better. "This is childish."

"No it's not. I want her to understand that just 'cause I

slept with a woman doesn't mean I want her or I'm going to jump her. It's dumb."

"Whatever, but you know how Sara feels. You promised to give her time. This doesn't solve anything."

"It's not just about how I feel, Ann," Sara began. "The Bible …"

"Sara, please. Go in the bathroom." Ann begged before flopping on the bed. "You two are going to drive me crazy."

Thalia moved from the doorway, and Sara walked by her and stuck her tongue out. Thalia rolled her eyes and laid on the bed beside Ann. "You can come to me for treatment. I'll help you when you're nuts."

Ann laughed. "You, psycho woman, are the last person I'd go to."

Sara came back out a second later, wearing the same top she had on when she went in. She threw the piece she had tried on onto her suitcase.

Ann sat up and leaned back on her elbows. "What happened to the new top?"

"Didn't like it." Sara smiled sheepishly.

The three women burst out laughing. "You two are crazy, crazy," Ann got up and yelled at the sky in mock frustration. "Why me?"

"Because you love us," Thalia hit her with the end of her bath towel as she got up and went to place it in the bathroom.

"Yes, for some strange reason I do." Ann agreed as Sara put her arm around her shoulders and they headed into the living room to wait for Thalia.

Ten minutes later, they set off on their trip to Ocho Rios. Halfway there, Thalia asked if they could forego the shopping plans and just head to the falls instead. Both Ann and Sara agreed.

They arrived at Dunns River Falls in the late morning. The piercing heat of the sun had gotten fiercer during their drive. Ann assured them that relief was soon in sight. She promised that once they hit the falls, they were in for one of the most exhilarating experiences of their lives.

"Is it better than sex?" Sara asked provocatively.

"All I can say is it will send tingles up and down your spine," Ann replied, falling in step with Sara's frivolity. And because she had promised Spice that she was going to flow more into freedom, she revealed to her friends, "I am going to take you to an area where if you position yourself just right, ecstasy is guaranteed."

"I was just kidding," Sara protested, though she had a curious smile.

"I'm not."

"Whoopee, what are we waiting for then? Let's get to it," Thalia said.

They got out of the car and headed toward the entrance to the falls. The closer they got to the gushing water, the more electrifying the charge in the air became. An onslaught of native men approached and offered their services as guides. Ann turned them down gracefully. She was confident that they could navigate the waters by themselves.

They walked down to the beach for their ascent up the falls. At the base, they joined hands and formed a chain link for the trek upstream. The gushing water carved out steps in the rocks that provided the footholds for climbers. It wasn't as steep as it seemed, however, the onrushing water was being forcefully carried by the current, which made it difficult to climb in any precise manner. And the rough surfaces were waiting to mark anyone who didn't traverse with adequate skill. Sara slipped a few times, but Ann and Thalia caught her before she was swept back down the falls. About halfway up, Ann pointed out the spot she had told them about earlier. It was still quite a little distance uphill. Sara was about ready to give up. The water seemed to be rushing down the rocks more forcibly than any place else that they had encountered so far.

Ann showed them once more how to place their feet against the tide and asked them to hang in for just a bit longer. After what seemed like an eternity, they finally got to the rock. Ann entered the whirlpool first and demonstrated how to straddle the cascading water. She braced her arms against the rocks and sunk her body into the rushing waters, allowing the powerful sprays to spout off into her pelvis. Soon thereafter, she called out to Thalia and Sara to come and join her. At first, they rolled their eyes in that 'you must be crazy' style. Minutes later though, when they saw how good a time Ann was having, they beckoned for her to come and get them.

After they had all taken turns, Ann asked how they liked it.

"My cup runneth over," Sara said in jest.

"Mine is full, but not yet running over," Thalia chided. "I still have room for one more."

"Why don't all three of us see if we can fit in there together," Sara suggested.

"The most innocent among us, Miss Sara, is always looking for an orgy, isn't she?" Thalia remarked.

Hands tightly interlocked, they slipped and slid back under the falls. Once again, the thundering waters caressed their throbbing hips. This time, standing in formation, a burst of electricity surged through Ann's hands, made its way through to Sara's, then meandered into Thalia's. They had no option but to surrender to the waves of rapture pulsating through their bodies.

The exhilaration slammed shut their eyes, locking each one of them into their own customized version of their bodies on fire. The nirvana was soon rudely busted by a guide asking their permission to bring his party of three women into their spot, shattering Ann's images of Spice lapping his tongue all over her body; tearing Thalia away from her ruminations with Lee; and splintering Sara's secret fantasies of running her hands through Marlon's locks.

They procrastinated for a while, not completely ready to give up their seventh heaven, then reluctantly continued on, slowly weaving and wiggling through a few more water cascades until they finally made it to the top. In spite of the physically demanding trail, their bodies felt reinvigorated and renewed, alive, and alert. Sara shared with them that being able to master the physical feat of the climb rekindled and ignited her old, adventurous spirit. There was no missing the sparkle of life in her eyes; it was infective.

THURSDAY

Rejuvenated and inspired by their wonderful time at Dunns River Falls, and knowing how much more enthralling Laughing Waters was—the other waterfall that Thalia had inquired about, Ann was determined to find someone to take them there. She asked a few of the guides, but they all acted as if they did not know what she was talking about. Ann was just about to give up, when she decided to try her luck with some of the young women selling crafts along the entranceway. Something about one of them struck her, even though she had received numerous "no's". She reminded Ann of Weston, the fisherman who had taken them to Emerald Key. As luck would have it, the young market woman, Mavis, told Ann that she thought she could help; her baby's father was a fisherman and had his own boat; he was across the street at his friend's shop. Just as she started to go get him, Ann's curiosity got the best of her. She asked Mavis if she knew a fisherman in Negril named Weston. Mavis busted out in a big smile and told her that not only did she know him—he was her father. Ann shook her head in wonderment at the coincidence, no, synchronicity of the moment.

Ann watched Mavis's stall while she went to find her baby's father. She wondered if maybe she would have come to the same place in life, being a market woman, if her mother had not migrated to America. She wondered if she could have been as skillful as these women needed to be, smiling always at those who treated them with so little respect. Ann was glad when Mavis returned a few minutes later, because she did not want to turn away any more sales, but there was no way she was going to beg any of those tourists to come to the stall. Mavis introduced Ann to Morris, a very attractive Indian fellow; he was very agreeable to taking them, especially after Ann told him how much she was willing to pay.

Ann joined Sara and Thalia over by the jerk pit, after she and Morris finished their negotiations. She pulled up a seat at their table, helped herself to some of their festivals and fried plantain and ordered a Red Stripe beer. After they ate everything in sight, they set off for the location where Ann had arranged to meet Morris. They found him sitting by his boat patiently waiting for them.

Thirty minutes after he helped them on board, they arrived at Laughing Waters. An armed guard approached them as soon as they stepped foot onto the beach. Lucky for them, it turned out that he and Morris had known each other since primary school. Since the property was not occupied at present, the guard told them that he would let them check out the waterfalls for a small price. He warned though that if his boss showed up unexpectedly, he would have to act as though he had not given them permission and ask them to leave. They all nodded their heads in agreement.

They took off their sandals and strolled barefooted through the glistening, white sand in the direction of the falls. Morris and the guard went and sat under a tree.

"Even though this is much more scaled down than Dunns River," Ann announced, "I find it much more picturesque."

"Sometimes good things do come in smaller packets," Thalia said.

"Is that what you told Reggie to reassure him?" Sara teased. They busted out in laughter.

"Why, are you saying that Reggie was not fully endowed and equipped?" Thalia replied.

Sara pointed to the skin on her hand. They burst out into laughter again.

"Wow," Sara said looking up toward the grand house whose main view was the cascading waters. "It must be like Shangri-la to wake up and have your own river and waterfall right there in your backyard. Don and I need to buy something like this."

"Why do you think I've been so happy these past few months? There may not be all the luxuries and technologies here that we take for granted back home in America, but I'm telling you, nothing can make you more content than being constantly surrounded by nature's beauty."

"We Westerners have it backwards, don't we?" Thalia added. "In our pursuit of materialism, all we have done is become slaves to our brand of science that is constantly trying to master and negate nature."

"Yes, but without the materialism that you're slamming, how do you buy your own private waterfall?" Sara was defensive of the lifestyle she knew she and Don shared.

"Sara, it can be a great thing to have lots of money, but you need to have an attitude of self-worth to accompany it. And, by that, I do not mean entitlement."

"True," Ann said. "Money should ultimately be about

bringing us not just things, but joy. I believe that whereas money cannot guarantee happiness, happiness guarantees comfort with whatever money we already possess or are visioning to. How happy are you guys?"

Sara did not answer that loaded question.

"I trust that because we are all god's children, no more, no less, the universe supplies us freely with all that we need to survive," Ann continued, trying to focus the discussion less on Sara and Don. "It is man who has created the money and ownership game."

"You can't be lazy though," Sara said. "God only helps those who help themselves."

"As a mother, I find it hard to believe that our creator, the greatest mother of all, would have some kids starve from nothingness, while others throw up from their gluttony and excess," Ann said. "Is the child who grew up in poverty responsible for the societal institutions that disregard her disadvantage and keep her in a cycle of depravity?"

"You and Thalia always say she when I say he," Sara remarked. "Why is it that you both need to make god a woman?"

"And why do you automatically assign her as a man with your pronouns?" Thalia replied. "Why don't you challenge yourself and ask why you unquestioningly accept her representation as male?"

"Ann?" Sara said ignoring Thalia's comments.

"I say 'she' deliberately so as to get us to pay attention to how we have masculinized our construct of perfection,"

Ann told her. "I always go back to nature to better understand life's mysteries; and what I have observed is that for most forms of life, both the masculine and feminine come together to create it. So ultimately for me, the creative force, god, allah, yahweh, whatever, encompasses both genders. I choose to use the feminine most of the times, because the feminine is usually the vessel and primary nurturer of life."

"This could be the one big exception," Sara said.

"The big, dirty trick," Thalia added.

"I won't argue with that," Ann said. "The truth is, no one knows. Unfortunately, most of us just go along with our cultural brainwashing from childhood. I try to incorporate and learn from all the different religious schools of thought, and not think that any one is more righteous than the other. I try to bring them together in one big quilt, because, as separate entities, they are nothing more than a piece of the patchwork of life."

"Hmm," Sara said. "It's an interesting argument, but I can't just let go of everything I've been taught."

"You are afraid that if you question God you will end up burning in hell, aren't you Sara?" Thalia asked.

"Hell yes," Sara replied. They all burst out in uncontrollable laughter.

"He or she, Sara, I don't think God wants any of us to stay in the dark. If we don't question, we don't learn." Ann's thought was a good way for them all to agree to disagree. "Lets go to the falls. We don't have a lot of time."

Gladly, they all got up from their sprawl on the beach and headed toward the beckoning waters.

"Don't be fooled by the calmer waters. Trust me, like every other riverbed, this one is just as anxious to rejoin the sea. I know from experience that the undercurrents here are really powerful."

"Let's not climb it all the way up," Sara was quick to suggest, after her experience at Dunns River.

Ann was happy to oblige. The beauty of Laughing Waters could be experienced in so many ways. They climbed only a couple of rocks, then sat under a small ledge and allowed the falling waters to pound lightly on their shoulders. As they began to relax, Ann offered a silent prayer that the liquid would beat out all the stubborn, remaining encumbrances that seemed to be cemented in and between them. She didn't want to be impatient, knowing how much they had been through in the short period so far, but her worry about Sara was deep, and she had no idea what her friend would get caught up in next. With her leaning toward staying in Jamaica, she worried that the physical distance would allow Sara to hide anything she knew Thalia and Ann would want her to get away from.

No words were spoken, except for an occasional, 'this is heaven' remark from one of them. In silent contemplation, they each surrendered to the bliss of being touched and massaged by nature's flowing waters. Ann was the first to open her eyes, and turned to ask her friends if the half hour had been enough for them. Even with her eyes closed, Ann could tell that Sara was shaken. Ann inquired what was wrong. Thalia immediately opened her eyes and agreed that Sara was upset about something.

THURSDAY

"While I was sitting here, a memory came back to me that I am very afraid and ashamed of," Sara said.

"Maybe if you voice, it you can let it go," Ann said.

"I guess there is no hiding from it," Sara said. "I am so ashamed to tell you about it, yet I don't know if I can keep it locked up anymore. It first started coming back to me about six years ago," Sara began to remember. She omitted to mention it was accompanied by her first suicidal thoughts. "Since then, it comes back and haunts me every now and then, but it's been getting more frequent lately. Sometimes I think I'm about to lose my mind."

"Stop holding on to it, Sara. It's not helping."

"I know that I am messed up and all, but please know that in my own way, I love you both," Sara said. "I don't know where to begin." Once again, Ann could feel the hurt little girl in Sara begging for release.

"At the beginning," Ann told her.

"Then put on your seatbelts ladies and get ready for a very bumpy ride," Sara said, fighting back the tears. She inhaled slowly and deeply. Something in her head was telling her not to speak, but she couldn't stop her emotions from pouring out. "Here we go," she said. "The beginning let's see, okay ... My mother was very good at being the minister's wife. To the outside world, we were the perfect family. But the truth is, it was hell growing up in my house. My mother was the light-skinned southern belle, and he was the dark, charismatic preacher. Deep down inside, I think that my father resented my mother's color and all the privilege that it brought her. On the other hand, my mother was angry with him for not treating her right; and she probably resented needing him and his money." As the words came out of her mouth, it dawned on her for the first time that the intense need that her parents had for each other was perhaps the reason why they had such a hard time loving each other. It frightened her to think that the same thing could be going on with her and Don, so she quickly let go of the thought and continued. "My brother and I were so dark next to my mother's fair skin, I can remember being out in public with her and people asking her if we were her kids. It would make her so angry. I'm not sure if it was because we weren't light like her, or if she hated how people treated us different from her because of our skin color.

"Anyway, there was a lot of anger going around in my house; my parents fought all the time. Whenever my father hit her hard enough to draw blood, she would lock herself up in the guest room. Sometimes she would stay away from us for days. During those times, the housekeeper would care for my brother and I during the daytime. At nights though, we were on our own. A lot of times, Elijah would get very scared; he would cry and pound on the door until Mom gave in and let him come in and sleep in the room with her. I stayed behind. I never felt that my mother wanted me. I once overheard an argument between her and my Dad in which she told him that if it were not for being pregnant with me, she would never have married a nigger like him. So I would stay in my room by myself crying, until ..." Sara paused and took another deep breath, "my dad started coming into my room."

Sara stopped talking all together. She began to hyperventilate. Thalia grabbed her hand and instructed her to breathe slowly. Ann massaged her temples and told her that she did not have to continue if she did not want to. Maybe that was what she needed to hear. It all came pouring out. As soon as she regained her breath, she shrank down and whispered, "Oh my god, I still remember the sound of his footsteps."

Sara began to hyperventilate again. She wondered if she should take Ann's advice and stop; she did not want to remember anymore.

"It's all so disgusting," Sara said.

"Were you the one who did the disgusting things?" Ann asked.

"No, I don't think so," Sara said. "But maybe I caused him to?"

"Sara, for god's sake," Ann replied, "you were a child; he was an adult."

"The first time he touched me," Sara said, "he told me that the reason Mom was sick was because she would not let him touch her and make her feel better. He said that if I did not let him touch me, I would get as sick as Mom. I was so afraid, I just froze. I stiffened my body and pretended I was in a coffin and he was coming to bring me back to life. He told me never to tell anyone. But one day, after I had heard him preach a sermon about Jesus raising Lazarus from the dead, I broke down and told Mom that Dad did scary things to me when I lay dead at night. We were away at the beach, she and I and Elijah. Daddy was not there. I begged for us to stay there, the three of us together. But she got very mad at me and told me that these thoughts were coming into my head because I was not saying my prayers at night. She warned me never to repeat the story again. We packed up and left the beach house and never went back. She didn't spend much time alone with me and Elijah." Sara felt stronger when she realized that, unlike her mother, Ann and Thalia believed her.

"Mom told me not to say those things, and Dad had sworn me to secrecy. He always warned that if I told, not only would no one believe me, but bad things would happen to me. When I never got to go to the beach again, I felt that was my punishment for telling. So I promised myself no one would ever know. From that day forward, I kept my mouth shut. I never again tried to tell Mom what was going on. In fact, I started liking it. Dad would give me anything that I wanted.

"This must have gone on for many years. Until the day he found out that my period had started, he stopped coming. I became furious with him."

Sara had to stop because she started to hyperventilate again. Thalia gently rubbed her head.

"You're still angry with him," Ann remarked.

"Yes," Sara said, "He pulled away from me very abruptly; I did not understand why. Luckily it was at the time when I had just started to have boyfriends. To spite him, I made sure that he knew that I was sleeping with them. My Mom must have known also, because one day she asked her sister who was a nurse at a Planned Parenthood clinic to take me there to get birth control."

"Didn't your Dad die when you were a teenager?" Thalia inquired.

"He did," Sara admitted. She was not quite sure if she was quite ready to tell this story; but it was too late to hold back any longer. She had begun to feel relief from her catharsis, and she was swept up in the magical healing.

"Elijah fell into the wrong crowd at high school, and began using drugs very heavily. There were several times when he got real strung out and was sent away to drug treatment. By some miracle, he managed to finish high school." Sara stopped; if only she could go back in time to the night of his graduation and change the course of what happened. Ann couldn't help but notice the frozen look upon Sara's face, so she inquired about what was going on.

Sara informed her that her heart always stopped when she thought about this part of the story. Ann reached over and placed her hands on Sara's heart; the warmth of her gesture propelled Sara forward. "The night of his graduation, after they got home, he and Dad got into a very heated argument. At some point, my brother went into our parent's bedroom, got Dad's gun, walked back into the guest room where Dad was, and shot him. He died instantly."

"Did you witness it?" Thalia asked.

"Thank God no, I wasn't home. You see, after the graduation ceremony, I went and spent the night at my best friend's house. I did not go home until the following morning. As we pulled up in front of the house, I had this eerie feeling that something was wrong. I could sense the gloom spilling out of the house. Sure enough, when I went inside, there was still blood all over. Mom was sitting on the sofa in a state of shock. She barely recognized me. She just kept mumbling that Elijah said that she wouldn't hurt anymore because Lucifer was dead."

"Oh Sara, I am so sorry," Ann said, drawing closer and hugging her. "I cannot begin to imagine how hard it must have been to lose your Dad so tragically at your brother's hands."

"It was hard. I felt so sorry for Dad; in spite of all that he had done. He did not deserve to die like that."

Ann inquired about the anger that she used to feel toward him.

"It turned into sadness. But after that, I got really mad at my mother. She refused to mourn for him. She became a new person after Dad died. The fight to try and get my brother acquitted filled her with an energy and purpose that I had never seen before."

Ann suggested that maybe her Mom renewed her broken spirit after she was released from a marriage that was so oppressive. Sara did not seem to buy it.

"Elijah was found not guilty on the grounds of temporary insanity and sent to a mental institution. To this day, Mom visits him weekly. She even started a support group at the institution for mothers of the criminally insane."

Thalia inquired when was the last time Sara saw her brother.

"I never ever saw him again. My last memory of Elijah is of him dressed up in his graduation robe, sporting a huge afro and wearing dirty tennis shoes. My mother and I made a pact that she would never tell me about what was going on with my brother, and I would never tell the authorities that he had often told me that he was going to kill Dad someday. I just never took him seriously."

"Of course you wouldn't," Ann tried to alleviate the guilt she recognized. "You were just kids."

Sara shrugged and continued. "When I was around eight, which would make him ten at the time, he used to make me play this game with him in which he would dress up in Mom's clothes and pretend to be a woman. He would try to get me to be the father and put some of Dad's clothes on, but I always refused. He would tell me to hit him hard, which of course, I did. I liked that. But then, he would get extremely angry and start shooting me with his play guns. He would tell me that I could not hurt him anymore because I was dead."

Sara could not hold back the tears any longer. Neither could Thalia, or Ann.

"Since a few years ago, he visits me every so often in my dreams. We are still playing the same game, only this time I get the gun and kill him and then myself."

"Oh Sara," Thalia said, "I used to think that no one else's pain could come close to mine."

"Now you see why I have avoided talking about this stuff," Sara said. "My whole family is a mess. No wonder I'm so messed up; but I must admit, being saved has been a big help."

"The most important thing is to let it out, Sara," Ann prodded. "There is nothing to be ashamed of. Your family's dysfunction is not an indicator of who you are. Who any of you are! You all obviously couldn't live together healthily, but it doesn't make any of you bad people. Your Dad was ill, yes, terribly so, but ..." Ann was at a loss for words. She was trying to make it easier for Sara to deal with her emotions about her dad, but Ann was fighting her own rage at him, trying to find some place of reason from which to operate. Though she had suspected something like this for years, the truth pierced her like a knife when she imagined the hell Sara had lived through all her life.

"I was so torn apart at my Dad's funeral," Sara said. "I felt so guilty. I remember sitting in the church and begging God for one of those Lazarus miracles, but no luck."

"Your Dad's death may have been a karmic way of releasing all the suffering that he brought to his family," Ann said. "He certainly killed the spirits of you, your brother and your mother."

"I have always felt responsible for his death," Sara said, not grasping the deeper lesson of what Ann was trying to show her.

"Take it from me," Thalia said, "you have to remember that it was not you who pulled the trigger."

"Still, it's hard because they were fighting over me," Sara replied. "On the day of the funeral, I overheard Mom telling her sister that the argument between Dad and my brother heated up when my brother told Dad that he was jealous of my boyfriends. At that point Dad told him that he did not know what he was talking about, because he was a sissy. That's when my brother apparently lost it and got the gun."

"Oh Sara," Ann said, "What a burden to be carrying all these years."

"I still pray for that miracle," Sara said. "That one day I will go home and see a new Dad smiling and waiting to hug me."

"So you tried to resurrect your Dad by marrying someone just like him?" Ann said.

"Oh …" Sara's mouth fell open, but she remained speechless.

"Sara," Ann filled the gap, "the day that you realize that you and your brother were the scapegoats of your parent's dysfunctional marriage, is the day that you will stop blaming yourself for all their behaviors."

"Earlier when I plunged my head under the falls and let the water beat down on my head, I imagined that the water was washing away my sins," Sara said. "So I could start anew."

"The only sin you are guilty of is not seeing and owning your power," Ann said. "You have given it away by blaming yourself for things over which you have no control."

"Sara," Thalia said, "You can reclaim your power now by believing that you did not make your Dad molest you. You were the victim of his need to exert his power over you, a powerless child unable to protect herself from his evil."

"I know but," Sara said, reflecting for a moment. "I also gave in to sleeping with Dad because when I let him sleep with me, he didn't beat Mom as much. So I've always felt like, like I knew what I was doing. In fact," she looked down at the ground and squirmed a little, "It's only now that I'm understanding the pain that I caused you when I slept with Don. Deep in the recesses of my mind, as unbelievable as it may seem, I really did think that I was doing the right thing. I distinctly remember Don complaining that you were always too busy and or tired for him. I guess he had forgotten what it was like during the third-year hospital rotations. I see now how my experiences set me up to behave in the manner that I did. I used sex to try and keep our little family together. That's what I was accustomed to."

Sara looked up and finally allowed herself to fully feel Ann's closeness. "Please believe that I have always loved you, then and now."

Ann looked deep into Sara's eyes, straight through to her soul. What stared back at her was a frightened little girl, around three years old. She hugged Sara and said to her, "It makes so much sense why you have such mixed feelings toward women. Starting from early on with your mother, and including myself, you have felt abandoned and not protected by us."

"Growing up, I always was closer to men than women," Sara reflected. "All my friends were guys, up until when I met you and Thalia; you were the first two women friends that I ever had."

"I hope that you didn't think I abandoned you also?" Thalia said.

"No. You, Thalia, are the one person who has always stood by me, no matter what."

"From now on," Ann said, "you can add me to that list." Turning to Thalia, "I owe you a big one Thalia, for making sure that we all followed through with this reunion."

"We can thank James for that. Every time I wanted to back out, or one of us tried to, I would remember looking at him lying so still in the coffin. Like my father, I'd spent a lot of time away from the people that I loved but was angry at them. Life's too short for that. Remembering both of them in the coffin made me realize that's not how I want to remember how much I love you guys."

"Well, you guys know how good I've been at locking up my pain and throwing the key away," Sara said.

"With my mother's death, I got stuck in the time and place that I closed myself off," Thalia said. "I kept time still after she was gone, and from then on, ended up locking myself in a cage where I never learned how to deal with loss."

"So many of us do that with our emotional traumas," Ann said. "I have done the same thing with James. I am still very much frozen in the moment right before he died. It is as if I am holding both of us there, stuck in fear and anger, not wanting to let either of us move beyond it."

"That's exactly how I felt with my mother's death, cynical as all hell," Thalia said solemnly. "That is, until the both of you helped me to face it the other morning." Thalia could literally feel how the negative space that the hurt had occupied in her for all those years was beginning to clear away and make room for more loving memories. "From now on, I'm going to hold Mom in my memory as she appeared to me the other morning with her beautiful spirit shining through. Not the grotesque one with the brains all blown to pieces."

"We all have to release the hurt regarding our mothers, and it is a continuous process; for there are many layers." Ann said, thinking about her own mother. Just then it occurred to her that her mother leaving her to go to the States to pursue a better material life was no less righteous than her leaving Ahsima to come to Jamaica in pursuit of a better emotional and spiritual life. They were both seeking to enhance an aspect of themselves, which they thought would ultimately benefit their children.

"Hopefully, one day I will get there with my mother," Sara said.

"I know that you have the strength to do so Sara," Ann said. "You have come this far. Be patient and trust that the universe will take care of you."

"It's hard to trust," Sara said.

"That's because the first person that you depended on to soothe, hold and protect you turned her back on your pain," Ann explained to Sara. "It's the same as being physically abandoned."

"Yes," was the soft concurrence.

"But one day, Sara, you are going to have to see your mom as just another human, full of contradiction and vulnerability," Ann said. "At that time, you will be better able to understand her choices, forgive her, and let the true love flow once more."

"I hope that I will be ready to let it happen soon," Sara said.

"Don't rush it. It'll happen when the time is right, just like so much of what we've talked about since we've been here. Who knows, if we'd shared these things with each other before, they may not have been as powerful as they are now; but then again, back then, we might not have been ready or equipped to help each other."

The thought was encouraging for Sara. She smiled and nodded at Ann, not feeling as inadequate in her spiritual growth as she had felt earlier.

Ann looked up and saw Morris gesturing to them "We need to get ready to leave. The sun is setting."

"Before we go, since we all seem to be in a 'clearing out the cobwebs' mood," Sara said turning toward Thalia, "I have one thing that I am going to face up to." Sara paused for a moment, shifted her gaze to the water, and said without looking up, "My brother is gay. She paused again, still not able to make eye contact. "He once told me that Dad knew and had made him suck his dick several times. It was after he had returned from one of the countless drug treatment programs, so, of course, I did not believe him and dismissed it as drug induced delusions."

"That could explain your fear of homosexuality," Ann said. "You experienced it in your family in a harmful and deceitful way."

"I don't know, but I just wanted you to know that I am trying to accept your lifestyle," Sara said lifting her head finally and looking at Thalia again.

"Just don't keep me waiting in vain," Thalia shared a smile with her.

They climbed down from the waterfall, grabbed their sandals that they had left in the sand, and hurried over to join Morris at the boat.

7

Friday

The treacherous drive across the mountains from Ocho Rios to Kingston kept Ann alert with her eyes wide open. She had chosen to make the drive early in the morning to avoid traffic. Unlike the drive along the coast—which was lined with serene skies, sedate blue seawater, striking coconut and palm trees, and wispy sugarcane blowing in the wind—the journey across the rugged mountains was hazardous. But beautiful in its own unique way! Ann particularly liked driving alongside the river, sandwiched in between stone mountains covered with lush, green trees on either side. They made her feel very protected, almost womb-like. The steep inclines and sharp, blind curves seemed symbolic of the dynamics that had been unfolding between her, Sara and Thalia during the trip. She prayed that the mountain air would help to evaporate the final remnants of the cloud that solemnly landed on them yesterday with Sara's revelations. Or perhaps the flattening of the ridges into the beautiful valleys and plains of Kingston would signal the return of their hopefulness about better days to come. Something had to give—Ann didn't want to spend their last two full days in painful contemplation.

Last night when they had returned to the villa from the falls, they were weighted down by the evilness of the human spirit. Refusing any company, Sara had decided to go for a long, solitary walk. Thalia spent a thoughtful hour in the sauna, while Ann swam laps in the pool. They knew Sara wanted more time alone when she had not returned for dinner. So the two shared a quiet, uneventful meal together, leaving Sara's meal on a warmer in the kitchen. She returned shortly after they had finished and gave them each a hug before they retired to bed. Listening to Sara patter around the kitchen, Ann realized she had returned from her walk with a brand new calmness. Ann dropped off to sleep that night, reassured that she did not need to worry about Sara.

As they got closer to Kingston, Ann's thoughts switched to her long anticipated reunion with Spice. She was amazed at how excited she was to reunite with a man she had only spent one night with. Nervousness flared in little spurts, but her talk with Thalia had convinced her to work on calming her fears. The only sensation that ran unfettered within her was eagerness. She couldn't wait to call him as soon as they got settled. It would calm her anxiety to know exactly when they would meet again.

Fortunately, the usual morning congestion had thinned out by the time Ann got to Red Hills Road, allowing her to pull up in front of her beautiful Mediterranean-styled townhouse complex in less than three hours. The rounded, rolling hills that enveloped her complex always reminded her of expectant breasts wanting to be suckled. Ann was happy to be back in Kingston. As idyllic as the other places had been, it always felt too surreal for her to feel totally alive. She loved the pent-up energy, in both the people and the sharply, jutting hills, of Kingston. Everything felt like it was ready to explode at any moment. The city's sights and smells—the sweetness and freshness juxtaposed right next to stench and decay—danced between extreme polarity—power and surrender, beauty and monstrosity. Ann loved it all.

The guard at the gate welcomed Ann back and handed her a note that had been dropped off earlier. Thalia and Sara were still asleep, so Ann quickly opened and read it with a pounding heart.

"Sweetness, I got up at the crack of dawn anxiously awaiting your arrival. I have to be at the studio this morning to meet with a potential promoter. Call me so that I can arrange to see you this afternoon. One love, Spice."

As Ann approached her home and drank in its familiarity, she welcomed the sanctuary that it always promised; and delivered. She noticed someone sitting on her verandah, but she could not make them out fully as they were somewhat hidden behind the bougainvillea. She made a mental note that she had to have the gardener trim them when next he came. When the person stood up, Ann recognized Cassandra.

"I bribed the guards into letting me in," Cassandra said, smiling at Ann as she pulled into the driveway and rolled the windows down.

"I am sure that it was no problem with that bewitching smile that you have," Ann replied stopping the car and turning off the engine.

FRIDAY

Ann nudged Sara in the front seat and Thalia in the back. "Welcome back to the land of the living," she told them.

"Was that Cass's voice that I heard?" Sara asked as she opened her eyes.

"Yes it's me," Cassandra said walking toward them. "I wanted to be here when you ladies arrived."

After hugs and kisses, Cassandra helped Sara and Thalia unload the car. Ann went ahead to open the door and check on her apartment. When she walked inside, she saw someone sitting on the sofa. He was lounging casually, like he belonged there. Ann's heart leapt half from fear and half from excitement.

"Spice, what are you doing here? How did you get in?" she managed to say.

"Is this how you are always going to greet me?" Spice asked, grinning from ear to ear as he stood and pulled her into his arms. He kissed her lightly as he knew full well that was all Ann was about to give him.

"Is this how you are always going to show up, out of the blue?"

"I did not trespass," Spice held his hands up in mock defense. "Aunt Cassie let me in." Before Ann could reply, Sara, Thalia and Cassandra entered. Possessively, Spice slipped his arms around her waist as she turned to her friends.

"Fancy walking in and finding that not only is there a man in the house, but you are in his arms," Sara said. "You have some explaining to do."

Ann quickly stepped out of Spice's embrace. She felt like a kid caught with her hands in the cookie jar.

"Auntie Cassandra is the one who is going to have to do the explaining. She is the one who let the man in," Ann replied, emotions flustered, cheeks blushed.

"I think that introductions are in order first," Cassandra said. "Thalia, Sara, this is my nephew Spice."

"I cannot believe that you two are related!" Ann exclaimed.

"Yes, unfortunately for me," Cassandra winked at her nephew.

"I don't believe it," Ann said, still not fully convinced.

"Believe it," Cassandra said. "Tuesday when I got back to Kingston, Spice told me about this incredible red-headed sistren that he had met down in Duncan. I immediately figured out that it was you. I was so glad. The very day I met you I wished this rambunctious man of mine would meet someone like you, but I don't meddle in things like that. I have faith that what is to be will be. And here you both are."

"Well, Mr. Spice," Thalia shook his hand. "You get many points by just being related to Cassandra." Thalia's gesture cracked the tension. Immediately Ann responded.

"I didn't mean to insinuate that you were not being earnest Cassandra. I am just in shock," Ann said apologetically.

"Yes, tell us all about it," Sara said, loving the intrigue that was unfolding.

"Miss Sara, don't start none won't be none," Cassandra laughed. "The long and short of it is that Spice's father is my oldest brother. After Spice's mother went to England to follow her dream of becoming a singer, my brother and Spice moved back into my mother's house. We basically raised Spice together, but, of course, it was I who really nurtured his artistic side and taught him everything that he knows."

"Now I see why I was drawn to you," Ann remarked. "You've got some Cassandra in your blood."

Spice smiled at her, pleased to hear her vocalize her feelings. When she looked away, realizing what she'd said, he decided not to embarrass her further.

"Let me be a gentleman and help you ladies with your luggage," Spice volunteered.

While Spice took the luggage upstairs and put them in the rooms per Ann's instructions, Cassandra and Ann went to the kitchen to start some coffee. Sara and Thalia followed him up to their rooms so they could freshen up.

"I am delighted that someone has finally lassoed you in," Cassandra said when Spice joined them in the kitchen.

"Auntie, do not give Ann the impression that I am some loose, out-of-control bachelor," Spice pleaded. "The only sin that I have been guilty of is wandering the earth, playing my music in search of my lost soulmate. Don't mess me up now that I have found her."

"I wouldn't do that," Cassandra said. "Just don't mess it up yourself."

"I know I won't," he said, looking directly at Ann.

"You should have at least introduced us," Ann said, ignoring Spice's challenge.

"I couldn't have," Cassandra replied. "Spice must not have told you that he and his band just got back from a four-month tour of Europe and Asia. Plus, he only just moved back to Jamaica this past year after living in London for over ten years."

"There is obviously a lot that we don't know about each other," Ann said.

"We got all the time in the world to get to the mundane issues," Spice declared. "Once you've had your time with your friends, I will do my best to monopolize your attention."

Cassandra was as pleased as Ann pretended not to be, "This is simply marvelous that you two found each other here in the homeland, especially since you've both been away all these many years," Cassandra remarked.

"Like you said, Auntie, what is to be ..." he trailed off as he leaned over and kissed Ann on the forehead. "I have to go. Please walk me outside." He said goodbye to his Aunt, and they left through the living room, running into Sara and Thalia.

"I'll see you ladies later," Spice said.

"I'm sure you will," Sara teased.

Thalia and Sara giggled at Ann's attempt not to smile. "Bye Spice." Thalia sang and winked at her friend. The two women locked arms and went to see what Cassandra was whipping up in the kitchen. Ann went outside with Spice.

Before getting into his car, he leaned against it and drew her into his arms. Her body instantly remembered the ecstasy. "Come to the club tonight?" he whispered in her ear.

FRIDAY

She had no time to reply. Quickly, they became swept away in an overwhelming desire to wrap themselves into each other's hearts. Not caring how many neighbors might be watching, she offered him the tongue that he was so longing to taste. His hardening self sprung her back to reality.

"I'll try. Now go away, Spice. You're making me crazy." She tore herself away and ran inside. In the doorway, she turned and smiled at him. He was still leaning by the car. She waved goodbye and he smiled.

"Likewise, sweetness. Likewise," was all he said before getting into his truck.

Ann returned to the kitchen to find the women engaged in lively conversation and making fried dumplings and plantains. She poured some coffee and sat with them at the table. She noticed that her appetite was gone; she had an unsettling feeling—she feared that she might have fallen too deeply in love with Spice in too short of a time.

"We were wondering if you were coming back," Sara teased.

"Of course I was," Ann replied a little defensively.

"Oops, we are being very sensitive, aren't we?" Cassandra said.

"I guess my nerves are a bit frayed," Ann said. "What with the surprise of seeing Spice again and under these circumstances of finding out about his connection with you, Cassandra. It all seems a bit unreal."

"Honey," Cassandra reassured her. "There is no set reality about how our lives will unreel. Not if we step up to the task and become co-creators of our dramas."

"The reality that I see," Thalia said, "is that you two are very much in love."

The other women all nodded in agreement. Ann felt as though they were ganging up on her.

"Ladies, I am still a widow in mourning," she told them. From out of nowhere, images of her wedding to James began to flash in her head. Ann struggled not to cry.

Cassandra reached out and captured her hand. "I know how much you loved him, daughta," she comforted her. "No other man will ever change that. But that does not mean that you cannot love someone else just the same. As a mother you should know that we are all capable of many loves."

Sara went over to Ann. "I am going to quote what you told me yesterday—we have to let go of the pain that wrenches and anchors us to the past."

"Maybe I have been telling that to everyone else because I've been struggling to do so myself," Ann said.

"You are right on," Cassandra remarked. "We oftentimes teach what we need to learn."

"I don't know what I would do without my sistah friends," Ann thanked them. "I love you all."

"See," Cassandra said. "It's possible to love in multiple."

"Remember what I said the other day Ann, you are lucky. Stop acting like you're cursed."

Thalia's sharp words were exactly what Ann needed to push away the tears. She had cried enough. She nodded.

"Well, welcome to Kingston. What do you all want to do?" she said trying to raise the energy she had lowered.

"Let's go into the town. We can have fun looking at some fine brothers like yours."

"You already found one, Sara. You just kept dissing him," Thalia snickered.

"Need to check out the women, Thalia?" Sara rebutted.

"Yes," Ann pretended Cassandra had asked. "They are always like this."

"Must be love." Cassandra smiled. "I'll be the tour guide. Ann, you coming?"

Ann yawned, reminding them all of her long, pre-dawn drive to get them there. No one tried to talk her into coming. "I need to run some errands," Ann excused herself. "Cassandra, I don't know how you were able to make all this with these bare cupboards."

Ann cleaned up the kitchen after they left and began making a shopping list. But, unable to ignore her fatigue any longer, she went to her room to rest before she headed out. Instead of taking a nap, she admitted that the chaos churning inside her head and begging for attention was draining her much faster than her lack of sleep. What she needed was a bit of quiet space as an antidote. Since she was planning to do yoga at sunset, having missed it at sunrise, she opted for meditation.

Determined to put distance between herself and her thoughts for the moment, Ann undressed, lit a few candles, put on the CD 'Om' by John Coltrane and sat on her mat, spine erect. Each time a thought appeared in her mind, rather than try to analyze it, she instead observed it. After a long while, the thoughts began to lessen. After she stopped breathing life into them, they disappeared from lack of sustenance. Eventually, the vacuum left in her psyche became filled with bliss.

She remained in meditation until a very loud and persistent knocking on her door startled her back to the present. She put her robe on, went downstairs and opened the door.

"Spice, what are you doing back here so early?"

"I couldn't wait any longer; I had to see you," Spice explained. "Are you going to let me in?"

"Of course."

As soon as he stepped inside, he pinned her to the wall and leaned against her. "I kept feeling you," he said, kissing her lightly all over her face.

"I am feeling you hard," Ann told him. She could feel his heart pounding through her chest.

"See what you do to me!" he tried to claim her mouth in a deep kiss.

"Wait, Spice. There's so much I want to know about you," Ann said, trying to put in check the passion that was quickly building between them. Even though she wanted desperately to have him hold and caress her, she was not ready to have him inside her yet. She wanted to talk, get to know him more. "I realized today how little we've shared. Like your relationship with Cassandra! Even though it's a good one, it's quite a surprise."

He didn't resist as she released herself from his embrace and led them to the sofa.

"There's not much to tell," he said, after they had both sat down. "I was about eleven years old at the time when we moved in with Granny and Auntie Cass. Granny died a couple years later, at which time Aunt Cassie took over the role of woman of the house."

"I still find it hard to believe that in the past five months that I have known her, she did not tell me about you," Ann said.

"Would it have made a difference?" he asked.

"Maybe," Ann said a bit coquettishly. "It might have given you some extra points. I will have you know that I am a great admirer of your aunt. She is a phenomenal woman."

"What about me?" he asked. "Am I a phenomenal man?"

"Well from watching you on stage, I would venture a yes," Ann decided to talk about his career rather than his sexual talents. "Even though I only got a listen while dodging an earful of pick-up lines, I'm pretty impressed by the way you make such a perfect fit out of reggae and jazz together. I've heard lots of fusion, but yours is like a whole new art form."

"So you just gonna dis the rude bwai's real talents," Spice said, pouting and pretending to be upset, though pleased at her observation. "Rude bwai will go for the ride then into the land of his musical genius." When she playfully shoved him, he accepted the compliment. "The first time I knew I was doing something special was when I found out that my dad was listening to my music when I wasn't home. That inspired me more than anything else. And the music filled the spaces my aunt couldn't when my mom left." He paused and reflected momentarily, "Outside of the special people in my life, there is nothing else I live for."

"I know. It's obvious in the way you sing."

"I'm working on something for you," he took her hand.

"Will I hear it if I come tonight?"

"It's not ready yet. Maybe I'll perform it in private first."

"How'd you get into jazz growing up here though? Is that what your mom sang?"

"Yeah." His sad smile was proof that he spoke from a special memory. "Before she left, I'd spend many days doing homework on the floor while she played the piano and sang. She knew I was pretending to concentrate on my work and would say things aloud like, 'hmm, the base in reggae and jazz do tend to have a similar do-do-dom beat. Yes, that's right. The difference is that in jazz the other sounds drift apart and do their own thing, whereas in reggae, they stay close and build upon each other.' It was funny, 'cause I drank it all in. But my dad would have flipped if he knew she was trying to teach me stuff. Even before she left, they would argue about her desire to sing. In the end, the fusion I create, it's what she taught me and more. In it I bring both seemingly opposite tendencies back together, like finding the point of convergence in very divergent states."

"I think she would approve, Spice. It's pure creative genius merging and molding what could be otherwise chaos into beauty."

He smiled.

"Do you miss her?"

FRIDAY

"Ah, yes and no, honestly." He responded to Ann's raised eyebrow, "Don't get me wrong. I wish she'd been around, I really do. I miss lots of things about her, but Auntie Cassie really was a class act in squashing my dad's resentment and making me feel loved by her. You know? It helped keep my feelings for her pure. I was angry at times, but Auntie made my dad deal with it without turning me against my mom. I think I could have a relationship with her if she walked through the door right now. It just would never be what it could, or should have been."

"Ever tried to find her?"

"I'm not that tight. I think I'll leave it up to fate. I don't think she's performing though. I always think I'll run into her on the circuit somewhere."

"How long have you been performing, Spice?"

"Went on my first big road gig when I was twenty."

"Wow. Pretty young."

"Yeah, but Aunt Cassie had my head screwed on right before I started out."

"Uh huh, you going to tell me you didn't enjoy the attention of the groupies?"

"Let's just say, I know when I'm in a relationship and when I'm not."

Ann rolled her eyes and smirked.

"Seriously," he made his case. "None of my ex-girlfriends can ever say I cheated on them. There was always enough other stuff that didn't connect. Or like my last girlfriend, other shit to fight about. You know?"

"What do you mean?" Ann asked.

"My last relationship was quite turbulent," Spice told her. "We really weren't good for each other. When it finally ended, I swore off women."

"That bad?" Ann asked.

"She was the kind of woman who doesn't know what she wants from men," Spice said. "She spent our year and a half doing her best to drive me crazy while she tried to figure it out. One day I wasn't macho enough, the next I wasn't sensitive enough."

"Really? I think your masculine and feminine energies are pretty well balanced. It's definitely a turn on for me."

"Well, that scared my old girlfriend," Spice said. "Especially when I tried to open up and talk to her. That was more intimidating than me trying to dominate the relationship."

"Where is she now?" Ann asked.

"Back in London," Spice said.

"Do you have any children?" Ann asked.

"None that I am aware of. But there really shouldn't be any. I have always practiced safe sex. You know that." She blushed, and he touched her chin softly. "You?" Spice asked.

"A daughter."

"How old is she?"

"Nineteen. She's away at college now. All grown up."

Spice read her correctly, "Miss her?"

"Terribly," Ann said. "But I am slowly learning to let her go."

"Don't ever learn to do that with me," Spice said. Ann reached over and held his hands.

"I want to trust that this is real," she said.

"Don't you ever doubt the sincerity of my feelings for you," he told her. "In this moment, which is all that we have, I am yours completely. Do you believe me?"

"I want to Spice, believe me, I want to," Ann replied. "But I have lived a bit longer than you my dear fellow, and have had a bit more lessons in the school of hard knocks."

"I hope that our age difference is not tripping you out again," Spice reassured her. "So you have lived a few more years than I. All that it means is that like fine wine, you are a bit mellower and more refined."

"You are as smooth as it gets," Ann replied. "I doubt that I am there yet, much less, ahead of you."

"Yes, you are woman," he said, placing a kiss on her forehead, "you are beyond smooth. Why else would my nerves be so wrecked after meeting you just a few days ago? If I am not careful, my senses are going to spin into overdrive. Then, before I can shift myself back into proper gear, I'll be running up and down the streets, all crazy and cross-dressed in a housecoat and slippers, calling out your name. Worst thing though, I'll probably be turning away all the pretty young things who think that they can turn me back into the real catch of a man that I used to be." Spice held his head in his hands and continued, "I can just see them now, declaring mi a madman to rahtid and locking mi up in Belleview!"

Ann was convinced that much of Spice's drama came from his aunt; as did his respect for and warmth toward women, she added. "Maybe it's your Auntie Cassie who put a spell on the both of us? I am pretty coo-coo about you myself."

"She is a witch, all right," Spice said. "There's none better."

Ann said. "Tell me more about your ex."

"Why?"

"I want to know if we're anything alike."

"Well, you're very similar in that you're both African princesses. But that's where any likeness ends. She was one based on status. I kid you not. She even acted with her secretary as if she were a lady in waiting. I was duly charmed. You, sweetness, are one of spirit. I feel the same peace reverberating off you that my aunt has. I've been looking for that for a while in a partner. I'm a slow learner, I guess, but I think I learned the lessons when I was with women whose energies were in the wrong places."

Ann did not need to hear anymore about her. Feeling a sudden desire to be covered by his touch, she pulled closer. He wrapped her in his arms and whispered in her ears, "Don't worry about the past. It is as it should be—over. Right now, right here, you are all the woman that I want. I want to make love to you again."

Spice got up from the sofa and dropped to his knees in front of Ann. He clasped her hands together in his.

"Royalty taught you well," she said, making light of his gesture, afraid to elevate his genuflection to the level of commitment that it suggested.

"This is not a fling for me Ann, it never was," he darted back "I really want to be your man."

Ann knew her mind was slipping from her control—as was her body. She was on fire to taste his spices. But she suddenly remembered that she had turned the Jacuzzi on right before she went upstairs to meditate.

"Let's go sit in the Jacuzzi," Ann suggested, hoping that the water would put a damper on the fire.

"I have had fantasies of making love to you in the water from the night that we first met," he said. "Before we go, I want you to lay on top of me and remind me of your special magic." While still holding her hands, Spice reclined backwards onto the floor, pulling Ann on top of him. Lying atop his pounding heart and bulging groin, Ann became forewarned of the volcano that was about to erupt. And she knew that nothing but red, molten lava would be spewing from his crater.

She sighted an escape route from what was sure to be deadly scorching. "I want to make sure that our connection moves into the spiritual plane, and does not stay stymied at the level of physical attraction." She rolled off from on top of him and lay by his side.

"You sound just like Auntie," Spice reluctantly succumbed, knowing full well the power of her teacher. "She must be teaching you well."

"Yeah, as part of her spiritual training, she has schooled me well in the art of tantric sex. Can I show you some of my stuff?" Ann tempted.

"I am always a willing student," Spice said.

"Then we're on."

Ann instructed him in the art of conscious breathing,

explaining that first they had to stop attending to all the noise and other peripheral distractions that kept their emotions and spirits from listening to and communicating with each other. Spice was not sure that he would be able to in the midst of his rising passion; however, he agreed to try.

"I will do anything for you, my sweetness," Spice said to Ann. "I will try to be patient." He lapsed into his Jamaican accent and continued, "but please know though that I am a full-blooded, extra hot, Jamaican brethren, which is why them call mi Spice. Mi nuh know if mi gone be able to have wi bodies so close and nuh want to be all up inside you." But he admitted in his British accent "I know that it is important to you that we go slowly and explore the other aspects of our connection."

"I am glad that you understand," Ann thanked him. "It's taking a lot of patience for me to wait too."

"Good," Spice teased. "Misery loves company."

"I must be inhaling some of your extra testosterone," Ann revealed. "Until you and I got together this week, I had been celibate for a long while, at least eighteen months. For a while there, I was very much in control of my sexual longings. But then again, I can't say that I was seriously tempted in anyway, that is, until I met you."

"I definitely like the results," Spice said, running his tongue along his lips. "Nothing excites me more than a hot mama, sizzling all over and burning me up!"

Ann chuckled a bit nervously. "It's still really hard to think of myself as a 'hot girl'. She decided to ignore his 'mama' reference and all that it implied about her age.

Somewhere deep within the dark recesses of her mind, being referred to as 'hot', was associated with being loose.

"Being sexually on fire is a sure turn on for me," he continued.

Ann did a quick check to try and pull out the source of her discomfort. "I guess all that Victorian indoctrination that Jamaican girls of my era were raised with regarding sex has left little residues of shame and guilt deep within me, in spite of my exterior persona of being the liberal, sexually explicit psychiatrist."

"The real shame, that is if any is to be had at all, is that you miss so much pleasure by not being fully in touch with the full range of your sexuality, north, south, east and west," Spice remarked.

"If this is to work in all spheres like you are suggesting," Ann continued cautiously, "then it has to be a wholesome love affair in which the both of us bring our full selves, mind, body and spirit to each other." She noticed that he was shaking his head as if in agreement, "Can we take such a journey together, Spice?"

"All the way," Spice told her. He took a deep breath, glad to feel that his libido was being transformed. "On this mini-excursion that we are about to take, I want to be your co-pilot. But since you're in the driver's seat right now, I am going to trust you to guide us home!"

"My pleasure," Ann told him, throwing all fears and caution to the wind. "Let's go upstairs." They walked hand in hand up the stairs to her bedroom. The candles were still aglow and emitting a faint suggestion of sandalwood.

Together with the Nag Champa incense that was also still burning, their olfactory pathways lit up their entire being with feelings of joy and ecstasy.

Ann invited Spice to sit on the rug by her bed while she put on an old Monty Alexander CD. Spice was extremely impressed with her selection. He marveled at the coincidence, for he knew that there was no way that she could have known that Monty, one of the first Jamaican musicians to blend jazz and reggae, was his role model and inspiration. "Woman, you are driving me wild and crazy," he said to her. "Come over here to me."

Ann joined him on the rug. "Oh no. Hot mama at the controls, remember?" she reminded him as he tried to pin her into a tight embrace. He loosened his embrace.

"Don't worry, I am going to touch you, but in a deeper way," she told him. Ignoring his playful sneer, Ann laid him on his back and massaged his legs and feet, being careful to avoid his groin area. When she could feel his sexual charge lessening, she gently pushed his thighs as far back as they would extend toward his head. After he was fully loose and mellow, Ann gently guided him into the cross-legged sitting position. She then sat in the lotus pose, facing him. They both stared into each other's eyes. "I see your soul Spice, and it is full of the sweet music that I am hearing."

"And I can see your soul too, Ann," Spice whispered back. "It is filled with words; I have this sense that you can paint pretty and soothing pictures with words."

Ann reached for his hands and massaged them, alternating between light and pressure-point strokes. After a short while, they both could feel the electricity flowing between their fingers.

Spice remarked, "This feels almost as erotic as having my groin stroked."

"Hold on, there is more to come," Ann warned him. She directed him to lie back down again and massaged the pleasure spots on the soles of his feet. Within a few minutes, Spice started breathing deeply. Ann turned him over on his stomach and massaged his lower spine until she could feel him squirming in ecstasy. "I am releasing your kundalini energy," she told him. She advised him to sit up as soon as he felt as if he was going to burst. "That will direct the unleashed energy upwards away from the pelvis and into your higher chakra centers."

"I hope that I do not explode," Spice said, sitting up quickly.

Ann directed him back to his breath. "Focus on your breath and take control of it. Within it lies the life force that helps us to transcend to our higher planes."

Ann took several, deep breaths with Spice to help him regain his composure. Exhausted, he fell back down on the rug; Ann cuddled up to his side. Donning her most soothing and beguiling voice, she guided him through a hypnotic visualization, connecting the colors of the rainbow to their corresponding energy levels in the body. Spice was totally relaxed and in the zone by the time she finished. He felt as though they had made love in the physical realm. "Tell you the truth, there is no way that I could muster up the energy to have sex now." He felt totally at peace.

Still lying on his back, Spice whispered in her ears, "A brother has to have a little take charge, so why don't you let me take you through my layman version of a soulful trip. You with me?"

"Of course," she smiled. She loved the comfortable give and take that was erupting between them.

"My little odyssey is to get in the Jacuzzi that we have been trying to get to for the past hour," he said smiling. "So, when we get there, I'm going to feed you the Bombay mango that I brought for you. It's in my knapsack somewhere. I couldn't resist, because the juice and flesh remind me of eating you. I'll cut the mango in half, scoop the flesh out with a spoon, put it on my tongue and then feed it to you. Then when the flesh is almost gone, we put the seed between both our mouths, and suck it until it's bare."

Ann loved how balanced his chakras seemed, and how fluidly he shifted between the higher and lower centers. She rolled over and kissed him. "That was really a soul-food journey," she told him. "And you know what, I think that I fell in love with you somewhere in the middle."

He smiled and held her tight. "That is such sweet music in my ears," he said. He closed his eyes once again. After several minutes of silence, he whispered in a very distant voice, "I am moving into a higher zone."

"What are you feeling?" Ann inquired.

"It's more than a feeling," he replied. "I can see myself drifting above my body. I have this feeling that you and I have been here together before." He stopped talking and drifted off into a very peaceful reverie.

Before she snuggled up beside him, Ann pulled the sheet from the bed and covered them both. She could feel a very intense charge swirling in between what was now becoming a very porous boundary in between their skins.

Ann awakened to a gentle tap on her shoulder. "I hate to do this to you guys, but it is after five in the afternoon," Cassandra nudged them both.

Spice jumped up, "Oh shit, I am late for my meeting," he said as he looked at his watch.

"Not if you hurry up and get going," Cassandra said. "When I saw your car in the driveway and realized that you were here and not there, I called Kalamu at the studio and told him that you were on your way. I know how important this meeting is to your career."

"Yeah, it is very important. This meeting is with an exec from one of the major record labels in London."

"This one with this sexy lady seems like it was more important," Cassandra kidded him.

"I sure hope that is not the explanation you gave them?" Spice blushed as he only just then realized that he was naked. He pulled the sheets closer, "Believe me, it's not what it looks like."

Ann remained silent, embarrassed too but happy that

she at least had clothes on. Cassandra noticed her discomfort and gave her a reassuring wink.

"Spice, don't worry about what I may or may not think, or what I may or may not have said," Cassandra said as she headed for the door. She turned back and gave him a playful grin. "It's not like I haven't seen it all before."

"You know best how to take care of me." Spice thanked her.

"You're my boy," Cassandra said, closing the door behind her.

After showing Spice his way around the bathroom, Ann went downstairs to join the other women. Even though he wanted her to stay and talk while he got dressed, she knew that her presence would be a distraction and delay him even further. She also missed her friends and wanted to hear about their day. She saw them on the back porch—Sara and Thalia were sitting in the Jacuzzi, in only t-shirts and panties; Cassandra on the lounge chair nearby, dressed even more sparsely in her bra and panties. Ann remembered that she still had her bikini on, so she slipped off her sundress and slippers and walked toward them. She smiled as she realized that she had missed her soulful, no lustful, mango treat with Spice. Thalia and Sara called out to Ann to come and join them.

Taking a seat on the edge of the Jacuzzi, Ann inquired about their day.

"Seeing that smile upon your face, I am sure ours was nowhere near as fabulous as yours was," Sara said, flicking water on Ann's leg's.

"Speak for yourself, Sara," Thalia interrupted, " I had a fantastic time."

"She was disgusting," Sara butted back in, feigning annoyance. "She was cruising all those pretty Jamaican women."

"I did no such thing," Thalia corrected her, happy to be able to talk about it without a fight. "I'm taken."

"Well, let me just set the record straight right now, because I know what you are all thinking," Ann said, "Spice and I did not have sex." Just then, Ann could hear Spice letting himself out of the front door. She was relieved that he did not come find them to say goodbye, because the air was raging with untamed estrogen.

"And I am a saint," Sara replied.

"And right you are," Cassandra piped in. "If only you would believe."

"No kidding ladies," Ann said. "If we had made it to the Jacuzzi like you all did, we probably would have, but we made another kind of love with each other; sacred sex; we allowed our spirits to convene. It was so powerful, we fell into a deep sleep."

"I swear, you are too deep for me sometimes, Ann," Sara said in amazement. "If I had a fine man like that hanging on to my every word, I promise we'd have done it, and not just once today."

"Well, we could always find you some young stud. There were plenty out today."

"I didn't think you'd notice men anymore, Thalia?"

"I certainly noticed Marlon, except he only had eyes for

you," Thalia turned it right back on Sara.

"Nice try, Thalia. We both know Marlon has nothing to offer me."

"Who's Marlon?" Cassandra asked.

"A local artist who showed us around in Duncan. Really nice guy."

"Nice? The guy was a complete gentleman, hot as hell and all over Ms. Thing there."

"You know, Thalia," Sara got out of the Jacuzzi, agitated, "It seems you really have a thing for Marlon. Maybe you should help yourself? I'm sure it's all the same to him." She began to dry off feverishly.

"I doubt that, Sara," Thalia laughed off Sara's attitude. "Anyway, after my experience with Lee, I'm not sure if a man will ever be able to make my clit jump or my heart smile again."

Sara was even more annoyed by Thalia's laughter. "Then I will just have to keep praying for you," she shot at her, before turning sharply and walking back inside the house.

"Seems as though Sara cannot take what she dishes out," Cassandra remarked after Sara left. Cassandra got up from the lounge chair and captured the space inside the Jacuzzi vacated by Sara's departure.

"In some areas she does not like direct confrontation," Ann said, "And Thalia loves to mess with her sometimes. They used to go at it all the time, but Sara doesn't handle it like she used to, you know?"

Thalia nodded her agreement.

Cassandra moved on to something else she'd noticed, "So Thalia, you said you are taken. Have you come to a resolution?"

"No. Well, yes. I think I need more time to deal with the reality of being in a lesbian relationship, above and beyond how I may or may not feel about her the person," Thalia admitted. "I think Lee also needs to think more about what this could mean for her career. I am sure that the public does not know that she is gay; black people still cannot deal with homosexuality. I also have to figure out how to deal with this issue with my son. He has always been and will always be the number one priority in my life."

"As well he should," Ann said. "That seems reasonable to me. What's the problem?"

"All of it," Thalia realized it was time to bring up the discussion she'd planned to have with Ann. Especially with Cassandra there who understood. "Lee is very spoiled and very used to having the things that she wants when she wants them. As much as I am intrigued and attracted to her, I do need the time. I was talking to Cassandra about feeling rushed on one hand, but on the other hand, feeling comforted by Lee because she really knows me well. She's a good friend; she was there for me to sound off on for a lot of what I went through with my divorce from Reggie. I know she understands what I need."

"Well, not if she's rushing you?" Ann clarified.

"True..." Thalia trailed off.

"But?"

"Well, I've been thinking about something Cassandra said that morning I was telling you about?" Ann nodded that she remembered what day Thalia referenced. "Even though Saturday night was the first time that Lee and I had slept together, the physical attraction had been there for quite a while. I was just in a lot of denial. I'm just not sure if the denial was about being in love with Lee, or being a lesbian. You know? Was I running from the fact that I have those kinds of feelings for women in general, or just for one human being who just happens to be a woman?"

"Hmm," Ann was thoughtful. "Well, I believe that we are all bisexual and have the potential to choose either pole. I am not surprised that you had been denying any of those feelings. It's not an easy thing to face. Plus, it could have gotten even more complicated by you thinking that you were being reactionary due to the ending of your marriage." Ann could tell from Thalia's furrowed forehead that her discourse had done little to take Thalia out of her dilemma zone. So she prodded on, "I don't want to downplay your relationship with Lee, but you don't seem very clear about your feelings for her."

"I know. Cassandra pointed out how having her in my confidence all this time may be setting the tone for our relationship. I've been giving that a lot of thought, and I can't say that she isn't right."

"Ah," Ann nodded and smiled at Cassandra. "An intercept relationship."

"See, I knew she would even have a fancy name for it," Cassandra spoke for the first time.

The two women smiled at the Sage. "What's that, Ann?"

"Don't mind, Cassandra," Ann pretended to shrug her off, "she likes to tease me about my western training. But this one actually comes from a theory one of my friends, Maggie, made up."

"Maggie from the arts council?"

"Yes, you remember her? She's tight. Anyway, according to her, when I was tempted to mess around once when James and I had some difficulties, she pointed out that by constantly confiding in this other person about what was wrong with my relationship with James, he figured out what to, or not do, to win me over. And voila! I foolishly thought that I found the perfect antidote to my problems." Ann smiled as she remembered how humorous Maggie was as she gave her the unsolicited advice. "She likened what I was doing to giving someone an open book test with all the correct answers underlined. If they have any modicum of intellect, Maggie said, the minimum they are going to get is an 'A'."

Thalia waded over to the opposite side of the Jacuzzi to get a sip of Evian, unsure if her thirst was from the heat of the water or the conversation. Could that be the case with Lee, she wondered. For, she had met Lee during a very difficult period shortly after her divorce from Reggie, and Lee quickly became her confidante and therapist.

"Well, Lee gets an A with several pluses," Thalia remarked, returning to her jet by the step next to Ann. "I don't want to make that mistake. But I don't want to keep pushing her away."

"I don't quite understand. Why do you think that you are pushing her away?" Ann asked.

"I won't commit to an exclusive relationship, and that seems very important to her," Thalia replied.

"If you don't want exclusivity, and she cares about you, why are you thinking that you are wrong for her not understanding? That's not fair." Ann asked.

"Beats me," Thalia replied. She pondered the question for a while then said, "I don't want you to think that Lee's a bad person, she really is not. Before we became lovers, only a few short days now, she was always a very dear and trustworthy friend, always caring and giving, and expecting nothing in return. She reminds me a lot of you, Ann."

"Well then maybe she is simply afraid to lose you, and that's why she's pushing so. But don't let her feelings for you get confused with yours for her. You don't owe her anything but the truth. If she's the friend you say she is, she will understand. But just don't string her along"

"That is absolutely what I've been doing," Thalia nodded in agreement, lifting herself up from her seat by the jet and sitting next to Ann on the edge. The water temperature had become unbearably hot. The force of the jet spray now seemed as if it was beating up on her; earlier, it was a welcome massage. "I've felt so guilty about falling fully in love with her, I've had my brakes on. I would love to keep seeing her intimately. I just don't want to commit to anything right now."

"Isn't it wonderful the things that happen when we release our fears and allow ourselves to be?" Thalia looked straight into Cassandra's eyes, remembering that she'd spoken very similar words in the caves.

"Cassandra. You are amazing." Thalia admitted that she had read her right from the start.

"With your level of insight, you will work it out as best fits your needs, Thalia," Cassandra took no credit, but continued to reassure her. "You just need some more time as you said earlier."

"Especially in relationship to my son," Thalia continued. "As I said earlier, he is number one."

"If Spice and I should become more seriously involved with each other, I too, am going to have to figure out how to handle things with Ahsima," Ann noted. "I don't want her to feel that I have betrayed her father. But for now, I am going to leave that worry until I meet it in the present."

"Cassandra, please help this woman to admit that she is madly in love with Spice," Thalia said.

"One day I am going to help her to remember," Cassandra said.

"What do you mean by that?" Ann asked.

"Wait and see," was all that Cassandra ventured.

By now, Thalia was feeling water logged and heavy-eyed, so she decided to get out of the Jacuzzi completely. Ann pointed out the cupboard that housed the towels.

"I know just what you need," Cassandra said.

"Do you really?" Thalia said mischievously, wrapping the towel around her.

"That and more," Cassandra replied mysteriously, getting out of the Jacuzzi also and joining Thalia by the cupboard. "For right now though, what you need is some ginger tea to bring your energy back." Cassandra dried off with the towel that Thalia handed her, then went inside to put on her clothes; she needed to go to her car to fetch her remedies. Thalia went inside too to put clothes on and search for Sara.

The women's departure and the growling in Ann's stomach reminded her that she had not eaten since breakfast. As much as she wanted to spend some quiet time in the water, she needed to find something to eat. So she dried her feet, put her sundress back on and went to the kitchen. The cupboards and refrigerator were still quite bare, for she had not made it to the market as she had planned to. There was not much choice, however she did manage to find some bun and cheese. Cassandra returned with several packets of herbs. In addition to making ginger tea, she told Ann that she was going to brew a special blend of bush tea for Sara from Cerosee, Ganja and Fever Grass. She confided in Ann that she was worried about Sara's low energy, and the lifelessness that settled in her eyes at times. Ann realized that she too had taken notice, but was afraid of probing too deeply into Sara's physical health; after all, she was only a psychiatrist. Sara and Thalia were the real doctors.

Thalia and Sara returned downstairs a while later. Sara announced that her evening nap was very refreshing. They all sat around drinking the tea that Cassandra made and exchanging light conversation about Kingston culture. Ann was pleased to see Sara's ravenous appetite, especially given her earlier conversation with Cassandra.

After all the bun and cheese and tea were devoured, Thalia reminded Cassandra of her earlier promise to take them up into the mountains to witness a very special African ritual that was happening up in the hills at night. When Cassandra explained to Ann that it was a Pocomania ceremony, Ann got very excited, for she had been trying to go to one ever since she arrived.

"Since I seem to be the only one who has not engaged in some relaxing endeavor, sleep or sex and beyond," Thalia commented, "I hope that I will be able to hang tough tonight."

Cassandra reassured her that the singing and dancing at the ceremony would totally revitalize her. "Those drums are so powerful, even the dead will be awakened."

Hearing the term 'special African ritual' immediately sent up a red flag for Sara. She was sure that it was just another code name for some kind of pagan ritual. But since she enjoyed Cassandra's company, even though she perhaps was some kind of a witch, Sara decided to ask Jesus to accompany her and protect her from the devil, who she was sure was going to be there. She would try to remember to make the sign of the cross every time she felt anything blowing against her.

Dusk began to roll in as they packed into Cassandra's jeep. Ann sat in front with Cassandra, Thalia and Sara in back. Thalia began snoring within minutes of hitting the road.

Ann thanked Cassandra for being such a gracious host to her friends. "No need to thank me," Cassandra told her. "Thanks for bringing them back into my life. We are all ..."

Her sentence was cut short by a truck speeding around the corner. Cassandra slammed on her brakes. Luckily they were all wearing their seat belts. Cassandra yelled out to the driver to blow his horn next time.

"Bitch, shut up and drive yu car," he yelled back. "Yu the one who fi get blown, but by a real man."

Thalia jumped up from her sleep, "Are we in an accident?" she asked, appearing quite confused.

Cassandra reassured her that everything was okay.

"I was having a weird dream," Thalia remembered. "My mother appeared to me, surrounded by a beautiful, silvery white light. She told me she had some place to take me. I told her that I did not want to go, because I was not ready to die. That is when the jolt and the chatter awakened me. And spared my life, I might add. Something tells me that if she insisted, I would have followed her."

"Life is but an illusion, a dream." Cassandra said. "Maybe if we all awakened from the hell that we have created here on earth, we would come to realize that the spirits of all those we love are with us all the time." She looked into the rearview mirror and caught Cassandra's eyes. "It could very well be that you are dead and with her now but don't know it."

"Are you trying to tell me that I am just dreaming and that basically we are all dead, or should I say, all alive?" Thalia asked. "Come to think of it, I have had the experience a few times of not knowing if I was dead or alive. It felt like I was in a twilight zone."

"A few of my patients have described that phenomenon to me also," Ann said. "I think that it is some kind of psychic phenomenon."

"One of the things that I remember my mother telling me before she died was that I was born with the veil," Thalia said. She pointed to the holes in both her earlobes. "The elders in my adopted village in Africa told me that these holes mean that I can hear spirits."

"You probably can," Cassandra said. "Not only can I see ghosts, I can become one; I can exist in both states."

"This is the point at which I am going to sign out of the conversation," Sara announced, making the sign of the cross. Even though her Church frowned upon Catholicism, she felt certain that for the sake of using it to rebuke Satan, she would be forgiven.

"Go on, Cassandra," Thalia said. "Ignore our religious fanatic please."

"You can call me whatever," Sara said, "I'll be praying for you all on Judgment day. I am going back to sleep, so please wake me when we get there."

"Judgment Day or the ceremony?" Thalia joked.

"Sara, you have my permission to tune Thalia and myself out right now," Cassandra told her.

"I have, so don't mind me," Sara replied.

"So please go on," Thalia begged Cassandra.

"The times that I choose the death form are mostly when someone in the light tunnel is in limbo about whether or not they should leave their body, and their spirit asks mine for help. In that instance, I experience their death for them. I am then able to come back and share with them what I experienced. If the journey felt light and exhilarating, it means that they had accomplished their life plan and are ready to move to the next level. This is when they transition into their reunion with the All and decide whether or not to physically reincarnate into another lifetime experience or stay in spirit form. In that case, I do not discourage them from going on. However, if the journey felt heavy and laborious, it means that they are using death as an escape. They are choosing to die rather than deal with the life struggle they chose when they were deciding on this current lifetime. If they choose death as an escape, they will have to start all over again. They'll be stuck in the same place, struggling with the very lesson they are trying to avoid. A kind of rebirth back into the same karmic lesson. Regardless of the difficulty, the lesson must be learned before they can move to a higher plane.

"That is fascinating," Ann commented, glad that Sara had removed herself from the conversation. "What do you advise them to do in that case?"

"I never give advice," Cassandra said emphatically. "I just tell what I see. Only they have the power to make that choice."

Thalia couldn't help but wonder how one got in contact with Cassandra if and when the need arose. "Do you have spirit-mail wiring?" she joked, as she always did when she wanted to mask the intensity of what was happening to her.

"An s-mail," Ann joked.

"All that you have to do is store this knowledge in your soul, in the default drive," Cassandra replied. "It will automatically activate whenever you will it."

"Again, being Ms. Practical," Thalia continued, "In order to have this service, would I have had to have known you and had this conversation with you?"

"That's the surest way," Cassandra said. "But I can also creep into your unconscious, even if you are asleep. I can come in a dream, or I can just get absorbed through energy vibrations."

"Well, even though I know that Sara is feigning sleep, please lock it into her soul too," Thalia begged. She could not help but observe her tendency to worry incessantly about the women that she loved.

"Thalia, your Mom had been trying to tell you for the longest that she was okay, but you would not let her in," Cassandra said. "I am glad that you finally did."

"How do you know that?" Thalia asked. She was even more fascinated to figure out how Cassandra knew that she was thinking of her mother right at that moment; the woman who was taken from her so abruptly and so unfairly. "What did Ann tell you about my Mom."

"Nothing," Ann promised.

"Thalia, for now, just trust that I know these things," Cassandra said, a certain finality creeping into her voice. "When you are ready to hear it, I will be the first to let you know."

Upon that command, they all retreated into silence as the dark cloud of night surrounded them. Ann tried to block out the mysterious sounds that popped up ever so often. At one point, Ann was convinced that she saw spirits floating by. She felt as if her sanity was being tested. Perhaps she should have done what Sara did and checked out. Not wanting to worry her friends, she kept her psychosis to herself.

After what seemed like an eternity, Cassandra stopped and parked the jeep in front of a house with two red flags flying at the front gate.

They were greeted by two older women, dressed completely in white, except for a red band around their waists. The contrast between their charcoal jet-black skin and white garments was striking.

"Welcome to the barn yard, Miss Cassie," the elder and statelier looking woman said. "Wi greet your friends also. I name Imogene and mi witness by mi side here name is Ms. Pearl." She turned to the rest of them and said, "We always walk two bi two, and so should you when you enter the main house. Follow mi up to the house and then we will go outside and begin. We wus waiting for you, Miss Cassie before wi get started."

"I came as soon and as fast as I could, Miss Imogene" Cassandra apologized. "My friends and I are ready to partake and witness."

"Then follow us," Miss Imogene said. "And remember, stay two bi two." The two women led them up to the main house. A very strong, sweet odor overtook them. "What is this that I smell?" Ann inquired.

"Khus-khus oil," Miss Pearl replied. "We splash it all over the house before the merriment begin."

"What is the ceremony about?" Sara said, making the sign of the cross. She was surprised but comforted to see Ms. Pearl make the sign of the cross along with her. She hoped and prayed that this was not some trickery by the devil, trying to make her comfortable before he began to ride them all.

"You soon gwan see," Miss Pearl said. She took them out to the back of the house where all the others were gathered. There were about twenty women there; all dressed alike in white dresses and red sashes. There was a big feast laid out on a table off to the side with a roasted whole pig with eyes still intact on the head. Surrounding it were pots of boiled wild yams and bananas. And of course, several bottles of white rum and aerated water.

Ann noticed that there was only one man present, the drummer. She asked Cassandra why.

"This is an issue of womanhood, so it is a ceremony for women only," Cassandra explained. "The folks believe that only the ones who know the experience of having a child, should be present. It is only because they need drumming why they permit a man to be present. They believe that the greater strength of men make it easier for them to beat the drum at the high, vibratory frequency necessary to contact the spirit world."

"Why are they contacting the spirit world?" Thalia asked.

Cassandra explained that it was a very special and unusual occasion. "What you are going to witness is a belated attempt to try and get rid of a duppy spirit, a kind of spirit de-possession," she said. "A young girl has been inhabited and made barren by the spirit of her older brother who was a stillbirth. The story goes that the mother became very depressed when her son died that she forgot to hold the nine-night ceremony that was necessary to send him off to the spirit world. So he just hung around the house and kept her company. When she gave birth a year later to a girl, he entered this baby's body and has been said to be possessing her ever since."

Cassandra pointed to the center of the yard, "You can't see her yet, but she is lying on a mat in the middle of the circle that the women have formed. She is dressed in white, and beneath, her body is also painted in white." Cassandra further explained how earlier in the day, the elder women prepared the young girl as if she was going to get married. They took her to the river and bathed her. Then they took her back to the house and gave her a final balm-bath. Next, they massaged her entire body with khus-khus water, the same fragrance splashed all over the big house. Lastly, they banded her all the way from her head to her feet with a white sheet, and sprinkled her again with khus-khus oil.

Sara stared in bewilderment. She was not sure which she was more frightened of, the roasted pig looking at her or the talk of spirits flying loose. Just as she was about to insist that they leave, the drums got so loud, no one could hear her even if she opened her mouth and spoke.

The drummer began singing in an unknown tongue.

Cassandra asked Miss Imogene's permission for Ann, Thalia and Sara to join the circle. "So long as them don't never look back when we start walking. We don't want to fool the duppy and have him turn and come back."

Cassandra noticed that Sara was a bit hesitant, so she took her hand and asked her to be her witness. It was definitely too late now for her to turn back. Sara decided to stay in constant prayer.

Four of the women left the larger circle and formed a smaller one around the young girl. With her body still fully draped, they lifted her up and raised her toward the skies. They muttered what seemed like a short prayer, and then placed her back on the mat. The drum roared once again, even louder. All the women began to sing as the four women in the center drew a circle in the ground around the young girl and sprinkled white rice and white rum around her. All the while, during the invocation, the women in the outer circle took turns leading the singing.

At some point, Miss Pearl beckoned for silence. She looked down to the ground. "Lord, wi here to send one of your spirits back to you; take him please because the dead have no place among the living. Mr. Duppy, we have plenty food here for you as we lead you on your way back home; eat and full you belly." She walked around the young girl and spoke in an unknown tongue. Next she called for Miss Imogene, and together, they raised the young girl up by her arms and stood her on her feet. She was still covered in the white sheet.

The women lined up two by two behind Miss Imogene and Miss Pearl and formed a processional. Sara and Cassandra, Ann and Thalia went toward the back. Two women lit several kerosene lamps made from soda bottles and handed them out. They then lined up behind Sara and Cassandra and reminded them that no matter what, they should not look back.

The moon and stars were hidden behind a eerie bed of thick clouds; they made their way briskly through the still, dark night. Occasionally, a peenie-wally darted by, lighting up the night with its instant flashes of light. After going for about three miles, they came to an abrupt stop in front of a banana tree. It was loaded with several bunches of green bananas. They all gathered around as Miss Pearl and Imogene stood the young girl along the tree, her back leaning along the trunk. Suddenly, Miss Pearl picked up a machete from under the tree, and with one clean swoop, cut through the tree, right above the place where the young woman's head was touching. Pouring salt onto the ground, Miss Pearl cried out, "Duppy, a only here-so you fi live from now on; a put a pimento stick right here to mark your spot for you. Go play with the other duppy them that live out ya so. Don't ever come back."

Sara was scared so shitless, she forgot to sign. Her body began to shake. Cassandra squeezed her hands.

Miss Imogene and Miss Pearl took the sheet off the young girl while the other women chanted, "Percy, you set free now." Miss Imogene then gathered some of the liquid oozing from the cut tree and rubbed it on the young girl's forehead. Miss Pearl told her not to speak a word until the morning. Then, one of the women shouted out, "Koo-min-yah, Koo-min-yah, Koo-min-yah".

Thalia asked Ann what that phrase meant. Ann told her that it was an old Congolese word to describe the process of building a final resting place for the dead.

The exorcism over, they headed back. This time there was no drumming or chatter. The walk back was in silence, as a show of support and respect for Percy, who was forbidden to talk until the following day.

When they reached the house, Miss Imogene gave Percy a mug of Ganja tea, and sent her to bed. Miss Pearl invited them to stay and join the eating and celebration that was about to erupt. Sara insisted upon leaving. If she had to hire a ride back on her own she was going to, she just could not bare to be in Satan's presence any longer. Sara would not budge. Knowing that there would be no way for her to leave on her own, Cassandra apologized to their hosts for leaving. They said their thanks and good-byes, and headed back to the city.

The three women were all fused in silence during most of the ride back. Cassandra understood their need to process what they had experienced in their own way. Only when they neared the city did she ask, "Do we still want to go hear Spice's band, or should I take you home?"

Ann opted for going home. She felt totally drained like everyone else.

"Spice is not going to be happy, but I will just tell him to blame me," Cassandra said. "I had no idea that we were actually going to walk to the duppy's burial ground."

"Cassandra, in spite of the intensity of it all, I am very grateful that you took us," Thalia finally remarked. "It brought me right back to living in Africa. I had the honor of attending similar ceremonies for the dead in some of the remote villages."

"I am glad that I witnessed it too," Ann said. "It brought back memories of when I was a little girl still living here in Jamaica. My cousin Delroy and I used to love to go with my aunt to the nine-night ceremonies that were held in the country. We were not scared of duppies like the other kids. In fact, we used to do all kinds of crazy things to try and see them."

"While we were standing at the banana tree, my mother appeared to me again," Thalia told them. "She held my hands and told me to come take a walk with her. For some reason I was not afraid to touch her this time. When I would dream about her as a kid, I always used to wake myself up because I was afraid to have her touch me. This time, I stretched my hands out to her and she lifted me up. We began to float above the clouds. We landed in a mountain that I recognized as the one overlooking the caves at Duncan. I saw myself being led by some of the village people to a tree. They told me that this was the tree of life; that in it was to be found the cure for many of our illnesses. They said that if I found a way to have people ingest its succulent leaves just as it was picked, it would help them build up their immunity to fight off many diseases."

"So when are you going to get to your true vocation?" Cassandra asked her.

"You are not suggesting that Thalia give up her medical career to follow some crazy dream to become a herbal witchdoctor, are you?" Sara had heard all she wanted to for one night.

"Yes I am," Cassandra said. "Many of the great advances in science occurred to people when they were in dream states."

"Then get to it Thalia," Sara said without conviction and in a very sarcastic tone. Maybe that would be her punishment for living a life without Christ. "Start looking for your tree." She wondered if all three women would end up with apple trees. Drifting off to sleep a few minutes later, she wondered what form their serpents would take.

It was very late when they arrived back at Ann's place, so Ann insisted that Cassandra spend the night. Cassandra agreed, hoping that Spice would figure out where she was. She did not want him to be worried when he got home and she was not there.

8
Saturday

Ann was awakened at dawn by the sound of the telephone ringing—the guard at the front gate calling to announce that she had a visitor.

She quickly threw on her robe and went downstairs. Upon opening the door, she barely recognized the man standing in front of her—bloodshot eyes reflecting the rising sun and clothes mimicking his come-feel-me-up untamed hair.

"Where's Auntie?" He asked, looking past her, speech loud and slurred.

"My god, Spice, what's wrong?"

"What the fuck do you care!" he hollered, stunning her sleeping senses with the stench of stale alcohol emanating from his breath. "Whey mi aunt deh?"

Ann was speechless, dumbfounded by his foul language and abrupt dismissal. It must be the alcohol that had set up a barricade between them—not allowing any of her love in, or any of his out, she thought. Or worse yet, an alien intruder had taken up residence in the man who, in less than a week, had gently pried her heart space open.

"Yu not goin answer mi?" His onslaught continued. "Mi jus want know if she dey ya or not; mi come fi get mi keys from her so that mi can get into mi house."

SATURDAY

Barely able to get the words out, Ann pointed to the den. "She's sleeping in there. Let me get her."

"Mi nuh need no help," he retorted, brushing her aside.

As he staggered past her, he bumped into the sofa and landed on top of it. Ann rushed to his aid, however he brusquely motioned her away, got up, and continued toward the den. Ann hurried back to the front door and locked it. There was no way that she was going to let him get back behind the wheel. But she knew that she had to be strategic, so as not to add any more fuel to his drunken fire. Feeling a bit mystified, she inhaled deeply, braced her shoulders and made her way back to the den; as resolutely as she could.

When she entered the room, Spice was standing over Cassandra and shaking her as she lay sleeping on the sofa bed. "Wey mi keys deh?" he prodded.

"Spice, why you bothering mi so early in the morning? What's gotten into you?" Cassandra sat up, reluctantly opening her eyes. No response was necessary. Similar to Ann's experience, she too was immediately assaulted by his intoxicated breath.

"Come on man Auntie, you know you have mi keys," he continued to shake her.

"Spice, get a hold of yourself!" Cassandra advised, holding his arms firmly. She couldn't recall ever seeing him tipsy, much less drunk and disorderly.

"Auntie, mi nuh want any lectures, just mi keys," he yelled, pointing his finger at her.

"Bwai, that don't give you no right to come in here trying to man-handle mi," Cassandra scolded him.

"I waited and waited ..." His voice began to trail off.

"I'm sorry that I forgot to bring your keys back to you last night, Spice," Cassandra apologized. "But you knew where to come and get them."

"Mi just tired and need to go to mi bed," he replied, a hint of contrition beginning to creep into his voice, now several decibels lower. Or was it fatigue?

"Then you better lay down beside mi right here 'cause there's no way I goin let you drive in your condition," Cassandra replied, voice stern and unrelenting. Ann let out a sigh of relief, happy that the admonishment was coming from his aunt and not her.

Spice sat down beside Cassandra. "I don't get any respect from you ladies, do I?" he asked, reverting to the Queen's English. "First, you lie and say you coming to the club last night; and now, you refusing to let me go home and get some peace and quiet." He shook his head in defeat.

Seeing the bend in his attitude, Ann seized the moment. She walked over from where she was standing in the doorway and went and sat beside him. "Spice, it's all my fault," she apologized, taking the full rap. "I was so exhausted after the ceremony up in the hills last night, I went straight to bed when we came home."

"Which is where your man was also hoping to be," he responded. "But no man, he got kicked to the curb, left stranded, waiting in vain."

Cassandra smiled, recognizing Spice's veiled attempt at working them. He always tried to collect as much pity mileage as he could; even before he could barely talk.

Ann smiled, sensing that the love energy had broken through and was flowing once more. "How can I make it up to you?" she asked penitently, placing a light kiss on his forehead.

Spice smiled, he too seizing the moment. "It is never too late to invite a wounded soldier of love into your bed," he suggested, planting a kiss on her lips. "Come give me some sweet making-up love to make the hurt go away." he licked his lips. "All I need is a spoonfull of sugar to make the medicine go down."

Ann smiled again, realizing just how much of a Jamaican man Spice was. Her experiences, both professionally and personally since she had been back were teaching her that no matter how incapacitated Jamaican men were, most were always willing to trod the pussy trail, even if it required that they limp on all fours!

"My bed is ready and waiting," Ann informed him, noting that his drunken rage had now evaporated into a drunken stupor.

Spice began to drift into a drunken nod. Cassandra shook her head up and down in her victory bob, glad that the struggle was over. It would only be a matter of minutes before he would be fast asleep; as she also hoped to be.

Ann and Cassandra stood up and helped Spice to his feet. They placed his arms over their shoulders and led him up the stairs to Ann's room. A few stumbles and near falls later, they deposited him onto the bed. Before they could finish taking off his shoes, he was fast asleep and snoring.

"I hope you don't mind if I lay right here and finish sleeping?" Cassandra asked as she flopped down on the bed beside Spice. "I really don't have the energy to go back downstairs. Spice is some heavy."

"My bed is yours too, Auntie," Ann wisecracked.

"You going to lie down too?" Cassandra asked.

"Not right now," Ann replied. "I am wide awake like a morning rooster."

"Unlike you, I'm a night owl," Cassandra said. "I am definitely not a morning person. I need my sleep." With that she rolled over, reached for the cover and pulled it over her and Spice both.

Remembering that Sara had been getting up quite early in the mornings too, Ann decided to go and see if all the commotion had awakened her. Sara had blamed her sleep difficulties on her surgeon hours and jet lag, however Ann felt that her marital stress was also a part of the equation.

Sure enough, when Ann popped her head into the guest bedroom, Sara was awake, sitting on her bed and staring at the door. "What was all that ruckus about?" she queried in as calm a voice as she could, hoping that Ann would not sense her inner terror.

Ann went and sat next to her and explained all that had happened. "If I were you, I would be lying right there next to my man," Sara responded. "He needs to know that you are there for him through thick and thin."

"So do you," Ann piped back. "And, you're awake; he's asleep."

"But I don't have what he got to make it all worthwhile in the end," Sara giggled. "Trust me, there is nothing sweeter than morning dick, girl; especially with a little booze on board." As soon as the words were out of her mouth, Sara regretted them. She did not want to stir up anymore of those old memories, especially now that they were right there under the surface. She needed to heed her pastor's counseling and work hard to bury her sinful past. She did not want to be haunted anymore by those earlier times when she had allowed herself to act like Eve, tempting and seducing men to come eat from her tree; come taste her apple.

"A little booze! If' that's the case, then he cannot hold his liquor," Ann exclaimed, blocking Sara's travels through the Garden of Eden. "Girl, Spice is so drunk, he couldn't get it up if all three of us went in there and ran around naked."

They both burst out in laughter. Ann was delighted to see that the empty, vacant stare that had taken up residence in Sara's eyes ever since the trip to the falls in Ocho Rios was beginning to recede. Her mood also seemed less numbed.

Suddenly, without any warning whatsoever, Sara's mirth abruptly switched to grief. "I don't know why I am doing this," she sobbed.

"Don't worry about why, right now Sara, just let your feelings flow." Ann wondered if telling Sara about Spice's drunken behavior had brought back painful memories of her abuse. Knowing that what Sara needed most was a nurturing and healing touch, Ann reached over and embraced her. She rested Sara's head upon her shoulders and asked the universe to use her as a channel to infuse and surround Sara with pure and divine love energy.

The light from the rising sun had just begun to seep into the room. Outside, the birds were busily engaged in their early morning calls. Rocking to the rhythm of Sara's heaving body, Ann found herself humming the nursery rhyme that she so oftentimes sang to her baby girl when she needed comforting: "Hush little baby don't you cry, Momma's gonna sing you a lullaby. And if the lullaby don't rhyme, Momma's gonna buy you the gift of time. And if time don't run away, maybe you will live another day." Those times with Ahsima always validated her belief that a mother's greatest duty, indeed, her highest calling, was to protect her young.

"It felt good to have you hold me," Sara remarked after her tears had slowed. "Hearing your heart beat next to mine made me feel very safe." Sara then pulled away from Ann's embrace and recoiled into the fetal position. Watching Sara curled in her primal innocence, the mother in Ann came face to face with Sara's child. Ann realized that what the wounded little girl still living inside Sara was searching for was someone to protect her; a task that her mother had been incapable of doing. With that realization, Ann felt herself being filled with unconditional love for Sara. She vowed then to love her fiercely and without judgment, from that moment forward.

Feeling the need to hold Sara once again, Ann laid down behind her, with her front lightly touching Sara's back. Ann then slipped one hand under her body and the other around Sara's shoulder. She wanted to make sure that Sara could still feel and hear her heart beating.

The silence eventually awakened Thalia. As soon as she opened her eyes fully and was sufficiently alert, she sensed the depth of the vibrations permeating the room. Feeling a need to share in the love that seemed to be flowing so freely around them, Thalia got up from her sofa bed and went over and lay next to Ann, adding another layer to their spoon. As all three women lay together on the full-sized bed, their bodies touched cloth to cloth in most places, skin-to-skin in some and bone-to-bone in others. They felt reassured by the feel of their frames against each other and by the familiar warmth of their physical closeness. Ann, Sara, and Thalia were finally together again in step. They were inseparable in their awareness that they were coming to the end of their reunion on the island, but the beginning once more of a lifetime of connectivity. Contentedly they lay crunched up against each other, motionless except for the breath, as one might imagine triplets in their mother's womb. Thalia drifted back into sleep again, joyful that she was sharing deep intimacy with women again without it being sexualized.

Ann was the first to wake up, hours later. She got up slowly, trying to slip from between Sara and Thalia without disturbing them. But as she sat up, the mattress shifted under her weight and they both stirred.

"Don't get up sleepy-heads, I'm just going to check on Spice."

"I hope he slept off that liquor," Sara said bubbly, her earlier blues nowhere in sight.

They heard a loud rumbling. Thalia burst into embarrassed laughter.

"Thalia! Is that your stomach?" Sara asked.

"You know it. I'm getting up. Ann, where are you taking us for breakfast."

Ann looked at the clock; it was almost noon.

"Girl, breakfast? It's lunchtime. Let me check on my man and I'll be right back."

Ann left Thalia and Sara to get dressed. When she went into her bedroom, Cassandra and Spice were still sprawled across the bed. Ann tapped her lightly.

"How did this happen?" Cassandra asked as she rubbed her eyes open. "How did I end up in your bed with this ugly nephew of mine."

"Do I hear someone calling me ugly?" Spice said, opening his eyes.

"Of course not, pretty bwai," Ann said.

"How come Auntie is in the bed and you are not?" he asked, looking around. "It should be the other way around."

"Let's see what you've got there that you don't want me to see," Cassandra teased, reaching over and motioning as if she were going to pull off his covers.

"I'm warning you," Spice said, "that's for my woman's eyes, and hers only."

"Bwai, I used to change your dirty diapers," Cassandra said. "Don't let me tell your secrets."

"I want to hear them all," Ann said, going and cuddling next to Spice. "But right now I have two hungry girlfriends to feed."

"How's your head?" Cassandra asked with motherly concern.

Spice stole a sheepish glance at Ann. "Which one?"

"You better use the one up top to work your way out of this mess," Cassandra warned him. "And by the way, when did you become such a boozer?"

"You know that I hardly drink," Spice replied. "This is the first in a very long time that I have ever been this drunk." He turned toward Ann with another of his beguiling grins. "Mi know yu less than a week and yu drive mi to the bottle already!"

"Spice, you better start taking some responsibility for your actions," Ann halfheartedly scolded him, all the while running her hands through his locks. "This is the last time that I am going to apologize for not showing up last night," Ann said, planting a kiss on his lips. "I really did want to be there."

"You should have. The ladies were swarming. I needed a shield," Spice boasted.

"Are you trying to blame your bad behavior on Ann?" Cassandra asked, noting the downturn in Ann's countenance.

"Whose arms and whose bed am I in right now?" he turned to Ann trying to set her mind at ease.

But Ann was not totally reassured.

She began rising off the bed, but Spice caught her arm, sensing her unrest. "In case you're wondering, no, I don't usually drink like I did last night. All these years on the circuit have taught me how to drink nice and easy. Last night though," he paused, "I did try and numb myself a little."

"Not the most reassuring thing to tell a psychiatrist."

He smiled agreeing. "Not saying I use it to cover my emotions either. I think you know by now I have no problem speaking from the heart."

Ann had to agree on that.

"Still it was ugly, I know. I'll keep myself in check next time."

Ann gave a small smile. She got up and took a few deep breaths. Spice had misread her real bone of contention. She didn't want him to realize before she could reestablish her grounding, so as not to lapse into jealousy. Luckily, before she had to say anything else, Sara and Thalia burst into the room.

"So, where is Mr. Spice taking us to eat?" Sara asked coyly.

"I know the perfect spot. A not-so-classy, but oh-so-tasty joint owned by a friend of mine's family. If you ladies will give me one second to kiss this beautiful redhead and freshen up, we'll be on our way."

"Or maybe you should reverse the order," Ann said, a hint of sarcasm tainting her usual goddess voice. "Freshen up then kiss!"

The chill sent them all on their way. Thalia and Sara went downstairs to make coffee while Cassandra went to the bathroom. Ann did not pry any further into Spice's deeds or misdeeds, and he volunteered no further information. Silence crept in between and around their egos to protect any further hurt.

After everyone was dressed, they packed into Spice's jeep and headed for downtown Kingston. The energy was still a bit polite, so Cassandra suggested music. Spice volunteered his soon to be released CD, explaining that it was a jazz journey chronicling varying Jamaican genres—from the more traditional folk and mento sounds, to the more popular ska, rock-steady and reggae.

"You are such a jazz aficionado, do you know Lee Coleman?" Thalia ventured, when the CD was finished.

"I've not met her in person, but I am a big fan," he told her. "She is one of the best jazz singers on the scene right now."

"That's her girlfriend," Sara blurted out.

"So then an intro should be no problem?"

"No problem man," Thalia replied, ignoring Sara.

Minutes later, Spice stopped the car and announced that they had arrived. He pointed to the restaurant.

"You're right about this being a hole in the wall," Sara commented, not wanting to get out. "Isn't it a bit dangerous around here?" The surroundings surely fit the profile of the crime-infested neighborhoods she had read about in the travel advisory. All the buildings were decrepit and dilapidated. Several were boarded up. The street was swarming with equally frightening people, talking in a language that she could not decipher.

"My best friend's father owns this restaurant," Spice reassured her. "I am a regular here; the folks look out for me and protect me all the time." Ann got out of the car quickly, ignoring his dash to open the door for her. So instead, he opened the back door. Sara did not release her hand from his when he helped her out; she was still frightened. He escorted her toward the restaurant. Cassandra, Thalia and Ann followed slightly behind. They were not afraid.

It was very evident that Spice indeed was a popular man in town. Folks hailed him from the moment they got out of the car until they got inside. Thalia commented on his celebrity status, but he quickly brushed it aside, "On a small island like this, it is easy to seem like a big fish."

Spice walked them all the way to the back into the office and introduced them to the owner, Mr. Chin. He welcomed them and thanked Spice for gracing his establishment with his friends. He called for a very attractive, young, cocoa-hued waitress, Rita, and told her to seat them in the most private spot in the back of the restaurant. On their way out, he admonished her to take good care of his very special guests. "You don't have to tell mi that sir," she said, flashing him a most endearing smile. "I always take good care of everybody, especially my regular customers."

After they were seated, she brought them menus. "Mr. Chandler, you going to have your usual stewed fish, or you going to change up today?" she asked.

Ann quickly picked up the double entendre.

"Rita," Spice replied, trying to play it off. "I am going to have whatever the red-headed lady orders."

As could be expected, she got to Ann last. "What would you recommend?"

"If I was you, I would have the stewed peas and rice," she replied. "Mr. Chandler eats that sometimes when we run out of the fish."

Ann admired her persistence. "Then that's what we will have," Ann said, winking at her. Unhurriedly, she walked away, purposely assuring that every move she made displayed her voluptuous curves.

"The day when women stop using their bodies as missiles is the day they will start loving themselves," Cassandra said.

Sara shuddered and put her hand to her head as if she was distraught.

"Sara, what's wrong?" Spice asked.

"Oh nothing, that white woman over there talking with that guy reminds me of what my husband Don is up to while I'm here on vacation. She is brave indeed to come to such an out-of-the way dive like this to hit on a black man."

Spice laughed hard. "I didn't even see them."

"What's so funny, Spice?"

"That's the last man that's going to be taken in by a white woman's charms. That's the man who schooled me when I was dating white women."

"You too?" Sara asked in disgust.

"Sure. Years ago, when I was living in England I dated white women.

"I'm sure that your fitting the stereotype of the tall, dark, handsome, dread-locked entertainer made you very attractive to them," Ann said. "They tend to like your type."

"I guess," Spice shrugged.

"Truth is nowadays, they go after all types, just so long as they have a big, black dick and money," Sara said.

"Sara, I don't think there's been a day in your life when you weren't talking about dick," Thalia teased.

"Be quiet," Sara said. "You don't want to admit that you are missing them. There is but so much fingers and tongues can do."

"If we weren't in public, I would show you what tongues and fingers could do. You would soon forget those big sticks and be moaning for soft, fleshy stuff."

"Thalia," Spice said, "You and I obviously like the same things."

"Thalia, I can't believe you said that," Sara said playing the innocent.

"Girlfriend," Cassandra said, "you started it."

"Well, I hope the food is coming so we can do something more important with our mouths. I'm starving. What's taking so long?" Sara moaned.

"You should know by now that we operate on island time here," Cassandra reminded her.

"The white lady has her food," Sara snapped.

They all looked over to see the waitress placing a plate of steaming food in front of the white woman. The brother talking to her stood up, shook her hand and walked toward them.

Spice stood up. "Kalamu!" he said. "I was waiting 'til you got done with your customer before I called you over."

As he approached their table, Kalamu's six-foot plus, statuesque strides reminded Thalia of Africa's finest Masai warriors. His finely chiseled, clean-shaven face and bald-head set him apart from the local men they had seen thus far. And upon closer examination, so did his Asian eyes. He shook Sara's hand as Spice introduced them. He paused with Thalia. His stare stripped her naked as he bent over her outstretched hand and kissed her fingers. The feel of his mouth against her skin landed her right back into the arms of Nala, the doctor whom she briefly dated before she left Africa.

"Aha, so you must be the famous redhead," Kalamu said when Spice introduced Ann.

"The one and only," Spice responded to Ann's pleased smile.

"Now I see why you were not answering your cell," Kalamu said to Spice. "I wouldn't want to be found either."

"Blame it on these three incredibly wonderful women," Spice said as he sat down.

"Men!" Cassandra said. "Always quick to jump at new raw meat and forget the old seasoned one."

"I meant to say four," Spice apologized.

"Women!" Kalamu rebutted. "They only show signs of caring when they think you are jumping ship."

"Wishful thinking, my dear fellows," Cassandra replied. "I am much more interested in the affection of these three incredibly wonderful women."

"And fellows," Sara added, "You have to come through her to get with any one of us."

"Why don't you pull up a chair and join us," Thalia suggested to Kalamu, ignoring Sara's newly invented policy.

"I have to follow orders and ask for Madam's blessings," he responded, bowing deferentially in Cassandra's direction.

"More likely our friendly waitress," Cassandra said. "She has been blowing us ice ever since we walked in."

"She doesn't welcome more than one attractive woman in her lair," Spice joked. "One, she being it, is definitely her winning number." Ann silently wondered if any part of his comments were meant for her.

"Yeah, Cass, you Jamaican sistren are definitely very catty," Kalamu said. "You all spray territory that don't even belong to you."

"When they have their scent on you, it's just a matter of time, as they see it," Spice continued. He and Kalamu gave each other the cannot-help-but-be-defeated-by-pussy-power look that is reserved for men only as they burst into laughter.

Kalamu pulled up a chair next to Thalia. He called out to Rita to bring them an order of fried bammy for starters, and each a cold Red Stripe beer. "Didn't Daddy tell you that you have to smile with all the customers, not just the men?" Kalamu winked at her, reaching out to hold her hands. She rolled her eyes and sucked her teeth, as she pulled away.

"Now that's a Jamaican woman for you," Cassandra said. "She can control a man just like she can a child—with the look, and the look only." Kalamu lowered his eyes in silence.

"Kalamu, Spice told us that Mr. Chin is your Dad," Ann piped in, trying to change the subject, and the mood. He shook his head affirmatively.

"So you are what is referred to here in Jamaica as half Chinese, aren't you?" Even though Kalamu hated to get into discussions about his racial background, for he oftentimes found it a way of diluting his ethnicity, he welcomed the diversion. He did not want to be put on the hot seat in regards to Rita's behavior.

"A bit hard to see, isn't it?" Kalamu replied. "Other than my eyes, it is hard to tell I have any Asian blood."

"And your hair when you let it grow," Spice reminded him.

"You can tell that my mother had some serious, black genes; they just about knocked Daddy's to the curb. Look how dark and tall I am." And handsome, Thalia wanted to add. Mr. Chin walked over toward them. "You calling mi, K?" he asked. "No, I was just telling my friends here about how you and your brother came to own this joint," Kalamu fibbed.

"What I admire about Kalamu's Chinese family is that they see themselves as Jamaicans, first and foremost," Spice remarked when Mr. Chin left.

"But dem must," Kalamu said. "As soon as dem open dem mouth, you know sey dat them come straight from right ya-so," he added in patois.

"How did they get here?" Ann asked Kalamu, curious to learn more about the Chinese migration to Jamaica.

Kalamu schooled them on the post-slavery arrival of the Chinese in Jamaica to work as indentured laborers. And the arrival of the second wave again in the 1900s when several ran away from communism in China. He flavored the history lesson with his own socio-cultural and political analysis: "For a long time the Chinese kept to themselves, not assimilating into the local Jamaican culture, except as was necessary to maintain their success as food merchants. They maintained their own parallel social, religious and educational institutions for the longest. It wasn't until the mid-1960s during an insurgence in Kingston in which local blacks revolted against Chinese shopkeepers that the issue of Chinese Jamaican loyalty and citizenship was brought to a head. Quite a bit of progress was made. Unfortunately, in the 70s, many Chinese families emigrated to Miami and Canada, fearing economic annihilation under Manley's socialist doctrine."

"Why didn't your father leave?" Thalia asked.

"The fact that my father married black and stayed married to my mother for thirty plus years until her death is the best reason that I can think of," Kalamu stated. "Most of his kind just had affairs and children with black women."

"Like the French did in Louisiana," Ann remarked.

"Why don't we broaden that concept and say like most European men did throughout the entire diaspora," Thalia remarked.

"So you see Thalia, your Dad wasn't so bad after all," Sara remarked. "He too married your Mom."

"Not bad, but not good enough." Thalia refused to totally forgive him. "Unlike Kalamu's Dad, he didn't hang around for the long haul."

"Not to change the subject, but where are you from, Thalia?" Kalamu asked.

SATURDAY

"I was born in New York, and I now live in DC."

"I did my undergraduate degree in New York before going to England," Kalamu replied. "I wish I would have met you then."

"Puleeze," Ann jumped in. "Like many so-called mixed race Jamaicans, you probably would be hanging around with the white folks in America."

"Ann, you are forgetting that Thalia can pass," Sara added.

"Sara, please let this gentleman know right now that you are kidding," Thalia insisted.

"She doesn't have to," he said tenderly. He reached over and rubbed her arms reassuringly, "I know a sistah when I see one, and you are definitely one hundred percent."

"Thank you," Thalia beamed, giving Sara a little snicker. "And you are obviously a one hundred percent and more brother."

"I man transcend all race and creed; I ain't no mongrel Cablanasian. I am a full-blooded Rastaman; yu overstand!" Thalia could feel Bob Marley's wisdom emanating from his being. "All this mixed race bullshit is being used as a divisive tool to create disunity and chaos among us," he continued to reason, but now slipping out of his rasta lingo. "It keeps us fighting among ourselves for the spoils."

"I choose to affirm myself as a black woman each day," Thalia said. "It is an active process that I am very proud of!"

"That's right, we have to be active in our own self-definition," Kalamu agreed. "We cannot allow the point of view of the white man's history about race to label who we are. His is a history meant to denigrate us, and in so doing justify their abominable and inexcusable behaviors toward us. Truth is, race is not a biologic reality; just a sociopolitical construct."

"Right on," Cassandra said, raising her fisted hand in the black power gesture.

Kalamu was about to add something when Thalia excitedly interrupted, "Stick a pin in it for a minute, I think I see our food coming."

"Surprise, surprise. I don't see the waitress," Sara said. They all burst out laughing.

Mr. Chin brought the food to their table himself. The aromas and vapors that greeted them were sheer gastronomic bliss. He did not explain Rita's absence, and no one cared to ask. Cassandra called upon the goddess Nut to purify and sanctify their meal—Thalia's lo mein with curried goat, Spice and Ann's stewed peas and black mushrooms over Jasmine rice, and Sara and Kalamu's steamed fish in oyster sauce. She asked that it not only nourish their bodies, but fill them with the sacred grace of the universe.

Once they took the first bite, the previously animated conversation was rapidly pushed to a backseat. Only an occasional comment on how good everything was, and a few "could I try some of yours?" could be heard. "This Jamaican/Chinese fusion is definitely slamming," Thalia remarked after all their plates were empty.

"Are we talking about food or ..." Sara asked teasingly.

"Look at how we cleaned the plates," Ann remarked, quickly changing the subject again. "We black folks certainly don't mix food and chatter."

"That's for sure," Thalia agreed. "We sure gave new meaning to the concept of not being able to do two things at a time."

"By the looks of it, you are doing just fine in the juggling department, Ms. Thalia," Sara continued to rib her.

Ann again diverted them from what was sure to be another discussion of Thalia's sexuality. "Guys, how and where did you meet?" she asked.

"We met in England. I was living there and Kalamu, who at that time was Vincent Chin, was doing his PhD in Anthropology at Cambridge."

"Anthropology, wow. That's a nontraditional choice. What was the topic of your dissertation?" Thalia asked.

Kalamu paused as a young Jamaican fellow came and removed the emptied dishes. Sara and Thalia exchanged smiles again at Rita's continued absence, but said nothing as Kalamu continued.

"First off, I chose anthropology, because as I see it, it is the truest form of the history of a people. I want to tell my people their true stories; especially those that can use our past grandeur to restore us to present power. My dissertation looked at the linkages between ancient Egyptology and the Middle Passage. Recently though, since I have gotten back to Jamaica, I have been focusing on the history of maroons. It is a history and herstory that you will not find in any of the classic textbooks." He looked toward Spice and continued, "So here Spice and I are, reconnected again."

"Yes and I have to listen to him blab about his intellectual aspirations all over again, but it's worth it. If I pretend to listen to his anthropological theories, he'll agree to play with my band. He's an amazing musician. In fact, he played congo drums on several of the cuts on the new CD."

"Multi-talented, hmmm," Thalia remarked. "Going back to your fascinating studies, who are the maroons?" She needed to return to intellectual territory and away from where her passions were trying to take her; deep into her lower chakras.

"They are the West African warriors who were captured by the slave traders, but were never enslaved," Kalamu explained. "From the moment they got on those ships and realized that they had been tricked by the white traders, they fought their way to freedom. The slave traders could not wait to get to land to get them off the ships. They immediately escaped into the hills and set up their own communities."

"Kalamu has a house in the hills close to the sites of the old maroon settlements," Spice said.

"Why don't you all drive up and visit? It's beautiful," Kalamu offered.

"Not so fast man, we already have plans," Cassandra said pinching Kalamu in the arm.

"Cassandra's taking us to a river up in the mountains."

"I'm hurt," Kalamu said. "But if you care at all about my wounded heart, you'll come to the club later on. I'm sitting in with Spice's band. I'd be inspired by such beauty in the audience."

"We can do that," Thalia said eagerly. "Right Sara? Ann?" The women gave the men their assurances.

A subdued Rita brought the bill to Spice. She asked if anyone wanted anything else without making eye contact. They refused and she placed the bill in front of Spice, turned on her heel and swished quickly away. Thalia grabbed the bill from in front of him and would not allow him to pay it.

"I can see that feminism is far away from these shores," she commented in response to Spice's insistence that he should have been the one to pay, as she carefully counted out the Jamaican dollars and left them on top of the bill.

When they went to the back to say goodbye to Mr. Chin, he handed Cassandra a couple bottles of freshly squeezed cane juice. Cassandra informed them that cane juice was very good for balancing the nerves, which is why she got her weekly supply from one of Mr. Chin's vendors. Sara asked to have some, acting as if she had forgotten that she turned her nose up at it when Ann bought her some in Negril.

Since it had gotten pretty late, Spice agreed to let Cassandra use his jeep for the trip to the mountains. This way, she did not have to go back to Ann's to get her car. He would hang with Kalamu for the rest of the evening until they both went to the club.

The men accompanied the women to the jeep. Kalamu opened the door for Sara and Thalia. While Sara climbed in, Kalamu slipped his card into Thalia's hands; she put it away quickly, hoping that the other women did not see. Before she made it to the jeep, Spice took Ann aside and said to her, "You better show up tonight, woman."

"Will I hear my song tonight if I do?"

"If you show up, you'll hear it after the set. It's a work in progress."

She kissed him lightly on the cheeks. "Make sure you clear out the best seats in the club because we will definitely be there."

Kalamu and Spice headed to Kalamu's car. Cassandra climbed into the driver's seat of Spice's jeep. As soon as they drove off, Sara began questioning Thalia about her flirtations with Kalamu. "Just a few hours earlier you told me that only pussy turned you on."

"Correct," Thalia rebutted "That's how I felt then; but this is how I feel now."

Sara gave her a quizzical look. "Now, I am totally confused."

"You think you are the one confused!" Thalia exclaimed.

"What did you feel with him?" Ann asked.

"I felt something special between us, but the situation is just not right," Thalia responded.

"And what about your feelings for Lee?" Ann continued.

"Still strong," Thalia admitted. "Which is why the situation is not right, at least not for now. That does not stop me from being attracted to him though." Thalia was silent for a while, before continuing, "Maybe my attraction to Kalamu has given me permission to not lock myself into too rigid a definition of my sexuality."

"Maybe it's good that you decided to take it slow with Lee for right now," Cassandra reminded her.

"Maybe seems to be the magic word right now, doesn't it?" Ann surmised. "It may be Thalia that you are just a lesbian who is in denial. Or it may be that you are a bisexual and are just now discovering your homosexual pole. Or it may be that you are a hot-blooded heterosexual who is just having a lesbian affair."

"The good news is that you don't have to figure it all out just yet," Cassandra told her.

"Amen," Thalia said, "Hear that, Sara. Stop riding me."

"Wishful thinking," Sara shot back. "But, not to worry, I am going to take my usual afternoon nap." With that, she rested her head on the seat rest and closed her eyes.

Ann was happy to see glimpses of the old Sara emerging—the light-hearted and quick witted Sara that she first met in medical school. The Sara that could always be counted upon to have a twisted sense of humor.

The drive up the mountains to Irish Town was steep and tortuous. As they zigzagged their way up the mountain road, Cassandra pointed out some of the magnificent views of the Kingston Bay down below. As had become the norm on all their trips throughout the countryside, a melee of scintillating sights and colors waylaid them: the always stately, blazing-red Poinciana trees; the jambalaya of multicolored bougainvilleas and hibiscus; and the wild and freely growing yellow daisies, green lilies, blue jades and irises, and violet and purple pansies.

Thalia was especially moved at the sight of the country women walking up the hill with items on their heads. She loved the humble strength that they exuded. Their bodies were just as sculpted and fit as the African women whose gracefulness she fell in love with when she lived in Kenya. Once again, these little snippets of rural Jamaican life were so reminiscent of her years in Africa. "It's so wonderful that these mountain people are shielded from much of the negative influences of Western society."

"Unfortunately, they also miss out on some of the positive technological ones," Ann remarked.

They finally arrived at their destination after endless sharp turns, few of which almost landed them head on with the approaching cars. Cassandra parked in front of a food shop where several people had congregated. When the women got out of the car, several onlookers rushed up to say hello to Cassandra. Their dialogue was so heavily accented with Jamaican patois, Sara and Thalia could not understand a word of the conversation; even Ann had to struggle to keep up.

Cassandra explained that this was the village where her mother was born and raised. "Mama brought us here very often because she hated her life in Kingston."

"Why was that?" Ann asked.

"The society women in Kingston shunned her," Cassandra explained. "You see, my dad, who came from a very wealthy mulatto family, left his upper class wife and married my mother. It caused quite a stir. In those days, men like my father just kept lower class black women as their mistresses; they never married them. But my dad, noble soul that he was, divorced his wife and married mom when he found out she was pregnant. She went on to bear him two more."

"Did he have any children with his former wife?" Ann asked.

"No," Cassandra replied. "I am sure that is one of the reasons why he left, because he always loved and wanted children. I am his first daughter. Like I mentioned yesterday, my brother, Spice's Dad, is the first child. Our younger brother was killed in a motorbike accident several years ago."

They walked for about a mile down a hillside dirt road to the valley below. On the way down, Cassandra conversed with several more folks. They all invited her and her companions into their homes for a bite to eat and drink, but Cassandra declined with a quick "we jus' eat."

They eventually made their way to a very lush and densely wooded area at the turn in the road. A feathery, hissing sound alerted them to flowing water close by. "Whenever I approach this river, the anticipation of all that is to unfold always gets me excited," Cassandra told them.

They climbed over a wall made of stone and crossed some very tall underbrush, before they finally caught their first glimpse of the river, snaking her way through the verdant foothills. Similar to Emerald Key, every possible variation on the color green, from pale mint to dark hunter's green was on display.

"My mother used to bring me here almost every Sunday," Cassandra told them, stopping for a while along the bank. "She buried our navel strings right here along the riverbank. She wanted the water spirit Yemoja to always watch over her children." Cassandra pointed to her mother's grave close by and invited them to join her in paying her respect. "She loved this place so much we buried her here. Before I go to the river, I always visit her. Please join me; my mother is a very open and loving spirit. She loves meeting new friends."

Sara picked a few wild daisies and handed them to Cassandra. "Cass, I don't think I'm up to it right this moment. Please place these on the grave for me." She walked away from the others and found a large rock to rest on.

Ann felt a rush of maternal love for Sara, similar to earlier in the morning. It was clear to her that Sara's mother's inability to protect Sara from abuse had been the source of Sara's inability to trust women. Ann could see how, in order to compensate for the loss, Sara did everything in her power to ensure that she never had to depend on women, even though deep inside what she most yearned for was closeness. So to protect herself from the engulfment she felt if women got too close to her, or the abandonment that she felt when they stayed their distance, she either drove them away before she felt too attached, or denigrated and devalued them when they went away.

Before leaving to catch up with Thalia and Cassandra, Ann ran over to Sara and gave her a big hug. She asked her to say a prayer for them all.

SATURDAY

At the grave, Cassandra reached into her backpack for a bottle. "We must first offer libations to our ancestors, those wise souls who can show us the way of Light," she said. She poured the spirits over the tombstone: *'Louise Mary Mouton, 1937-1972'*, then asked them each to call out the names of their dearly departed—Thalia called out her mother; Ann, her Mom, Dad and James. Cassandra then knelt at the side of the grave and placed Sara's flowers on it. Ann and Thalia remained standing, each one resting an arm on Cassandra's shoulder.

A tear rolled down Thalia's face as memories of her mother's funeral came charging into her consciousness. She realized how much she had missed by not visiting her mother's grave. "As soon as I get back, I am going to New York to visit my mother's grave," she declared. "I have never been back since the funeral, almost thirty-five years ago."

Ann hugged her, a tear rolling down her face too. "We are all weeping inside for our mothers."

Cassandra got up and hugged them both. As they stood within the silence of their own pain, they surrendered and released the hurt of the many losses they had suffered over the years, allowing serenity and tranquility to flow into their newly opened spaces.

Ann took a deep breath. She rubbed Thalia and Cassandra's backs. "Thank you two so much. I needed that." Knowing that she was bursting with emotions that needed more release, Ann excused herself to practice her daily meditation.

When Ann walked away in search of her Bodhi tree, Cassandra put her arm around Thalia and invited her to come sit on her mother's grave with her. "Thalia, let me tell you a secret. My mother is one of the great earth spirits. And when your mother passed, she became a great earth spirit too. So here, let's sit and welcome our mothers' spirits back to us."

Ann chose her spot under a mango tree close by. It was laden with buds soon to give birth to the coming season's jewels. She remembered Spice telling her how he was going to seduce her with mangoes. She wondered if the mangoes were going to come from this tree, the one bearing fruit beside his grandmother's resting place.

A beautiful yellow-tailed green bird flew by and pecked at a mango blossom, reminding Ann of James. Birds were his favorite animals. Ann smiled as she recalled the many times that he would come home from a trip and get upset with her or Ahsima because neither one had remembered to fill the bird feeder. When the bird flew over her head, Ann felt as if James' spirit was contained in its brilliantly colored plumage and soaring all above and around her. The burning in her heart slowly began to dissipate, escaping along her spine and up through her crown chakra. And, in the space that opened up, she felt herself being transfused with the energy emanating from the entire universe.

Her body began to twitch. She needed to move. So, she kicked off her shoes and did a few yoga asanas. Yoga was her dance with life. As she laid in the child's pose, she heard Cassandra calling out to her to come and go for a bath in the river with them before it got too late. Feeling refreshed and totally renewed, she frolicked through the grass on her way to meet them. To her surprise, when she approached the rock where Sara, Thalia and Cassandra were sitting, all three women were naked.

"I cannot believe my eyes!" Ann exclaimed. "How did we get to feeling free so quickly?"

"Blame Cassandra," Sara said. "She reminded me that I was created in the image and likeness that God wanted me to have, and for some strange reason, I stopped feeling ashamed about having my body seen or touched."

"Give thanks to Yemoja and her mermaids," Cassandra said.

"And here I was thinking that it was because you're not afraid of me being as attracted to your body since I still found the male anatomy appealing," Thalia said, half joking, half serious.

"As Ann said earlier," Sara poked back, "maybe is the magic word."

"Touché," was all that Ann could muster. Silently however, she thanked the Great Spirit for all the divine miracles that were transforming them all.

Ann quickly took off her clothes and followed Cassandra into the water. Sara, then Thalia entered next. Halfway across, Sara lost her footing and slipped. Frightened, she yelled out for help. Thalia was right behind her, so she quickly grabbed her under her shoulders before she slipped all the way under the water. From then on, Thalia held Sara's hands and guided her across to the miniature waterfall where Ann and Cassandra had already taken a seat.

They made room for each other, allowing the water to beat their heads and massage their backs.

"There is another story that I must tell before we all go our separate ways," Cassandra said, breaking a long silence. "It goes back even further than the one I shared with you in the caves."

"Let's hear it," Ann said anxious to partake of Cassandra's wisdom.

"Around the year 200 AD, in a small village in Ethiopia, the women would gather along the banks of the Nile every full moon at midnight to celebrate and give thanks. They were led in song and dance by the high priestess Sarantha, in praise of Isis, their creator, who blessed them with children and food. Men were never allowed to attend, except for the few who served as musicians.

One night, in the midst of one such celebration, strange-looking men with pale faces and stringy hair invaded their gathering. These men stopped the dancing and forced everyone back into the center of the village. There, they killed all the males, including the children; the two musicians were spared however, because they were dressed like women for the ceremony. Next, the strange men raped as many of the young girls as they could. When they were finished with all their pillage, they bound Sarantha's hands and took her with them. Se, the drummer and her lover, tried to rescue her as she was dragged away on a horse. He was stabbed mercilessly in his chest.

Janius, the general and leader of the invasion fell in love with Sarantha on the journey back to his homeland up North; he loved her dark skin and wide hips. When they arrived, he declared her his concubine and took her to live in his primary home. He lavished her with fine jewels and clothes, but kindness could not cure her blues. She missed her daughter, lover, people and their customs. In the beginning, she oftentimes tried to run away, but she always found herself lost in the strange terrain. She did not know where she was nor was she sure which direction she had come from. Her feet failed to lead her in the right direction. Whenever she was found, the strange men would bind her wrists and carry her back to Janius.

In an attempt to make her love him, Janius built her a temple like the one he found her in the night they raided her land. He thought this small, profound reflection of home might make her happy. He was right. Soothed by her temple, Sarantha's blues began to lift. After a while, she even came to love him—almost as much as she loved Se, her old lover. Yet no matter how much Sarantha had grown to love Janius, she refused to bear his children. Whenever she found herself with child, she aborted Janius' seed with extracts of myrrh.

One day, the king's wife became very sick. Word spread that Sarantha had special powers from the gods, so the king summoned her to the palace. He begged her to heal his dying wife. In her temple, Sarantha called upon Isis to infuse her with the wisdom of healing. Isis guided Sarantha to a willow tree. Sarantha made a brew of the willow's bark and placed a few drops upon the queen's lips. As the willow-bark brew saturated the queen's royal mouth, she opened her eyes and arose *from her deathly sleep.*

The next day, the queen was completely healed. The townspeople celebrated for thirty-five days. The queen made Sarantha an attendant in her royal court and appointed her the task of training royal healers. Sarantha chose seven women to be her disciples. As the women learned the wisdom of the sun and moon, Sarantha grew in power and influence. Within years, everyone had forgotten Sarantha's arrival as a captive and revered her as a powerful holy woman.

Many years later, a new religion that had only men at the center swept through the land. A few generals, who had grown tired of the king's deference to the power of women, embraced the new religion and started a bloody battle to force all the townspeople to adopt the new ways. The king and Sarantha's husband refused to become converts, so they were killed.

The new generals put out an edict that anyone who did not convert risked having their heads cut off. Sarantha and her disciples went underground. One night, during the secret moon gathering, their makeshift temple was raided. The commanding general threatened to have all the women killed if they did not rebuke their worship at once. One of the priestesses screamed in defiance. The general grabbed her and attempted to rape her. As he fumbled with the priestess' skirts, Sarantha summoned her Isis warrior power within. She seized the general's sword from his waist and stabbed him through his groin. She then cut his penis off and threw it into the pot of burning frankincense. He bled to death.

The following morning Sarantha set her house and temple on fire. She bribed a few of the remaining loyal men to take them back to her homeland. After all those years of refusing to show her the way home, the men nobly escorted her and her disciples South in honor of the dead king. As they neared familiar terrain, a new joy overtook Sarantha. The length of her absence did not diminish the love she felt for her homeland. She was very happy to be returning at last. She hoped her daughter might still be alive and prayed that they might make a home for themselves in the land of her birth.

Sarantha and her disciples eventually reached her village after several weeks of travel. Famine, illness and death had decimated the village. The only face she recognized was that of Sau, the other musician and sole person remaining from the old circle. His face twisted into a painful smile when he recognized Sarantha. When Sarantha asked for her daughter, Sau's eyes went blank. In trembling tones, he informed her that he had married her daughter when she came of age. Together, they hoped to repopulate their land after the invasion. Sarantha demanded to see her daughter right away. Sau opened his arms helplessly. His voice faltered as he told Sarantha that her daughter died giving birth to their first child. The news filled Sarantha with overwhelming grief. She did not want to lay eyes on her grandchild, for she did not want to ease her hurt. Without even a glance at her disciples, she ran to the river and threw herself back to Yemoja."

"That's it for now ladies," Cassandra. "It's getting late."

"Why do the main characters, the women in particular, all die in your stories?" Sara asked

"So that they can live again," Cassandra replied.

"Do you think that we are all dying in our stories?" Thalia asked.

"A Buddhist friend once told me that at the moment we signed up for life, we also did for death," Ann added.

"As usual, I don't get it," Sara said.

"You will, when you are ready," Cassandra told her.

"That probably won't happen until I'm on my dying bed," Sara replied. "Then it will be too late.

"And if we all don't hurry and leave soon, that could be tonight for all of us," Cassandra said, looking up at the darkening skies.

"What!" Sara yelled.

"I am just joking, but seriously ladies, I don't know if you have noticed, there is no electricity around here. We didn't carry any lanterns and our clothes are on the other side of the river. We need this little bit of sunlight remaining to find our way back to the main road." The women took heed and followed Cassandra across the river as quickly as they could.

The walk back up the hill was much less strenuous than they expected. Several of the villagers were still sitting on their verandas or standing at their gates as they passed by. The conversations were much briefer this time as the women hurried to get back to the car before dark.

They reached the shop at the top of the hill just before nightfall. It had now transformed itself into the center of a loud and zesty street party. There was dance-hall music blasting from huge speakers, and several men standing around outside drinking rum. A few approached them and tried to make conversation, however Cassandra quickly dismissed their passes.

The drive down the mountain was more frightening than ever. Ann kept light conversation going with Cassandra to keep her alert. For the most part, Thalia and Sara remained silent, their mouths half-opened with fear.

When they arrived back in Kingston, Cassandra stopped first at a vegetarian restaurant owned by some of her Rastafarian compatriots. They invited them to smoke a spliff with them and eat, but Cassandra declined. Instead, she ordered the ital stew, callaloo, rice and festivals to go. She did not want anything widening the gulf between Ann and Spice. Not if she had anything to do with it.

They pulled up at Ann's complex a little after eight o'clock. The guard at the front gate told her he had a large package that a gentleman left for her. Since there was not much room in the jeep, he promised to take it to her as soon as his buddy got back from his break. Ann shook her head, wondering if this was another one of Spice's attempts at making up.

The women were indeed happy to be home. The exhilaration they left the river with had worn off revealing hunger and fatigue deep inside. The answering machine light was blinking when they got inside. Ann sat down to retrieve the messages while Cassandra went to the kitchen to organize the food, and Sara and Thalia went upstairs to wash up. The first message was from Spice warning that if they did not come to the club, her punishment was going to be twenty lashes with his tongue. Ann grinned, thinking that was the kind of sentence she could live with. He also mentioned that Kalamu was looking forward to seeing Thalia again.

The other message was from Lee. "Thalia," Ann yelled. Thalia ran down the stairs.

"Lee called. She asked you to call her back as soon as possible." Thalia nodded and turned to go into the kitchen.

"Thalia! You're not going to call Lee back?"

"Lee can wait. It's only one more day until I return to D.C. This is my time with my girls. Let's eat."

As soon as they sat down and began eating, the doorbell rang. Ann ran and opened the door, food in mouth. The guard had brought the package like he had promised. By the looks of it, Ann figured out that it was a painting. Given how huge it was, Ann asked him to place it in the living room. Her name was on the envelope, but when she opened it, the salutation was to Sara. Remembering that Marlon had promised to get the painting to Sara before she left, Ann called all the women into the living room and handed the letter over to Sara. Seeing that all the women's eyes were expectantly awaiting the contents of the letter, Sara hesitantly began to read out loud: "Sorry that I missed you. Here is the painting that I promised. I hope that you will like it. See you again, one day soon. Until then, I present to you, the Emerald Woman."

"He just won't let it go, will he?" Sara said, shaking her head.

"Maybe true love persists in spite of resistance," Thalia remarked.

"Speak for yourself," Sara said.

"Be honest, didn't you feel a little something for him?"

"Nothing strong enough to make me leave home," Sara replied.

"I hope that it is a happy one," Cassandra said.

"Don and I have a lot of problems," Sara admitted, "but at least they are very familiar. I am not about to venture onto any new playing field right now."

"Sara, can you truly say that his infidelity and abuse does not bother you anymore?" Ann asked.

"It does, but more important than what he is doing, is that I am not ready to let that white woman win and take my husband from me. I made him who he is, and I'll be damned if I am going to turn over the goods to her," Sara said.

"Be careful that you don't get hurt in the process," Cassandra warned again. "The goods sound like spoils to me!"

"I know that you are worried about me, all of you. But Don has promised to change. It's only fair I give him a chance."

"But why should he?"

She was startled by Cassandra's question. "What do you mean?"

"Have you given him a reason to change? Are you asking him to change or just expecting him to?"

"Of course I am ..." Sara stopped mid-sentence as she really thought about the question. "He said he would Cass. You don't think I should believe him?"

"I think you should recognize he is human." She paused and realized Sara was truly listening. "If you give a man, a woman, anybody everything they want; a good life, home, car all that. Plus, they have a good job and all, and they cheat on you. And you take them back with open arms each time, why do you think he will change? He has everything."

"Including his personal punching bag," Thalia had to add.

Ann was pleased to see Sara thinking, Cassandra had gotten much further than she was able to.

"He is your husband, yes. But he is human. Ask for something from him, Sara. After all these affairs, the battery, demand something for yourself. Stand up and let him know he doesn't get his happy image if you're not happy." When Sara still had no words, Cassandra bailed her out. "You have a long trip home to think about this. Open up your gift."

Sara hesitated. "Someone else has to do it for me."

"To borrow my favorite Jamaican colloquialism, 'No problem man'," Thalia volunteered.

Ann went to the kitchen and got a pair of scissors. She and Thalia carefully removed the many layers of wrapping while Cassandra and Sara looked on.

"This is incredible!" Thalia cried out after they took off the final wrapping.

"Sara, I have never seen you look as ravishing as you do in this portrait," Ann remarked.

"This is the work of someone who sees the divine beauty in you, Sara; you should pay attention. This picture is a work of love," Cassandra advised.

Sara remained quiet. She could not quite see what they were all raving about. For even though the face of the woman in the picture was hers, it seemed unreal. It was much too perfect. And she couldn't quite get with the dove atop her head. Nor the way her entire face was painted in green and gold.

"Don't you have anything to say for yourself?" Thalia asked after a while.

"Marlon must see me through rose-colored glasses," Sara said, grasping for words to cover her returning anxiety.

"That's a man who sees all the way to your soul," Cassandra insisted. "It's not just about your surface beauty. He loves your total being."

"Cassandra, if the man loves me, it's because he does not know me," Sara retorted.

"Sara, I am no psychiatrist, but what I just heard you say is that you are not a lovable person, and that is not true. We three women love you," Thalia said, going over and giving her a hug.

"I loved you from the first moment I saw you, sick and pale as all hell," Cassandra added, giving her a hug too.

"If you allow yourself to meet the true Sara, you would be filled with love for her," Ann said, getting into the group hug.

"And how do I do that?" Sara asked, choked-up by the outpouring of love that she was receiving.

"You've already begun," Ann told her. "The first step is self awareness, and you are halfway there."

"What makes you think that?" Sara asked unconvinced. She still felt as if she was in a perpetual state of emotional miasma.

"Because you've been sitting with yourself and with us these past several days, looking at a lot of the hurts and fears that you had buried deep inside," Ann reassured her. "That's step one."

"And step two?" Sara asked, still unconvinced.

"Step two comes with letting go and accepting what was; but at the same time knowing and trusting that you have the power to create what is and will be. But first though, you have to traverse beyond your ego, for it is always trying to keep you from going beyond fear."

"Ann is so right on," Cassandra interjected. "It is only when you let go of ego that you can meet your soul. And when you meet her Sara, you will find that she is the perfect Christ-like being who is your true being and who you have been, are and will be forever."

"Then there's hope," Sara said, shaking her head solemnly, her earlier frown dissolving into a smile. "Maybe one day I will see me in the painting. But, until then, Ann, would you keep her here in Jamaica for me? It will be too complicated to take it home; you know, with getting it repackaged for the plane and all …"

Ann read beyond the excuses, but let it be. "Done deal," Ann replied. "Emerald Woman, Sara, goddess of love and beauty, will be hanging in my living room until you come and get her."

Just then, the clock struck nine, followed almost

immediately by Thalia's growling stomach. They went back to the dining room and finished the meal as quickly as possible. Ann had promised Spice to be at the club no later than ten.

An hour or so later later, they arrived at Club Merrytunes. So as to avoid the crowd lined up outside, Cassandra took them through the side entrance. Inside, the hypnotic sound of Spice Rum and the Chasers had the dance floor jamming. The walls were lined with couples locked together in what seemed to be a motionless grind except for an occasional pelvic gyration. In addition, there were several men, the majority of whom sported dreadlocks and cut-off tank tops or open shirts exposing their lean and mean bodies, drinking Red Stripe beer or Guinness Stout and dancing by themselves. Thalia wondered if this was a derivative of the African custom of men dancing in circles with each other, or simply a present day cultural camouflage for men dancing with each other in a homophobic society such as Jamaica.

At first look, they could not find any seats in the house; all the tables were taken. So they pushed their way through the crowds toward the band. It wasn't until they got to the very front right next to the stage that they got Spice's eye. He motioned to them to sit at a table that was occupied by a lone woman. Cassandra explained that the woman was Jane, the executive from the English recording company that was trying to sign Spice's band. Jane welcomed them to the table, telling them that Spice had asked her to save a seat for them.

Woman's intuition immediately notified Ann that Jane was Spice's temptress the previous night. Ann was both disappointed and surprised, given Spice's declaration during lunch that he had gotten over his attraction to white women. Ann had to struggle with Sara to claim the chair furthest away from Jane.

As soon as they sat down, Spice announced that his next song, Third World's 'Now That We Found Love' was dedicated to his new love. Ann found herself feeling slightly irritated and mistrustful. Even Spice's crooning at the end in his sexy baritone voice, "I have found love, and I know what to do with it. I am going to take love, and give love back," did not melt her ice. Nor did the champagne that Jane ordered for the table.

Next came Bob Marley's 'One Love'. Cassandra, noting Ann's withdrawal, suggested that they all go and dance. Jane bowed out gracefully, invoking jet lag and tired feet. Ann was glad to see that she at least had some limits about when not to compete.

"In order to reach that higher zone of 'one love', we must start right here with ourselves," Cassandra shouted above the music as they walked onto the dance floor. Somehow, maybe because of a week of self-contemplation, Marley's message of universal love was lost on them. All three women personalized 'one love' to their immediate circumstances—Sara wondered if she would be able to hold on to the loving feelings that she was beginning to feel for Don again. Thalia wondered if she could possibly achieve 'one love' status with both Lee and Kalamu. And Ann wondered if Spice wanted to share his 'one love' with her and Jane.

They danced together for several more songs. Eventually, their display of feminine freedom caught on. Soon, several of the women who had been sitting by themselves got up and joined them. Not long afterwards, a few of the men who were watching found themselves being drawn into the circle.

The band closed out the set with Black Uhuru's 'Solidarity'. Ann thought that this was a most fitting tribute to the newly reformed bond of love, respect and unity among them all.

Spice stepped down from the stage and joined them. He held Ann's hands and began heading toward their table; Jane was still sitting by herself. Ann intercepted and instead asked him to step outside for a few minutes. She needed a breath of fresh air and to clear her head about Jane.

"Only if yu goin rub up in the dark wid mi," he tried to make light of Ann's terse attitude. Ann did not respond. Instead she slipped his arms around her and asked him to show the way. On the way out, Ann noticed that Kalamu had joined her three women friends, plus the other woman, Jane.

Outside, a brilliant, blue velvet sky, inhabited by a sparkling half moon and countless, twinkling stars greeted them. Ann went straight for the gusto. She was tired of the dull aching that she had been feeling all day. "I don't usually find blondes attractive, but I must admit that Jane is quite stunning. No wonder she was tempting you so last night."

"She is tempting all right," Spice admitted. "But I never took a bite."

"So why all the drinking?"

"If not the apple, then why not some grape juice?" he joked "For see it ya now—here is this stunning blonde parading pussy in my face, and I don't want to touch it. I guess I was bemoaning the loss of my bachelorhood."

"And what stopped you from touching it?"

"Woman you're not hearing me. I am in love with you."

"That doesn't stop most men."

"Sweetness, I represent Spice and Spice only!" he proclaimed, thumping his clenched fist on his chest. "I am not most ordinary men," he insisted.

Something about the steadfast resolve of his own unique and separate manhood made Ann realize that she was dumping past traumas onto him. So she owned up to her projection. "Twenty years ago, Spice, in circumstances similar to this, another man professed instant attraction and love. A few months later, he was in bed with one of my best friends. Even though it is forgiven, it is not forgotten. The scars are still there as a reminder."

"All that I can say is judge me on my own shit and not his. Believe me, I do have a lot; so don't add anyone else's, please, baby, baby please!"

Ann could feel his sincerity in spite of his levity. It brought forgiveness to her heart. "We're cool now Spice. You have to remember that a lot has happened in a very short time. I need a little time to absorb it all." She hugged him tenderly. "This is all the rubbing that this black woman has to give right now," she teased.

"Then to add insult to injury, I seem to have landed us right back to the black man and white woman issue." He pulled her into his arms as close as he could. "I can see how and why that upset you, and I am sorry," Spice apologized.

"I don't want you to get the impression that I am dissing white women carte blanche, so let me say this real quick before we have to go back inside." The band was beginning to warm up. "I hold no anger against individual white women, Jane for example. I respect her humanity. I have issues with her only if she doesn't take the time and effort to deal and struggle; and if, in her laziness, or should I say arrogance, she perpetuates collective group behaviors that oppress us as a race."

"I hear you all the way," Spice nodded in agreement. "Since I am going to accept the deal with her company, we're just going to have to find a way to manage it all. And I'm confident that you will educate and bring her along. She has a real positive vibe, you might be surprised."

"Good. Maybe my karma is to find effective ways to help white women undo racism," Ann pondered out loud, looking up to the heavens. "Just maybe." Just then, a shooting star zoomed across the skies.

"Make a wish," Ann told Spice.

"And yours better have me playing a significant role in it," he replied.

"Only if you play me significantly too," Ann shot back. Little did she realize that their wishes collided as they ascended up high and landed back upon a star; shattering the boundaries that were still hovering between them.

"I love it when you get a little possessive," Spice said as they began heading back inside. "Shows me that you are still a yardie in spite of all your New Age cool."

"So this is your twisted way of justifying why you need to make me jealous!" Ann replied, giving him a loving shove. Not having the time for what would surely turn into a philosophical discussion, Ann made a mental note that she needed to further explore Spice's knowledge base about metaphysics and religion. She needed to correct his assumptions about New Age thinking—that what was being labeled New Age by westerners was simply a rebroadcast of African and other Eastern old age wisdom.

"It wasn't me," Spice joked, unaware of Ann's higher, internal quandary. It was she. And trust me, she got the message real clear that you are my queen."

"I never knew that your name is Shaggy too," Ann chuckled.

Kalamu and the band were still warming up, so Spice had time to escort Ann to the table. Taking a seat, this time it didn't matter where, Ann was overcome with joy—joy at the re-found friendship with her girlfriends, and joy at the newly found romance with a man friend. As he walked away, Ann pulled him back and whispered in his ear, "The rhythm of the river is flowing inside us all."

"I can't wait to get flooded," he replied.

Thalia and Sara did not look up from their conversation. Ann wondered if they were punishing her for leaving them and going off with Spice.

"Where's Cassandra?" Ann butted in after being ignored for several minutes.

"She gave Jane a ride back to her hotel," Sara said.

"They seemed to hit it off quite well," Thalia added.

Before Ann could ask Thalia exactly what she was meaning to imply, Kalamu went over to their table, a mischievous grin on his face. "What's up?" she asked him.

"I've come to fetch Thalia," he replied.

"Excuse me?" Thalia had a surprised look on her face.

"Well, a little birdie told me that Thalia was an incredible singer," Kalamu explained. "So when Spice asked if we wanted to have a karaoke jam, I said that I knew just the person."

"That little birdie doesn't happen to be sitting to my left, does she?" Thalia asked.

"Okay, so I told Kalamu that you were an incredible singer when you went to the bathroom with Cassandra," Sara confessed. "But I did not think that he was going to act upon it. At least, not so quickly."

"Then you need to be the one on that stage!" Thalia refused adamantly. No way was she going up next to Spice and his band; they were in the big leagues.

"Pretty please?" Kalamu coaxed. Thalia would not budge. "Do this for all the women out there who are trying to find their voices," he persisted. Thalia wondered just how much Sara had told him about her being a lesbian, for he seemed to know which tactic would disarm her.

"If you put it that way, how can I resist?" Thalia said, a hint of shyness creeping into her usually self-assured voice. "We've spent all week trying to overcome our fears and shame, so I guess this is the test."

"That's right girl, you can do it," Sara said encouragingly.

"Remember the performance that you did with the choral group at your hospital when Ahsima and I visited you in Africa, Thalia?" Ann reminded her. "You were fabulous!"

"That was eons ago, and that was the minors, compared to this," Thalia said, getting up slowly. Hesitantly, she allowed Kalamu to escort her.

Walking on stage, Thalia realized that this was her opportunity to bury the havoc that the awful night at the beauty pageant continued to wreak in her psyche. Per Ann's earlier lecture to Sara, she was aware that she had made it through step one—becoming aware of and releasing her fear. Now was the time for step two—to accept the past and recreate her self anew. And most important to her was to reclaim her voice, one of the most beautiful legacies from her mother. Taking a deep breath and lifting her chest high, Thalia went over to Spice and asked if they could play her selection. He assured her that it was one of their standards. She walked to the upper deck of the stage where the drummers were and sat on the ledge closest to Kalamu. She could see his eyes gleaming with pride and beaming with encouragement. She cleared her throat a few times, and closed her eyes. Visions of her mother and Lee leaped into her being, lodging into her throat. Thalia took a deep breath, dug deep into her vocals, and cut her voice loose. Out came the most fiery and sweltering reggae rendition of 'Smile, Sara, Smile' that many in the club, including the band, had heard.

Thalia ended the song to a rousing applause from the crowd. They begged for more, but she knew that she had come to her limit. Too much was happening in her head all at once, and she did not want to tip over the edge, into mania. She graciously took her bow.

Before the ovation ended, Sara rushed onstage and kissed Thalia. "Thanks for my song."

"Be careful how you kiss a lesbian, you might like it!" Thalia quipped, giving her a big hug. To Thalia's surprise, Sara pulled her closer and said, "No matter how many girlfriends you may have, I will always be your number one woman." Thalia was stunned; she had no comeback; only a few silent tears.

Ann stayed seated, giving Thalia and Sara the space to have their special moment. As she observed the closeness that had erupted once again between Thalia and Sara, Ann thought that she finally understood Thalia's attraction and devotion to Sara. Just maybe Sara was a living symbol of Thalia's mother—two very melancholic women, cut off from the essence of their majestic, black beauty.

Cassandra returned to the table, while Sara and Thalia were still locked in their embrace.

"You sure were gone a long while," Ann remarked. "You missed Thalia's performance of her lifetime."

"There will be many more to come," Cassandra said in a very mysterious voice.

The band began playing Burning Spear's 'African Woman' as Thalia and Sara walked back, hand in hand, to the table. Before they could sit, Cassandra pulled Ann up and announced, "My women have all come back to me. Let's all go dance and give praises to the most high, Isis, mother of Jah, Jesus, Buddha, Allah." The three women did not fully grasp all that she was saying, but they were not seeking answers; they were just being. So they danced until the wee hours of the morn.

The club eventually emptied out after several final drum rolls. Cassandra proposed a trip to the beach to watch the sunrise, before going home. She met with no resistance because by then, everyone's sleep deprivation had cycled into mild euphoria. Ann welcomed the idea, thinking that it would be a perfect ending to Thalia and Sara's visit. She also thought that it was a great way to preempt the potential confusion about who was sleeping where and with whom.

Ann, Sara and Cassandra rode with Spice in his jeep;

SATURDAY

Thalia rode with Kalamu in his sports car.

It was still dark when they pulled up by a clearing alongside the St. Thomas Road. Spice informed them that the beach was only a few feet away from the road. Cassandra, Sara, Ann and Spice climbed out of the jeep making their way and finding a spot, while Kalamu and Thalia brought blankets and a flashlight.

They spread their blankets and laid down, Spice next to Ann, Kalamu next to Thalia, and Sara next to Cassandra. Kalamu lit a spliff. He shared with them that in ancient times, Ganja was a very sacred herb that was used in rituals for opening up the seventh chakra and connecting to universal Oneness. "I invite you all to live in the spirit of the most high, Jah, Rastafari," he said solemnly. He took a big inhale and passed it on to Thalia.

Thalia took a toke. "I give thanks for beginning to remember how to live from and within my soul," she said. She passed it to Cassandra.

Cassandra took several puffs. "I give thanks for reconnecting with my soul sisters," she said. She passed it to Spice.

"I give thanks for finding my long, lost soulmate," he said. He passed it to Ann.

Ann thought for a minute, then said, "I give thanks for relearning that the soul never dies," She passed it to Sara; she graciously declined.

"I'm just thankful to be alive right now," Sara said, "and that's as profound as it gets for me.

"That's profound enough," Cassandra told her.

"What perfect timing," Ann said, looking up to the skies. "She is about to give birth to the day."

The blessed firmament began to lighten, changing from deep purple to lavender. Pink and orange streaks began to appear in the eastern sky. Minutes later, the blazing golden ball made its grand entrance.

They laid in silence, occasionally broken by the sounds of the animals awakening, and watched the sun's coming. By the time she completely crossed the horizon, everyone had become victims of their sleepless night. They could barely keep their eyes open. Only Spice and Ann lay awake wrapped in each other's arms, listening to each other's breath. Ann sighed and smiled. He looked around at her and asked, "Thinking about James?"

"How did you know?"

"You always get this soft, sad smile when you talk or think about him."

"You never mentioned it before."

"What's there to mention?"

Ann thought about that for a while as she stared in wonder into his eyes. Suddenly, James' words that night she first met Spice came back to her, "Don't worry, our love will never die." Just as quickly, the answer to her struggles against her feelings for Spice came to her. She closed her eyes as the peaceful revelation washed over her. There was no need for her to fight to hold on to James. With Spice, James would always be protected as a part of her. A silent tear or two stole their way down her cheek. Spice, knowingly did not ask. He could feel the peace exuding from her body. Instead he began to hum:

Is one night enough to say that I love you?
Is one night enough to promise my heart?
She looks at me with eyes searching for lies.
But the truth in my heart cannot be denied.

One night
One outstanding night
One night
One night that stands out
One night
Cursed by time

Redheaded vixen lit a fire in me
Well-aged wine poured over my spice
Time whispered to her to run it's too early
But time knows not love when it bloom in one night

"Spice, is that my song?" she turned around in his arms, a broad smile plastering her face.

"What do you think?"

"I love it."

"Like I said, it's a work in progress. When you hear it to music it'll be much better."

"It doesn't get much better than this, Spice."

"Damn right," he smiled back and kissed her long and deep. Spice started to pull her more intimately to him, but she had to stop knowing where things would head.

"We have tons of time. I have to get my girls home so I can get them to the airport."

"Once they're on that plane, I claim you for good."

"Yes, sir." She offered no resistance. Spice kissed Ann again and laid back. He let his tired eyes slip closed and joined the rest of the sleeping posse.

The morning was still peaceful and undisturbed, however, the sounds of cars along the roadway began to steadily build up. Out in the distant waters, a few fishermen were making their way inland from their morning's catch. Ann could feel herself getting teary. She was going to sorely miss her sistahs. She loved the warmth and intimacy that they had reopened for themselves. No one, no man, was ever going to come between them ever again. She was free of the pain of the past. For the first in a very long time, she felt wholly alive.

Ann became filled with a strong longing to have a few moments alone by the water with her friends. So she tapped Thalia and Sara lightly on their shoulders.

"Let's go for one last stroll on the beach," she suggested. To her surprise, they offered no resistance, as if sleep had been pushed aside by the adrenaline of their rapidly arriving departure.

"Let's start with a farewell hug," Ann said. They wrapped their arms around each other and lingered there until the pain of their separation was replaced by the joy of the wondrous living that lay ahead.

Arm in arm, they strolled along the water.

"As I stared into the water a while ago, I saw us all, our

past and our future, wrapped in the stories that Cassandra told us," Ann said, breaking the silence after several minutes.

"Funny you should say that. As I ran my feet through the sand, I had this feeling of déjà-vu," Thalia remarked. "A flash back and forward to some kind of communal living."

"That's interesting," Ann remarked. "Cassandra and I have been talking about the possibility of developing a spiritual retreat center where black people from all over the Diaspora could escape to for some real soul renewal and spiritual awakening."

"Earth to my sistah friends, please re-orbit into our present moment and let us use these last moments to talk about where we go from here," Sara suggested. "A lot has happened in a very short space of time."

"Great idea," Ann agreed. She thought about it for a second then stated, "My greatest lesson this week is that in any given moment, we always have the opportunity to choose the path that best allows us to create happy moments, no matter the past." She took a deep inhale then continued, "So I am choosing to give Spice and I a chance to grow. Who knows, maybe I will make Jamaica my home again. It sure feels like James has returned me to my paradise lost."

"And for me," Thalia said, "I have learnt that courage is what brings us closest to freedom. So that path is going to lead me back to Lee. As much as I enjoyed the energy with Kalamu, I am even more committed to giving Lee and I a chance to be. And it's not just about my desires; I feel that I owe her that much; she is such a giving person. And if it does not work out, I want it to be because our paths were not complimentary; not because someone else created a detour."

Sara nodded. "I don't know which road I am choosing, but it definitely is leading straight back to Don," she said. "What I did learn, as small and obvious as the lesson might seem to some, is that I do have choices, that there are other paths; that I do not have to stay. That's a big deal to me."

"And me too," Ann smiled at her.

"I'm so glad I came, you know? Whatever happens from here ..." She quickly looked at Thalia and Ann, then looked away. But not before they saw the tears start forming and felt their own.

"True," Thalia's voice was thick.

Ann took both her girlfriends' hands and held them close to her body. She sighed. She was satisfied.

The sound of fishermen chatting as they returned inland from their catch brought them back to the ordinary reality of their time and space—two women had planes to catch at noon. They looked out and watched the men briefly. Even though they were quite ambivalent about whether they should stay or go, all three women knew that the time had come to depart this leg of their group excursion into island glory. But there was one thing about which they felt no confusion—where, and with whom they were journeying on their road less traveled. And in that moment, they tasted their freedom. For, all three women had claimed the courage to surrender to their path of truth.

9
A Year Later

It was a picture perfect day as three women stood on the beach Emerald Key. There was not a cloud in the azure blue sky above. A gentle wind was blowing as if to dry their tears. They were thinking the same thing to themselves at the same time: How do you say goodbye when one of you has come to the end of the journey?